# VILE SPIRITS

# VILE SPIRITS

A Mystery

John MacLachlan Gray

Douglas & McIntyre

1 2 3 4 5 — 25 24 23 22 21

Douglas and McIntyre (2013) Ltd.
P.O. Box 219, Madeira Park, BC, VON 2H0
www.douglas-mcintyre.com

Edited by Pam Robertson
Text design by Carleton Wilson
Printed and bound in Canada
Printed on 100% recycled, FSC-certified paper

Supported by the Province of British Columbia

Douglas and McIntyre acknowledges the support of the Canada Council for the Arts, the Government of Canada, and the Province of British Columbia through the BC Arts Council.

LIBRARY AND ARCHIVES CANADA CATALOGUING IN PUBLICATION

Title: Vile spirits / John MacLachlan Gray.
Names: Gray, John, 1946- author.
Identifiers: Canadiana (print) 20210239573 | Canadiana (ebook) 2021023962X
   | ISBN 9781771622776 (hardcover) | ISBN 9781771622783 (EPUB)
Classification: LCC PS8563.R411 V55 2021 | DDC C813/.54—dc23

*I do not believe that men can ever feel so pure
an enthusiasm for women as we can feel for each
other. Ours is nearer to the love of angels.*

—Catherine Sedgwick

*Evil draws men together.*

—Aristotle

# PROLOGUE

VANCOUVER, DOMINION OF CANADA, SEPTEMBER 1925

YET ANOTHER ROYAL VISIT
Ed McCurdy
Staff Writer
*The Evening Star*

Having swallowed a snootful of liquors
Arrested in garters and knickers
Ne'er to be crowned
He's Canada-bound
While all of Westminster snickers.

Nothing gives this reporter more astonishment than our province's appetite for royal visits, and our eagerness to foot the bill.

Over the past year, Vancouver's capacity for obsequious toadying has brought us a parade of dukes, earls and lords (English, Scottish and Welsh) whose unearned wealth and family history somehow renders them holy; by all appearances, a title and an overbite will confer sainthood on a toad.

No bridge, building or ship can be considered safe until christened by an English nobleman. No civic anniversary is worth observing without the presence of an aristocrat with a chest full of inherited gongs.

Our current occupant of the welcome mat is His Royal Highness The Prince George, whose purpose is, nominally, to pay homage to the city that bears his name—when the truth of it is that the prince has been temporarily exiled to our remote corner of the empire while the London press makes a meal of his latest indiscretion.

Over the past few months, His Highness has provided the public with a veritable smorgasbord of succulents: ill-advised affairs with married women, a fondness for alcohol in quantity, and a taste for morphine and cocaine—the latter courtesy of one Kiki Preston, an ex-patriot American socialite known as "the girl with the silver syringe."

The most recent disgrace has to do with a sighting of the prince, accompanied by the playwright Noël Coward, both in a moist and windy condition, swanning about Soho in women's clothing.

Mistaking them for prostitutes, a policeman invited the two gentlemen to the constabulary, where things were quickly sorted out—but not before some anti-royalist on the force alerted London scribes. Having been proclaimed on the pages of the *Tatler* and the *Daily Mail*, Westminster must now ensure that the event does not enter the pages of history.

But here in the colonies, a Royal is a Royal. British Columbia's ruling class welcomes any opportunity to host the prince and to bask in the royal sun, courtesy of the taxpayer.

# PART I

*News is what a chap who doesn't care much about anything wants to read.*

—Evelyn Waugh

# CHAPTER 1

ATTORNEY GENERAL GORDON Cunning awakens with his newspaper spread over his legs like a blanket. He fishes out his handkerchief and mops his forehead. He should be in bed, but his failure to attend would be used against him for months.

It will require several martinis to get through the evening.

Nestled in a wingback chair, in an inconspicuous corner of the Crystal Ballroom, he watches the bunting-draped ceiling quiver in an updraft, then surveys the vast, brightly lit space containing tight clutches of men in black suits, smoking cigars, cigarettes and pipes, and bellowing at one another, while servers in tuxedos sidle sideways with the agility of snakes, balancing drinks trays overhead...

*Where was I? Ah, yes.*

The guests present are mostly farmers, small businessmen and village lawyers, many of whom have travelled hundreds of miles for the occasion, shuffling nervously from foot to foot, perspiring in Sunday serge coats adorned with decorations pulled out of dresser drawers and polished by their wives. Their thick-soled, practical boots scuff the Persian carpet (the size of a tennis court); their sausage fingers clutch glasses of whisky and rum for dear life.

These are his constituents, whom he has wooed and won in two elections and coddled like cats in between. But just because he represents them doesn't mean that he has to *like* them...

*Where was I? Ah...*

*Closed my eyes for a moment, should be in bed...*

He thinks he might have a touch of the flu—inevitable when you shake hands with so many workmen and breathe the stench coming from their lungs. Looking over the assembled guests he envisages swarms of germs, swimming from nostril to nostril through the damp, smoky air...

*And here he comes.*

A hush descends on the room as His Royal Highness The Prince George—wearing tweeds, not ermine—arrives with his royal retinue. A fawning mob converges around him, their faces glistening with anticipation, hands outstretched like oars from a slave ship.

For some reason, Attorney General Cunning can't quite summon the energy to join them, or even rise from his chair. A torpid feeling has taken over, along with a headache and an upset stomach. If he weren't so tired he would make an appearance, if only to pass his germs to His Highness.

Perhaps another martini will inspire him to action.

The first opportunity to grip the royal palm goes to representatives of Canadian Pacific Railway, whose indentured Chinese have succeeded in uniting Canada from sea to sea. They are followed by the ex-military pecking order, led by Vancouver's two generals, Newson and Armstrong, whose bespoke suits drip with medals and ribbons that shimmer brightly while they glare at each other like executioners, bristling with mutual hatred. Then along comes the premier and members of the executive council (Cunning really should be among them), then members of the upper bureaucracy. Ah—there is Clyde Taggart, good old Clyde, teammate, drinking mate, resolute supporter, best friend a man could have. A pity about the LCB...

*Where was I? Ah, yes. The campaign.*

Running for re-election was a miserable, dirty business. Miserable, because it's no fun having to appeal to Scottish voters in an itchy kilt, with a bulky, hairy sporran drawing attention to one's privates. Besides, he has never been fond of Scotch (it tastes like disinfectant); however, his usual martini might be seen as effeminate.

And the campaign turned nasty, deteriorating into questions of personal character. And yet, voters in the riding had every right know the truth about Fergus Hendry: Can an unfaithful husband be trusted to keep faith with his constituents? It was hardly Cunning's fault that Mrs Hendry overreacted the way she did—by publicly denouncing her husband and throwing him out of the house—because the other woman in the affair was her sister-in-law.

All in all it was a nasty business, unsavoury and unfortunate. But that's politics. And a win is a win, even by a margin of forty votes.

Ah. Another martini cocktail has arrived: a fresh, frosty glass beside the polished brass lamp, flashing drops of condensation— and in the proper glass, an inverted pyramid perched atop a transparent stem, improbably tall, with an olive inside, blurry as though seen through a screen...

*What's going on now?* It seems as if the room has thinned out. The prince must have returned to the Royal Suite, which means it is too late to get up and shake hands...

Sparks flicker behind his eyelids. His headache has got worse. Someone has dimmed the chandeliers.

No more martinis tonight. Best stay put and rest until the dizziness and queasiness fade, then make an inconspicuous exit and head up to his suite...

*Where am I?*

He must have fallen asleep again. He opens his eyes—

And is surprised to find that they are already open.

# CHAPTER 2

A MEMBER OF the cleaning staff discovered the body next morning when he noticed that the sleeping man had yesterday's newspaper spread across his lap.

After checking for vital signs, out of respect our man fetched a tablecloth with which to cover the corpse. He then spoke to his superior, who telephoned the manager, who telephoned his secretary, who telephoned Front Desk, who telephoned the hospital, who telephoned the police.

Nestled in an inconspicuous corner, the shrouded form could be mistaken for a statue protected by a dust cover—maybe a fish.

Detective Sergeant Calvin Hook sighs and lights an Ogden's, his first of the day. Another dead body: a hundred and sixty-some pounds of meat to be identified, diagnosed, transported and buried.

Hook saw his share of them at Rugeley training camp: men blown up during grenade training or shot with their own rifles (some by accident, some not) or skewered in bayonet practice or struck by a motor car or fallen off a horse, kicked by a horse, bitten by a horse or trampled under a number of horses, or dead because of having cut themselves on a nail. You didn't have to have fought at the Somme to get your full ration of dead bodies.

The disposal of war dead wrecked the French economy. Every family thinks their boy is special, to be buried with his name on a piece of stone, never to be forgotten—which is fine when people died at a normal rate, but in the *millions*?

Where do birds go when they die? Why can't humans be like birds and just disappear?

He can smell Constable Quam standing behind him. Some might call it a stink, but it isn't really. Quam doesn't stink, he *smells*.

Every day he smells of something different—always a faint

but distinct odour, not necessarily repulsive. Today it's sour apples; yesterday it was ear wax.

Hook turns to face Quam, staring back at him with the eyes of a cow, the stance of a bull and the round forehead of a newborn child. Hook speaks in his Royal Canadian Army voice, the Redhat voice that could stop a fleeing AWOL in his tracks—not to exert authority over the constable but so that his words might penetrate the man's thick skull.

"Very well, Constable, let us unveil."

"*Unveil*, sir?" The word seems to frighten him. His little eyes glitter with moisture.

"Unveil, yes. To see whether it's a body or a work of modern art."

Constable Quam's brow furrows, with not a flicker of comprehension. "Oh I wouldn't know much about art, sir."

"I'm talking about the sheet, Constable! The bloody piece of cloth covering the corpse!" Hook takes a moment to calm down. "Remove it, please."

Hook hasn't yet decided whether Quam's mulish incomprehension is due to mental impairment, mental inertia or a combination of both. Perhaps overzealous bodybuilding deprived the constable's brain of the energy required for what is commonly known as *thinking*.

Plus, he didn't serve.

Hook knows just to look at him that the man has never used a weapon other than at target practice. His fists certainly, but you don't fight a war with your fists.

And of course the question follows like manure follows a horse: *Why the hell not?* Was it brain impairment of some sort? Does the Vancouver Police Department recruit imbeciles who are too stupid to be conscripted?

In Hook's view, this might indeed be the case. By the end of the war, men of Quam's stature became a fixture of the force—burly man-bashers who learned to enforce the law under the War Measures Act, when a policeman could arrest a citizen on a hunch, then beat a confession out of him and it would stand up in court.

Such methods are no longer acceptable in peacetime. Police forces must adapt accordingly. But for men like Constable Quam, it isn't easy.

To deal with the situation, to ease the transition from war-time to peacetime police work, the Police Board called for a pro-gram of "professional upgrade" in which these officers were to become familiar with concepts such as *habeas corpus* and the presumption of innocence.

With a recession in progress, however, the city refused addi-tional funds for such "professional upgrades," in order not to burden the hypothetically hardworking taxpayer. The chief of police was ordered to assign the retraining program to lower-tier officers—as an unpaid contribution, like marching in funeral processions or playing in the brass band.

Any shift in the way of things is bound to produce unintended outcomes. In this case, VPD Chief Lionel Barfoot saw the "retrain-ing program" as an opportunity to keep the peace among the regulars by making Hook's life as difficult as possible.

The recent piecemeal amalgamation of scattered municipal police forces in the region by the Vancouver Police Department had disrupted the established pecking order. VPD regulars were understandably resentful of officers like Hook, who had been promoted over their heads after having been lured away from the Point Grey detachment.

The upshot is that, in return for a new rank and a minuscule increase in salary, DS Hook has Constable Quam attached to him like a wart.

But there's no turning back. Calvin Hook is a married man now. He is responsible for someone other than himself. He must accept that Quam has entered his life and is not going away any-time soon.

Hook flicks a kitchen match with his thumbnail and sets fire to his second Ogden's of the day.

"Mr Quam?"

Seemingly, the constable's mind has wandered off someplace else, or nowhere. His hands dangle from his sleeves like boxing gloves with fingers.

"Yes, sir?"

"Are you hard of hearing, Constable? Please remove the bloody sheet!"

"Right away, sir!" Quam turns sideways to squeeze his torso between the chair and a tree fern; in doing so he jostles the side table, which in turn upsets the brass table lamp. Reaching out to steady the lamp, he nudges an empty martini glass with his sleeve, causing it to tumble onto the carpet and the stem to break in two.

Quam gets down on one knee, retrieves the two pieces of glass, examines them without interest and lays them on the side table.

DS Hook shuts his eyes and massages the bridge of his nose with thumb and forefinger, doing his best to relax.

"Shall I take the sheet off now, sir?"

"Yes, Mr Quam. If you would."

Quam grips the tablecloth by two corners, whisks it off as though he's a magician's assistant and drops it at Hook's feet— once a death shroud, now a pile of laundry stained with wine and gravy.

Quam peers at the body as though it were a dead animal in a ditch. "Sir, is this someone familiar?"

"It's Gordon Cunning, Mr Quam. The Attorney General of the province. The boss."

LEANING AGAINST THE railing a few yards away, breathing asthmatically due to the tobacco smoke in the lobby below, McCurdy cleans his spectacles with his handkerchief, gazes up at the shreds of limp bunting dangling from the ceiling and withdraws his notebook from a side pocket. Opening it to a blank page, he steps forward for a closer look at the body.

Though well acquainted with the Attorney General, he scarcely recognizes the figure in the chair.

Known for his impassioned speeches and barbed exchanges with members of the Official Opposition, Gordon Cunning roared through one ministry after another, as Speaker of the Legislature, Minister of Labour and, until now, Attorney General. Cunning was the political equivalent of a Duesenberg— sleek and quick, putting rivals in the ditch.

This is not that man.

The man in the overstuffed chair leans slightly forward and gazes upward and to the right, as though watching some passing bird. His mouth, bluish-purple, is stretched into a rictus of a smile, all the more grotesque because his dental plate has come loose; it no longer adheres to the roof of his mouth but hangs suspended in mid-bite, creating the impression of two mouths, one on top of the other. The hand that shook thousands of palms and waved at cheering crowds is now a white talon, squeezing the chair arm as though he is on a roller coaster.

McCurdy wishes he had stayed in bed.

Corpses are a reporter's bread and butter to be sure, but their value hinges on who they are, how they died and under what circumstances.

Paradoxically, in this circumstance, Cunning's prominence wrecks the story. By the looks of him, our man suffered a seizure of some sort, which can happen to anyone, no scandal there. And to publish a photograph of a cabinet minister in this state would invite accusations of partisanship, cynicism and bad taste.

Important Man Dead—that is the story.

Since he walked several blocks to get here, McCurdy makes a token attempt at a lede: *Neither instant nor lingering, though surprising nonetheless...*

*Surprising?* He rips the page from his notebook, balls it between his palms and lobs it into a brass ashtray.

You win some, you lose some.

Thanks to tipoffs from DS Hook, McCurdy is usually first on the scene of any potentially newsworthy crime. In return for this service, he supplies information to bear on whatever case the sergeant might be working on. It's an unwritten, unspoken agreement that both men will deny to the end.

But not every tip pays off. In this case, the potential scoop is just another dead politician.

A bit early in the day, but McCurdy feels like a drink.

DS HOOK TAKES a last drag of his second Ogden's, flicks the end into a brass ashtray and gestures for Quam to grant the Attorney General a shred of dignity by returning the tablecloth to its former position. The constable doesn't respond.

"Mr Quam?"

"Yes, sir?"

"Cover the goddamn corpse."

The constable's eyes water slightly. "No need to swear, sir."

"Quite right. Carry on." Hook turns toward the bar and catches sight of McCurdy making himself at home. A bit early in the day, one might think, but the reporter's indulgences are well known.

A pair of white-coated attendants from Edwards Funeral Home arrive with a furled stretcher. They lay the stretcher on the floor in front of the armchair and attempt to slide the body downward, only to find that it has stiffened in position. After a moment's discussion, they manoeuvre the corpse sideways off the chair onto the carpet and shift it onto the stretcher so that it lies on its side in the foetal position, hands outstretched like the claws of a dead bird.

An attendant shakes out a crisp white sheet and covers the corpse; now the shrouded shape beneath could indeed be a piece of modern sculpture, or a machine having to do with agriculture.

"WELL, IF IT isn't Ed McCurdy!"

Having struggled to the top of the marble stairway, red-faced and out of breath, Max Trotter spots McCurdy with his fat glasses, his thin moustache and his soiled tailored suit, here first. Snookered again. *How does he do that?*

"A bit early for a nip, Ed, wouldn't you say?"

McCurdy already sensed an enemy present. "Actually, Max, I'm here for a witness quote from the barkeep. Basic reporting— if you practised it, you'd still be with the *Sun*."

"In fact I'm with the *World* now, a higher word rate. The *World* is based on fact you know, a step up from the *Star*."

"No more red-baiting then, Max? No more temperance whoring? Taken the pledge? Life of purity from now on? Trotter, your hypocrisy is appalling."

"It's called journalism, McCurdy. You should try it sometime."

Trotter lights a cigarette and heads back down to the lobby. "Have fun, Ed. See if you can find a rhyme for *corpse*."

McCurdy knows that word of his alcoholism will spread anew, like the opium rumour and the cocaine rumour. If the trend continues, he'll be the only drug fiend in town.

He leans toward the white-jacketed bartender, whose pink jowls and white moustache radiate the required English bonhomie. "Excuse me, sir, but what is that chap at the other end of the bar drinking?"

"The gentleman is having a Bloody Mary, sir. It's one of the new drinks we serve."

McCurdy senses a note of disapproval, to be encouraged. "Just another faddish cocktail—like the martini."

The bartender leans closer to speak in a near whisper, not to be overheard by certain parties.

"With these drinks it's all about the look, sir. I tell you, it's the American influence—what the devil is this penchant for ice? They want ice in everything. They insist on beer just this side of freezing!"

"I take it that Mr Cunning enjoyed the occasional martini."

"Very much so, sir. I don't know where that glass came from, though."

"What do you mean?"

"We've been serving the cocktail in tumblers with crushed ice and a lemon slice. We ordered martini glasses from New York, but they haven't arrived. And there have been complaints, let me tell you, sir. Without the proper glass they say it's nothing but a puddle of gin."

"It's the times we live in," McCurdy says. "Packaging is everything."

He takes out his notebook, writes three words and tears off the page.

THE LIFT DOORS open like vertical eyelids; the cage is swept aside and the manager emerges. He has a little moustache and is dressed in a vested lounge suit with a bow tie. As he approaches DS Hook he manages a sour, twisted smile so insincere that it virtually says out loud: *I trust you will be leaving very soon.*

"Good morning to you, officers. You have everything you need, I think? We do not wish to alarm our guests."

Though Hook has taken an instant dislike to the man, he can appreciate his concern. Whether the hotel is a Michelin five-star or a fleabag in Hogan's Alley, the longer the police remain on the premises, the more rumours will spread and the more skittish guests will become.

DS Hook produces his warrant card. "I am with the Vancouver Police, sir. And might you be the manager of this hotel?"

The manager's accent originates in Quebec but is sufficiently Parisian to convey sophistication and taste. "I am Manager Bernard Tremblay, Officer, and I bid welcome to you. Anything we can do for speeding things up will be welcome, I say this."

Reaching into his pocket, Hook trades his warrant card for his tin of Ogden's and produces a fresh cigarette. "We don't want to put you to much trouble, sir, but we do need to look at Mr Cunning's—"

Before he can finish his sentence, the manager extends a room key and gives it a shake for emphasis, in order to show off his gold Hamilton watch.

"*Voilà*, officer. The key to Mr Cunning's suite. It lies on the eighth floor."

"Our inspection shouldn't take more than a few hours, if all goes well."

"Very good. You may return the key to the concierge. Now if you are having no need of me further—" He turns, starts to walk away, then stops and turns back, remembering that a human being died in that armchair.

"The hotel is shocked and saddened by Mr Cunning's decease, I say this. A valued guest of long standing, there is no two doubts about it."

With a sigh and a tilt of the head, Manager Tremblay frowns at the empty chair whose arms are spread as if to say, *"What was I supposed to do?"*

"We are extending deepest condolences to the family—and flowers, of course."

Hook maintains his official expression, though he would like to grab both ends of the manager's moustache and pull. But that would set a bad example for Quam, who is currently loitering by the stairs with his finger up his arse.

"On behalf of the Vancouver Police Department, I thank you very much indeed, sir."

A brisk nod and another smile, not far from a smirk: "You are most welcome, *monsieur*. If you are having any further concerns, you may connect my office without hesitating."

Hook turns toward the bar where McCurdy is working on his second Bloody Mary. The reporter throws a nod in his direction and raises his glass, as though proposing a toast.

GORDON CUNNING DEAD
Cecil Harmsworth
Staff Writer
*The Beacon*

Last night's gala reception at the Hotel Vancouver for His Royal Highness The Prince George took a bitter turn this morning when hotel staff discovered the remains of Gordon Cunning, Attorney General for the Province of British Columbia, in a corner of the Crystal Ballroom.

"We didn't notice him right away. He sort of blended in with the fabric," said janitor Stanley Flemming. "He was sunk so deep in the chair it was almost like he was part of it. I only seen him when I stooped over to dust a lamp."

Up until Monday, Gordon Allen Cunning's political career seemed like one triumph after another. Elected to the Legislature in 1916 by the voters of Omineca and re-elected this last year (albeit with a narrow margin), Mr Cunning has served in succession as Speaker of the Legislature, Minister of Labour and, until yesterday, as Attorney General.

Among observers in Victoria it was thought that, should Premier Gulliver choose a graceful exit after his well-deserved humiliation at the ballot box, Mr Cunning was the obvious choice to succeed him, having assembled an impressive list of allies through the generous distribution of patronage plums, courtesy of the taxpayer.

For others, Mr Cunning will be remembered as the man who brought "moderation" to the province and, with moderation, new sources of tax revenue—as well as, observers note, new opportunities for patronage and graft.

Mr Cunning's physician, Dr Lloyd Kettle, pronounced the cause of death to be peritonitis brought on by an inflamed appendix. "He complained of abdominal pains from time to time. We contemplated some tests, but he was a very busy man."

Plans for a ceremony and a parade are underway at the Provincial Grand Lodge, of which Mr Cunning served as Grand Master for BC and the Yukon.

"Gordon Cunning was a bright star in the Liberal Party," reads the official statement. "It is a great loss to the province."

A government spokesman, speaking over the telephone, added: "Mr Cunning was a smashing orator, a jolly fine administrator and an all-around capital chap. He will be terribly, terribly missed."

# CHAPTER 3

SEEN THROUGH DIAMOND-SHAPED windows, the iron cage appears from above with surprising speed, along with a pair of sharply creased trousers, a set of brass buttons and a white glove.

DS Hook has never been comfortable riding in elevators. The devices didn't exist in his hometown of Waldo, where even a second floor was a rarity; nor were lifts needed in the barracks and tents of Rugeley base. On one of his trips to London he might have seen one clanking its way up and down, but any able-bodied man could reach his desired floor well ahead of the lift.

The things travel much faster now, which is a misery for anyone who was taught at an early age that what goes up must come down—a fundamental understanding of physics that, whether going up or down, triggers danger warnings and visions of plummeting helplessly to one's death, trapped in an oblong box.

The doors open. Nothing for it but to get in.

Sensing Quam watching closely behind, therefore keeping a stiff upper lip for appearance's sake, Hook takes a last drag of his cigarette, crushes it in a brass ashtray, straightens his shoulders and steps inside.

(*Where will it end, this appetite for labour-saving devices? Once people take lifts for granted, will they want moving sidewalks? Is this what the war was for?*)

"Constable, which floor was Mr Cunning on?"

"'fraid I don't remember, sir." Quam chews an imaginary cud with not a glimmer of interest.

"Eighth floor, please." Hook glares at his assistant, a rebuke Quam either misses or ignores. The constable's fruity aroma fills the tiny space, overcoming the pong of stale tobacco.

"Certainly, sir." One white-gloved hand sweeps the grille closed, the other reaches for the rheostat handle, and Hook braces for their ascent.

The lift attendant wears a uniform appropriate for a London tram operator, with adornments suitable for a luxury hotel—a double row of polished buttons, red piping on the seams, a pillbox hat, everything in order and ready for inspection.

In contrast to his crisp turnout, the lift operator's face has the sunken weariness of a man who has seen too much and has kept too much of it to himself. It's the face of a man who served in the trenches—which, it is said, aged a man one year for every week on duty.

Already the normal tension between any three men in a tiny, softly lit room has become palpable. Hook imagines an interrogation room, with the rheostat lever operating an electric torture device.

The lift operator pushes the lever and the car begins its ascent. The abrupt speed causes Hook's stomach to heave.

"Is a pity about Mr Cunning, if I may say, sir," the lift operator says.

"I completely agree."

"A man of accomplishment."

"Were you acquainted with the Attorney General?"

"Mr Cunning was regular passenger since six years. We spoke from time to time."

The lift operator stares dead ahead as the floors swish by.

"Did you happen to notice anything about Mr Cunning's state of mind over the past little while? Did he appear worried or frightened or out of sorts?"

"Many people are nervous on lifts, sir—including yourself."

"I meant something out of the ordinary way of things."

"No, he is normal. On the go always—though he complained of having a touch of something."

"You mean like a touch of the flu?"

"We don't use that word, sir."

"Of course. I expect the Spanish flu is still on the minds of your guests."

"They are saying it outkilled the war. Only a rumour it takes to empty a hotel."

"Where did you serve?"

"Hundred and Second Battalion, sir."

"Out of Comox?"

"Correct, sir. Mobilized in '15."

"Wounded?"

"Cambrai, sir." The lift operator knocks his white-gloved hand against the wall. "Is made of wood halfway to the elbow. Stopped a bullet from an alley-man. They used the guillotine."

"Well, soldier, at least you survived—unlike many."

"Yes, sir. That is true, I suppose. For what purpose I am not sure."

"Many men would agree. Not much use for combat training these days."

"True, but is not necessarily so."

A pair of hard blue eyes flash like stones from a jeweller's shop.

DESPITE THE NUTRITIONAL value of tomato juice, McCurdy feels like eating breakfast.

It takes a full twenty minutes navigating through the mass of pedestrians headed to work to cover just three blocks from the Hotel Vancouver to Maxine's Lunch, which is across the street from his lodgings on Granville. He takes his usual seat by the window, chiding himself for violating his normal schedule: stimulants in the morning, depressants at night...

If the martini glasses hadn't arrived, then where did it come from—the broken one he saw with his own eyes?

With no further information, he decides to put the question aside for the moment, stir up the pot to see what surfaces. When a man like Cunning dies unexpectedly, it's a matter of hours before the rumours start flying—and who knows, one of them might actually be true.

Beckoning the rather pretty new waitress in the white apron and cap, he orders coffee, bacon, sausages, eggs, black pudding, baked beans, tomatoes, mushrooms and buttered toast, banishing from his mind the mental image of Gordon Cunning's outstretched claw and detached denture.

He wonders what chain of cause and effect might lead to a man dying alone in a public place, drinking a martini. He wonders if compiling an enemies list might be worth the time and trouble, or perhaps it would be better to adopt a wait-and-see attitude and stand by...

Savouring the taste of relatively fresh coffee, he gazes out the window, where unemployed veterans loiter between buildings, smoking. Everyone gravitates to a specific place, and McCurdy has been watching them for over a year, gently crumbling, thanks to the meagre support from Veterans Affairs.

Lately, however, things seem to be looking up for these forgotten men, with various small business dealings taking place between supposed vagrants and some of the vehicles and pedestrians who happen to pass by.

Across the street, just such a transaction is taking place now: while McCurdy slathers beans and egg yolk onto a slice of toast, a green Avalon Dairy wagon pulls up by the curb, the driver's side window opens and, as though by pre-arrangement, a hand reaches out to receive a number of paper slips from three unkempt gentlemen. In return they receive what looks to be currency and then return to their customary spots.

Orders for booze and dope, no doubt about it, however early in the day.

Without a word having been exchanged, the driver's window shuts, the reins are given a shake, the patient, blinkered horse lifts up a set of hooves the size of dinner plates and the wagon trundles on, leaving behind a steaming mound of shit.

# CHAPTER 4

LOCATED AT THE northwest corner of the building at the end of a carpeted hall, the Alexandra Suite consists of sitting room, living room, dining room, bedroom and bath; DS Hook inspects the soles of his boots before continuing, like a child about to enter the front parlour.

"Say, aren't guillotines French, sir?"

"In the field they used a smaller version. Quicker and more efficient than a bone saw, with less splatter."

The constable flinches. Civilians flinch easily.

Hook pushes the light switch, causing a series of shell-shaped wall sconces to cast a warm glow over an arrangement of imitation Chippendale furniture, a popular choice that conveys Britishness and is immune to criticism.

"Don't touch anything with your bare hands."

"Fingerprints, sir?"

"Yes, Mr Quam. And, in your case, breakage."

"I suppose you mean the martini glass, sir. It was not my fault."

"Quite."

"So we are treating this as a crime scene?"

"For the time being, yes."

Quam thinks about this. "I suppose every scene is a potential crime scene, depending on the people present."

For not the first time, Hook wonders whether Quam's remark was very deep or very stupid. He decides on the latter, lights an Ogden's and examines the slip of paper McCurdy slipped into his side pocket.

*No martinis served.*

Hook thinks about the martini glass. Did Cunning supply his own? Otherwise, whoever served the martini must have planned

ahead. Perhaps McCurdy has something to say. He's an inveter-
ate bullshitter, but some of his bull hits the mark.

"Right, let's get to it then. Mr Quam, you are to search the
bedroom. See if you notice anything suspicious."

"Such as what, sir?"

"If we knew what it was in advance, it wouldn't be suspicious,
would it?"

"I agree, sir. Nothing is suspicious until it is."

"Oh come on, you might as well say that everything isn't suspicious until it isn't."

"Yes indeed, sir, that as well," Quam says, heading for the
bedroom.

Alone now and able to concentrate, Hook surveys the sitting
room. Nothing seems out of place; in fact the room looks as
though the maids have prepared it for the next guest—except
for an area in front of the bay window looking toward Grouse
Mountain, a niche occupied by a walnut writing desk topped
by irregular stacks of paper—documents, reports, newspaper
clippings—piled around a brass banker's lamp.

He crosses to the desk and pulls back the chair—an executive's chair with curved arms and dark brown leather upholstery designed to assure the sitter that his comfort is of utmost
importance. He sits down and rifles through the mounds of
unsorted paperwork. Apparently Cunning was no detail man,
rather the sort who spends time staring at the mountains and
making plans.

Hook gets up and crosses to the bedroom, where for some
reason Quam's legs are sticking out from under the bed.

"Mr Quam, are you hiding from someone?"

"What?" The muffled voice might just as well be coming from
the floor below.

"What are you doing down there?"

"I think I found something, sir."

While Quam reverse-crawls from under the bed, Hook opens
a side table drawer and extracts a Gideon bible. Clamping his
cigarette between his teeth, he flips through the pages, causing a
number of twenty-dollar notes to flutter onto the table. He wets
his finger and counts them out: a hundred and twenty dollars.

By now Quam is on his feet, holding a near-empty bottle of

clear liquid. "It rolled under the bed to the side, where you might put a chamber pot."

"Very observant, Constable. And did you search the drawers?"

"Every one of them, sir. Nothing to report there."

Hook holds up the notes and the Gideon bible. "People stash money in books, Mr Quam."

"By stash, sir, do you mean he was keeping the money hidden?"

"That would be one interpretation, yes."

"I keep my money in my wallet. That's hidden enough."

"Bully for you, Constable. Do you think it possible that this money is reserved for payment to someone who comes to his suite, someone who provides a good or service?"

"Oh, I wouldn't know about that," Quam says, scratching his armpit. "It's a lot of money to spend on room service."

"But not for other services, surely? Of the female persuasion?"

The constable's cheeks acquire a rather fetching blush: "Beg pardon, sir?"

"You're a bachelor. Surely you've had some dealings with working girls."

"Only to arrest them, sir. Begging your pardon, but I find your suggestion shocking."

Hook feels an urge to thrust Quam's head into the drawer and slam it repeatedly; instead, he points at the bottle in his hand. "What is that you're holding?"

Quam hands it over. "It's a bottle."

"You don't say." Hook reads the label: *Patterson's Silk Hat Martini Cocktail*—one of many so-called tonics from pharmacist's shelves, popular during Prohibition. The heel contains maybe three fingers of clear liquid.

He wonders whether Cunning might have discreetly ordered liquor brought to his suite, to be paid for in cash—with Patterson's Cocktail as a standby for a rainy day. With paid informants at every liquor store (the People's Prohibition Association employs a stable of them), an Attorney General who campaigned as a moderationist can scarcely be seen buying liquor on a regular basis.

At the same time, with martinis available in the hotel lounge, why resort to Patterson's Cocktail?

WHILE THE CONSTABLE roots about the dresser and armoire, Hook inspects the bathroom, which wouldn't be out of place in a hospital for royalty: a spotless sanctuary of marble and porcelain, equipped with a tub that would accommodate a small family, a massive pedestal sink, a chrome towel warmer, a steam radiator and multiple towels as puffy and soft as whipped cream.

Opening the water closet, Hook steps into an immaculate cubicle with a small frosted window and an electric fan for ventilation; an image comes to mind of infantrymen squatting over holes in the ground, bent double to avoid snipers...

*How long have I been staring at this pokey little window?*

This has been happening more frequently of late—situations in which he looks at a thing and suddenly he remembers the war. Even more alarmingly, the experiences that come to mind aren't limited to his own, or even to scenes he has witnessed: bursts of machine-gun fire tearing a man in half; entire platoons blind and choking to death; foot rot, lice infestation, rat bites: events he "heard about somewhere" can burst into view every bit as vividly as any memory. In the army you hear stories. They seep into a man's bones, like family lore from the Old Country.

Next to the flush toilet, a metal stand embraces a stack of multiple-ply paper sheets with a soft, flannel-like finish. Hook removes several sheets, folds them in two and slides them into his breast pocket; Jeanie will find them a welcome change from the usual Izal loo roll, whose edges can cut a person's arse to shreds if he's not careful.

Across from the water closet and beside the marble sink (with gold faucets), a hardwood table contains a brass stand carrying a straight razor, shaving brush and a bowl of Taylor's Lavender Shaving Cream. Next to it is a chamois-lined, zippered leather toilet case containing a silver-backed hairbrush and toothbrush holder. He examines the toothbrush—a Koh-I-Noor, the brand Jeanie buys.

He must let her know that, in one respect at least, they travel first class.

The top shelf of the recessed medicine cabinet contains a bottle of aspirin, a bottle of Wildroot hair oil and a tin of Ex-Lax. On the next shelf down, a bottle of Bromo Seltzer and another of Mrs Winslow's Soothing Syrup, a cocktail involving baking powder, ammonia and—until the recent legislation—morphine. The bottom shelf holds more Patterson's products: bottles of Patterson's Pepp, Patterson's Male Bracer and Patterson's Kick (*"To Get You Going"*).

He dumps half the aspirin tablets into the side pocket of his tunic (he is running low), and furtively shuts the cabinet door—to face a nondescript policeman with an unsatisfactory moustache and the eyes of a boy from Waldo who wanted to be a motorcycle acrobat. He removes his cap, notes his receding hairline and quickly puts his cap back on.

"Sir! I think you might want to take a look at this."

Returning to the bedroom, Hook finds Quam at an open armoire peering at the suits and haberdashery: cap-toed Oxfords, spats, club ties, all muted and unobtrusive, the garb of a man who wishes his clothing to be recognized only by people who can afford it themselves.

However, the constable's focus is on the shallow wooden case of bottles sitting on the hat shelf.

"There are more bottles, sir."

"I can see that. Bring them down, then. But cover your hand with your handkerchief."

"Are we worried about fingerprints, sir?"

"Do we want *your* fingerprints, Mr Quam?"

"I think not, sir."

"Well, then."

Using his handkerchief as a mitt, Quam brings down the case and sets it on the bed. It contains three bottles of Patterson's Martini Cocktail. Presumably the fourth was under the bed.

"Constable, I want you to return these bottles to the station, secure them under lock and key, then take the one from under the bed to the BCPP."

"I beg your pardon, sir, I hope you don't mean the Provincial Police." Quam appears alarmed, probably by the prospect of actually *doing* something.

"Correct, Constable. Take it to their shiny new lab and we'll see what they can make of it."

"Sir, did Mr Cunning not die of natural causes?"

"Well, he didn't die of old age. Let's move on, shall we? At the time of death, our man had been drinking martinis. Now we see that a bottle labelled Patterson's Martini was under his bed. What do you make of that?"

"Nothing, sir. Pure coincidence."

"Or it could have been a pun."

"A *pun*, sir?"

"Oh, never mind."

Quam's eyes grow watery: "Detective Sergeant, I hope you appreciate the paperwork involved in requisitioning all this lab service."

DS Hook's jaw has become so tense that he wonders if it's beginning to crack. "Indeed. Most inconvenient having to do one's job."

Constable Quam's eyes narrow: "I believe that sounds like sarcasm, sir."

"Oh does it really? How strange."

"Sir, I should caution you that sarcasm is frowned upon in the VPD. There's an unwritten rule that officers should refrain from taking the piss."

"Do you mean it's a tradition, like saluting?"

"It's just not the thing, sir. If you don't mind me saying so, a good punch in the mouth is more acceptable."

DS Hook is well aware that he is the new man in the constabulary, and that members are expected to demonstrate loyalty to the force—sometimes in preference to the law. In Hook's case, such devotion has not yet presented itself, to his colleagues or to himself; he is an outsider, arbitrarily promoted and parachuted into a senior position.

Quam has long been established as one of the gang, and has the advantage.

While seated alone in the staff room with his tea, Hook has often watched Quam in conversation with other constables, exchanging gossip and sports stories, with periodic bursts of unpleasant laughter at someone other than themselves.

To succeed in this new position, Hook will have to put out of mind the VPD's earned reputation for incompetence and venality. (Not unlike the army, really.)

He takes the last aspirin from his tin, chews it to a bitter powder and swallows it down. "Mr Quam, the government has funded a shiny new crime lab. Surely the BCPP will be eager to put it to use."

"I wouldn't know about the workings of the BCPP, sir."

Hook's mind is suffocating. He needs space to think clearly. To exchange ideas with Quam is like having glue pumped through his ears and into his brain.

"What about a spot of lunch, sir?" Quam says the word *lunch* as though chewing on it. "Twenty minutes for a Downy Flake and a coffee?"

"Good idea, Mr Quam. But there's one thing I need you to do first."

# CHAPTER 5

THE TWO DOORS slide open and DS Hook uneasily enters the lift. "Mezzanine floor, please."

He feels vaguely sheepish about having put the constable to a wall-to-wall creep search of the floor, embarrassed by the satisfaction it gave him to hear Quam's knees crack on the way down.

"Mezzanine. Certainly, sir." The lift operator pushes the rheostat handle and the vehicle starts to plummet, and Hook's stomach is a clenched fist.

"Do not worry, sir, it will soon be over."

"Quite." Hook winces: Do these cramped quarters enable the occupant to read the visitor's thoughts? "By the way, I'm Detective Sergeant Hook."

"I am pleased to meet you, sir. Sark is my name."

They shake hands—Hook with his right hand, Sark with his left.

"A quick question, Mr Sark. Did Mr Cunning take deliveries?"

"Deliveries of what, sir?"

"Anything really. Packages, documents, that sort of thing?"

"On daily basis. By courier from Victoria."

"What about sundries? Books? Magazines? Bottles? Any personal visits? Did he have any visitors? Female, perhaps?"

"Sir, it is central policy of the hotel to protect the privacy of our guests. There are twelve policies, we obey them or—" The lift operator mimes throat slitting with his good hand.

"Then I take it Mr Cunning had dealings to be private about. Oh well, I suppose we all have something to hide."

"The human being is complicated machine, sir. Like us all, Mr Cunning was man of many parts."

Having stopped at the mezzanine floor, the lift operator reaches and the cage squeezes open.

"Mr Sark, were the cable to break, what would happen if we jumped up and down? Would it give us a fifty-fifty chance of survival?"

"No, sir. In either case you can spread us on sandwich."

"I was afraid of that."

"It is not to worry. A small box going up and down is safest place in the world."

Hook's headache is back. He reaches into his side pocket, pops two pilfered aspirin in his mouth and chews them to powder.

IN THE HOTEL manager's outer office he faces a pretty young woman (even without makeup) operating an Underwood typewriter with unsettling speed. Beside the usual wire baskets of foolscap, a cradle telephone stands within reach; behind that is a small Chinese vase containing what look to be forget-me-nots— an emblem for girls whose swains were overseas in the war.

She looks up with a smile that would be pretty if it had any happiness in it; in this case, it is the smile of someone who has been told to smile.

"Good afternoon, sir. How may I help you?"

As she greets him, her fingers still tap the keys and the type bars strike the platen, creating a distinct rhythm, like a tap dancer gone mad. The presence of a policeman seems to have no effect on her speed whatsoever. DS Hook can only stare at her two-tone fingernails, moving like the legs of tiny burlesque dancers.

"Sir?"

Returning his gaze to its proper position, he displays his warrant card and executes his most cordial smile. With an effort he avoids looking down past the crucifix around her neck just above the frilled bodice of her blouse. This is a good Catholic girl who would not take it as a compliment.

"I'd like a word with Mr Tremblay, miss, if you don't mind."

"Yes, sir. And who shall I say is calling?"

"I am Detective Sergeant Hook. It's about the Attorney—"

Before he finishes his sentence she gets up, crosses to the inner door and pokes her head inside. A short exchange follows, impossible to overhear. DS Hook averts his gaze from her derrière, preferring to examine the huge photograph on the wall to the left—a portrait of honourables in top hats and long black coats standing in front of the main entrance, and below it a description of the eminent men attending the Hotel Vancouver's opening, with a note that the picture was taken in 1916.

Ah, 1916: with Europe a slaughterhouse, the CPR saw fit to build the grandest hotel in the empire.

"Mr Tremblay will see you now."

To go with the manager's three-piece tweed suit, his office conveys a sense of solidity and continuity, with club chairs of chocolate leather, a brass banker's lamp and a desk as heavy as a roadster, topped with a silver-and-leather desk set. With the oak wainscotting it all comes together as a unit—like the interior of a luxury auto—except for the two black candlestick telephones placed side by side like twin long-necked birds about to quack.

"What is it that I can do for you, officer?"

The manager occupies a swivel chair not unlike the Attorney General's desk chair, seven floors above.

Just to annoy him, DS Hook takes a moment to examine the huge oil painting to his right, across from the arched window—a rectangle filled with vertical blotches of black and green, like a waterfall dispensing dead fish floating in stomach bile and blood pudding.

"Ravishing, is it not, officer? It is a Milne. A very important artist."

"Don't know much about art I'm afraid, sir."

A pause while the manager extracts a Gitanes from a silver case, and DS produces an Ogden's from his crumpled packet.

On the wall behind the manager's chair hang photos of eminent men—Charles Lindbergh, Neville Chamberlain, Somerset Maugham, Babe Ruth—each inscribed with a brief statement about having had an enjoyable stay.

"I shan't keep you long, sir. Any man with two telephones must be a very busy man indeed."

A barely perceptible flinch: "It is the modern age, officer. The Hotel Vancouver is a modern business."

"Do you talk in both at once? Do you hold meetings over the telephone?"

"Ha, ha, that is I think a joke?"

"Just curious—something I haven't seen before."

"People on the important call do not like to wait."

"So you *do* hold meetings—with a receiver on each ear."

"Is this the reason for your visit, *monsieur*? To discuss the telephones?"

An uneasy pause. The manager lights his French cigarette with a silver desk lighter; Hook flicks a kitchen match with his thumbnail; smoke blows in two directions, creating a bluish haze above the desk.

"Quite right, sir. To the business at hand, which of course concerns the sudden demise of the Attorney General."

The manager sighs, shakes his head, sucks his cigarette and blows a melancholy plume from deep within his lungs: "It is all a dreadful business, *monsieur*, I am sure you will agree this is so. Mr Cunning was a valued guest."

"As I understand it, a guest who rented his suite at a yearly rate."

"Of course. A member of the Executive Council cannot do government business always in Victoria. This is normal, yes?"

"Was the Attorney General an acquaintance, sir—or might I say, someone you knew personally?"

"*Moi*?" The manager marvels at Hook's stupidity. "Not of me, *monsieur*. But a friend of the hotel, that is so."

"Is there anything you can tell me about Mr Cunning's personal habits? Any regular visitors? Did he entertain frequently?"

"Of course, it is impossible. Our duty is to protect the privacy of our guests."

"A dead man is no longer a guest, Mr Tremblay."

"It is, am I to say so, a technicality."

"Sir, I salute you as a man of principle. Of course, the stand you have taken will drag out the investigation—"

"What is it you mean, *drag out*?" The manager stubs out his cigarette unnecessarily.

"Issues have come up that must be resolved before we can vacate the suite."

"What questions are you questioning, please?"

"It is departmental policy not to discuss an open case with the general public."

The manager produces a report in the afternoon edition of *The Beacon*: "'Cause of death to be peritonitis brought on by an inflamed appendix.' Officer, what is to investigate? I ask this."

"Mr Tremblay, on viewing the remains, did you yourself see evidence of such an illness? For example, did Mr Cunning puke or shit himself?"

The manager colours slightly. "Sergeant Hook, it is outrageous you are holding the suite empty on your vague suspicion. I will issue a complaint."

"That is your right, sir. But surely you can't have booked the suite already—with a year left on the government lease and the bed still warm, so to speak?"

"A hotel is a business, *monsieur*, not a mortuary."

"It may also be a crime scene. In fact, I expect we'll have to seal the room."

"*Seal the room?*" Seeing the manager flush with alarm, DS Hook's headache eases somewhat—or it could be the aspirin.

DEATH OF A MODERATIONIST
Much Uncertainty in Cunning's Wake
Ed McCurdy
Staff Writer
*The Evening Star*

Disciples of wet and of dry
Bid him a sullen good-bye
And who will succeed
Mr Cunning to lead
The dominion of watered-down rye?

He served as House Speaker and Minister of Labour. Re-elected three times, as Attorney General he presided over the ministry responsible for law and order, not to mention the Liquor Control Board, which trumps the Department of Finance when it comes to the province's fiscal health. The late Gordon Cunning may well be remembered as the most gifted politician in British Columbia's history.

A fine speaker with a resonant singing voice (his "Danny Boy" at a funeral drew tears from the deceased), the veteran politician cut a handsome figure in a kilt (*He ha' a brawny set of legs on 'im!*), so that his outward Scottishness made up for his upbringing in the southern United States.

At the same time, it must be said that, in fighting for and keeping his seat in the riding of Omineca, Mr Cunning tended to battle his opponents with a pair of sharp elbows, and became a divisive figure in Williams Lake during the last election by conducting an unusually vicious campaign.

Yet such setbacks were but potholes in the road to greater glory.

Throughout the plebiscite he was at the forefront of the moderationist army, which cemented his position as Attorney General, whose domain now included a bureaucratic empire called the Liquor Control Board of BC.

Naturally, Cunning's moderationist position drew the personal enmity of the Woman's Christian Temperance Union and the People's Prohibition Association, as well as Presbyterians and Baptists—and continued, despite subsequent efforts to appease, with a set of restrictions that might have been crafted by Nellie McClung.

Meanwhile, the new restrictions on liquor production have infuriated manufacturers, while hoteliers chafe at the new drinking laws and consumers of alcohol complain about high prices and low quality in government stores.

In the end, Mr Cunning's attempts at reconciliation succeeded in making enemies of just about everyone.

The one group well satisfied with the new regulations are the bootleggers, who have seen no drop in demand, having maintained an overwhelming advantage in price and quality. For the black market, business has never been better.

But who will take up the challenge, with Cunning out of the picture?

Among observers one name stands above all others: Boris Stalker, the newly elected MLA for Vancouver City.

Supporting this opinion, other sources in the Attorney General's office report a rumour to the effect that Clyde Taggart, a Cunning loyalist (and some say, his Svengali) is about to walk the plank.

One thing certain: Cunning's death marks the end of an era.

With so many enemies, it seems almost absurd that the Attorney General should die peacefully in the Hotel Vancouver, with a martini glass by his side.

# CHAPTER 6

GENERAL VICTOR NEWSON, member of the Legislature and owner/publisher of *The Vancouver Evening Star*, occupies a corner suite on the top floor of a brick cube, with windows overlooking Pender Street.

His office could be taken for a command post, having no carpet and nothing on the walls but a map of the battle zone. Since the election, the electoral map has been replaced by a street map with red dots indicating liquor outlets, as though Vancouver has the measles; a livid rash spreading over the downtown core, diminishing to isolated pimples at the edges.

In the field, the general was known as Old Lime Juice, for refusing his men their customary tot of rum before climbing over the top to be blasted to bloody bits. Civilian life has not changed his leadership style other than to increase the level of bombast, and give free rein to his hazardous whims.

"Sit down, lad." Already McCurdy can feel Newson's stare burn through his forehead, exploring for ulterior motives.

McCurdy takes the only seat available: rock hard, straight-backed, with legs that seem to have been sawed off so that the seated visitor is forced to look up to his host.

Custom built to look like a field table, Newson's desk is strewn with notes in his tiny, tight handwriting. Before him sits a pile of blank foolscap, and a field artillery shell containing a bouquet of sharpened pencils. Broken pencils litter the floor—not with broken leads, but broken in two.

For Newson, having lost a plebiscite and then won a seat in the Legislature, the past few years have been a mixture of victory and loss. Throughout the war it was victory or death—General Newson's victory, someone else's death. In peacetime, however, with his glory years behind him, comes a creeping awareness that the day will soon be at hand when other people will be alive and he will not.

Someone must pay for this.

THANKS TO MCCURDY'S chair, Newson looms overhead, elbows braced, arms splayed like a human field gun.

"'The hottest places in hell are reserved for those who maintain their neutrality in a time of moral crisis.' Who said that, son?"

"It's from Dante's 'Inferno,' I think."

"You're wrong. It was General Haig. I heard him say it with my own ears. He was talking about the Swiss."

"If the Swiss are in hell, then where are *we*?"

Lately, McCurdy has heard himself blurt such phrases often, remarks he wishes he could haul back into his mouth. Of course, it might be the powder he takes as a bracer for meetings such as this.

But the general doesn't seem to have taken offence, in fact doesn't seem to have heard him at all. Instead, he has moved on to another thought.

"Son, is it right for a man to be judged in heaven and not on earth?"

"It seems unfair. But even so, I should think hell is sufficient punishment."

"Wrong again, son. Hell is too good for some people."

McCurdy is beginning to suspect where this is going. The general isn't about to call a truce just because his enemy is dead.

"Sir, if you're referring to the late Attorney General, now that Mr Cunning has pegged out perhaps it would be better to—"

"Bury the hatchet? Let bygones be bygones?" Newson would sneer if had an upper lip. "Thanks to Crooked Cunning and his goddamn moderation, the Liberal Party is a cesspool of graft. What is to come next? Government whorehouses?"

"The bible calls for judgment—in heaven *and* on earth. And we will do our part, lad. We *will* do our part." On the word *will*, the general stabs his desk with a forefinger, splitting the nail; he doesn't appear to notice.

"Sir, it sounds as though you propose to use Cunning's death to fight the temperance issue all over again."

"Well put, lad—but on a wider field. We are going to war against Gordon Cunning and his whole gang of moderation mercenaries. And you, sir, will lead the charge." Newson's two fingers become a pistol aimed at the reporter's face.

He was afraid of this.

During the war, General Newson was known for his astounding casualty rates, thanks to night raids on heavily fortified positions; it was Russian roulette for the troops, with the general well out of danger framing a report that would fetch a commendation, if not another gong.

Having no idea where else to go, McCurdy continues the military metaphor: "And what's our strategy, sir?"

"For the present, we keep our powder dry. As my top writer, you are to stockpile ammunition. Soon I intend to desert the Liberal Party and sit as an Independent.

"Then we go at them lad—guns blazing!—and force an election.

"Timing, lad." For some reason the general taps his temple; beads of blood leak from his split nail, unnoticed.

"If you don't mind my asking, sir, what then? Bowser and his Conservatives form a government—What is the point? Where are you going with this?" And a glimmer of understanding comes to him.

The general sits back and makes a tent with his long fingers; a lipless line widens into what might be a smile.

# CHAPTER 7

THIS IS MCCURDY'S first venture into the newly built Kingsway Hotel, whose "beer parlour" is the first establishment in town specially designed to accommodate the new regulations.

He has never seen anything like it.

In preparation for the meeting, he has taken a table in a section labelled *Ladies and Escorts*, separated from the all-male herd by a fence made of thick rope, strung through low wooden posts and whitewashed to achieve a nautical look that is entirely abandoned within, as the rope barrier becomes a corral, complete with a wagon wheel chandelier. The tables are the standard terry-covered discs, each with a salt cellar in the centre to "wake up" a stale keg.

Outside the white rope, ranks and files of terry-covered tables stretch to the wall in what might be best described as a drinking factory.

Already, the Ladies and Escorts section has acquired an unsavoury reputation as a sexual marketplace; when McCurdy explained to the waiter that he was about to meet a lady, the waiter made no attempt to hide a smirk.

Since he entered the Kingsway, he has felt as though someone is watching him, like an itch in the nape of his neck. If Miss Wickstram doesn't arrive soon, he will be thrown out of the Ladies and Escorts section, if not out the door.

Late, as always, the more inconvenient the better. He knows she does this on purpose. Swallowing his annoyance with the remains of a pint, he takes pencil in hand and takes notes:

HEAD: *A Drinking Factory for the Working Man*

The upper classes raise a glass
In dens of gilt and teak

While working dogs must gulp their grog
In quarters cold and bleak.

LEDE: The Kingsway Hotel, so new the paint is wet, was specially designed to comply with the new drinking regulations.

BODY: For Liberals, a master stroke. Prohibitionists approve. Make beer by the glass nasty & as expensive as possible.

SUBHEAD: A Hotel in Name Only.

Towels, soap rarely present. Capricious maid service. Sheets changed grudgingly. Room service a myth.

SUBHEAD: A Miserable Place To Drink.

Long, barn-like area. Rows of tables the size of the palm of your hand. Terry cloth the colour of blood. Two spine-breaking chairs.

Decor—none.

Entertainment—none.

Games, food, singing—none.

SUBHEAD: Class Warfare?

Upper-class private clubs (ex. Terminal City Club), home cellars stocked with imported whisky, wine from California. Versus beer by the glass, the only drink working men can afford.

TAGLINE: To discourage working-class drinking, a venue designed to ensure that nothing distracts a man— from drinking.

Pocketing pen and notepad, McCurdy stands to pull back Mildred's seat. "Better late than never, Miss Wickstram."

"Better never than here, Eddie. Why don't they just drink from hoses, like autos at a petrol station?"

Mildred has arrived in a flimsy dress that shows altogether too much skin for the premises, and a severe Egyptian bob that could have been cut with a pair of gardening shears. The last time he saw her, she was in a suit, vest and tie. Neither look is to his taste.

She removes a beaded cigarette case from her purse, extracts a Turkish cigarette and lights up with a mother-of-pearl petrol lighter. The plume of acrid smoke reminds him of a burning tyre.

"First off, you owe me ten dollars for Noël Coward."

"Nothing like getting to the point, is there? It took up a single paragraph. Surely five dollars is sufficient."

"That wasn't our agreement. Locating a source, a night letter from London—don't be a chiseler, Eddie. The Prince is halfway to Australia. You're going to need new shit to shovel. You will need information you're not prepared to locate."

McCurdy has no good reply to this. "A spot of blackmail, I see. How classy. Such elegance."

Hovering over them, the waiter sports a smudged apron, a paintbrush moustache, patent leather hair and a tray loaded with glasses of beer and balanced on one arm, each glass filled precisely to a painted white line just below the rim, the official dosage. He places two "railroad servings" (two glasses each) on the table and removes McCurdy's empties.

The reporter gives him sixty cents, tip included. With an insinuating lift of one eyebrow, the waiter leaves the Ladies and Escorts section, pausing at a nearby table to share a private joke with a worker stained black from the creosote plant who could be mistaken for Al Jolson.

"Why did he look at me like that?"

"He thinks you're a woman of easy virtue."

"Do I look like a woman of easy virtue?"

"It's the bare arms, I think."

"Don't be an animal. It's a tea dress. I'm invited to a ladies' book club in Kerrisdale. I didn't have time to wear something more appropriate."

"Like a lumberjack shirt, you mean."

"A good choice, here at least. Surprising, how much one can learn if one fits in visually—like a real reporter, gathering information as opposed to buying it, that sort of thing."

"A bit snide, coming from someone who trades on guests' private telephone conversations—and at the classiest hotel in the empire."

"Eddie, as one who types up General Newson's crap, I wouldn't go on about ethics in modern communication."

She drains a third of a glass in one swallow, then dabs foam from her upper lip with a lace hanky—gently, so as not to smear her lip gloss.

McCurdy takes a long drink, deliberately leaving foam on his moustache, and leans forward, confidentially: "In any case, I have an assignment. What you so delicately like to call 'shit to shovel.'"

"First let me see ten dollars." She presents her open purse, a mouth waiting to be fed.

Resentfully, he opens his wallet, extracts five two-dollar notes, and slaps them onto the table like playing cards.

She wrinkles her nose. "Devil's dollars? Is that all you have?"

"Superstitious, Millie? Gone native, have we?"

She tears off a corner of each bill to ward off bad luck, then folds them into a side pocket of her purse. "So what vile business is it this time, Eddie?"

Reflexively, he checks for eavesdroppers. "I need material about our late Attorney General and his cronies."

"Such as what?"

"You tell me. You've been eavesdropping on him for ages."

"Among others. I'm not a voyeur."

"Indiscriminate eavesdropping is equally indecent, I should think."

She smiles, while giving him the stink eye: "Have you known boredom, Eddie? Real boredom? Try saying the same three sentences over and over for nine hours, with a twenty-minute lunch break and two ten-minute tea breaks, and some biddy walking back and forth behind you policing your posture and *cheerfulness*. Do that six days a week for, oh let us say, a year, for joke wages. Then see if if you can muster the will to articulate a sentence other than 'Please hold, I'll connect you now...'" Mildred lights another cigarette with the last one still burning under his nose.

"Your fury is chilling, Millie. The voice of the loyal servant who puts poison in the soup."

"Oh fuck off Eddie, just tell me what you want."

"That's a big question, but for the moment it's this—" He produces a folded piece of newsprint from his breast pocket. "The general has opened a new front in the war on drink. He says I'm to lead the charge."

He tosses the folded newsprint across the table. "This should give you some idea."

THE REAL PRICE OF ALCOHOL
## Citizens Demand Second Plebiscite
Editorial
*The Evening Star*

Since the defeat of the prohibitionist cause, it has become clear to all that rescinding it was an ill-considered blunder.

It is now understood by sensible men that the vote's timing put the People's Prohibition Association at a crippling disadvantage. The conviction of Commissioner Farris on bootlegging charges handed peddlers of alcohol the opportunity to push through a vote before the scandal could be put into its proper context.

Thanks to rogue officials, an isolated incident and a lack of judgment on the part of unsophisticated female voters, the most farsighted legislation in BC history lies in ruins, and hoodwinked citizens have been left to stew in their own juice.

Now government coffers have swollen, thanks to usurious taxation enabled by the weasel word *moderation*. The public good withers in an atmosphere of venal opportunism.

It is hardly a matter of great surprise that alcoholism is rife throughout the city. At beer halls such as the Kingsway Hotel, children freely partake of six per cent beer when they should be attending school.

It appears that alcoholism is a disease contracted not just by individuals, but by governments as well.

Mr Cunning's sudden demise is a pity, for he can no longer be held accountable for the harm he has done.

Mildred folds and refolds the clipping into a lozenge and flicks it away. "Newson is losing his mind."

"Do you think it's that bad?"

"Look how he mixes his metaphors."

"Of course he mixes them. Who doesn't?"

She looks about, theatrically. "I don't see any schoolboys around. It's a creation of his fevered brain."

"Newson has always chosen the facts to fit the picture."

"Isn't it a bit unusual for a member of the Legislature to

denounce his own Attorney General—his *late* Attorney General? Not to mention his own party."

"For the general, nobody should exist but him. That is his worldview."

"A bit like you, Eddie?"

"Please darling, don't go Freudian on me."

"Fine. So let us sum up: at the general's deluded whim, you are prepared to undertake a campaign of character assassination against a corpse."

"That's correct, Millie. Actually, it's not such a tall order. Since the liquor legislation came into effect, just about everyone has simply loathed Gordon Cunning. There's a ready market for unflattering stories, true or not."

"All the news they want to hear, that sort of thing."

"Supply and demand, Millie. Unless you're a Communist."

"You're the most cynical man I've ever met."

"It was just an observation, no need to get shirty about it."

"Fine. So the first line of business is to prove that Mr Cunning was a hypocrite."

"Correct."

"To be frank, for a politician that doesn't sound newsworthy or interesting."

"To start, look at it as a character study from a specific viewpoint. The Drys want to hear that he was an out-and-out drunk—and he did drink, sometimes immoderately, which is a start. This could lead to other contrasts between word and deed. And we mustn't be afraid to branch out—a sexual indiscretion would be ideal, given the way he squeaked out a victory last election. I see it concluding on a cautionary note—a *What If He'd Lived*? pipe smoker about our man's corrupting influence on everything he touched... Why are you looking at me like that, Millie?"

Again, the smile and the stink eye: "Eddie, your soul is curling up at the edges, like a dry leaf."

SHE LEAVES THE beer parlour, alone—a bit imprudent in this part of town—but it is still daylight and it is not as imprudent as being seen with McCurdy, who has become a magnet for loathing in some quarters, some of it intense.

Had he not failed his eye test (any eye test), McCurdy would have made a fine assassin. Perhaps that is what he is.

The trolley from Burnaby shrieks to a halt in front of her—one of the new models made of steel and not wood, with the steering wheel on the left-hand side. The driver pulls a heavy lever that causes the doors to fold open, letting out a waft of warm, stale air.

Mildred reaches for the railing, places her foot on the bottom step, braces and heaves her body inside. Like most machinery, the trolley was designed for male proportions. A women of five-foot-three must board like a monkey climbing a tree.

As the doors are about to close, she looks back, waves to the familiar shadow in front of the Kingsway Hotel and then turns to drop seven cents into the chute.

The driver watches her carefully. She can feel his eyes running up and down her bare arms like dirty fingernails. When she meets and holds his gaze, he smiles placidly and turns to examine the windscreen.

Crab walking down the aisle between leather seats, she passes a man seated by each window, either staring at his reflection or dozing with his mouth open. Some faces are so dirty they defy the whole concept of a "white" race. Even the clean faces aren't really white, but pink and beige, some with prawn-coloured blotches.

Which one will she sit beside? Whose body odour will she inhale? Which one is a masher with inadvertent hands?

For reassurance, she pats her purse, containing the self-defence tools recommended by a new friend—a longish hat pin and a metal comb with sharpened teeth.

YOUR SOUL IS curling up at the edges, like a dry leaf. What in holy hell did she mean by that?

This is not the first time McCurdy has found himself brooding about something Mildred said. She seems to have taken it upon herself to make him uncomfortable—or rather, more uncomfortable than normal.

After deep-breathing fresh air outside the Kingsway Hotel, he heads for the street, mulling over his wasted life thanks to Miss Wickstram. In his preoccupied state he fails to notice the two men in checked suits and derby hats until they appear just ahead of him, a wall of muscle and fat.

"Good evening, gentlemen."

"Did ye serve, arsehole?" The larger of the two has a flat tone of voice and a slight lisp.

"Sorry, but I think you might be mistaking me for one of the waiters."

"In the war, ye feckwit. Did ye serve in the fecking war?"

McCurdy lifts his eyeglasses from his nose as evidence: "Refused, I'm afraid. Blind without them. Tried my best."

"So ye're the bugger who ain't served, slagging the royal family."

"You mean the piece on Prince George? Good grief man, that was two columns ago!"

One derby hat turns to the other, as though to translate: "This is the fecker who stirs trouble and slags his betters."

"Surely you saw that the piece wasn't about His Grace personally. It's about the aristocracy, the class system, inequality in general—"

A footballer's straight arm snaps his neck back hard enough that he stumbles, trips over the second man's outstretched leg and hits the sidewalk.

"Told you he was a pinko. Put the boots to him, Paul!"

Not a good thing to hear when you're lying down.

Remembering some advice from a unionist of his acquaintance named Sparrow, the reporter covers his face with his arms, his neck with his wrists and hands, and takes the foetal position to avert injury to his vital organs and private parts. The right kidney will just have to fend for itself.

As they go to work, the men chant what sounds like a football yell, punctuated with boots to the organs.

*Fecking bastard!*

*Did you serve, four-eyes?*

*This is for the Somme!*

*Go back to China!*

*Stick* this *up yer fecking arse, arsehole!...*

*Add this to yer bell end, ye bloody bugger bloodclaat.*

AFTER AN UNCERTAIN amount of time, they stop. (His union friend assured him that, eventually, they become tired and bored.) To be on the safe side, he remains in the foetal position, for they might be waiting for him to unclench in order to put the boots to his nuts, while at the same time he wonders how he managed to put himself in this position. You write something, you get paid, then you write something else and get paid for that. How is the writer to know that he is creating a monster?...

"I reckon it's okay to get up now, suh."

He opens his eyes to see a logging boot in front of his face, below a pair of brown wool legs and, above that, what his blurred vision takes to be a plaid shirt.

Paul Bunyan has arrived.

The ribs crack painfully as McCurdy rolls onto his side. An arm is stretched out above him, pointing at something. The hand is holding something solid. Nearby he hears the voices of his attackers, muttering to one another as they retreat to the hotel.

He fumbles for his glasses, only to find they were snapped in half. Holding one lens in front of each eye, he peers about, feeling like an insect on its back.

The man standing over him holds a firearm—a pistol, small enough to fit in a pocket.

"Anything broken, suh? Bleeding anywhere?"

McCurdy takes inventory: ribs, cracked but not broken; bruises will throb tomorrow, not to mention the back, which wasn't in great shape to begin with—

Startled by the shadow overhead, he looks up through his makeshift monocles at the clean-shaven, not unfriendly face before him.

"Thank you for asking, sir. I do seem to be in one piece."

"Glad to hear it, suh."

McCurdy's saviour extends his left hand and levers him to his feet; the right hand is holding the firearm by his side, with the nonchalance of a mechanic with a monkey wrench.

McCurdy takes a seated position. A moment ago, he felt like an insect; now he feels like a toad. "I must say, you are a very persuasive fellow."

"Just a matter of making things clear. Folks respond to plain speaking."

"I suppose. Especially when one is armed."

The pistol disappears into a side pocket. "Don't know what you mean, suh."

"Neither do I," McCurdy replies, relieved that the thing is now out of sight.

The young man smiles. He has crinkles at the corners of his eyes. He has good teeth. *Un-English* teeth.

"The rascals kicked you in the head. Bound to be a mite confused."

"It would be much worse if not for you. My brain thanks you. My kidneys thank you."

"Glad to hear you're in good fettle, Mr McCurdy, suh. These pikers' brains are thick as old barn wood, but they can do damage." The hand pulling him to his feet belongs to a card player or a pianist, certainly not a workman. "The name is Johnston. Hollis Johnston." He smiles with those excellent teeth.

"Glad to have met you, Mr Johnston," McCurdy replies with utter sincerity.

"Seems these fellers took a dislike to you."

"An occupational hazard. I'm with the *Evening Star*."

"Is that a local paper?"

"It is. So you're from out of town?"

"Yup—doing a piece of work is all."

McCurdy takes a few uncertain steps toward the street; Johnston takes his arm. "Steady now, Mr McCurdy. Trolley should show up soon. I'll walk you to it."

"Come to think of it, I think I'll spring for a taxi." McCurdy gestures toward the chattering yellow Studebaker in front of the hotel entrance.

"Suit yourself."

"Thanks again, Mr Johnston, for rescuing me from my readers."

"You betcha." With a quick nod, the young man with the pistol heads back to the Kingsway Hotel, like the Sheriff of Stone Gulch—*straight* back. Clearly, he didn't just happen by.

And how did he know his name?

# CHAPTER 8

WHEN YOU MARRY a woman, you marry her cooking.

Coming from the north part of England, Hook's wife has acquainted him with a whole new food vocabulary: *stottie cake, rumbledethumps, tatty 'ash, pease pudding...*

At present, he is working through a plate of tripe and onions. When he was stationed at Rugeley, the very idea of eating the lining of an ox's stomach would have been enough to put him off his lunch; but when one is smitten by a woman, the taste buds alter. And he is grateful not to face Scottish cookery—oats, internal organs and root vegetables in such quantity that Scotsmen tend to look like root vegetables themselves.

Jeanie puts out an Eccles cake for dessert, pours two cups of strong tea, sits in the chair opposite and watches him eat, with a look of satisfaction that nearly breaks his heart. Whatever she makes, he will eat. He'd eat dog food just to see that look.

"Tell me a story, ducky," she says, resting her chin on her hand, one elbow on the table.

Hook wishes she wouldn't call him that childish name, but he dislikes *Calvin* more these days; seldom is the social gathering where some wag doesn't note that he is the namesake of the US president, forcing him to smile and chuckle. Momentarily he has an urge to reach out to the person and strangle him.

So "ducky" is fine.

Every evening she asks to hear something about his day, something interesting, something they can discuss, anything really— and he is happy to oblige. So he becomes the storyteller—sadly, because he has the stories to tell.

"Pet, this is more like a riddle: Why did the hotel man have two telephones?"

"I can't imagine," she replies, then grins: "One for each ear?"

For the second time today he imagines Tremblay with ear pieces sticking out both sides of his head, like a dog responding to a whistle.

"And there are many men who talk through both sides of their mouth," Jeanie adds.

She's made him laugh twice already. He gets up and leans across the table for an awkward kiss. "Shall we discuss this in another room?"

"You have another curious story to tell me?"

"Let's the two of us make one up."

Hook is sometime troubled by the thought that Jeanie finds him more interesting than he really is. In his own opinion, he is a man with a mediocre brain, filled with mediocre thoughts. But like most veterans, he has a collection of experiences—his and others'—that make him *appear* interesting.

He has begun to suspect that "soldier's heart" is contagious. Even his dreams contain scenes of trench warfare he has never seen himself.

Small wonder that returning soldiers exhibited an unwilling-ness to relate their war stories at home—because many of their most troubling experiences didn't happen to them but to others, yet they left scars as deep as shrapnel...

The two of them lie naked under the coverlet, her cheek on his chest, his hand stroking her hair; he is pleased that his wife has a traditional woman's body, isn't one of those stick women you see today.

"That was lovely," she murmurs.

"It was very lovely. We must do it again soon."

She frowns slightly. "Do you think it possible that the two telephones serve different purposes?"

"If that were so, pet, they would have two different numbers—which would require two separate lines both in and out. And they would both need to go through a switchboard—"

"Ducky, do you think your friend the reporter might ask his friend the hello girl? Mrs Lampman says that's where all the rumours come from."

"I shall mention that to him. You're such an intelligent girl. I find that exciting."

She looks down at the small tent in the quilt. "I can see that.

Whatever are we going to do?"

He turns to the bedside table and examines the empty packet of illegal contraceptives he bought from the barber (*Something for the weekend, sir*?), which were once issued to the troops for free, and are now a luxury at a dollar apiece.

"What do you think, ducky? Shall we chance it?"

A MORE DEADLY DRINK
"A National Experiment in Extermination"
Max Trotter
Staff Writer
*The Vancouver World*

Following the unfortunate death of Attorney General Cunning, fundamental questions bother reasonable minds: Was the diagnosis of peritonitis premature? If he had suffered from an "inflamed appendix," why was there no talk of its removal?

More disturbing is the fact that, on the night he died, Mr Cunning was at a function serving alcohol.

What was he drinking at the time, and could it have contributed to his death? Was tainted alcohol involved—and if so, was the Prince himself in danger? Such a possibility would be good enough reason for authorities to let sleeping dogs lie.

It is understood that corrupt practices go with the alcohol industry like flies and rotten beef. (The People's Prohibition Association make much of this.) Yet reports such as the recent shocker from the *New York Herald Tribune* suggest that, in America, the cure is not just worse than the disease but a disease in itself—a disease that may have spread north.

A year ago, Prohibition officials in the United States reportedly set out to discourage the drinking of alcohol by poisoning it with wood alcohol (also known as methyl alcohol), like the most unscrupulous moonshiner.

As might have been expected, bootleggers simply continued to sell whatever hooch was on the wholesale market so that, for drinkers, suffering that went well beyond a normal hangover became the cost of feeding the beast.

When consumption failed to decline, prohibitionists, undeterred, decided to adopt a firmer approach—by doubling the poisonous component. Public bulletins were distributed with a warning: "Three ordinary drinks of this illegal substance may cause blindness, while four may prove fatal."

Yet as one might well imagine, many affected individuals failed to take such a monstrous threat seriously. Bootleggers are not chemists and are unlikely to test their product for harmful ingredients; and for the confirmed alcoholic, even the prospect of terrible harm will not separate a man from his poison of choice.

To no one's surprise, over the months since, the body count in America has ballooned to more than two thousand dead.

Charles Norris, chief medical examiner of New York City, called the measure "our national experiment in extermination." American prohibitionists argue that law-breaking alcoholics deserve no pity. A headline in the *Omaha Morning Bee* asks, "Must Uncle Sam Guarantee Safety for Souses?"

Seymour M. Lowman, assistant secretary of the Treasury in charge of Prohibition, all but rejoices at the casualty figures: "Inferior elements are dying off fast from poison hooch. If the result is a sober America, a good job will have been done."

Canada and the Mother Country take a different view.

Sir William Hogg, Minister of State for Health, has voiced the government position that "the United States has embraced extreme measures that exceed the bounds of common decency."

Whenever some mania preoccupies our neighbours to the south, Canadians are asking: Has the sickness spread north? Is it possible that Mr Cunning was served American bootleg liquor, smuggled into Canada and sold under the table?

And if so, who will be next to die, before police take notice?

207 Government St
Victoria, BC
September 2, 1925

Dearest Millie,

Yes it's me! Grace! I am so excited & thrilled, I imagine
I shall be very incoherent!

I found your address by pure coincidence, just this
week.

A girl at the telephone exchange sat next to me at
church. We were talking about our trips west, and I
happened to mention you, and she said that she once
worked beside you at the Hotel Vancouver—can you
imagine such a coincidence???

It has been more than two years, Millie! So much
has happened! So much to tell!

Please write back soon and tell me that you are the
same Mildred. I shall be ever so upset if you're not!

Heaps of love,
Grace Rideout

# CHAPTER 9

MILDRED REREADS GRACE'S letter on the tram to Kerrisdale. They haven't seen each other since they parted at the Victoria ferry. As a fellow immigrant, Grace was her first female friend. For a single young woman, female friends, let alone interesting female friends, are thin on the ground here. Unless one is a flapper, loneliness is the general rule.

Kerrisdale is a town on the cusp of Shaughnessy Heights, inhabited by people who make a good deal of money but not as much as people who live in Shaughnessy. No doubt both will one day be absorbed into the expanding amoeba called Vancouver.

In any case, a book club in Kerrisdale, while not as posh as a book club in Shaughnessy, is a big step up in society for a hello girl with a room at the YWCA.

The Harlan Crombie residence is a hulking structure in the Swiss Cottage style (which is anything but cottage-like), on a corner of Wilson Road. It's a dwelling suitable for the ambitions of the head of the house, whose career, word has it, is about to reach its ascendency.

Her education at Badminton School taught Mildred never to enter an unfamiliar environment without doing proper preparation. Via library search, she learned that Crombie went to posh Heriot, a Scottish private school known to excel in the sport of caning. Upon emigrating to Canada, he dealt in real estate, first in Toronto, then on the West Coast—where he struck gold.

In Vancouver, where success in real estate is a matter of knowing the right people, Crombie, with his public school manners and posh Edinburgh accent, cultivated mutually advantageous relationships with members of the Board of Trade, the Chamber of Mines and the Ministry of Lands.

Thanks to countless rounds of whisky and golf, our man developed an uncanny knack for anticipating decisions by the Great Northern Railway and the CPR. His recent coup was to predict the location of the new Second Narrows Bridge, the only route from Vancouver to the North Shore that will accommodate a motorcar. He was able to buy up most of the land around the projected site as part of a syndicate that included George Worrell, the roads superintendent for North Vancouver, and an unnamed silent partner.

Currently the syndicate has acquired a substantial stake in the Grouse Mountain Highway and Scenic Resort Company, which plans to develop a luxury snow-ski venture.

Crombie can not be faulted for a lack of ambition—nor can Mrs Crombie, who was successful in corralling the Vancouver women's vote for Boris Stalker. *Behind every great man...*

The Crombie parlour is Scottish and old-fashioned. The furniture is arranged around the perimeter, leaving room in the centre for what, traditionally, would be a coffin—a space now occupied by a huge wrought-iron coffee table in the modern Art Deco style, brand new and emphatically out of place in this atmosphere of pursed lips and gloom.

That particular item of furniture, together with Mrs Crombie's moon manicure, causes Mildred to view her hostess as a woman who longs to "break free" (a common expression since the War)—a desire made all the more intense by her husband's extended absences in Victoria attending committees, writing and giving speeches, glad-handing his way to the upper tiers of power.

Mildred suspects that Mr Crombie will have something to say about that table. Soon it will be back in the showroom, awaiting the next frustrated housewife who wants to "break free."

Though slightly overweight, Mrs Crombie is a handsome woman with a regal nose and exceptional posture, accentuated by a hobble skirt down to the ankle—all the rage in London, five years ago. There is a certain vagueness to her affect that Mildred doesn't remember from their previous meeting.

Mildred's tea dress proves a success, which is to say it is quite daring compared to her fellow guests, who are in head-to-toe chiffon, like wedding cakes with waistlines. Having situated their enhanced bulk on the parlour chairs, they share sideways glances at Mildred's bare arms, as though she has three of them. She is beginning to suspect that she is not so much a guest as an exhibit.

Introductions ensue: Carol Oliphant, Julia Budge and Audrey Glenlyon are married to an optometrist, a banker and the manager of McKim Advertising. All are members of the Beaver Club and St Andrew's Presbyterian Church.

From Scottish history class, the surnames tell Mildred a different story. As septs of the MacDonalds, the Oliphants and Budges are unlikely to trust a Glenlyon, after their treachery at Glencoe in 1692.

Who knows what centuries-old conflicts are contained in their *maiden* names?

Between glances at her sleeves and neckline (Mildred might as well be a seated mannequin), the women talk among themselves.

*Alga, your new table is splendid, I must say.*
*Wherever did you find it?*
*At William Worrall.*
*Of course, the Select Collection.*
*Yes. I felt like a bit of a change.*
*Good for you, Alga. It gives the room dash.*
*Though I shouldn't like everything modern.*
*Too cold.*
*Not to mention a bit gaudy.*
*Not cozy at all...*

She would hardly classify the room as cozy. Other than the table from William Worrall, the furniture is a testament to the Scottish craving for physical discomfort. The carved lions in the back of her mahogany chair have been expertly placed to poke one's spine just so.

It then occurs to Mildred that none of the ladies seems to have brought a book to the book club, nor is there a bookshelf in sight.

Soundlessly, the maid-of-all-work appears pushing a Jacobean tea trolley containing what must be fifty pounds of silver and china, plus their contents. First she sets out a silver-plated sugar and creamer set, a rack, a waste bowl and a tea egg. Next, a set of Shelley teacups, saucers and plates embossed with the fish, bell, tree and bird of the Glasgow coat of arms. Next, a metal pot full of water, a metal trivet and a paraffin warmer. Next, the teapot, placed off-centre beside a three-tier tea sampler containing warm scones, cookies, finger sandwiches and assorted pastries.

Chan Jingheung works as precisely as if she were arranging a bouquet. Afternoon tea is much like the *gongfu chah*, but with less ceremony and more equipment. She goes about her work with an expression of pleasant non-comprehension, to assure the *gwai poh* that she isn't listening in.

*They didn't! Surely you're joking!*

*I simply didn't believe my eyes.*

*And in a public place.*

*With children present.*

*Did it ever occur to you that such creatures exist?*

*Back at home we would never have put up with it...*

As the conversation rattles on, as per her role as hostess, Mrs Crombie pours with exaggerated concentration. The air is aflutter with overlapping voices as they pile their plates with sugar- and fat-based delicacies.

For a few short moments the only sound is of slurping and chewing; then the conversation sets sail again, with its cargo of complaints about health, servants and the weather.

Steam rises from every cup—except for Mrs Crombie's.

*Strange.* Mildred wonders about that.

207 Government St
Victoria, BC
Sept 6, 1925

Darling Millie,

Your letter was dear—I am just so overjoyed that you are you!

When we parted, my separation from you was so grievous to be borne that I might have died of lonesomeness were it not for Gwendolyn, though she has a bevy of admirers to occupy her time.

Perhaps because we sent in our applications at the same time, we are both employed in the same building, just in different offices—Gwendolyn with the Attorney General, and I with the Liquor Control Board, which is not a bit as exciting as it sounds.

I am so keenly aware that you are so near and yet so far! I don't know how, but I will manage to visit you one day, by hook or by crook. I am not at all jealous of your new American friend, who sounds charming, if intimidatingly direct.

But I promise I shall be ever so cross if you do not love me, as I do you!

Your eternal friend,
Gracie

Gwendolyn and Grace crossed the Atlantic together in a third-class, four-bunk cabin on the *Royal George* from Avonmouth to Halifax. From there they had planned to travel by train to Victoria, where they had secured government employment by correspondence.

Of the two other girls in their cabin, one remained in bed seasick, arising only long enough to go to the bathroom or throw up in the commode, while the other had a posh accent that offended Gwendolyn, whose family were devoted Socialists in Birmingham.

As a public school girl from London, Mildred had worked at Command office in Whitehall, and exhibited a level of sophistication and fearlessness Grace had only witnessed in moving pictures.

On the transcontinental train from Halifax, Mildred occupied the more expensive lower bunk, which had a window, and she would invite Grace to sit with her and watch the country go by. Gwendolyn preferred to socialize with the workmen in coach, especially the young fellow who turned bright red when she entered but could barely bring himself to speak for shyness.

Grace and Mildred would lie across the bed, staring out the window as the train slithered through ravined alleyways and endless forests and then across an immense flatness, while listening to the rhythmic chewing of the iron horse in front and, beneath them, the syncopated rhythm of metal wheels over tracks.

While they were together, the miles and the hours flew by. Thanks to Millie, Grace no longer views boredom as the normal state, but a girl doesn't have many such friends and nobody has come to take her place.

CHAN JINGHEUNG GLANCES at her employer for direction. Mrs Crombie responds with neither approval nor disapproval.

Mrs Oliphant speaks as though taking up the task of managing the hostess: "Oh Alga, more scones. That would be lovely if there are any left."

"Perhaps there are more bird's nest cookies too," Mrs Budge suggests.

"Yes, yes. Chan, just get them, would you please?" Her employer's tone indicates that she has lost her *sanfen*. For Mrs Crombie, such snapping is not normal. Friends envy Chan Jingheung for her courteous and thoughtful employer, but lately Mrs Crombie has seemed *bushi* and off-balance. Beneath the paint and enamel, her lips and fingernails are blue. She spends much time in the bathroom, with no sound of running water.

Had she been consulted, Chan Jingheung would have advised against this gathering. Mrs Crombie should not be seen like this. Since the election, rumours have spread that Harlan Crombie's wife is a secret *jaugwei*. Already Mr Crombie has lost face. When he telephoned from Victoria last evening, the voice she overheard amid the crackle and hiss was like the roar of an angry beast.

She also heard her employer saying that he is in line to be appointed to a high position with the Liquor Control Board, so a scandal would be especially harmful.

It is a complicated situation, but what will be will be. *Seuhn keih zihyin la.*

"LADIES, MAY I introduce you to our guest, Miss Mildred Wickstram—a Badminton girl, an opera buff, a Londoner and, I must say, a bright spark, with the most *refreshing* ideas... most refreshing if I do say so..." Mrs Crombie pauses, having lost the thread.

She was looking forward to introducing this young woman to her group, if only because it implies a wider circle of acquaintance than she really has.

The opportunity presented itself a fortnight ago at the Opera House, when the smartly dressed young thing took the seat next to her on a single ticket. An unaccompanied young woman with the better sort of accent is a rarity in this savage city.

During intermission they seemed to "hit it off." Mrs Crombie doesn't ordinarily make conversation with strangers, but her husband had become engrossed in a discussion with Boris Stalker. Should she interrupt or distract them, she would hear about it at home.

Miss Wickstram proved knowledgeable about an extraordinary number of interesting things—trends in London, hemlines, moving pictures, the royal family—and said sharp, witty things about public figures, comments she would love to have said herself if she'd dared.

The encounter left Mrs Crombie in a bittersweet mood.

For the wife in a joyless marriage, the presence of a modern young woman can bring on a sort of buyer's remorse—a feeling of misgiving, as though one has failed to secure value for one's investment in time and drudgery.

Throughout the afternoon, Mrs Crombie does her best to follow the conversation and to interject a comment that has some relevance to the subject at hand—which shouldn't be so difficult, given the subjects discussed.

*And isn't it a pity about Norah?*

*Still, no need to make a scene at church.*

Lately she has found it a major chore just to get out of bed and get dressed, much less run the household. And she needs spectacles— another certain sign of creeping old age. Watching *Ben-Hur* at the Strand on Tuesday, she had trouble making out the title cards.

In fact, she will just close her eyes a few moments and let the others talk among themselves...

*Her husband is a beast.*

*Of course he's a beast, but there is a time and a place for everything.*

*Sometimes it is better to keep oneself to oneself, but that's not the way, these days.*

*Not among the young people.*

*I wonder about the young people.*
*Take it all for granted, they do.*
*Never saw war.*
*Never had to do without.*
*And the girls smoking cigarettes.*
*It's the moving pictures.*
*During last week's sermon when Reverend Nicholson said we*
*should see* Ben-Hur, *I thought I'd die.*
*The hero is a Jew, Mabel, can ye imagine?*
*With Jesus in a supporting role.*
*Blasphemy it is, that's the truth of it.*
*Reverend McDougall thinks it will bring more young people to*
*church.*
*Surely he could have suggested something more wholesome, like*
The Wizard of Oz—
*Too fanciful, Julia. And a whiff of heresy as well.*
*Surely a wizard is more wholesome than* Ben-Hur.
*Carmel Myers—did you see what she had on her?*
*Nothing left to the imagination there.*
*And she's a Jew you know.*
*Who? Carmel Myers?*
*Aye. Of the Jewish persuasion.*
*Oh dear, I didn't know that.*
*Hollywood is full of Jews.*
*And DPs most of them.*
*A clever people.*
*Very good with money.*
*Did you know that Clara Bow has bright red hair?...*

"What do the young people say about the Jews, Miss Wickstram?"

Mildred's mind has wandered off. "I beg your pardon, Mrs Oliphant? Which Jews do you mean?"

"Why the Jews in the moving pictures, of course."

When faced with a loaded question, the Badminton girl smiles innocently and switches to a neutral topic—but what might that be? The perfume selection at Woodward's? Bargains at the Army & Navy? Does she know a recipe?

An uncomfortable pause drags on. Mrs Glenlyon bites into another Hydrox cookie while Mrs Budge gazes into her teacup.

Mrs Oliphant examines her manicure. They are not going to let her off easily.

*When in doubt, appeal to the hostess.* "Mrs Crombie, your scones are to die for. Did you make them yourself?"

"I think I made them, yes." Mrs Crombie replies as though her mind has left the room.

"Oh Alga, of course you did. As one surely must," Mrs Glenlyon says.

"Chinese cooks knead them to death," observes Mrs Oliphant.

"Aye, they have no feel for pastry," adds Mrs Budge.

"D'ye see what they call a bun?" continues Mrs Glenlyon. "A lump of dough is what it is. The Chinese overknead everything."

All laugh, except for Mrs Crombie: "What do you say, Alga?"

Clearly, Mrs Crombie has not been following the conversation.

"Alga, you sound strange—and my dear, you do look pale."

Mrs Crombie struggles to her feet. "If you will excuse me, I believe I shall visit the ladies' room."

They watch her retreat and exchange worried looks.

"Alga seems unwell, I fear."

"Something she ate, d'ye think? Or *drank*?"

"Ah. Well, we mustn't judge the poor soul."

"Phooey. She should be in Victoria by her husband's side, like the other wives."

"If he wants her there."

Mrs Oliphant is just about to continue with her thoughts on the duties of a political wife when the maid-of-all-work reappears in the doorway.

Chan Jingheung hesitates before jumping into cold water. Of necessity, she speaks English—reasoning that she would have to if the house were on fire.

"Ladies, please you must come now, quickly!"

Mildred wonders whether the guests are more shocked that Chan Jingheung is speaking out loud, or that she is speaking English and not pidgin, or that she is giving them orders and not the other way around. They remain in their chairs, momentarily stunned, while Mildred follows Chan Jingheung into the hall.

Mildred rushes over to the staircase, where Mrs Crombie lies stretched out on the floor in a shape defined by her hobble skirt—at first, Mildred thinks she may have tripped on it. She kneels beside the inert body, brushes aside the ruined coiffure to uncover her neck and presses the artery with three fingers.

"Miss, where is the telephone?"

"It is in the study. Please, I will show you."

Mildred struggles to her feet (damn these Louis heels!) and follows Chan Jingheung to the study at the front of the hall, past a clutch of frightened women with nothing to say.

Chan Jingheung remains silent, eyes on the floor, hoping that the ladies will forget her impertinent outburst in English.

At last they mobilize: Mrs Glenlyon fetches a tea towel soaked with cold water, which she applies to Mrs Crombie's forehead; Mrs Budge loosens Alga's bodice and Mrs Oliphant removes the shoes, to no avail.

In the study, Mildred places a call.

*Hello, operator speaking. CAstle exchange.*

*Operator, here is CAstle 135. TRinity 211, please.*

*Edwards Funeral Home. Please hold while I connect you.*

AN ODD COINCIDENCE
Untimely Deaths Give Cause for Concern
Ed McCurdy
Staff Writer
*The Evening Star*

A matron who's married to power
A political man of the hour
Developed a notion
For Patterson's Potion
And now they're both pushing up flowers.

In war, many people die at a time and in similar circumstances. In peacetime, other than a derailed train or a sunken ship, such an event is a rarity.

So when two prominent persons—the Attorney General and the wife of a deputy minister—perish just a few days apart, it is inevitable that the city would grow rife with speculation. One of the more outlandish theories is that the two victims were lovers who died in a suicide pact, like a middle-aged, overweight Romeo and Juliet.

That is the wonder of a rumour: it can be based purely on the fact that one victim is a man and the other a woman.

More plausible rumours exist, however—one of which has to do with their reputed taste in restorative tonics.

According to a source in the police department, sometime before his death Mr Cunning is believed to have imbibed Patterson's Silk Hat Martinis. For the rumourmongers, it can hardly be coincidence that in the case of Mrs Crombie, one of the ladies present reports a partially empty bottle of the same stuff, in the upstairs bathroom next to the sink.

Thus, the Patterson's brand has become a factor in both investigations. Mr Patterson may be required to subject every one of his many products for analysis.

Whether Mr Cunning's death can be attributed to a flaw in the product or to deliberate contamination remains to be seen—leaving the possibility that, if the victims died by the same poison, the culprit may have been something other than American hooch, as Mr Trotter has suggested.

Apparently public interest in the two deaths is not shared by the Vancouver Police Department, which has declined to perform autopsies, sources say, despite being urged to do so.

"Such measures are a drain on public resources," was Chief Barfoot's response to questioning. "The VPD will require more evidence before taking such a course. A time of austerity is no time to undertake a wild goose chase at public expense."

As for Mrs Crombie, an autopsy would also require an official family request—which has been forwarded in writing by her bereaved husband. According to a knowledgeable observer, the Crombie request was strongly critical of police inaction thus far: "We do not understand the police's unwillingness to reach a conclusion and put the family's mind at rest. It flies in the face of human decency."

For the present, the Crombie family, and the public at large, must make do with a diagnosis of "heart failure"—a general term that describes the final stage of most deaths, in war and in peace.

If contaminated Patterson's products were to be found in the possession of both victims, then two open-and-shut cases could become one.

After two weeks of seeming inaction, one question prevails in the public mind: Are the Vancouver Police up to the challenge? To judge by their conduct of the Janet Stewart case last year, this reporter sees little reason for optimism.

# CHAPTER 10

THE TWO POLICE officers head from the station to Yaletown on foot, a good half-hour walk. The journey would take ten minutes by motorcycle (traffic permitting), but the thought of Quam's arms about his waist causes DS Hook's sphincter to rise.

As Hook remembers it, the Patterson building once housed the California Wine Company, a blending and bottling plant. With the onset of Prohibition, rather than close down production entirely, the owners opted to keep the business barely breathing as the Sunset Vinegar Company, whose new mission was to turn an alcoholic beverage into a condiment and cleaning product. Perhaps inevitably, Sunset eventually fell into receivership and went belly up for good.

The visionary who brought this whole enterprise back to life was Cormac Patterson, an entrepreneur from the Prairies, who built and ran the only hotel in Shaunavon, Saskatchewan. (Sadly, Patterson's Hotel burned to the ground, cause of fire undetermined, fully insured.)

Patterson arrived in Vancouver in 1920 and, in scouring the city for business opportunities, earned his reputation as a businessman of genius when he happened to discern that the Prohibition Act, as written, failed to mention tonics, bitters and other "cures" containing alcohol. Nor did the act make any reference to cocaine.

Patterson saw an opportunity, and pounced.

He bought the Sunset Vinegar Company and its equipment for a song, and rededicated the plant to the production of patent medicines, based on the fact that a by-product of vinegar production is ethanol, and renamed the company Druggists' Sundries Limited. In the way that Marmite, a by-product of brewer's yeast, became a product in its own right, the aim of Druggists'

Sundries was for its products to occupy a space in every pharmacy and every medicine cabinet.

The company's first offering was Patterson's Stomach Bitters and carried the branding *Guaranteed To Contain None But The Purest Ingredients Compounded In A Scientific Manner*. Its label featured a set of crossed skeleton keys (*The Keys To Good Health*), implying that the product had the blessing of both the Pope and St Peter and thus appealing to Catholics and Protestants alike.

At Hook's previous constabulary, fellow officers bore witness to its efficacy in aiding digestion; Chief Quigley was never without a bottle of the stuff in his desk drawer, ready for use. (Of course, that was when cocaine was as legal as aspirin.)

As with any patent medicine, the efficacy of the Patterson's product depended on consumer confidence more than it did on the ingredients themselves. Based on an old American recipe created to sidestep state temperance laws, Patterson's Stomach Bitters consisted of aromatic oils, anise and coriander, as well as the all-important vegetable bitters, emulsified in forty per cent alcohol to preserve the medicinal properties of the vegetable extracts, and to maintain therapeutic potency. (By coincidence, its taste reminded consumers of a peaty highland Scotch.)

Patterson's Stomach Bitters proved a resounding success. Throughout Prohibition, in many temperate homes, no evening meal would be complete without several draughts of that pleasant cordial.

As they turn onto Homer Street, the two policemen discuss strategy, with limited success.

"Constable, as a person of interest we must approach our man carefully, for he is a smooth customer."

"Patterson is Irish, sir. The Irish are a sneaky, lazy, drunken race—but they are excellent dancers."

"Was that a figure of speech, Mr Quam?"

"A what, sir?"

"Your reference to *dancing*. What did you mean by that?"

"I should say a jig, mainly. Or step dancing, with arms like posts..."

Hook chews a couple of aspirin; he feels a headache coming on.

DRUGGISTS' SUNDRIES COMPANY
Home of Patterson's Cocktails
Deliciously Palatable, Full Strength,
Satisfying and Economical

Next door to the Firestone Tire and Vulcanizing Shop on Homer Street, a windowless brick wall contains an enormous billboard advertisement, but the entrance itself needs no signage thanks to the odour of vinegar—brewery-like, but with an acidic bite that catches in the back of the throat. As the two policemen enter the unmarked door and climb the stairs, the pong becomes thicker and more pungent.

"Sir, are you sure it is safe to breathe?"

"Remember Wipers, constable. Piss in your handkerchief, cover your nose and carry on."

"Wipers, sir? What sort of wipers?"

"Ypres, Mr Quam, was a battle in the war."

"Of course when you pronounce it that way..."

The second floor is a lofty, factory-like space occupying the entire second and third floors of the building. Along three walls, overhead platforms support an unbroken line of kegs and a bank of fuel drums above that, underneath a series of enormous wooden vats. All of which are barely visible, thanks to a bewildering criss-cross of suspended pipes connected to a tangle of hoses, down to an elongated, U-shaped assembly counter, where men in felt hats and dungarees administer to an endless procession of bottles, to be filled, corked, labelled, packed in cases, loaded onto a gravity roller and transferred to the rear of the building, near an open freight elevator operated by rope and pulley.

As they approach the bottling station, they can hear a man shouting curses upstairs, audible despite the clatter and whine.

Directed by a tall man who is operating a corking apparatus while scratching a rash on his neck, they climb a set of iron stairs to a landing, where Quam knocks repeatedly on a thick metal door behind which is the source of the shouting.

"He doesn't seem to answer, sir."

"Yes, Mr Quam. Could it be because he can't hear you?"

Quam gives him an offended look.

Hook takes a moment to chew up two more aspirin from his side pocket as though they were mints, then twists the door handle and gives it a sharp push. The door abruptly lurches open and the two policemen nearly stumble into a single room occupying a corner of the building. The decor is reminiscent of a banker's office, with heavy oak furniture and a wall containing what look to be ledgers but may be the spines of books glued to a board, as with many home libraries.

It is the office of a man who desires respectability. Thanks to profits not unassociated with bootlegging, Vancouver contains many successful men with more money than stature, who try to compensate with their office furniture.

Semi-reclining in a swivel chair, Cormac Patterson is hollering into the telephone with the candle in one hand and the earpiece in the other. To go by his repetition of the phrase *Sue the bastards!*, Hook gathers that the person on the other end is a lawyer. The mention of McCurdy in this context catches his ear.

He takes a moment to size up their first person of interest in the case. Stocky, muscular and with an enormous head, our man would be handsome were it not for a long-ago broken nose, and an inflamed carbuncle on his left cheekbone that looks as though it might burst momentarily.

Remembering the itchy rash that blotched the bottling-line worker below, Hook reminds himself that the fermentation process involves fungi and germs. He blows his nose into his handkerchief and glances at Quam, who is scratching his bottom while examining a print depicting John L. Sullivan. The opposite wall contains an array of posters advertising Patterson's Pepp (*The Greatest Bracer You Ever Drank*), Patterson's Jazz Cocktail (*The Mystic South American Drink*), Patterson's Tonic-Port (*For Invigorating Health*) and, of course, Patterson's Silk Hat Martini Cocktail.

Patterson slams the earpiece nearly hard enough to break the cradle: "That bastard and his fecking rhymes!" Looking up, he sees Constable Quam for the first time. Rising to his full height of five-and-a-half feet, Patterson sticks out his chest like a bantam rooster who sees another male chicken on his patch: "And just who in the feck are you?"

The constable turns his attention away from the painting with a frown: "I am Constable Quam, sir, here on official business."

"Don't play the nance with me, boyo." Patterson steps in front of the desk, thrusting forward the latest edition of the *Evening Star*: "Look at this piece of shite! Ye feckers have half the city thinking I'm poisoning me customers!"

Quam swivels his bulk in Patterson's direction. "I'll thank you not to address the police in that tone of voice, sir."

"Oh so you don't like my tone, do ye? Such sensitivity!"

"And we don't react well to sarcasm, sir." Quam's eyes have begun to water.

Patterson moves a step forward, fists clenched.

Quam moves to meet him. "Sir, I'm giving you a caution."

Knowing from experience where this exchange is headed, Hook attempts to intervene: "Mr Patterson, I assure you that our inquiries..."

Too late. In a remarkably smooth motion, Quam lands a roundhouse uppercut to Patterson's solar plexus that has the man on his knees on the Persian carpet, retching.

"Constable, for the love of God, what have you done?"

Quam faces his superior with glittering eyes. "I felt threatened, sir. I exercised appropriate force."

Patterson is making short rasping sounds, like a saw working through a piece of lumber.

DS Hook shoves the constable aside, kneels down beside the president of Druggists' Sundries Limited, takes his arm and levers him to his feet and back in his chair, where he sits with his head between his knees.

"Keep your head down, Mr Patterson, sir, take deep breaths, you're just winded is all." Hook looks up at the constable: "Well, you've made a bloody mess."

"Shall we charge him with assaulting an officer, sir?"

"No, Mr Quam, we will do nothing of the kind." Hook's jaw muscles have locked; he can feel his teeth about to splinter.

"Bottom drawer!" Patterson gasps. "Bottom right!"

Hook opens the drawer, removes a half-full bottle of Kilvannon and a tumbler, uncorks the bottle and pours.

"Fill it to the brim, damn ye! Surely ye at least know how to fill a glass!"

The two policemen stand by as Patterson bends over the desk, leans on one forearm and pours the contents of the glass straight down the neck, adding, "Fecking idle buffoons."

Hook turns to his assistant. "Mr Quam, are you acquainted with the laws on police brutality?"

"Not as such, sir."

"Thought not. Read them as soon as possible."

Patterson pours himself another three fingers, while Hook tries to make amends.

"We do apologize, Mr Patterson, both for the press coverage and for this—this unfortunate incident." He glares at Quam, whose expression remains firm.

DS Hook's official apology seems to have a calming effect. With difficulty, Patterson reaches across the desk, removes a Robusto from a mahogany humidor, bites off the tip, spits it on the floor and sits back in his chair, awaiting a light. His complexion is less apoplectic now, and the boil on his cheek has faded from coal-black to maroon.

Hook lights Patterson's cigar, then the fresh Ogden's that has somehow found its way between his teeth. He once saw an officer drop dead after a similar blow to the solar plexus, during a fracas in the mess at Rugeley. (Sixty men in the room, and nobody saw a thing.)

"Constable, I don't care what fucking excuse you lard it up with, if you do that again you will leave the force, either voluntarily or due to a crippling injury."

"Sir, in all fairness—"

"Shut up, Quam. Just shut up."

Patterson puffs his cigar, astonished at the sight of one policeman upbraiding another for punching a citizen, rather than pitching in himself.

"Well since yer here, ye might as well seat yerself."

"Thank you, sir. Mr Quam, as you were." DS Hook takes a seat, puffs his cigarette and tries to think of something to say. A murk of cigar and cigarette smoke settles in, masking the pong of fermenting vinegar.

Hook takes out his notebook and pencil, finds a clean page, then smiles across the desk. *Just a friendly public servant seeking facts...*

"If it's of any comfort, sir, we have no indication yet that the Silk Hat Martinis in question were adulterated. Samples are at the lab awaiting analysis—aren't they, Constable?"

"As we speak, sir, they're awaiting transfer."

"And while we await, the brand goes down the toilet!" Patterson drains his glass, whose effects put him in a more reflective mood. "Well Jesus, it's not as if it's the first time."

Hook replies, "That's the press for you, sir. They'll do anything for a headline." (No need to mention that McCurdy's information came from Hook.)

Patterson relights his cigar. Hook lights another Ogden's. Constable Quam sneezes into the arm of his tunic, a practice acquired during the Spanish flu.

Patterson continues: "Last time, word was that we put saltpeter in the tonic so a man can't get a boner. Sales of Patterson's Pepp hit the dirt for two months."

"I'm not a lawyer, sir, but surely they can be sued for slander and defamation."

"Ha! That's how it is with rumours. There's no beginning or end to them. Before the saltpeter, it was said that Patterson's Nerve Invigorator caused Parkinson's disease. The names are similar, don't you see. Before that, Patterson's Relaxing Cordial turned people into dope fiends."

"Who do you suppose is behind these attacks?"

"Who in the feck *isn't*? When the province was dry, it was just the government on our arses. Now with Repeal, it's the Drys, the Wets, the bootleggers—and worst of them all, the LCB. With Prohibition we were criminal suspects, don't ye see, but now we're *competition*." He spits the word out as though an insect somehow flew into his mouth.

He pours himself a fresh whiskey. "Will ye have a drop for yourself, officer?"

"Thank you, sir, but we're on duty."

For the second time, Patterson looks up in surprise at another rare statement from a policeman's beak.

"It seems Mr Cunning was fond of martinis."

"Ye're right, officer, and here's to him." Patterson drains his glass and pours just a splash more. "An early supporter. Gordon Cunning was that rare investor who *believed* in the product, and

God love him for it."

"As the minister in charge of the LCB, didn't that amount to a conflict of interest?"

"For certain it would—if Druggists' Sundries was in the booze business. But we're not. We produce remedies, not liquor."

"Would it surprise you to know that Mr Cunning had several bottles of your products in his possession?"

"Not a bit. Samples were part of the original shareholder agreement—to dodge the tax, don't y'see."

"And was the product delivered, sir?"

"The investors didn't come and get it themselves, Officer."

"Did he order your martinis specifically?"

"Aye, he was especially fond of them." Patterson's eyes grow misty: "Said it tasted almost like the real thing. It was his enthusiasm that first put us on the shelves. And as for investors, he brought half the Lodge in with him—and everyone made a pretty penny!"

"Can you tell me who actually put the case of product in his hands?"

"All packages were to be left at the front desk, to be delivered by a lift attendant known for his discretion. A politician in Mr Cunning's position can't be too careful."

AS THE TWO policemen walk in silence down Hastings, past Leonard's Cafe and the Strand Theatre, Quam continues his justification for punching Patterson in the stomach. "He's an unstable personality, sir. The suspect moved toward me in a threatening manner."

Hook stops to admire a parked Hudson Super Six with fresh new whitewall tyres. "Constable, tell me what identifies him as a suspect. Surely he'd have to be damned unstable to poison his own product."

Quam stares down at the cigarette ends in the gutter, as though looking for inspiration. "What about the martini glass, sir? If it didn't belong to the hotel, it belonged to *somebody*."

"Such as whom, Mr Quam?"

"Did Mr Cunning bring it down with him, do you think?"

"Do you mean the way some snooker players bring their own cue to the game?"

Quam's voice takes on the mewl of a cornered puppy. "People can be very picky about the proper presentation, sir."

"In any case, someone must have served it to him in the ballroom."

"That is true. There was no buffet."

"In any case, the manager has called a staff meeting first thing tomorrow. We'll speak to the waiter who served the victim—or more probably, we won't."

Quam's eyes have started to water again. "It all seems awfully complex, sir. And we've not had our lunch."

As they continue down Hastings, both policemen are grateful for the New Westminster tram, whose rumble and clang preclude further discussion on the topic, and provide Quam with the opportunity to slip into Con Jones's Tobacco and Billiards for a chocolate bar, while Hook lights an Ogden's under the Don't Argue sign and observes a pair of swells in bag trousers and straw boaters that look to be made of breakfast cereal.

Seen through the plate-glass window, men in shirtsleeves bend into islands of light to make their shots, while the silhouettes of idle men lean forward with elbows on their knees, smoke rising from their fingers, a flattened cloud hovering just overhead.

Quam emerges, chewing on an Oh Henry!; Hook takes a last deep drag from his cigarette and flicks the butt into the gutter—each man, in his own way, thinking about something.

US SPEAKER TO ADDRESS PPA RALLY
Hundreds Expected to Attend
Cecil Harmsworth
Staff Writer
*The Beacon*

On Wednesday next, Vancouver will welcome Rev Daisy Douglas Tyler, the charismatic American temperance activist, who will address a rally of the People's Prohibition Association at the Vancouver Opera House.

Her record makes for an impressive document.

As leader of the YWCA, Miss Tyler led the campaign that produced a Dry victory in Muncie, Indiana. She served as president of Indiana War Mothers and was the first woman vice-chair of the Republican Committee.

As a life member of the WCTU, she co-founded the Indianapolis chapter of the Anti-Saloon League. She organized the first chapter of the Queens of the Golden Mask, to mobilize women in the fight against alcohol, prostitution and wholesale immigration and to promote social welfare and racial purity—in which interest Miss Tyler founded the Indiana chapter of the Better Babies movement.

An avid campaigner for women's sports, Miss Tyler won second place in the National Small Bore Rifle Championships at Camp Grant, Illinois, three years in a row, competing against seasoned war veterans.

As featured speaker at the annual meeting of the People's Prohibition Association, Miss Tyler will address the evils of alcohol on many levels, from the individual drunkard and his family to its weakening effect on the white race.

South of the border, Miss Tyler has been known to draw audiences of up to fifteen hundred.

According to Reverend McDougall of the PPA Advisory Board, "Miss Tyler will reinvigorate the movement, and prove well worth her not inconsiderable fee."

CAstle 135 speaking, Crombie residence. Are you there?

*Operator speaking, CAstle exchange. I have Victoria on the line, GOvernment exchange. Complete the connection, please.*

SWITCH

*Crombie residence. Are you there?*

*Here is the Office of the Attorney General, Mr Crombie. I have Mr Bertram Bliss on the line. I will connect you now.*

SWITCH

*Harlan Crombie here. Are you there?*

*Hello indeed, Harlan. I hope you are well.*

*Thank you, Bertram, I am as well as can be expected, thank you.*

*Ah yes, of course. My sincere condolences on the passing of your wife. Allison was—*

*Alga, actually.*

*Alga was a fine, fine woman, who worked like a horse on the campaign. Much appreciated by Mr Stalker, I can tell you.*

*Thank you, Bertram, Mrs Crombie would be gratified, I'm sure.*

*And may I say, chuffed to know that the transition is going swimmingly.*

*Yes, indeed.*

*And so to the business at hand. Just to be clear, this is an unofficial call.*

*I quite understand. Discretion is always to be advised.*

*We must always assume other ears are listening.*

*That is my understanding as well.*

*Harlan, the Office believes it to be only cricket before we make a public announcement to notify all parties directly affected.*

*I'm aware of the policy, Bertram. I was with Mr Stalker when it was discussed.*

*Then let us move on. This is all in confidence, of course.*

*Of course.*

*My call is about the Liquor Control Board. It has often been said that the LCB entails too much liquor and not enough control.*

*I believe it was I who said that.*

*Quite. Jolly good. Well said.*

*Bertram, we have discussed the remedy. Enhanced measures on illegal sales.*

*Special circumstances.*

*A heightened response.*

*Measures whose provenance is not open to unauthorized persons, so to speak.*

*I'm familiar with closed files, Bertram. No need to spell it out further.*

*Quite. Jolly good. Which brings us to the reason for my call. To make a long story short, Mr Stalker has decided that you are the man to lead the effort—to give the board a new sense of mission and purpose.*

*Bertram, please inform Mr Stalker that I'd be honoured to serve.*

*There's a good chap. It will be a bloody great challenge to ginger up public opinion—without, shall we say, overdoing it.*

*Aye, indeed so. In fact, the job may require an outside consultant— an expert in public persuasion.*

*As long as they can be trusted, Harlan. Is there someone you have in mind?*

*In fact, I do. Her name is Daisy Douglas Tyler. She could sell ice to an Eskimo and she has the PPA wrapped around her little finger.*

*Capital. Jolly good. Absolutely top drawer.*

# CHAPTER 11

IT WAS KNOWN as "Chinese Heaven," until even members of the Asiatic Exclusion League grew tired of the joke.

And yet the tradition remains, and the balcony at the Pantages continues to be effectively off-limits to Europeans; as a result, it has become an ideal refuge for *gwailo* who don't wish to be seen by other *gwailo*.

Especially handy are the loges going down both sides of the the balcony, like small enclosed boats. Illicit trysts are known to occur there, evidenced by the aroma of cigarette smoke, perfume, sweat and other excretions.

McCurdy listens to the piano player in the pit perform the last few bars of "By The Light of the Silvery Moon" while the last stragglers take their seats below. The upcoming motion picture, *The Clash of the Wolves*, will feature a dog named Rin Tin Tin, a German Shepherd rescued from the trenches who has achieved stardom as a symbol of loyalty and valour.

Hook is late.

In preparation, McCurdy has taken a pinch of white powder to sharpen his senses and to tolerate the newsreels to come.

Fox News may be a product of Hollywood professionals, but he often wonders if the lineup was assembled by a madman—a disjointed nightmare in which horrors flash before one's eyes, juxtaposed with laughs and oddities, so that the events of the day become a vaudeville show, a chorus line in which the dancers kick every which way.

A cone of dusty light shoots down from behind the balcony, and on the screen below appears a procession of plump men in plumed Tyrolean hats marching down a narrow street like an army of yodellers. Above them, women lean out of windows waving Austrian flags and blowing kisses. And a crush of pedestrians on the sidewalk follows along, the whole throng making its way to a cathedral, there to be blessed by a bishop.

McCurdy gets out his notebook, spreads another line of white powder on the cover and sniffs as the scene switches to Saudi Arabia, where mausoleums and domes in Medina have been levelled by explosives in a government program to combat "excessive veneration leading to *shirk*."

Then it is back to California, where a female "beach censor" in a coat and a black straw hat uses a tape measure to determine whether a girl's swimming suit falls within standards of decency. The young woman in the suit endures this with a long-suffering, contemptuous expression, rolling her eyes at the camera.

So much for up-to-the-minute world news, McCurdy thinks, blowing his nose into his handkerchief.

"Sorry to be late, Ed. I had to get out of uniform, and Constable Quam has been on my arse like a burr."

"Constable Quam? Is there an Oriental on the force?"

"Of course not. The name is Scottish, as usual."

"Then I should think it would be *McQuam*. John McQuam, say. Mind you, Albert McQuam has more gravitas."

DS Hook gives McCurdy the once-over and gets the picture. "Ed, may I speak plainly?"

"I'd rather you didn't, but I know you will."

"What have you got into now? Is it the opium again?"

"No. I have to work for a living."

"Ah. So you've picked a new poison?"

"Just a brain tonic is all. Nothing like it to bring out one's latent mental pep."

Hook lights an Ogden's. "So you've gone from opium-eater to dope fiend."

"It's also good for numbing the nose against cigarette smoke."

"Well if you're snorting gagger, please do it out of my sight— surely you know that cocaine is illegal now."

"I shall take that under advisement."

DS Hook produces a mickey of rye from an inside pocket. "Care for a nip? Or is rum too legal for you?"

"Delighted. It'll put me in a nautical mood."

On the screen below, a boat named the *Josephine K* is swarmed by men in suits. Crates of an alcoholic beverage labelled *Golden*

*Wedding* are being unloaded. Above and behind them is the pilot house, windows blown out. Two men in white carry the body of the captain on a stretcher down an almost vertical stairway.

"Calvin, does it ever occur to you that there's a lot of *arresting* going on these days?"

"Yes, and not always the right people being arrested."

"Puts the lie to the *fight for freedom* wheeze, doesn't it?"

"You can't blame everything on the war, Ed. Especially you—not having served."

"That's right, Calvin, kick the blind man."

"In any case, we're here to talk about the Cunning business, remember?"

"I know—his demise has surpassed land speculation as the topic du jour. Some of the rumours are versions of *Macbeth*, starring one rival or another. Others are versions of W.C. Fields: *Drowned in a vat of martinis? O death, where is thy sting?*"

"My wife Jeanie heard one at church, to the effect that he was poisoned by an assassin hired by the Drys."

"That's one of many, yes. Another is that he was poisoned by an assassin hired by the Wets."

"Both possibilities make sense: he betrayed them all with the liquor laws, in one way or another."

"And, of course, there are the stories about Patterson's Cocktail. Rumours promoted by the government, I expect. Anything to draw attention away from the LCB hooch. Enough legal rye would kill an ox."

"Should I add the LCB to the list of suspects, then?"

"I'll try and smoke Taggart out of his hole. He runs the place, after all—for the time being, at least. But he's devilishly good at avoiding press—except when he wants it, of course."

Hook fires up an Ogden's, ignoring McCurdy, who is ostentatiously fanning his face. "Just curious, Ed—is there a rumour that Cunning died of natural causes?"

"Not a one. Where would be the fun in that?"

On the screen, an army of girls in black skirts and white blouses, arms extended in the crucifix position, perform knee bends in a grassy stadium, reviewed by a beefy man in a dark coat, backed by men in black shirts and breeches. Thousands are cheering in the stands, waving handkerchiefs and Italian flags, while Mussolini doffs his fedora hat, baring a head shaped like a ball-peen hammer.

The scene changes with a title card proclaiming "Meanwhile In Merrie England": Miss Rotha Lintorn-Orman, a boyish woman with close-cropped hair, at a meeting of British Fascist Women, calls for a paramilitary Girl Scout movement, while an ex-camel veterinarian named Arnold Leese inveighs against British Fascists as "kosher fascists" who refuse to attend to the "Jewish question."

"You can never trust posh women with hyphenated names," Hook says.

"Especially when they dress like men," McCurdy replies.

Then a new segment begins, with no connection to its predecessor, in which a mysterious spotlight plays over a deserted city street at night, followed by a daylight scene in which tall buildings collapse in plumes of dust.

The title card reads, "Death rays will wipe out cities when the next Great War takes place..."

"By the way, Ed, can you think of a reason why a man would have two telephones?"

"One for each ear?"

After another pause for refreshment, Hook and McCurdy continue their discussion about the death of the Attorney General.

"Seemingly it's all about who controls the Liquor Control Board," McCurdy says. "With profits at every stage of the food chain, liquor has become something like fifteen per cent of government income—not to mention party patronage and slush funds. The Attorney General is more powerful than our lame-duck premier—and for that matter, so is the chairman of the LCB. They go together like Tweedledum and Tweedledee.

"Except that Tweedledum has a gun pointed at Tweedledee's head."

McCurdy leaves the possibilities open because that is as far as his thinking takes him. He would like another jolt of powder.

For his part, Hook wonders what a "lame duck" is. So many new expressions these days—who can keep track? "And on the list of persons of interest we also have Mr Patterson."

"The name Patterson seems to come up regularly, doesn't it? Actually, I did some research on the matter."

"Oh come on, Ed. Don't tell me you were in the library, poring through the stacks."

"Very well then, yes, I did pay for some information. But I had to commission a researcher, which amounts to the same thing."

"Not exactly, but continue."

"Of course, it always went without saying that a Jazz Cocktail would be drunk for the alcohol."

"Obviously. It's just as obvious that someone was being paid off to turn a blind eye."

"Not necessarily. That is Patterson's genius. When the PPA sued the government to ban Jazz Cocktail from the shelves, our man countersued—and won. Apparently, according to the *Oxford English Dictionary, cocktail* refers only to a bird and a cock-tailed horse, while *jazz* is either music or sperm. Nothing in either word implies the presence of alcohol. In the meantime, Jazz Cocktails became so popular that people developed a taste for the product as an end in itself. Of course, it could also have been the other ingredients—sharpened with a dash of cocaine, of course."

"Cocaine is illegal now." He sees what his companion is sniffing and his eyes roll upward. "For God's sake, Ed, put that away. I've reminded you twice. I just reminded you a minute ago."

"How can you be so sure it's cocaine?"

"It's white powder, what else could it be?"

"Well for one thing, it could be *eucaine,* which is substantially the same thing. Veterinarians stock it in quantity, and it's all the rage. Tried it myself and it's not bad, though best taken with an alcoholic beverage—unless diluted, it will rot out your septum in no time."

McCurdy blows his nose into his handkerchief, with a honk that turns heads in the balcony. "And as for relaxants like Patterson's House of Lords, now that laudanum is verboten, one can explore the bromides—combined with alcohol, the effect has an appeal all its own."

"You're saying that these substitutions keep Patterson one step ahead of the legislators."

"Of course, Calvin. That's the remedy business in a nutshell."

"So two random consumers died of something contained in Patterson's product? Is that what you're saying, Ed?"

"That's one line to take, but it could still be tainted hooch from the States. I'm betting on Patterson for the present, but it'll take more than a suspicion for the chief to spring for an exhumation and autopsy."

DS Hook gets up from his seat and steps out of the booth while Fox News grinds randomly on. "No offence intended, Ed, but sometimes I think you newspapermen are like maggots."

"Maggots are used to treat infection. I shall take it as a compliment."

"In any case, my subordinate and I paid a visit to Mr Patterson. He was speaking to his lawyer at the time. You were mentioned."

McCurdy places the bottle neatly under his seat. "People are so touchy these days. I do hope he's a suspect."

"'fraid not. A slippery customer, but I doubt that he's murdered anyone. Not on purpose, at least."

"A pity."

On the screen below, thousands of white-sheeted figures with pointed hats parade in rank and file down the National Mall in Washington, as a title card reads: "Citizens gather as one hundred thousand members of the Ku Klux Klan, bearing crosses and American flags, march toward the Capitol Building to cheers and the stirring strains of 'The Liberty Stable Blues'..."

DUnbar exchange. Are you there?
*Operator speaking, SEymour exchange. Castle Hotel calling.*
SWITCH
*Taggart residence. Are you there?*
*DUnbar exchange. Castle Hotel calling.*
*Please make the connection.*
SWITCH
*Here is the Taggart residence. Hello.*
*Here is Ed McCurdy of the* Evening Star. *I should like to speak to Mr Taggart, if I may.*
*Mr Taggart is not on the premises. Shall I take a message?*
*Am I speaking to Mrs Taggart, madam?*
*I am Mrs Taggart.*
*I wish to speak to Mr Taggart about the LCB's response to Mr Cunning's death—and his own response as chairman.*

*I wouldn't know about my husband's professional associations, Mr McCurdy. You'll have to call the office.*

*I've called the LCB countless times, Mrs Taggart, I assure you. He is always either in a meeting or out of the office.*

*Perhaps it's a hint that he doesn't wish to speak to you. But again, I wouldn't know—I'm just his wife.*

*I was hoping to get a personal statement from him about Gordon Cunning. I'm led to believe they had a close association. Perhaps Mr Taggart has some insight into Mr Cunning's customs and habits.*

*My husband and Mr Cunning did enjoy a long association. They went to college together. On the rugby team, I believe.*

*How would you characterize their relations since then, before his unfortunate passing?*

*For the third time, Mr McCurdy, I wouldn't know. My husband's business with the Liquor Board is none of my business. And now I shall ask you to mind your own business. Thank you for your call, Mr McCurdy. Goodbye.*

She returns the earpiece to its cradle. "Clyde, that was a reporter. He wishes to speak with you."

Taggart is lying on the sofa, having spent a restless night. "Well they would, wouldn't they? The rumours are everywhere. It looks as though Stalker's bastards have won this one."

"I know it's a blow, darling, but with Gordon gone you're well out of it. I do admire your ability to adapt to changing circumstances and turn them to your advantage."

"Thank you, darling, and you're quite right. That's politics. One must adapt, change one's plumage and carry on."

# CHAPTER 12

IN THE HOTEL Vancouver next morning, the two policemen meet at the bottom of the fire stairs, near the employee cafeteria. Today the constable smells like lemon oil. "Mr Quam, while I conduct interviews, I want you to go to the changing rooms and check the lockers."

"What am I to look for, sir?"

"Suspicious objects."

"What if the lockers are locked?"

"Then you can't open them, can you?"

"And if the locker contains someone's personal effects?"

"Try not to steal anything, Mr Quam. And leave the under-wear alone."

"That was uncalled for, sir."

With little or no enthusiasm, Quam heads down a stifling, poorly lit hall with pipes six inches overhead, and everything painted the green favoured by prisons, mental hospitals and public gymnasiums—supposedly for its calming effect, but more likely because it can be purchased at a deep discount through war surplus.

Surrounded by that all-too-familiar hue, DS Hook takes a moment to calm himself. Last night Jeanie woke him up because he was shouting in his sleep—warning someone, she said. He remembers what was about to happen; it was something dread-ful. Then she put her bare arms around him, and whatever the nightmare was, it went away.

Three days into their so-called investigation, the main object-ive is the elimination of possibilities: What wasn't done and who didn't do it?

In the cafeteria, the tables have been cleared and the chairs are occupied by the eight servers who were on duty throughout the royal reception, together with the avuncular bartender (with the impeccable whiskers of a true professional), and of course Mr Tremblay—tweedy and waxed, standing just inside the door like the maître'd of an expensive restaurant.

Whether out of habit or nervousness, everyone is smoking; the tin ashtrays are already full, at eight o'clock in the morning.

Unsurprisingly, in their civilian attire the waiters look like what they are outside the hotel—underpaid men in shiny ten-dollar suits, holding cloth caps in their fists and with a gloomy expression on their faces; while the women, in cheap but fashionable cloche hats, stare into compact mirrors and refresh their lipstick.

The staff are gloomy and skittish, perhaps because the usual purpose of such a meeting at this time of the morning is to announce that someone won't be joining them today as they have been sacked. Personal worries overshadow the prospect that the Attorney General may have been murdered, let alone that the murderer may be one of them.

The manager drops his cigarette on the linoleum floor and steps on it. "Ah, Officer Hook. I wish good morning to you."

"And to you, Mr Tremblay. On behalf of the department, I thank you for your co-operation."

"We are all wishing a speedy closing to this matter and pleased to co-operate with the authorities." He turns to the assembly, who look back without interest. "Is not this true, gentlemen, and ladies, of course?"

Heads indicate unenthusiastic assent; unpaid overtime is one thing, but it's a bit much to have to look happy about it.

With a flourish, Mr Tremblay produces a list, and a roll call follows—*Mr Ryan, Mr Provan, Mr Fleming, Mr Bugden...*

All servers on the day in question being present and fully accounted for, Mr Tremblay nods briskly, returns the document to an inside pocket and prepares to make a quick exit.

"Gentlemen, we meet to discuss the sad events of Saturday while the memory is fresh. I am here with Sergeant Hook, who is asking the questions. I will leave you to him. After, there is coffee for you, free of charge. And I bid you good day."

The manager inclines his head in a sort of twisted bow, then turns and heads toward the elevator with the haste of a man coming up for air, leaving DS Hook to face his semi-hostile audience.

"Good morning, ladies and gentlemen. And thank you for agreeing to what will be a quick meeting. My first question: Who was it that served Attorney General Cunning on the night of his death?"

He waits. The only sound in the room is coming from his own laboured breathing in this smoky, unventilated room smelling of disinfectant and overcooked coffee.

"Quite. If that's the case, I hope you weren't planning anything for the rest of the morning—"

Suddenly, hands shoot up all over the room.

What follows are a series of recapitulations, from eight near-identical points of view, of the events in the Crystal Ballroom that evening, and the information is not productive. The barkeep can only reconfirm that the hotel indeed served martinis, but not in martini glasses. Not a single waiter remembers (or will admit to remembering) having served the gentleman occupying the overstuffed chair in the corner. The two servers who noticed Mr Cunning at all can't recall seeing a martini glass, as it would have been obscured by the fern. The others, veterans at their trade, noticed nothing but the tray in their hands, having done their rounds like automatons with fixed smiles on their faces.

One waiter, whose name (Merten or Morton) Hook didn't catch, does remember having seen someone in a waiter's uniform standing nearby.

"A wiry gent, about your height I s'pose."

"What did he look like, sir? Hair, facial hair, any unusual features?"

"Clean-shaven fellow. We're understaffed for such an event. I took him for one of the part-timers."

"Or not," interjects the man next to him. "Anyone can buy a cheap tux."

"Did you note any distinguishing characteristics, sir? Anyone?"

"The bloke had patent-leather hair, pushed back like Monte Blue in *Peacock Alley*."

Hook has never seen *Peacock Alley*. "What colour?"

"I thought it was reddish. Or reddish-brown. Or brown."

After a series of similarly fruitless queries, DS Hook thanks the staff for their co-operation. Chairs scrape against the linoleum as the men and women rise, stub out their cigarettes, put on their caps, snap their purses shut and shuffle to the urn for their free coffee.

In the hall, he is met by Constable Quam, who has something like a smile on his face, and is holding up a near-empty bottle of Gilbey's gin. "I found this in an empty locker, sir."

"Excellent work, Mr Quam. This will join its fellows in the lab—let's find out what's in it."

"Sir, do you think someone did it on purpose?"

Again, Hook wonders if Quam's question was very smart or very stupid—and the same might be asked of the person who left the bottle behind.

DAISY DOUGLAS TYLER SPEAKS
Transcription in Full
Rev Angus McDougall of Highland Church
for
*The Beacon*

My Canadian friends, I bring greetings from America, birthplace of the Anti-Saloon League, to the People's Prohibition Association of Vancouver—fellow soldiers, in what may be the most ambitious campaign in human history.

Your own Nellie McClung led you into battle, and you gave it your all. And I assure you that America cheered you on.

And believe me, my friends, to lose a battle against an army of greed, corruption and vested interests is nothing to be ashamed of. In fact, it's a badge of honour—and from the vigour I sense here in this room I know that, although you might have lost a battle, with God's help you will win the war!

"Why will we win?" you ask. Because the other side is for the selfish individual and his momentary desires—while our side is for the family.

The family. The fundamental building block of civilized society, without which we are reduced to a state even lower than the savages.

Is that why God created Mankind? Is that why Man was given dominion over the earth—so that we can live like apes and cannibals?

And so I say to you, in the words of that immortal hymn: *Onward, Christian soldiers, marching as to war!*

My friends, anyone with half a brain knows that alcohol is an insidious, habit-forming drug.

And for those who need proof, the science is clear. Just as strychnine tears down the spinal cord, alcohol destroys the brain. The brain: the seat of reason, willpower, morality and brotherly love.

And the destruction doesn't stop with the present generation. This vile spirit damages the cells responsible for the transmission of genes to our children.

And the result?

The result is enfeeblement, passed from one generation to the next. The eminent authority Dr Caleb Saleeby referred to alcohol as *racial poison*. Why? Because alcohol reverses the very principle by which Mankind has risen from savagery to civilization.

*Is that what we want for the white race?*

No, you say. And so says Mother Nature.

Mother Nature will not tolerate a reversal of her evolutionary principle. She will exterminate any creature, any species, any race, whose fitness declines. It is a principle that has held true since the dinosaurs.

I emphasize that it is Mother Nature—not Father Nature, but *Mother* Nature!

It is we mothers who know, all too well, that the greatest harm done by alcohol is to the people who have never tasted it.

A child is not born with whisky in its mouth. A child cries out to its mother for milk, not gin.

In the years since the war, we have heard a good deal about "personal liberty" and "freedom of choice." Fine, mouth-filling words. But when it comes to alcohol, "personal liberty" means the freedom to soak a man's brain with liquor until he becomes an irresponsible, dangerous, evil-smelling brute.

95

"Personal liberty" is not for his wife, who endures his blows and curses. Nor for his children, who grow up neglected and wanton. "Personal liberty" is not for the woman who walks downtown at the risk of being raped by some drink-crazed savage.

And so I ask you, What about the innocents? Where is *their* freedom?

Like you, we in America summoned up the courage to put it to a vote—which, by God's grace, we won. And so America began the delicate, difficult, dangerous operation of extracting alcohol from the body politic.

Five years later, we see light ahead.

There have never been so many abstainers as there are now. More and more people are choosing to follow the dictates of science, the Bible and common sense. The tide of battle has turned, and we are winning—and so will you!

My dear Canadian friends, our two Christian nations march shoulder to shoulder. We are Soldiers of God, ready to do battle. The torch is afire! Together we will hold it high!

May God bless you all.

# CHAPTER 13

WHEN THE FRONT door to the Crombie residence finally opens, Hook is looking down at a tiny, silent Oriental woman in a black blouse and a spotless white apron, who is looking back up at him with frightened eyes.

He does a slight bow and presents his warrant card: *"Nei hou. Ngodeih gingchat, ngodei yahplai, ok?"*

*"Neideih yahplai la."* she replies.

Of necessity, DS Hook switches to English. "I do apologize, miss. When it comes to Chinese I just reached the end of my rope."

She smiles faintly and dips her head. "I am happy you have made a good start. But I regret my employer is not here."

"I understand. But perhaps we might come in anyway."

"You wish to search the house, sir? If so, I am most sorry but Mr Crombie must be consulted."

"The police will take full responsibility, miss. Mr Crombie has given us his support."

"But I am responsible, sir."

Standing behind him, Constable Quam awakens from his slumber. "Shall I get her out of the way?"

"You want to punch her in the stomach, do you?"

"Sir, I object to that."

"I apologize, Quam, you're right, it was uncalled for."

He turns back to the little person in the doorway. "We only wish to see the bathroom, miss. Nothing will be disturbed. You see, we are most concerned about what may have caused Mrs Crombie's death."

"Ah, yes. I understand. I too am concerned. Please come in."

The two policemen follow the maid-of-all-work as she glides down a cross-hall lined with prints of Edinburgh, Loch Lomond and Ben Nevis, as well as the Crombie coat of arms with its gloomy tartan.

Quam is, as usual, two steps behind. "Where did you learn Chinese, sir?"

"From a Communist."

"A Chinese Communist?"

"He was inscrutable, that's true."

"It is upstairs, sir," she says. "I will leave you now." With a slight bow, she disappears into what is probably the kitchen, as the two policemen climb the stairs.

"Sir, did we really get Mr Crombie's permission to enter the premises?"

"I was speaking in general terms, Constable. He has voiced support for law and order. Besides, the Dry Squad do this all the time and he's all for it."

Upstairs, they reach a dark, L-shaped hallway with three closed doors (bedrooms no doubt); the bathroom and water closet doors at the far end are slightly ajar, otherwise the hallway would be in pitch darkness. Hook smells floor wax and musty pajamas—the smell of bedridden convalescents and an extended absence of sexual activity.

The bathtub's feet are made to resemble lion's paws; the floor is covered with linoleum, patterned to imitate hexagonal porcelain tiles; the sink rests on a pedestal like a column from the Acropolis. A corner cabinet is topped by a vase depicting an animal with enormous antlers, and containing a bouquet of silk flowers that seem near death, even though they're artificial. Hook approaches the wooden medicine cabinet above the sink, without looking at himself in the mirror.

"Constable, see what's in that other cabinet, will you?"

"What am I to look for, sir?"

"Suspicious liquids, Mr Quam."

"Poison liquids, sir?"

"Well I wouldn't expect a skull-and-crossbones on the label."

Hook opens the medicine cabinet. From the upper shelves he takes out and examines two bars of La Parle Obesity Soap, jars of Radior Cream and Odo-ro-no, a tin of Encharma cold cream powder by Luxor, and a half-full atomizer of perfume. To judge by the bottom shelf, it seems that the effort has taken a toll on

Mrs Crombie's health: Rexall Orderlies laxative, Anusol suppositories, a tin of Bayer Aspirin, a box of Dr Chase's Nerve Food, a bottle of Hamlin's Wizard Oil and a packet of Dr Batty's Asthma Cigarettes.

Overall, Hook is struck by the dearth of masculine products. Unless he doesn't shave at home, Mr Crombie must spend his nights elsewhere. On the other hand, with or without Mr Crombie at hand, Mrs Crombie seems to have spared no effort to make herself soft and fragrant—perhaps she *was* having an affair...

He closes the cabinet (without looking at the man in the mirror) and turns to Constable Quam, on his knees before the corner cupboard, having emptied it of its contents: spare rolls of Scott Tissue, an enema kit, an electric vibrator and, on the bottom shelf, tall bottles of Emerson's Botanic Bitters, Riker's Beef, Wine and Iron tonic—and, as Hook expected, a half-full bottle of Patterson's Silk Hat Martini Cocktail.

"Something else for the laboratory, I think. Be sure it's properly labelled."

"I'll take it to them, sir, but they're already complaining about the workload."

"My heart bleeds for them."

"If I may say so, sir, I don't really think that's true."

A PROFITABLE CRUSADE
Ed McCurdy
Staff Writer
*The Evening Star*

O welcome the Damsel of Dry
The Yankee came down from the sky
With the God-given grace
To better the race
And bid all our boozing goodbye.

Rev Daisy Douglas Tyler, the celebrated American speaker, has come to town, courtesy of the People's Prohibition Association.

Miss Tyler's fee, said to be not unadjacent to a thousand dollars (a PPA spokesman refused to confirm the amount, terming it a "private matter"), has raised eyebrows among some, but the association can well afford her price.

Since the plebiscite, the People's Prohibition Association has never been stronger. The organization is so well funded by disgruntled Drys that it is now staffed by professionals and not volunteers. Temperance is no longer a movement, but an industry.

And as with any industry in the public market, promotion is key.

Wednesday evening at the Opera House, before an audience of 900, Miss Tyler did not disappoint. She swept onto the stage like an opera diva, in a nurse's uniform that might have been designed by Coco Chanel, topped by a blue military-style cape as light as a cloud. Her dark hair was curled and gathered like a Greek goddess; her makeup was a testament to Max Factor; her feet hovered over four-inch heels that made her to appear statuesque, despite her compact physique.

And a bravura performance it was—peppered with rhetorical tricks worthy of a Barrymore. When she lifted her arms as though to bless the audience, the position emphasized the fetching line of her bodice—a look that one male audience member termed the "bee's knees." Indeed, her entire affect seemed calculated to arouse, in the way that a callow youth is aroused by a comely, authoritative schoolmarm.

The speech itself, which may be read in its entirety on the pages of *The Beacon*, combined Miss McClung's WCTU rhetoric with Miss Tyler's passion for eugenics—the movement that would cull defectives from the human herd and breed a superior race.

To go by her reception, the audience at the Opera House seem to have received their money's worth—if not the whole story.

As it appears in the programme, Miss Tyler's record of achievement is an impressive one, highlighting her leadership of the Indiana WCTU, the Indiana War Mothers and the Better Babies movement.

Strangely absent from this list of honours is the fact that her Queens of the Golden Mask is more commonly known as the Women's Ku Klux Klan, in which her title was Imperial Empress, until she resigned last year after facing and denying charges of personal enrichment.

This enterprising temperance maven, suffragette and racial purity advocate allegedly pocketed eighty per cent of a steep initiation fee, while investing in businesses that manufactured Klan robes, a Klan bible called the Kloran, as well as "Klan Water" for certain rituals—all compulsory equipment for the new member.

Not that she has gone to any great lengths to hide her affiliation with the Klan—nor should she, given its burgeoning Vancouver membership under the leadership of the Grand Goblin, Maj Luther Forrest.

While in the city, she has quietly taken up residence at Glen Brae mansion, now known as the Imperial Palace of the Knights of the KKK, as a guest of Major Forrest, who hasn't done badly for himself either.

Having organized Klan chapters in Washington and Oregon, Major Forrest has wheeled his vacuum cleaner north to hoover dollars from chumps in "Kanada"—including, it is said, an alderman, several policemen and at least three members of the Legislature.

One doesn't know whether to laugh or cry. Is there no end to our gullibility?

# CHAPTER 14

NEWSON HOLDS OUT a copy of today's *Evening Star*, folded open to display a quarter page. "I'm beginning to wonder about you, lad."

"Wonder in what way, sir?"

Newson glares down at him over the edge of his battle table; it puts McCurdy in mind of a wolf about to devour a rabbit.

"The editorial position of this paper is emphatically on the temperance side. You know this, lad. You knew it when I hired you. Always has been and always will be."

He thrusts the offending piece forward in front of the reporter's nose: "Do you have a good explanation for this? I tell you lad, there had better be."

McCurdy anticipated this meeting well before the *See Me* note arrived, and had ample time to prepare a reply. As a writer he might hold his line of work in contempt, but it doesn't follow that he wants to be fired. His sight gravitates to the Union Jack in the corner:

"Daisy Douglas Tyler is an American, sir. Do we really want Americans to take charge of the Canadian temperance movement?"

General Newson flinches at this unexpected rejoinder. He pulls the paper back, squints at the article, lays it down on the desk, squints at it again. A pause follows, as he leans back in his chair, making a steeple of his long fingers, deep in thought.

"Please continue, lad. You interest me."

"Knowing your sharp mind, sir, I'm sure you quickly picked up on the fact that not only is Miss Tyler American, but so is the Ku Klux Klan. I, for one, find this alarming. Surely the paper's editorial line is that Canadians should be masters of our own house."

Newson reflects aloud: "Those bloody Americans. Joined the war three years late, and to hear them you'd think they won it single-handed."

"That is so true, sir. And I don't think you led the fight for a sober, white, British province, only to hand the reform effort over to our friends in the south."

The general's eyes focus inward, like a sleepwalker. "That bastard Armstrong..."

"Beg your pardon, sir? Do you mean Gen Hector Armstrong?"

"The snake married a rich American, made his money by selling out the west to Yankees. Alberta is the forty-ninth state now, thanks to that traitor."

"And, of course, we mustn't forget that Gordon Cunning was born in Missouri."

Newson rises to his feet and slaps the table so hard that a miniature Red Ensign flag topples over. "By God, you've hit upon it, lad! The Americans are an insidious race, sneaky as Chinamen—look what they did to Mexico. We must stand on guard on all fronts."

"Absolutely, sir. It's another kind of invasion—an invasion in spirit, co-opting our national struggle."

"*An Invasion in Spirit*—now there's a headline for you!"

"Gordon Cunning may have been a scoundrel, but he's *our* scoundrel. I'd hate to think the *Star* is about to let the Americans denounce him on our behalf."

"Couldn't have put it better myself, son. I can see that you have the bit in your teeth. Forward!"

# CHAPTER 15

THE PLATE GLASS window next to DS Hook's desk takes up three-quarters of a wall separating two offices.

The larger office is a warren of desks and chairs where every ashtray overflows, and where the smoke is so thick it has divided itself into tiers, like cloud banks after a storm.

A hive-like atmosphere predominates—men in and out of uniform darting this way and that, leaving a pong of armpit sweat and tobacco in their wake. At the telephone exchange near the entrance, two young women field and direct calls from the public. While the noise level may be alarming to visitors, its inhabitants don't hear it anymore.

The smaller office on the far side of the glass is a zone that unequivocally belongs to Chief Lionel Barfoot, a humourless Glaswegian who plays the tenor drum with the Police Pipe Band, and is skilled at making advantageous alliances. He is also a decorated veteran (DSO and bar)—an ambitious man who is still in the process of learning that sending men to kill people is easier than sending men to keep the peace.

The chief is testament to the fact that it is possible for a man to be a competent officer and a bullying windbag at the same time.

In this inner office, Barfoot takes meetings with conspicuously important citizens; it is also where departmental commendations and tongue-lashings take place for all to see, like a silent photoplay without subtitles.

DS Hook has just been summoned into that room, and it is a certainty that he is not about to be given a medal.

At present the chief is in conference with a conspicuously important citizen—Harlan Crombie, a balding gent with pink jowls, in a suit from London and a club tie from a public school.

Both men are puffing on pipes and engaged in what looks to be friendly banter, the sort of talk one has while waiting for someone.

In this case, they are waiting for DS Hook.

Bracing himself, Hook pulls open the door and steps inside: "You asked to see me, sir?"

As Hook approaches the desk, Barfoot stands—"Ah. There you are."—then immediately seats himself again. There is no chair for DS Hook.

"Harlan, let me introduce you to Detective Sergeant Calvin Hook. Hook is new with the detachment, which may explain part of the problem."

"If anything will," Crombie says, and relights his pipe.

"The deputy minister has come with a complaint, to the effect that you and your assistant barged into and searched his house, without permission and without a warrant."

"And terrorized my household staff." Crombie points at Hook's face with the stem of his pipe as though it were a pistol. "This is more than an imposition, sir, it's an outrage!"

"I quite agree," Barfoot says. "On the face of it, a demotion is in order. Mr Hook, what do you have to say for yourself?"

"Sir, we asked to speak to Mr Crombie, and in his absence were about to go on our way, when the constable suffered an attack of gastritis. I made a decision, based on Mr Crombie's unfailing support for the police—in particular, the Dry Squad..."

"Thank you, Detective Sergeant, I believe we have heard enough. And your response, Harlan?"

Crombie shakes his head. "Most improper. But under the circumstances, nothing will be gained by taking this further."

"You may be overly generous, Harlan, but if you wish to let bygones be bygones, that is your prerogative."

The flint in Crombie's stare tells Hook that he may have secured a temporary reprieve, but he will pay for this.

"Detective Sergeant, you're a lucky man," Barfoot says. "But if you so much as set foot on Mr Crombie's property again, you will forfeit your badge."

# CHAPTER 16

HAVING DETERMINED NEVER to enter the Kingsway Hotel again, McCurdy and Miss Wickstram have agreed that in future, rather than undertake a futile attempt at anonymity, they would impersonate a pair on a date. She accepted this on two conditions: that any physical contact be restricted to hand-holding and that, as the gentleman, he would foot the bill.

Naturally, McCurdy is ambivalent about this arrangement and suspects that Mildred is playing some sort of sadistic game. But here they are nonetheless, in the Ladies and Escorts room at the Alhambra Hotel, spooning with gritted teeth. (Typically, she has chosen the most expensive cocktail on the menu.)

McCurdy decides to get right to the point: "Apparently the manager of your hotel has two telephones. In your professional experience, what might the second one be for?"

"One for each ear, perhaps?"

"Very funny. An associate would like to have a definitive answer. If we may."

"I shall have a look. Incidentally, your invoice for information on Miss Daisy—who is far from a Miss, by the way—comes to ten dollars. Fins please, no counterfeit sawbucks."

Smiling coquettishly, she leans back in the wicker chair (the decor features an outdoorsy motif), lights one of her putrid Meccas, sips her Hanky Panky and enjoys his discomfort.

Mounted on the wall above her head, a big-horned sheep and a bison watch with glassy indifference as McCurdy painfully extracts two banknotes. It's like tearing out wads of his own hair, yet he manages to smile. "Millie, I hate to admit this, but your research has opened up new lines of inquiry."

"Why thank you, Eddie. How sweet. And congratulations for getting your piece past Old Lime Juice."

"Newson dislikes Americans even more than he dislikes alcohol. He has never forgotten 'Fifty-four forty or fight.' Everywhere he looks, the Yankees are upon us."

"Fifty-four what? Is that a football yell?"

"Something like that, yes."

Having drawn a ghost of a laugh out of her, he presses further: "So Millie, I take it you have found a source other than the public library."

"More than one, actually. The lines are buzzing over Miss Daisy and the Klan. Some say that the Klan is behind Cunning's death, that they brought poisoned hooch from America and fed it to him."

McCurdy gets out his notebook. "Interesting. Who told you?"

"Fuck off, Eddie. Where would we be if I coughed up my sources?"

Predictably, such an expletive from a well-dressed, attractive woman attracts the interest of, among others, a table of college men in blazers and Oxford bag trousers; it also seems to have drawn the interest of an athletic young woman seated at the bar, in a chemise and bobbed hair, no doubt waiting for her date.

To appease the audience, McCurdy takes her hand and smiles like a fond suitor. "I meant it as a joke, darling."

She laughs, girlishly. "So did I, darling."

He starts a genuine laugh, but winces.

"They broke your ribs, didn't they, Eddie?"

"Cracked a few, yes, but they've just about healed by now. It would have been far worse if it weren't for a young American chap with a pistol."

"How fortunate. Like Wild Bill Hickok, coming to the rescue."

"Remarkable timing. It was almost as though he was ready and waiting."

# CHAPTER 17

WHEN THE PERPETUAL autumn rain starts and various meteorological forces take over, low clouds stack against the mountains trapping the air so that the smoke from eleven sawmills remains captive for weeks at a time. In this season, with its stench of rotten fish, spoilt vegetables, decayed wood, horse shit and rotten eggs from the gasworks, a visitor might think the city to be one enormous wharf.

Especially prominent is the smell of creosote. In the Northwest, rot is as inevitable as death. It's the enemy you will never overcome; you can only beat it back by coating everything with creosote.

Since arriving in Vancouver, DS Hook has grown accustomed to the city's stink—an attractive, manly smell if somewhat poisonous, like the smell of gasoline, mothballs and gunpowder.

He has become so used to the taste of air at the back of his throat that, as with Scotch, he can distinguish its components. Tonight the air tastes of sweetened tar. At other times he detects notes of burnt rubber and smoked meat.

He lights an Ogden's—pleasant, manly and, doctors say, good for the system as well.

As he does for his meetings with the reporter, he is wearing street clothes so as not to draw the attention of the taxi drivers who surround the hotel and are currently seated on their fenders, awaiting customers, smoking cigarettes, selling condoms to pedestrians and trading the telephone numbers of sporting women.

Leaning against a lamp-post with a clear view of the staff entrance, Hook looks over to Granville Street, where pedestrians herd past the Radiophone sign for the second showing of *The Phantom of the Opera* at the Capitol. He'd like to see it himself, but Jeanie is afraid it would keep her up at night. (Given her husband's profession, Jeanie prefers to avoid entertainment that invokes fear.)

The lift attendant emerges twenty minutes after the end of his shift, in an eight-dollar suit and a tweed cap. While riding in the lift, Hook judged him to be in his late thirties, but now he appears much older, for his walk has the old man shuffle and stoop. His left arm swings by his side, but not so the right arm, which he has thrust into a side pocket to keep it from waving about on its own.

Hook crosses the street to head him off: "Excuse me, Mr Sark, sir, I wonder if I may—"

Immediately he realizes his mistake, as the lift attendant does a fast about-face, fists up, on guard, ready to fend off the enemy.

Hook holds up two open hands in the traditional gesture of harmlessness. "Easy does it, sir. Sorry to startle you."

The lift attendant takes a deep breath and relaxes somewhat. "Ah, it is you, Officer. I apologize for that. It is old habit."

"In any case, Corporal Sark, it was careless of me."

Sark tilts his head sideways: "Why you say *Corporal*?"

"Snipers are usually corporals."

"And how you know I was a marksman?"

"For one thing, your fondness for enclosed spaces."

"Ah. Yes, I can see that."

They head north on Howe Street. DS Hook has encountered a good deal of odd behaviour during and since the war, usually based on outmoded precautions. Here is a man whose avoidance of open spaces has put him in an upright coffin, going up and down for a minimum of eight hours a day.

As they approach Georgia Street, Hook turns to say something—and finds nobody there.

He thinks he knows what's up: a sniper may be trained to kill, but his life depends on his ability to disappear. So he retraces his steps until he reaches a patch of lawn containing a large shrub with a slightly enlarged shadow; the lift attendant has positioned himself so that, in this light, he appears to be part of the shrub itself.

"Did you see something suspicious, Mr Sark?"

He replies in a low voice, with calm urgency. "Devonshire Apartments. Seventh floor. Second window west."

Hook scans the floors and windows in the Devonshire. (*The Last Thing in Apartments*, according to an advert in *The World*.) In between a pair of partially drawn curtains he can make out the silhouette of a man whose elbow is sticking out at shoulder height.

"I think I see him, Mr Sark."

"And do you see rifle? Port position?"

"It could be a rifle, yes. But from the motion of the arm, I think it may also be a man brushing his teeth."

After a pause, the lift attendant emerges into the street light. "Is not possible to be too careful."

Hook recalls that snipers rarely suffer from shell shock, but can display unique long-term symptoms, each one a version of soldier's heart: compulsive checking for enemies, extreme reactions to sudden noses, rituals of all kinds, not to mention a wariness of human beings in general. Snipers, like Redhats, were a despised group and a common object of irrational "morning hate," and had as much to fear from their fellows as from the enemy.

To achieve some sort of rapport, Hook scours his brain for other facts about sniper duty. "It looks as if you're used to having a spotter."

"I did not lose a single one."

"You lost an arm, though."

"It was a lucky shot."

Momentarily, Hook envisions the Front as a forest occupied by snipers with rifles and wirelesses, on the hunt for each other.

"I suppose you had the Ross rifle."

"The Ross was good rifle, yes."

*Interesting.* Hook decides to push him a bit: "Was it really? I heard otherwise. The Ross rifle is notorious."

"Doesn't take crack shot to hit a man eating his lunch, sitting on a pile of wood." In the lamplight, the lift attendant's aquamarine eyes are focused on a point far away.

DS Hook gets the picture and moves on. "I wonder if you might tell me something more about Mr Cunning."

"We had no acquaintance outside the lift. This is frowned on by Mr Tremblay."

"I'm not surprised. Still, anything that comes to mind could be useful."

"Mr Cunning was contradicting gentleman."

"Do you mean that he contradicted other people's statements?"

"No, himself he contradicted. In his taste."

"What sort of taste do you mean, Mr Sark? Booze?"

"He was fond of patent medicines. They often are."

"What do you mean?"

"A habit could be this or that. Alcohol, cocaine, opium, codeine, bromide, women—it depends on the need to go up or down."

"Which direction did Mr Cunning prefer?"

"All of them, sir. Mr Cunning had a variety of visitors. Some official, some not so official."

"Friends, would you say?"

"Business connections is more like, I would say."

# CHAPTER 18

LIKE MANY WORKING-CLASS establishments, the Lumberman's Club is a place you can't imagine ever having been new. It might have surfaced intact from some prehistoric cave, steeped in every liquid a human body can produce, cured by eons of spilt alcohol and tobacco smoke, every surface weathered by boots, elbows, cigarette burns and workmen's hands, the air itself redolent with generations of evaporated sweat and damp wool. The result is not entirely unpleasant, like the smell of a barn, a blacksmith shop or a motor garage.

McCurdy occupies a stool at the bar overlooking a half-filled room the size of a small restaurant, its tables scarred with overlapping ring marks, covered with poker chips, cards, glasses and ashtrays, and surrounded by silent men in tweed caps, wrinkled lounge suits and logger's boots. Each player regularly glances from side to side as though someone might be pulling a fast one, then checks his hand to be sure his cards haven't somehow been switched for others, then keeps them face down on the table or tight against his vest.

Each man wears his hat, and many their coats as well; when making a fast exit, it's a shame to leave one's belongings behind.

All of which is seen through a haze so thick you'd think a beekeeper was smoking a hive.

McCurdy sits at the bar across from the bartender, Truman MacBeth, an ex-miner with a blackened nose, submarine skin and a jaw that could chew open a can of beans, who wears a battered brown Derby and a dishtowel over his shoulder that could pass for a mechanic's rag.

"My usual, Truman, and one for yourself. Everything jake?"

"'cept for the frigging bulls in plain clothes. Cy Steele sold a bottle of rum to two young fellers who turned out to be the fecking Dry Squad. Beat the shite out of him, then threw him in the clink."

"The gumshoes are hard to recognize now. I'm told they're recruited in Alberta and moved around the province."

"Like the fecking secret police in Russia. Cy is doing three months in the caboose. Mind, Dotson will keep him on at full pay. No such luck with this joint. With me behind the bar we go by the letter of the law. Nobody gets past the door without a signed membership. Nothing but lumbermen here, no sir, not while the city is crawling with informers."

"Maybe this is the epidemic of rats City Hall is on about."

"Like the rats, yes. Down by the harbour I seen wharf rats the size of raccoons."

"Max Trotter did a piece on it. Staged a photo of the mayor walking his cat around English Bay. Trotter is lodged so far up Taylor's arsehole—"

"And when there's trouble, Mayor Taylor loves the camera." Truman sets down a glass containing a finger more than the usual serving.

"Any new rumours about the Cunning case, Truman? Not that there's a shortage."

"It's said that Cunning was bumped off by Stalker. That he has goons to do his dirty work."

"The Dry Squad at it again is what I heard."

"Wouldn't be surprised. When you can't trust the government or the police, it makes a man suspicious generally."

"You're right. Like someone is following you all the time. I get that feeling often; it came over me just today, as a matter of fact."

Two whiskys later, McCurdy eases down the steps in front of the Lumberman's Club, crosses the sidewalk and pauses to steady himself against a light pole. More than once he has relied on poles to get him home safely, holding until balance is restored then flinging himself forward with enough momentum to grab onto the next before pitching face-first onto the sidewalk. Tonight is not one of those nights, however—he's had just enough lubrication to get him into a writing mood.

He checks the clock above the Cal-Van neon across the street—a quarter past ten, early yet. Might be good to take a walk and think his way through a piece on the resurgence of bootlegging—not despite the plebiscite but because of it, thanks to legal rotgut that costs an arm and a leg. Leaning on the lamp-post, he takes out his notebook.

A shrill *ping!* next to his head nearly splits his eardrum, followed by a *crack!* from some distance away, and he is on all fours, by instinct.

Though this has never happened before, he knows what it is. He remains frozen, hands splayed over the cobbles, heart racing, unable to move, like a rabbit in the presence of a predator.

He often wondered how he would react in such a situation. Now he knows.

Suddenly stone cold sober, he manages to stand up and examines the lamp-post: a bright stripe has been scored into the metal at eye level, as though someone scraped it with a rat-tail file.

Shaking, he holds onto the lamp-post, contemplates running for his life, then thinks better of it and scrambles back up the steps to the shelter of the Lumberman's Club.

Behind the bar, Truman is pouring a round of shots someone lost on a bet.

"Welcome back, Ed. Jesus, you look pale. Not going to ralph, are you?"

"A double please, Truman. I'm afraid someone just shot at me—"

"I'll get the mop."

# PART II

*If politicians and scientists were lazier,
how much happier we should all be.*

—Evelyn Waugh

# CHAPTER 19

IT MIGHT SEEM counterintuitive to place the capital of British Columbia on an island thirty miles off the mainland, yet it seemed the thing to do when Fort Victoria was preparing to fend off an American invasion and Vancouver didn't exist.

Seventy-five years later, the city is an homage to the Mother Country and a haven for British immigrants who want as little as possible to do with the rest of Canada.

One might think Grace would feel quite at home.

Crossing the expanse of lawn, sometimes she thinks she is in *Alice In Wonderland,* as though Queen Victoria, with her crown, her sceptre and her bronze décolletage were about to screech: *Off with her head!*

Above her, wisps of wet cloud swirl about the golden statue of Captain George Vancouver, perched atop the octagonal dome of the Legislature building.

Approaching the oak-lined committee room, silver light filters through wet leaded glass, barely illuminating a space not unlike the interior of a cigar humidor.

At a long table sit the three men with sole discretionary power over the legal importation, manufacture and sale of alcohol in the Province of British Columbia. Each man was selected by the Attorney General for his "exemplary character and reputation," as required in the Government Liquor Act of 1921.

Unnoticed or ignored (perhaps both), Grace takes her place at a student's desk in the corner, the dunce in the class, and resigns herself to another afternoon of transcribing their self-serving shite.

Today she senses tension in the room—and smells it, thanks to Mr Munn's imperfect personal habits.

This is the first board meeting since the untimely death of the Attorney General, and Gwendolyn seems to think the LCB is anticipating a big change. Before his sudden passing, Attorney General Cunning installed Clyde Taggart, a political operative and Cunning loyalist, as chairman. Mr Beaven and Mr Munn have disliked Taggart from their first meeting, when he announced his intention to "drain the swamp."

Grace assumes this to be some sort of metaphor having to do with the inner workings of the department. In her position it would be unwise to inquire further.

She is paid to serve, not to be nosy.

At the head of the table, Clyde Taggart glances at his pocket watch, then rises to his feet with an unlit cigar between his fingers. Impeccably tailored, he has the build of an ex-athlete and is rather handsome despite a cauliflower ear.

The atmosphere is, as usual, less than convivial. Mr Taggart is a man who is used to being disliked. Grace suspects that he sees it as part of the job.

"Gentlemen, before approval of the minutes, after the tragic death of Gordon Cunning I think it behooves us to call for a minute of silence."

After a lacklustre "Hear! Hear!" Munn and Beaven stand up and fold their hands in front of their watch chains. Grace wonders if it would be respectful or presumptuous of her to stand up as well, but rather than draw attention to herself, she stares at her blank sheet of foolscap, pencil at the ready, like a china figurine.

The silence seems to last a good deal longer than a minute. Outside, raindrops rhythmically tap the leaded glass like the tips of little fingers.

In the foolscap margin, Grace draws a headstone bearing the initials RIP.

Beaven and Munn exchange comradely nods across the table, implying that the death of the Attorney General wasn't the worst thing that could have happened.

Ever since the end of Prohibition, the two men have enjoyed a cordial relationship, despite their opposing constituencies. Mr Munn, with his thin white hands and face like a weasel, is on the board of the People's Prohibition Association. Mr Beaven, whose skin is the colour and texture of melba toast, is a corporate lawyer for the Reifel brothers—rum-runners of long standing who have become rich beyond imagining. Since the plebiscite the two have found common cause: both regard bootlegging as a menace, and both have an interest in obstructing any change to a system that has served them well.

Chairman Taggart clears his throat and calls the meeting to order. Grace readies her pencil. However, before they can move to the first order of business, the door to the committee room opens and a receptionist, after poking her nose through the crack, tiptoes into the room to whisper into the chairman's ear.

Taggart's eyebrows narrow. "Oh really? Yes, of course, Miss Witherspoon, please show him in. Gentlemen, it seems we have been favoured with a visit from the acting Attorney General's office."

And here it comes: Grace knows perfectly well what is about to happen, having been informed this morning by Gwendolyn, who works in that office and is just as bored with her job.

The unexpected visitor is a gentleman of perhaps forty who might have stepped out of the London Stock Exchange, the sort who carries a furled umbrella and thinks soft collars in the civil service will lead to the downfall of Britain.

Chairman Taggart manages a tight smile. "Gentlemen, we have been flattered with a visit from Mr Bertram Bliss, our deputy minister."

In the margin, Grace draws a snake.

The two shake hands, outwardly pleasant but wary. Beaven and Munn mutter a greeting, then reseat themselves and light cigarettes. Taggart remains standing; otherwise, the visitor would tower over him.

"And to what do we owe the pleasure of your visit, Mr Bliss?" A certain edge underlies the chairman's smooth baritone.

A practised speaker, Mr Bliss pauses to make momentary eye contact with each gentleman in turn. Impeccably groomed, his skin appears buffed—in fact, he could be a duplicate of himself out of Madame Tussaud's. Even his moustache could be made of paraffin, there being no evidence of the individual hairs involved.

Mr Bliss speaks the way members do in the Legislature, as though delivering a memorized speech.

"Chairman Taggart. Mr Munn. Mr Beaven. Frightfully sorry to barge in on your deliberations, but Mr Stalker insists that we follow one cardinal rule: before any public announcement is made, departments affected by the decision must be notified. This is, I think, only fair game, would you not agree?"

Mr Beaven and Mr Munn agree, although their enthusiasm is restrained. ("Fair game," in Canadian usage, is about being sportsmanlike; however, to the British it identifies a grouse that is fat enough to shoot.)

Though the chairman remains outwardly calm, his features have begun to gather at the centre of his face.

Satisfied with his progress so far, Mr Bliss heaves a sigh to indicate sadness. "We in the Attorney General's office remain in absolute shock over Mr Cunning's passing." He turns to the chairman: "Special condolences to you, Mr Taggart, as a colleague and a close friend."

With a curt nod, Taggart sets fire to his cigar with a silver lighter while the rest of the three-man board respond with nods of sober agreement: *Yes indeed, dreadful shock, dreadful shock, simply dreadful.*

Bliss shakes his head slowly, as though deep in thought—*Such greatness gone forever*—then returns to the present. "All the same, as I believe they say in Hollywood, 'the show must go on.'" He chuckles at his American reference. *How contemporary!*

"I believe you said you had an announcement," Chairman Taggart says.

"I beg your pardon?"

"If you can kindly make this reasonably short, we do have an agenda."

Bliss remains as placid as ever. "Quite right, Chairman Taggart, time flies and all that. I shall get straight to the point."

"Thank you, Mr Bliss." The chairman smiles with gritted teeth. Grace can see that he suspects something is up.

Mr Bliss exhales through pursed lips, the innocent bringer of bad news.

"Of course it goes without saying that change is never entirely welcome for everyone, and it goes without saying that change in no way indicates dissatisfaction with those persons affected—"

"Yes, yes, it goes without saying. Mr Bliss. You have staked a claim on our attention, now kindly get to the goddamn point."

"Quite. Just so." Mr Bliss sighs as though to say, *let's get this over with*, and clears his throat.

While Mr Bliss makes his announcement, Grace observes the way Chairman Taggart creates a buffer of smoke between himself and the speaker.

"Tomorrow morning, every newspaper in the province will report that Premier Gulliver has appointed the Honourable Boris Stalker, MLA for Vancouver City, to the position of Attorney General for the Province of British Columbia. I myself am to continue in my capacity as deputy minister. After due consideration, Attorney General Stalker has, in turn, appointed Mr Harlan Crombie to the position of"—Mr Bliss sighs regretfully—"chairman of the Liquor Control Board." After a slight pause to allow this to sink in, he continues. "In this capacity he will replace our current chairman," he nods to his left, "Mr Clyde Taggart."

With a sad smile, he addresses the man at the head of the table: "Of course, it would be an understatement to say that the Attorney General is frightfully grateful for your service. He wishes to schedule a meeting, perhaps later this week, to discuss the future.

"That said, gentlemen, I shall not detain you any longer."

Mr Taggart quietly sets his cigar on the ashtray rim. Taking advantage of the shocked pause, Mr Bliss eases his way out, like a cat burglar.

"Bliss, you squalid bastard!" Taggart makes a move toward the deputy minister, who hops sharply out the door and shuts it behind him.

Taggart turns back into the room, leans on the table and takes a moment to catch his breath. His teeth are clamped so tight that Grace wonders if his jaw might break.

Miss Witherspoon's frightened face reappears through a crack in the door: "Mr Chairman, was there anything more—"

"Get out!" And the door slams shut as though blown by a gust of wind.

Seated at her desk in the corner, Grace scans her shorthand notes for errors.

She wonders what Gwendolyn will have to say.

UPON THEIR ARRIVAL in Victoria Harbour, Grace and Gwendolyn spent their first few weeks at the YWCA, then took a room at Mrs Croft's Rooming House for White Women. Mrs Croft was a smug, religious biddy and a vicious bully who opened the doors at seven, locked them again at nine, and any girl locked out could seek other quarters next morning.

And she spied. When Grace came home from work, her undergarments were never folded quite the same way.

So the two began looking for a regular flat, where one could come and go as one pleased—only to have prospective landlords demand proof that two single women in a flat do not intend to run a bawdy house. How is one supposed to prove that?

Miss Carr came as a welcome, if peculiar, exception.

A sturdy woman with watchful eyes, she explained right off that she raised sheep dogs and kept a monkey, and if they objected to monkeys and dogs, then there was really no point in seeing the flat.

The fact that Grace's family raised sheep in the Lake District elicited a grunt of approval. Gwendolyn wasn't comfortable with monkeys, having seen them do disgusting things at the London Zoo, but she managed to keep it to herself.

The flat, though small, was clean and had decent furniture, and in any event an eccentric landlady seemed a more attractive proposition than hideous Mrs Croft, let alone a tattooed land-lord with duplicate keys.

Once settled in Miss Carr's boarding house, at Gwendolyn's insistence the two girls set about attending every mixed social available—Baptist, Presbyterian, Methodist, even Catholics were not out of bounds.

Grace quickly grew weary of these occasions, and not just because she is plainer and men aren't keen to look at her—instead, they look past her, as though someone more attract-ive might be just over her shoulder. At a Methodist gathering, a young man kissed her and slipped his hand around to where it didn't belong, and not once did he meet her gaze.

She thinks it might be the glasses, but suspects it to be more than that.

Their initial assumption upon arrival was that, in the absence of prospective husbands at home, there would be excellent hunting here, in this forest of men. Now Grace thinks that may have been a mistake. Quantity doesn't equal quality, and in Victoria the available men seem to be low down, stuck up or Chinese.

During their first week they were warned that Chinatown is a warren of wooden sidewalks with trap doors through which a girl can fall into a cellar, to be made a white slave or a member of some dreadful harem. Some said that pagan rituals take place, where people are hypnotized into doing unspeakable things.

Grace thinks a trip to Chinatown sounds exciting compared to a date with a local gentleman.

Gwendolyn is not discouraged. Bold as brass, she goes to dances at the armoury and the Crystal Garden, or moving pictures at the Royal, or a play at the Capitol, and never without a strong arm to lean on. (At times she dresses more like a flapper than a civil servant.)

For herself, Grace would rather stay home with the dogs, the monkey and Miss Carr.


### STALKER CONFIRMED AS ATTORNEY GENERAL
#### Cecil Harmsworth
#### Staff Writer
#### *The Beacon*

Vancouver citizens who are concerned over the current state of the city will welcome the appointment of Boris Stalker to the position of Attorney General of the Province of British Columbia, to replace the late Gordon Cunning.

As Reverend McDougall of the People's Prohibition Association was heard to comment: "Praise the Lord, the province is back on track."

Mr Stalker's entire career could be described as a "crusade" against alcohol, drugs, gambling, vice and unchecked immigration.

As commandant of the Vancouver Frontiersmen, he played a prominent role, at some personal risk, in pacifying left-wing radicals during the General Strike of 1918. As a member of the Asiatic Exclusion League and the Citizens' League, he spearheaded the campaign that brought about the historic Chinese Exclusion Act of 1923.

As a Vancouver alderman, Stalker drew praise from groups such as the Woman's Christian Temperance Union for his tenacity and zeal in patrolling the city's drinking places with an eye to infractions. At City Hall, with reporters present, he regularly dominated council meetings with reports of gambling, brawls, prostitution and, on one occasion, plying schoolchildren with whisky.

Continued Reverend McDougall, "With Stalker at the helm, we are on the path to reform."

AN INVITATION

On Friday, September 11, 1925, an informal reception will be held at the IMPERIAL PALACE OF THE KANADIAN KNIGHTS OF THE KU KLUX KLAN, 1690 Matthews Avenue West, at 8 PM.

You are PERSONALLY invited to attend. On presentation of this letter at the door, the holder will be conduced into the Aulik of the Grand Goblin, Maj Luther Forrest, who will be present to welcome visitors and to share insights and observations as to the objects, ideals and purposes of the Vancouver Klavern.

Klaliff Ambrose Walker
Imperial Officer of the Provincial Kloncilium

GOD SAVE THE KING
KEEP KANADA BRITISH

# CHAPTER 20

MILDRED HAD NO difficulty obtaining an invitation to the event. Every branch of every fraternal body in the city received them in the mail—Masons, Foresters, Moose, Orangemen, Elks—rumour has it that even the Ching Wing Chun Tongs received one, albeit in error. She managed to obtain a copy from the Independent Order of Odd Fellows by posing as a visiting Rebekah from London.

After passing through a wrought-iron gate with gold rosettes, she pauses to admire the extended grand verandah situated between the excessive domed turrets that caused Glen Brae (the property's original name) to be nicknamed "the Mae West House," a reputational blot that lowered its rental value to $150 a month.

She is greeted at the door by a gentleman draped in a white satin robe with a maple leaf beside the KKK insignia, complemented by a dunce's cap with a tassel dangling from the tip. He gives his name, but it is overshadowed by his title—*Klexter*. Mr Klexter seems slightly put off by the fact that she is a woman (the only one present, she expects) and a bit late as well. She considers making a joke of it, but he seems not in the mood.

Her escort shows her into the drawing room, a cavern of beams and wainscotting lit by a chandelier with bulbs like moons as well as a ten-foot cross lined with red electric lights and dominating the far wall. With a Union Jack draped overhead like the ceiling of a tent, the room contains perhaps a hundred men in rows of wooden chairs, heads bowed and hands folded, while a man she recognizes as Reverend McDougall, in his black suit and clerical collar, steps in front of the cross to lead the audience in prayer. Behind him, also with heads bowed, are four men in white robes and pointed hats, seated like a choir on either side of what must be the Grand Goblin himself in a silk robe lined in gold with red piping and the Klan insignia on his chest.

Reverend McDougall, in the ministerial drone of a true Presbyterian, recites what Mildred assumes to be the Klan prayer:

*Our Father and our Almighty God. We acknowledge our dependence upon Thee and Thy loving kindness toward us.*

*Keep us in the blissful bonds of fraternal union, of clannish fidelity one toward another and of devoted loyalty to this great institution.*

*Give strong minds and ready hands as warriors, serving our nation, striving for the protection of our women, our children and for the continued dominion of the race. We ask these blessings through our Imperial Savior, Jesus Christ. Amen.*

After a chorus of amens, Reverend McDougall steps back to exchange places with the Grand Goblin, Luther Forrest, who removes his conical hat to reveal a small head shaped like a lightbulb, precariously balanced on a long, thin neck. His thinning hair is plastered to a shiny scalp, above a nose like the edge of a ruler.

"Thank you, Reverend McDougall, official Kludd for the Vancouver Klavern. And welcome all, to this klonvocation."

Mildred is starting to become tired of all these *K*s—the sort of trick you see in advertisements for burlesque shows.

After waiting for and receiving silence, Forrest leans forward and lowers his voice, as though about to confide in a group of dear friends, while a pair of colourless eyes flick about the room gauging the response as he undertakes what is obviously his standard stump speech, honed by repetition, like a singer with his signature song.

From time to time, the eyes swivel from side to side as though alert to the possibility of an ambush.

*Gentlemen, welcome to the Imperial Palace of the Grand Knights of the Ku Klux Klan. I extend special greetings to members of the Freemasons, the Odd Fellows, the Orangemen and the Kiwanis Club.*

*Friends and neighbours, a bit of history: when the Founding Fathers of Empire conquered the Papist French, here is one question they never once asked themselves:*

Who are we?

*And why did they not ask that question? Because the Canadian identity was understood. It was understood that Canada meant a British Canada.*

*An English-speaking Canada.*

*A white Canada.*

*But now that question—Who are we?—has become not only relevant, but urgent, now that thousands upon thousands of Orientals are pouring into our country in an uncontrolled horde, bringing with them their alien loyalties, their alien customs—and, let us speak plainly, their racial vigour.*

*Why "racial vigour," you ask? Because that is precisely what we are losing, thanks to spiritual lethargy, moral laxity—and alcohol.*

*Friends, our social fabric is literally soaked with booze.*

*Anyone with half a brain knows that alcohol is a personal and social contaminant that ruins lives and families.*

*But in truth, alcohol is very much more dangerous than that.*

*The eminent authority Dr Caleb Saleeby has designated alcohol as "racial poison." Why? Because alcohol reverses the very principle by which mankind has risen from savagery to civilization. Alcohol is the lubricant of human devolution.*

*Thus, the question* Who are we? *has become a question of life and death.*

*My friends, all human beings are part of something. All humans come from someplace. We say, "These are my parents. This is my family." You have parents. I have parents.*

*And by the same token, you and I are part of* a *race.*

*Ours is the Nordic race, and we have a story to tell—a story about the Greek philosophers, about the Christian faith, about British laws, about freedom and the American way of life. It is a story about* a *people: Its spirit. Its values. Its blood.*

*As you and I are only too keenly aware, our values are not Chinese values. Nor are they African, Jewish or Slavic values.*

*We of the Nordic race believe in Honesty. Temperance. Hard work. Education. Healthy bodies. Healthy families. Good neighbours. And we believe that the Bible is the word of God.*

*These are the values of the Ku Klux Klan.*

*We are Christian warriors in the service of Christ the Lord, and of God's will. We invite you who share our values to join us in the struggle for a white, British, Christian Canada.*

*Already hundreds upon hundreds of your fellow citizens have become naturalized—have joined our Christian army in the fight.*

*Why? Because we know that as foreign races swarm across our borders in ever-increasing numbers, bringing with them their foreign values, unless white Christians unite against the foe, push back the deluge and instill our values in our young people, our race will not survive.*

*I invite you to join our sacred brotherhood, at a cost of pennies per week. As part of our community outreach, we invest all funds in local business enterprises, charitable societies and sports facilities. Be assured, the monies you provide will fund worthy projects and community improvements.*

*Membership forms can be obtained at the door. Our Klexters are standing by.*

*Thank you, and God bless you every one.*

The room erupts with applause and cries of "Hear! Hear!" Forrest acknowledges his audience with a modest bow, waits for silence, then turns to the open side door.

"Stewart, you may come in now."

A gangly, shy young man of about sixteen joins the Grand Goblin onstage, dressed in a khaki shirt, a black tie, a Sam Browne belt and an overseas cap; all war surplus except for the Klan insignia on the chest—a medieval cross with a drop of blood in the middle that makes Mildred think of the Red Cross.

Using the young man as a mannequin, Major Forrest announces the formation of a Vancouver chapter of something called the "Khaki Shirts"—*devoted to young men's fitness and health, to erecting a bastion against the temptations of alcohol, promiscuity and inbreeding...*

Now Mildred has lost interest, as she usually does whenever a sermon becomes a sales pitch.

The men in the room—and they are all men, the air reeks of sweat and baked-in cigar smoke—remain transfixed. They nod their heads to one another as though Forrest has clinched the argument. As though immigrant railway workers, house servants and grocers are marauding heathen hordes who must be held off with swords and battle axes.

She eases out of the room as inconspicuously as possible, while the audience is too enrapt and the speaker too full of himself to notice.

The main hall would comprise the entire floor space of a normal house. A huge stained-glass window at the far end depicts some sort of rural scene. She crosses the hall to what she supposes is the sitting room. It is completely empty, just a plastered space trimmed with carved joinery made of wood from Indonesia.

Just around the corner, down a hall to the lavatory, she takes note of a second door to the meeting room, slightly ajar. Standing beside it as though awaiting her entrance is a figure she recognizes—barely, for she bears little resemblance to the goddess who spoke to the PPA.

Theatre audiences given a backstage glance are often alarmed at how a stage beauty can prove disappointingly plain without costume and makeup. This is emphatically so in the case of Daisy Douglas Tyler. With her hair in a bun, spectacles on her nose and in a dress that would have been out of fashion ten years ago, Miss Tyler could easily be taken for a schoolteacher or the spinster daughter who has spent her life caring for her parents.

Aware that someone is watching her, Miss Tyler casts a wary glance in Mildred's direction. The two women have barely time to exchange a mutually suspicious nod when Miss Tyler, hearing her name called, enters the room with the purposeful strut of a pigeon.

Mildred takes Miss Taylor's place next to the door and listens as she recites a list of famous men and women, brothers and sisters in the fight against alcohol, then a series of alliances achieved with the Anti-Saloon League, with evangelical churches, with the police and with civic and state governments in Indiana, Colorado, Washington and Oregon. She speaks in a modest, unaccustomed-as-I-am murmur, like a loyal secretary reciting facts as required, leaving the drama up to the men.

One mention causes Mildred to take note: Miss Tyler refers to a "fruitful" meeting with Mayor Taylor, Alderman Garbutt and

Chief Barfoot, as well as upcoming appointments in Victoria, implying that she has established provincial connections as well.

It occurs to Mildred that Eddie will snap at this like a terrier. Surely he must be growing impatient, having been fed nothing new in days.

Mildred has heard quite enough. But since she is here, and with the hallway empty of white-sheeted figures, she decides to take a look around.

AT THE HEAD of the broad, carpeted staircase a hollow silence envelops her, emitting the sound of vacancy—and with decor to match: no carpet, bare plaster walls and a musty, tired smell, as though the house is disappointed by what it has become.

The light from downstairs fades as she makes her way down the hall. The wall sconces are dark; she sees a light switch but isn't prepared to be discovered just yet, so she moves on.

On either side, doors to what must be bedrooms gape open, their windows opaque with soot, while one room contains racks of white gowns and stacked cartons of, she supposes, Klan paraphernalia.

A locked door. Exactly what she was looking for, if *looking* is the right word in this light. Dropping to her knees, she fishes out her lighter to determine the type of lock, then retrieves the equipment supplied by Holly, her American friend, who possesses skills Mildred never dreamed of.

You learn from people. It took Holly just a half-hour to teach her how to pick the front lock of her room in less than a minute—a procedure involving two bobby pins, one straightened and the other L-shaped.

As instructed, she inserts one end of the L-shaped pin into the keyhole, closes her eyes and feels about until it detects the lock bolt, which she moves with the aid of the straightened bobby pin. She gets up on her feet, turns the knob, pushes—and the door opens.

Strips of street light sliver through Venetian blinds so that she can make out a jewel-toned oriental carpet, rattan furniture and a plantation-style four-poster bed that only needs a mosquito net to evoke Louisiana. In the far corner sits a clawfoot bathtub partially obscured by a Japanese screen depicting two painted birds with legs like black sticks of bamboo.

In the other corner sits a small French-looking desk below a corkboard on the wall. She reaches the desk, fetches her lighter from her purse, flicks it in front of her and can make out a publication entitled *The Patriot*, two pamphlets—*Smash the Reds and Pinks* and *Jews: Bolshevists of Ancient History*—and a book entitled *The Revolt against Civilization: The Menace of the Under Man.*

On the corkboard, someone has arranged a tier of rectangular cards using map pins, like a depiction of a family tree. Using her lighter, Mildred can see that they are government calling cards, many with gilt lettering. Nearing the peak of the pyramid, in the upper right-hand corner of one of the cards, someone has drawn a black circle in ink...

"Something I can assist you with, ma'am?"

Startled by the voice behind her, Millie drops her lighter on the floor. She turns but can only see him in silhouette, for he has turned on the hall lights. Even so, she recognizes the bulb-shaped head above the little papal cape, and of course the American accent.

"Actually, sir, I was looking for the loo."

"*Ectually*? he says, imitating her accent. "I doubt that, sugar, I surely do. By my lights, you were sneaking around looking for something."

"Well, I must admit that the house is a *frightfully* interesting piece of architecture. One could not help but wonder what it is like upstairs."

"You have a very classy way of talking, don't you? You are a classy Becky. I bet you like it *classy*."

He moves into the light from the window, smiling in a way she recognizes from past experience and does not like. She starts to leave, but he sidesteps, blocking her path. "I saw you watching me downstairs. I was watching you too. I had the same thought you did. And now that we're here..."

He steps closer to within a foot. She looks up at her robed captor, like a choir boy before a priest. "Actually, I came upstairs purely out of curiosity—"

"*Ectually*," he repeats, teasing, delighted with the situation. "*Veddy* well then, *dahling*. Let Lord Luther show you what's what..." He grips both her shoulders, turns ninety degrees and, gently but firmly, pushes her backward, in the direction of the canopied bed.

"Please let me go. Please let go of me..." One part of her mind is trying to think of a way out, while the other part is shrieking at her, *You're begging! How embarrassing!*

He eases her backward, crooning in a syrupy baritone: "*Let you go? Why ever would I do that, sugar? We're here together, you and I. We both know what we're here for. Because I* know *you, sugar. I* know *what a woman wants. No need to be coy. We both know that down deep what y'all want is a good screwing.*"

*Goddamn it! So that's what's happening!*

He backs her up until the bed nudges the backs of her knees. "Just lie back and enjoy it, sugar." He pushes firmly, her knees buckle over the edge of the bed and she is flung backward. Before she can turn sideways and roll off, he pounces full-length on top of her, and now he is kissing her neck while prying her legs apart, and by the way he does it, she can tell that he has done it before.

*Control your breathing. Keep calm. He's all instinct now. The reptilian brain is unstoppable but easily fooled...*

Though layers of fabric separate their naked bodies, she feels his erection as he performs spasmodic saw-like motions against her pelvic bone and continues to kiss and nibble her neck, while she stares at the ceiling, breathing his odour of shaving cream, brilliantine and sweat, and tries to think.

"Oh sugar, you are so... luscious."

*Get him to relax. Put him off his guard. Watch for an opening...*

With one hand he gathers up his robe, at the same time reaching awkwardly with the other hand to unbutton his trousers.

She forms a plan. As though aroused into submission, she relaxes, strokes his cheek, caresses his throat with her left hand, moans with pleasure.

"Oh, yes. Yes..."

"Oh, sugar..."

All at once, having stiffened her finger and thumb into a Y, she straight-arms his chin, forcing him to pull back without entry; meanwhile, her right hand fumbles in her open purse, finds her sharpened comb, takes it out and rakes it straight across his forehead, producing a gusher of blood that covers his eyes like a shallow waterfall.

With a wail of panic he jerks backward, giving her sufficient room to slide out from beneath him, roll to the side, tumble onto the carpet, scramble to her feet and run for the hall.

Reaching the main stairway, she glances back—and here he comes, face sheeted with blood, his hands outstretched like a sleepwalker, caroming from one wall to the other. She descends the main staircase, trying to appear unhurried and calm, a visitor who has just been taken on a delightful tour.

Outside the house, past the wrought-iron gates, the road is lit by a hard-edged moon with the texture of raw silk.

# CHAPTER 21

SETTLING IN BEHIND her desk in the corner of the oak-lined conference room, Grace retrieves her foolscap and sharpened pencil, ready to listen and transcribe.

As always, the board members didn't seem to notice her arrival, though perhaps they felt a slight breeze as she passed by. Having been their official stenographer for months, she is invisible—which isn't entirely unpleasant.

When Grace was a child, someone once asked her, *Which would you prefer—to fly, to breathe under water or to be invisible?* She had no hesitation in saying that invisibility would be her choice. (She wonders what Gwendolyn would choose—flying perhaps, to travel more quickly from one party to another.)

*Meeting: (DATE, TIME)*
*Present: Crombie, Beaven, Munn*
*Subject: Progress report*

As she dashes off preliminaries in shorthand, she notes that the atmosphere in the room has become more relaxed without Mr Taggart. More collegial. No more talk of "appointments based on merit" or "nephews on the payroll."

Mr Beaven and Mr Munn are now seated on either side of the chairman at one end of the table. It seems as though the LCB is no longer a board, but a club.

Grace, remaining invisible, prepares to take down every word.

Having called the meeting to order, the minutes of the last meeting are approved without anyone actually having read them. She could have given them a page from *Mrs Dalloway* and nobody would notice the difference.

Chairman Crombie clips his gold fountain pen onto an inside pocket and straightens the papers before him, checks his gold pocket watch and returns it to his vest pocket, glancing down to be sure that the gold chain drapes correctly from the buttonhole. His thinning hair is precisely combed, and he is clean shaven, exposing a set of lips she finds unsavoury.

"Gentlemen, to begin, Attorney General Stalker salutes you. The LCB has accomplished much, and in a short time.

"As we move forward, Mr Stalker has defined our mandate as, and I quote: *To play a special role in enforcing the liquor laws, advising and assisting the Vancouver Police and the Provincial Police as a de facto arm of law enforcement commensurate with the war against bootlegging."*

Grace writes it all down in shorthand, with comments in the margins. She finds the term *special role* unsettling in its vagueness; thanks to school Latin, *de facto* worries her as well, implying powers unmentioned in print; and she wonders about the deliberate introduction of the term *war*.

The chairman continues: "Which brings us to the main issue before us. I regret to say that, despite all our efforts, the current set of regulations are not up to the challenge. The time has come for a more authoritative, vigorous approach to policing."

The other board members nod solemnly as though great truth has been told, but Grace suspects that they don't entirely understand what is being proposed—which is, essentially, a return to what she remembers as the Defence of the Realm Act, which covered everything from food rationing to dog shows, and allowed for the arrest of persons of "hostile origin or association."

She prepares for the chairman to continue with the usual litany of alcohol abuses and tragedies (she knows them by heart), but Crombie's speech is interrupted by a discreet knock on the door, which is already sufficiently ajar to admit Miss Witherspoon's angular head and shoulders.

"Mr Bliss is just outside, sir. You asked to be notified of his arrival."

"Quite right, Miss Witherspoon. Well, don't keep him waiting, my girl, show him in!"

Everyone stands as though for a magistrate. Mr Beaven extracts his silver cigarette case and lighter and lays them down at the ready; Mr Munn stares at his white hands, splayed out on the table as though to measure the length of his fingers. (The last time they had a visit from Mr Bliss, he entertained the board by firing its chairman. It would not be oversensitive to wonder who will be next to feel the axe on the nape of his neck.)

It's not just the ever-present ennui that has produced a sense of déjà vu: looking over her notes, it's clear that Mr Crombie was marking time before the performance to come. In the margin she draws a stick man with a high hat, a cane and a monocle, like Mr Peanut.

"Chairman Crombie. Mr Munn. Mr Beaven. Gentlemen, I fear that once more I have barged in on your important work. The Attorney General sends his apologies as well. Please seat yourselves, no need no stand on ceremony."

Beaven and Munn mutter diplomatic niceties. In the margin Grace draws a smiling skull.

"As you know, Premier Gulliver—we're all jolly glad of this—has reassumed his duties, and his first measure was to reorder the chain of command, starting with his appointment of Mr Stalker as Attorney General.

"Our office staff, with Mr Cunning having left no instructions, and with no family to consult, undertook to prepare for the new occupant. In removing Mr Cunning's files, documents were found containing sensitive material."

Munn puts up his hand like a precocious schoolboy, while the other hand scratches a spot on his chin: "Mr Bliss, might this involve Communists?"

"An excellent question, Mr Munn. Without revealing specifics, it would be legitimate to say that some documents may or may not point to seditious tendencies."

Beaven butts out his fourth Gold Flake. "I'm not surprised. If you ask me, it's high time to clear the province of radicals."

Chairman Crombie lights his pipe and appears thoughtful. "A worthy objective, Mr Beaven, but I expect that we can all agree, in these unsettled times, that discretion is paramount. Mr Bliss, please continue."

"Thank you, Mr Chairman. A committee has been struck to determine the placement of Mr Cunning's papers. In the meantime, they must be kept secure. The Attorney General has entrusted the LCB with this task, under the leadership of the gentleman to my left." He nods at Mr Crombie, who nods back.

In the margin Grace draws two snakes, entwined, for it is clear that another agenda is at work as well.

Crombie responds: "It is an honour for the board to be put in a position of trust. Please have the files delivered to this department, and our people will see that they are secure."

"Jolly good, gentlemen. Tickety-boo. Then I shall leave you to your work."

Millie dearest,

I must confess that sometimes I quite hate it here, and to think you are less than sixty miles away pains me no end—the ocean is such a bother!

When I feel low in my mind and Gwendolyn is out with one of her fellows, I play with Miss Carr's dogs. They are my rescuers when it comes to loneliness. One can have a cry in their fur, and an all-but-invisible pair of black eyes peer at you through the fringe, to reach deep inside.

Did I mention that our landlady is an artist? I have heard that people in Victoria simply loathe her paintings. They see them as dreadful things that an Indian savage could paint.

But just imagine, a woman putting herself in league with Turner and Constable! It has caused me to view Miss Carr other than as an irascible old maid.

Still, she can be devilishly secretive. A fortnight ago, I entered her studio to report a plumbing problem, and Miss Carr hastily draped a sheet over whatever she was working on. Other paintings were stacked against a wall, but with only the backs showing.

Despite her eccentricity, she is the sort of person one takes a problem to, knowing that the answer will be pertinent—such as the day I was about to drown myself out of sheer boredom. Miss Carr's advice was: "Try and learn something. Anything, really. It will occupy your mind, and you will never know what good it will do until later on."

And Millie dear, where you are concerned, I have taken her advice. As you suggest, I shall keep my eyes open and shall keep you abreast. You are right, it is so much more exciting to be a spy—one looks and listens in a whole new way! Between Gwendolyn and me, I suspect we see more than anyone, being invisible.

For example, today I learned of plans to put the LCB virtually in charge of the police, and that our late Attorney General Cunning kept files of a "sensitive nature." It was my place to put them under lock and key, and in so doing I "accidentally" took a glance at the first few pages, but other than Mr Taggart's name it was mostly columns of numbers. I shall find a way to have a better look.

And I love you, dear, as you are aware, no end!

Yours always, Gracie

# CHAPTER 22

SEATED IN BED together, wearing very little and propped up on pillows, Millie rereads a letter from her friend in Victoria while Holly skims through *The Daily World*. A tea tray lies on the bed between their feet, from which they have been drinking tea made on her electric hot plate, and eating scones and jam from Notes down the street, like a comfortably married couple on a Sunday morning, except with less clothing.

(At the YWCA, although the matron doesn't permit gentleman callers, an overnight female visitor is perfectly acceptable.)

"Take a gander at this, Millie. Hundreds of folks poisoned drinking booze in New York."

Mildred puts down her letter to scan the article in question. "It says the government hired scientists to poison it."

"Yup. And the bootleggers hired the same scientists to make it drinkable again. So I reckon the Feds decided to up the stakes."

"It's like a game of euchre."

"Poker more like, with human chips."

"Which makes it a bit more than a game, I think."

Holly puts down her newspaper and laughs. "Sugar, you'd be surprised how serious men take their games."

Mildred's smile disappears. "Please don't call me that."

Holly puts on a serious face—with her short hair she could be a teenage boy who has come across an injured animal.

"I am sorry, dear, hush my mouth. And there you were just starting to cheer up. It's funny how a word can turn to poison in the mind." She leans over, plants a kiss on Mildred's lips and gives her a hug that lasts a long time.

After a while, Mildred pours herself another spot of tea. "Oh it's all right, love. I take back my objection. I don't want others having to tiptoe about, afraid to utter a word that might set me off. Somehow that would mean that he succeeded in what he wanted to do."

"Even so, I better switch to *honey*. This stuff can haunt you for a long time. Thanks to my Uncle Boone, the smell of chewing tobacco still makes me want to throw up."

"Actually, I think I've become allergic to brilliantine."

"Well at least he didn't run to biting you."

"Why? Was that a possibility?"

"The Imperial Wizard in Indiana liked to bite. The girl Stephenson murdered had bite marks all over."

"Really?"

"Really. I reckon you can't make up that stuff."

"I must say, it would make me extremely wary of Klansmen in Indiana."

"Wariness is always good policy, honey. This thing that happened to you isn't like lightning. With a good-looking gal it can strike twice, even a third time. Are you sure you don't want to learn to shoot?" She takes the pistol from the bedside table. "It's very light—here, take it, the safety is on."

"I'd prefer not to, my dear. But I must say that I wish I could fight with my fists."

"No. You don't want to mess up these pretty hands. Let me see those hands..."

A pause follows, in which neither speaks.

"Oh my. You have me feeling quite chuffed now."

"Don't know what that *chuffed* means, but it sounds swell."

After a time, they rearrange themselves and continue their previous discussion.

"In Britain the consequence of extreme drunkenness is a night in gaol, not a civil war over drink."

"We Yanks like a war. Peps us up. How many nations have a flag with a poisonous snake?"

"Blimey. Should I be afraid of *you* then?"

"I don't reckon so. We Americans prefer to kill each other."

"Nice of you to keep it among yourselves."

"Mind you, we fought the Brits for a spell. But that was a long time ago."

"Well then we must kiss and make up."

"Yes. Let's."

"You do know that this is illegal, dear."

"We Pinkerton's agents deal with crime, not morals."

Later, Mildred tries once more to contact McCurdy on the telephone. It seems obvious that for some reason he has gone to ground.

She doesn't know why she cares. The man has never inspired anything but intense ambivalence. But over time, for some reason she has come to feel *responsible* for him.

And she has information to sell.

WORKING AT THE switchboard next morning, while automatically plugging jacks, flipping switches and saying the same two sentences over and over again, Mildred wonders over the protracted silence from her oldest client. During her twenty-minute lunch break, she tries one more time to contact McCurdy.

No answer.

She hangs up after three rings for the sake of the operator—operators hate having to sit around waiting while somebody's telephone rings twenty-six times. (That is Mildred's personal record; the caller had taken time to visit the loo.)

Getting up for a stretch on her afternoon break, she pauses behind Myrtle Bee's station and, glancing over her shoulder at the switchboard, she notices something unusual:

To avoid misfires, it is standard procedure for operators to insert a detached plug in an unused circuit. On Myrtle's board, the port to Room 342 is open—and Room 342 is, in fact, a storage room. It has no telephone at all.

*Curious.*

At the end of her shift, after freshening up with a washcloth and eau de toilette and putting on her fall coat, Mildred emerges from the staff entrance, blinking in the light (though the day is by no means sunny), and takes a moment to breathe the aroma of horse shit, automobile fumes and sawdust—which she finds preferable to the switchboard room pong of varnish, perfumed soap, body odour and bad teeth.

Turning east, she heads down Robson to Granville and from there to the Castle Hotel, a three-storey structure with a mixed reputation, just across from the New Orpheum.

In front of the hotel, she stops to admire the massive vertical neon and, below that, the electric message: *A Man's Home Is His Castle*.

Or so he may think.

The lobby smells of floor wax and palm leaves, not disinfectant; the floor is covered with patterned tile, and not scuffed linoleum. Intact lounge chairs are lined up like soldiers. The wall plaster appears dry, free of cracks and mould.

Potted palms divide the room to graceful effect, while a sign directs ladies to a Cozy Ladies Rest Room, together with a drawing nicked from a furniture store advert. A line of text introduces Mrs Kahn, *The personal supervisor, who gives special attention to ladies travelling unattached.*

However, some things do remain constant no matter how posh the hotel, and one of them is the expression on a desk clerk's face whenever an unaccompanied woman requests a gentleman's room number. These chaps must attend classes to achieve that ever-so-faint expression of snide knowing.

Using her poshest vowels, Mildred replies to the desk clerk with the withering *Thank you very much indeed* that Badminton girls were taught to adopt at mixed socials whenever a gentleman needed frosting out.

In front of McCurdy's door, she knocks several times, to no response. She doesn't fancy a set of bruised knuckles, when intuition tells her that, dead or alive, he is in there.

The lock is even flimsier than the one at the Imperial Palace— in fact, it seems rather pointless to lock the door at all.

The door clicks open within a minute. Stepping into the room, already she can hear him snoring.

Of course he would snore.

Through the bay window, the multicoloured neon signs give the room a lurid cast even in daylight but she can see that the carpet is relatively new and not tarred by suspicious stains, nor is the wallpaper peeling in the corners. To her right, a door leads to a private bath; next to it, a steam radiator emits a comforting hiss.

All in all, the hotel's amenities provide evidence (as though one needs any) that hack writing is more lucrative than poetry.

By the room's decoration, it appears that McCurdy has made himself at home, to the extent that the furniture arrangement is an improved version of his previous digs. The tiger oak desk has been moved to the window alcove with the most comfortable chair facing it; on the walls hang the same photographs of Sassoon and Dickens, and the priest with the cross balanced on his nose.

On the floor near the dressing table, standard hotel prints of the English countryside lean like dominoes against the wall.

Next to the bed is a nightstand containing a lamp, a stopped clock, a long-stemmed pipe and a pair of spectacles. The telephone has been placed on the floor to make room for a copy of *Ulysses*. (As far as Mildred is concerned, the book was published as a cure for insomnia.)

She recognizes a faint sweetish smell, neither tobacco, nor hashish, nor muggle.

The man lying on the bed, seemingly asleep in his threadbare jacquard dressing gown, is also familiar, though in a somewhat reduced version. At the best of times, McCurdy seems to regard eating as a nuisance; from the look of him, it appears as though he has decided to quit the habit altogether. As well, his skin has taken on a tubercular pallor she has seen before.

She sits on the side of the bed, lights a Turkish cigarette and blows smoke into his face, a smell she knows he detests. His nostrils twitch. After an unattractive snort, the eyes open.

"Miss Wickstram. What are you doing in my room?"

"I haven't heard from you in a dog's age, and you're usually such a pest."

"I'm not entertaining visitors at present."

"I can see that. I thought you might have taken a shelf in an opium den. Now I see you've done the next best thing."

"These are my private quarters. I don't remember giving you a key so that you could snoop about while I was asleep."

"I picked your lock. A friend taught me how."

"Is he a thief, this friend?"

"Not as such. Quite the opposite, really."

"In any case, please go away now."

He closes his eyes and crosses his arms on his chest; the face transforms into an imitation of a death mask, with arms. She gets up, exits the room and walks down the hall, leaving the door ajar. Downstairs, as she passes through the lobby, she gives the smirking desk clerk her frigid Badminton stare.

In Maxine's Lunch across the street she orders a chicken club sandwich, wrapped to take away, and coffee in a Dixie cup. Men. Even in a business relationship one ends up running errands for them.

"SIT UP, LAZY bones. Time to eat." How she dislikes playing nurse, but someone has to do it.

McCurdy's eyes form slits. "Eat?"

"Eat. Surely you remember eating. Chewing, swallowing—like smoking, but different."

"I'm not in the mood for jokes." His eyes close again, as though he's nodding off.

"If you don't sit up, I'm going to pour hot coffee on your groin."

The eyes open again. Reluctantly, seal-like, he wriggles up to a seated position. "You've always been a bully. And a blackmailer as well."

Using a framed print of flowers as a bed tray, she unwraps his sandwich and places the Dixie cup in his hand.

He tastes the coffee and grimaces. "This coffee is lukewarm."

"That's because you can't be trusted with hot food. By the way, if I may ask, how long do you plan to lie in bed muggled?"

"I haven't decided yet," he says with his mouth full.

"You do know that when you run out of money you'll be out on the street. Hotels are fussy when it comes to unpaid bills."

"I've taken that into account."

"And you owe me thirty cents for lunch."

He finishes his sandwich and coffee. She removes the framed print from the bed, replaces it on the floor against the wall, tosses cup and wrapping into the wastebasket by the desk, returns to the bedside and sits, watching him carefully. She contemplates telling him about the incident in the Imperial Palace, but decides she isn't ready to discuss it with McCurdy—he might find it titillating, which would force her to sever their acquaintance for life.

She decides to imitate a police interrogator in a movie: "Okay spill it Eddie, what's your problem?"

He closes his eyes again and pretends to be asleep. She lights another cigarette and blows more smoke in his face. At length, he sighs as if to say, *You're not going away, are you?* and opens his eyes.

"If you must know, somebody shot at me."

"Metaphorically or literally?"

"What?"

"Was it criticism or bullets?"

"The latter. Shot at me when I was leaving the club."

"Do you mean the Lumberman's Club?"

"I have no other club, you know that. Don't badger me for details."

"Did you report this to the police?"

"What do you take me for?"

"Someone with a brain in his head. I could be wrong."

"The answer is no. I came here, locked the door and took something to calm my nerves and collect my thoughts. That was... some time ago."

"Always playing the hero."

"You're such a comfort. Go away now." He removes his glasses and returns them to the nightstand, using his blindness to put distance between them.

After igniting another cigarette, she gets up and looks around for an ashtray. Finding none, she retrieves the empty coffee cup and returns to his bedside.

"Being afraid to go outside, I assume you've been taking delivery from Chinatown."

"I order by telephone. It's part of the luxury package."

"And who is your chemist this time?"

"I maintained my connections. They were happy to hear from me."

"What's the appeal, Eddie?"

"I dreamed of almond blossoms. Of little painted cups full of golden tea, of a golden voice calling my name—it wasn't your voice."

"In any case, now that you're back in the stinky world, let's work our way through the story. You were shot at, or think you were shot at, you became terrified, then embarrassed at being terrified, then you retreated into a dope haze. I must say, most people would have reacted similarly. For myself, I'd be *under* the bed."

"It's different for you."

"And how is that?"

"You're a woman. On you, fear is attractive."

"Well thanks awfully."

"Men are supposed to exhibit courage under fire. In the army they call cowardice *getting the wind up*. Well I got the wind up. I froze on the spot. On the front, men like me were put against a wall and shot."

"Yes. That must have taught them a lesson."

His right hand flutters over the nightstand, feels for his glasses, wraps the temples around his ears and looks her straight in the face. She knows this to be one of his stage tricks, that he is well aware how huge his hazel eyes look from the other side of the lens.

"Put yourself in my position, Millie. The streets of downtown Vancouver are lined with men who spent years getting shot at on a regular basis and watching other men turned to bloody tissue paper. And here is the acerbic social critic who managed to grovel his way out of doing his duty, now unmasked as a snivelling coward. Can you imagine what Trotter would make of that? Let alone *The Beacon*! And what then, Millie? I'll tell you what: either I get out of town and freeze my nuts off in Winnipeg, or I blow my brains out with a borrowed shotgun."

"You reporters always exaggerate. You were refused because you're blind. I've seen thinner jam jars than those things on your face."

"They'll say it's all a pretense. It's how I evaded service." He lays back on the pillow as though exhausted. Behind the spectacles, the eyes close.

"In any case, Eddie, while you've been sulking beneath the covers, I've acquired an informant within the LCB, who has come upon something quite big—in fact, there's hope for a major scandal, if someone has the nerve to break it."

After a pause, one eye opens, then the other. "A major scandal, you say?"

"Mr Cunning kept files on people—including Clyde Taggart."

"What sort of files?"

"I shall find out. It wasn't a Christmas list, that much I can tell you. But first we discuss my fee."

# CHAPTER 23

"SOMEBODY SHOT AT you, Ed? Jesus Christ, did you identify him?"

Before this piece of information dropped, Hook and McCurdy were discussing the Terminal League, and how the Asahi will fare against Collingwood.

"*Identify*? Calvin, I just told you I didn't see him. It was a sniper."

"Are you sure you didn't imagine it, Ed? Into the powder perhaps? Some of the eucaine Patterson is so keen on?"

"As I told you, Calvin, snorting eucaine rots the nose. My system was clean as a whistle—a drop or two of whisky was all."

"Still, you only heard what you *thought* was a shot."

"Okay, fine. I heard something *like* a shot. Yes, I know, it could have been a car backfiring—except that it came from above and I heard a metallic ping nearby. When I looked in the direction of the *ping*, it looked as though something had grazed the lamppost next to my ear. Calvin, I'm losing patience. Do you think a man doesn't know when he's been shot at?"

Usually they do, Hook has to admit. The two men pass the bottle back and forth twice. McCurdy's flimsy evidence hovers in the air like a fart.

On the screen, a man with sad eyes and a waxed moustache, draped with gold braid and a chestful of gongs, inspects a line of troops; this is followed by an item in which a representative of the Catholic Legion of Decency denounces the moral degeneracy in Hollywood movies, along with a series of stills depicting underdressed women.

"Is this another item about Italian fascists ogling girls in gym wear?" Hook has trouble making sense of newsreels. Increasingly, they resemble the dreams he has on bad nights, when he wakes up screaming.

"No, Calvin. The ladies are in California. The Fascist is Greek."

"Ah. Thank you, I've been meaning to bring that up."

"About women's hemlines?"

"No, the lift operator at the hotel."

"What does he have to do with anything?"

"Mr Sark is Greek. It took me a while to realize that. And yet he claims to have been wounded at the Somme."

"And how is that implausible?" The reporter takes a delicate swig from the bottle, then passes it back.

Hook sighs at the persistent ignorance of the folks back home.

"Come on, Ed, think: Greece was *neutral*. The country joined up at the last moment to cash in on reparations, hardly lost a man. The Greeks are a sneaky race, always plotting behind your back."

"I suppose people say that about Indians as well. And of course the Jews."

"Not necessarily. Oppenheimer was the most popular mayor the city ever had. He could have run dead and buried and still been re-elected."

"Oppenheimer was an exception, Ed. There are always exceptions." Hook wipes the neck of the bottle with one hand before taking a slug; with McCurdy's personal habits, you never know what germs he might have picked up.

"Getting back to your original point, Calvin, how do you know that Mr Sark is Greek? Did he tell you that himself?"

"I know Greektown well. They have their own way of speaking English, as do Orientals. They ask questions as if they're statements, and vice versa. They don't know how to use the word *the*. Not to mention another thing about Sark—"

"You're going to complain about his smell are you, Calvin? Like you do with your assistant?"

"No, it's what he said about the Ross rifle. He praised a rifle that blows up in your face."

"Ah. Even I know about the Ross rifle."

"A dead giveaway, really." Hook lights his third Ogden's. He remembers men whose faces were blown apart by their Ross rifles. The wounds healed eventually, but the faces were hardly faces anymore.

"The only true thing I know about Sark is that he was a sniper."

"How can you tell?"

"They acquire a certain look, and he has it. Surely you don't think *he* shot at you? You don't even know him."

"Some louts who didn't know me from Adam gave me a dreadful thrashing just a few weeks ago—over a column I could scarcely remember writing. Maybe I spoke disparagingly about elevator operators at some point. I understand Greeks hold grudges for generations."

"You can't offend Sark; his English isn't good enough. Besides, he has contributed to the investigation, if you can call it that. He's the only witness to Cunning's habits who might be willing to open his beak."

IT IS ALWAYS surprising to come out of a matinee and find that it's light outside—enough light that McCurdy decides to take a shortcut home. South on Carrall, he turns down the alley joining Hastings and Chinatown.

Alleyways tend to echo, so the muffled curses coming from down the way were more than audible. Were McCurdy on the ball—and he should have been, having had the boots taken to him before—his first instinct would have sent him scampering back to Carrall right away.

But no, his mind was on something else. Now he is standing between two trash bins looking at two bruisers in greasy serge suits who are in the process of robbing a portly man with a bleeding nose; and by the time he can make out their faces, they are looking right back at him—with the look of men who don't like being interrupted.

For the second time in a week he has walked into a violent situation, but he doesn't freeze in fear this time; instead, a more familiar instinct activates in his brain: to bluff. Seemingly on its own, his mouth begins to move and, remarkably, words issue: "Gentlemen, in a spirit of fairness, I thought I should warn you that the police are on their way."

Bruiser One lets out a snort, while Bruiser Two produces a barrel flask of amber liquid from the victim's inside pocket.

"Go feck yourself four-eyes. We *are* the police."

The bottle smashes at McCurdy's feet, splattering his trousers with sour whisky and broken glass.

HAVING FIRST STOPPED off at his hotel to change, McCurdy enters the Hotel Vancouver, proceeds to the lift and waits to one side until the doors slide open; after checking to see that there will be no other passengers, he hops into the car at the last moment.

Barely glancing in his direction, the lift operator closes the cage and awaits instructions.

"Tenth floor please."

"Certainly, sir. Tenth floor." The lift operator's gloved hand pushes the rheostat handle.

The reporter attempts an intimidating look (which isn't easy with glasses) and decides to get right to the point. "I believe you are Mr Sark?"

The elevator whirrs by each floor. "Yes sir, that is my name."

"Mr Sark, I have a question: Did you shoot at me?"

The lift operator eases back on the handle. He seems amused. "Shoot at you, sir? Why would I shoot at you?"

"You're missing the point, Mr Sark. I'm not asking about your motive. I'm asking whether you did it. The why will come later."

The lift operator turns to face him, shoulders thrust back; his crystal eyes have narrowed slightly. "And you, sir? Who are *you*?"

"Ed McCurdy of *The Evening Star*. I'm writing a feature for the Saturday edition. It's about fraudulent veterans taking jobs away from men who served their country. I thought you might like to comment, Mr Sark—whose real name is, I believe, *Sarcos*."

The lift operator abruptly pulls back the rheostat lever and the car comes to a halt between floors, more abruptly than necessary.

"Where you get that name?"

"It's in your file. A matter of public record, if one bothers to look it up." (McCurdy maintains a firm gaze, despite the fact that there is no such record; he made a guess based on scanning the telephone directory under the BAview exchange.)

"And what else is on my file, sir?"

McCurdy notes that the doors are still shut. The air is thick with something other than tobacco breath. The lift operator glares at him like a dog assessing a prowler, and it occurs to McCurdy that a man could do considerable damage with that wooden arm, now that they are alone together in a little box.

Out of caution, his mouth starts to qualify his last statement: "By *file*, of course I don't mean literally, but as a sort of metaphor."

The lift operator looks him straight in the eye; it is like having one's brain poked with an icicle. After a disconcerting pause, he pushes the rheostat and the car continues upward.

"What do you say is this metaphor? You interest me."

"Of course. You don't use metaphors in Greek, do you? Sergeant Hook told me to watch for that."

Our man relaxes slightly. "Is this the policeman asking for Mr Cunning?"

"Yes. We're old acquaintances. We sometimes discuss this and that. Your name happened to come up in the conversation."

"Why did you not tell me you are friend of Hook? What is this about shooting at you?"

"I was shot at, outside the Lumberman's Club."

"This is another of your metaphors?"

"I wish it were. Mr Hook has described you and your war experience. The word *sniper* came up."

"That is a bad word to many people."

"If the shoe fits."

"What is this about shoes?"

"Were you indeed a sniper during the war?"

"The important answer to your question is no, I did not shoot at you. Proof is you are still alive."

McCurdy doesn't have a ready reply for that.

"Will you be getting off here, sir?"

"No, we can return to the lobby now."

"As you wish." He pushes the rheostat lever and the lift begins to plummet.

"By the way, Mr Sark, I have a small favour to ask—I could use your help with something."

"I am not surprised."

THEY MEET BEFORE dusk, beneath the street lamp in front of the Lumberman's Club. McCurdy is, by means known only to himself, more alert than usual and has an enhanced ability to see in the dark.

Sark is clearly not enthusiastic about the project. "Please pardon, Mr McCurdy, but this seems like you are doing blackmail."

"That's putting it a bit strong, Mr Sark. Everything you say to me will be off the record. You can take my word for it."

"I believe your word more easily than I believe your newspaper. Now please explain this shooting." He looks at his pocket watch. "I have one hour only. I am on double shift."

McCurdy takes up a position beside the lamp-post so that the elongated scar in the metal is about even with his ear. "This is the spot."

"And from where did you hear this shot?"

"I wouldn't know a shot from a blown tyre. What I heard was a metal object striking the post, exactly here." He slides his forefinger along the metallic gash.

"Stand where you are, please." The lift operator takes a pencil from his pocket, places the pencil sideways over the scar, then with one eye closed he sights along the pencil and down Hastings Street East. After a moment, he stands and points as though about to cry *land ho!*

"Do you see there?"

"See what? Where?"

Sark points with his good arm: "There. Flat roof. Building with Coca-Cola signs all over. That is where your shot was fired, my friend—if there was shot. Now we go take a look."

McCurdy is not eager to venture onto a roof with a Greek sniper. "Is this entirely necessary?"

"You have shot rifle, surely?"

"No, I didn't get the chance. I was rejected." He points at his lenses with two fingers. "The eyes, don't you see."

The lift attendant gives him an exasperated look. (*A man who has never shot a rifle!*) "It is surely amateur shooter who would miss at that distance. We check and see if he has left us souvenir."

They walk east and across the Main intersection until they are standing across the street from the building in question, a three-storey brick shoebox next door to a barbershop, with the Pastime Confectionery on the ground floor, two floors of apartments and a flat roof.

"There is fire escape behind. Come. Be brave, is not so high."

They head down a cobbled alleyway cluttered with bottles, tin cans and ancient newspapers. Electrical wires sag like clotheslines overhead; young spruce trees shoot up between the bins through holes in the cement, like a resistance group infiltrating the occupiers.

Halfway down to Gore Avenue, McCurdy sees a woman standing beneath a lamp, in a cloche hat that obscures all but her chin. She is smoking a cigarette, like a cinema woman of the street.

He takes out his notebook and writes: *War or peace, everyone has a costume. Service workers as actors, playing a version of themselves...*

Sark nudges his arm. "Write later, please. Not now."

As they pass, she makes no attempt to solicit. McCurdy wonders if he looks like a plainclothes copper.

The lift operator turns and lifts his hat: "Good evening, Selene."

"And to you, Dimitri."

"I hope is going well for you."

"Slow, I think," she replies. "People are sad tonight."

"Ah yes, Selene. There is much to be sad about."

"No more than usual, surely."

"Maybe so, maybe not. But sometimes it seems so."

Her eyes turn in McCurdy's direction. She takes a drag of her cigarette and smiles with carmine lipstick. "Come and see me sometime."

They continue down the alleyway. "I can't believe she actually said, 'Come and see me sometime.'"

"Selene watches too many photo plays. Is not a good thing."

"I take it then that you two are... acquaintances."

"We are in same neighbourhood, this is true."

Sark abruptly turns to the fire escape on his right. "This is the one."

"How do you know?"

"Is next to Horse Shoe Barber. Bruno cuts my hair."

THE FIRE ESCAPE has rusted badly. With any surface exposed to constant rain, the slightest chip will spread like a skin disease, and in this case the supports seem to have cancer.

McCurdy tests the floor at the first landing to avoid crashing through the iron grid. Above him the lift operator is climbing without having to grip the railing. (McCurdy's palms are scraped to bleeding.)

He has never liked heights. He would rather poke his eye out with a stick than climb a mountain.

At the edge of the roof, Sark kneels down carefully to inspect the surface, then silently points to a faint footprint in the tar.

Of course. Tar retains heat. The last week has been unseasonably warm.

The lift operator drops to a crouch—either for a better look at the footprint or as a precaution against other snipers. "Your friend has small feet," he remarks, then follows an almost invisible trail across the roof to the southwest corner, where there are more tracks in the tar, as though the shooter—if that's who it was—deliberately left a physical memory of himself in action.

Sark drops to one knee to examine a gouge from the toe of a boot, a dent the shape of a knee, and another small footprint just ahead. He runs one hand along the top of the ledge: "No marks of elbows. Was short person." He runs his finger along an elongated dent in the tar.

"Short? Do you mean in height?"

"Tall person uses elbows as tripod. Short person uses ledge itself."

"So I take it you have shot from the roofs of buildings."

Sark holds up his white-gloved wooden hand. "You think war injury made me civilian again, nice medal, nice peaceful life? Is so Canadian. Nice soft politics, no shooting necessary."

Peering over the knee-high ledge, McCurdy imagines the path of a bullet, shot through the air toward the Lumberman's Club.

The lift operator stands up to stretch his back, shaking his head with weary contempt. "What did I tell you? Is complete amateur. Maybe shoots squirrels for practice. Now..."

He crouches again, scans the perimeter, then zeroes in, the way a spotlight focuses on a target. He steps forward, crouches, then straightens up with a copper object in his fingertips.

"It is from a thirty-oh-six. Not a Mannlicher-Schönauer, and not your terrible Ross rifle." He seems amused. "A Springfield. Mr McCurdy, I think your enemy is American."

"Mr Sark, I think I owe you a drink."

THEY SIT AT the corner table McCurdy favours for private conversations. On its scarred and burnt surface Sark places the bullet

casing on its end like a miniature umbrella stand. (McCurdy has
already taken the lift operator through the customary membership application; Sark is now an honorary, one-armed lumberman so that Truman can relax.)

McCurdy returns from the bar with a double whisky for himself and a tumbler of ouzo on ice for his guest.

The lift operator raises the glass into the light, savours its
anise aroma and watches the liquid around the shards of ice turn
milky, as though a genie were about to appear above the glass.

"Is hard to find ouzo here. Some make it at home, but that is
vodka and licorice, not ouzo."

"With the Liquor Commission in charge, it could just as well
be licorice and antifreeze."

"This Liquor Commission. What is that?"

"A government department that tells us what to drink and
what not to drink."

"Ah. Generals are now doing this in my country also." The lift
attendant takes another gentle sip.

"Mr Sark, I don't wish to stir up bad memories, but where *did*
you fight?"

"Is not especially interesting. One of those shitty, vicious little
wars between shitty, vicious little countries. Who has even heard
of Thrace? At first we were in all the newspapers. But when
Great Powers go to war, what war can compete for attention?"

"You fought the Serbs, was it?"

"And Bulgarians. Serbs and Bulgarians are homicidal beasts.
We kill them whenever we can."

"That sounds like a good policy. Where were you wounded?"

"At the advance. Constantine wanted Sofia like Paris wanted
Helen. But Sofia was not Helen, did not appreciate his advances.
At Kresna Pass we were ambushed by 2nd and 4th Armies firing
from above us all at once. My arm was taken. Then wars ended
and we went home to fight among ourselves. I was on Lieutenant General Gargalidis side..." He shrugs as though nothing more
need be said—and more ouzo slides down the neck.

"Gargalidis sentenced to death, and I am immigrant to Canada. My sponsors Uncle Gustave and Uncle Nick had job for
me on paper but not real job, so I look. I know how to wear
uniform, whichever country no matter. I am veteran, whichever

war no mention. And lift operating is perfect work for one-armed men."

"Do you have plans to return home?"

"Someone must shoot General Pangalos first—a better shot than your friend on roof."

McCurdy proposes a toast: "To inaccurate snipers and one-armed men."

"And death to all dictators!" the lift attendant says with surprising intensity, then drains his glass and pushes back his chair to leave.

"One thing more before you go," McCurdy says. "I still need to know about Gordon Cunning. About his—"

"Mr McCurdy, it is hotel policy—"

"Officer Hook thinks Mr Cunning was murdered. I thought you'd want the investigation to be as brief as possible."

Sark looks at his pocket watch. "I have shift coming. If I may offer one advice: your sniper may be amateur, but he has more than one bullet."

"We mustn't assume the shooter is a *he*..."

Sark shakes his head sadly. "In these times, I fear that is true."

### NEWSON CROSSES THE FLOOR
Max Trotter
Staff Writer
*The Vancouver World*

As of yesterday morning, MLA Victor Newson has broken with the Liberal Party and will be sitting as an Independent. The result is that the situation in Victoria has become volatile in the extreme.

Following last election, seats at the British Columbia Legislature numbered as follows: Liberal 24, Conservative 17, Provincial Party 3 and Labour 3. With a Liberal Speaker of the House, Government and Opposition were at an even split. Just one vote on the Conservative side and the government would be defeated.

Hence, as he is now sitting as an Independent, General Newson will wield the power of life or death over former colleagues. Should he join the Opposition on a single non-confidence vote, the government will fall. The general can act as executioner or kingmaker by raising his hand.

When asked whether he has lost faith in the premier, Newson replied, cryptically: "No man named Gulliver ever survived the war."

Indeed, since his return to Victoria, Premier Gulliver is increasingly seen as a liability in the Liberal quest to rebuild their support. Officials, speaking on condition of anonymity, admit to increased caucus pressure for the premier to resign.

In the meantime, there emerges a public groundswell of support for Attorney General Stalker.

When asked about it, Mr Stalker's deputy and spokesman, Bertram Bliss, replied: "The Attorney General's response is that the challenges facing his ministry should be more than sufficient for any man."

Dearest Millie,

I tried my best, but as a spy I am a dismal failure!

I formed what I thought was a clever plan. Yesterday evening, I returned to the Legislature. I told the security guard that I had left my glasses on my desk and was nearly blind without them.

Since he had seen me in the building before and I had a key to the office, he let me enter. He even steadied me when I pretended to trip over the doorsill.

In the darkened hall, with nobody going up or down the halls and the stairway, for a moment I couldn't find our office door; I stumbled about until I managed to find the door, push the key into the lock and slip inside. As with rest of the building, the office was dark, except for street lights leaking in from the street. Having anticipated this part, I retrieved the kitchen matches I had filched from Miss Carr's stove.

Dropping to my knees, I unlocked and pulled open the drawer, and looked at one sheet from the file—when, at that moment, I heard a set of keys rattling in the hall, and a man's voice!

Someone was about to enter the office!

Millie, my heart pounded with such force that I thought I might die on the spot! I replaced the sheet, blew out my match, silently closed and relocked the file cabinet and crept along the carpet looking for someplace to hide, until I found my writing desk and crouched inside the knee-hole.

As the visitor opened the door, I waited for him to switch on the lights—then surely they would see me if they weren't blind! I was about to stand up and tell my prepared story about looking for my glasses—and why was I looking for my glasses in the dark? I was in a dreadful pickle!

But for some reason he did not switch the lights on. I was safe, for the time being.

Then they spoke, very quietly—which was when I realized that there were two of them, and that one was female. This was followed by the shuffling of feet, as they entered Mr Crombie's office.

There followed a long silence. Thinking back, I expect that they might have been kissing!

Holding my breath, I crept out from under my desk and looked toward the office but saw nothing. Then they began to speak in regular voices, and I could hear them perfectly while they proceeded to do certain things I could not envisage, let alone describe. And I swear that the male voice belonged to Mr Crombie:

*Daisy, I'm afraid this business with Forrest will end badly. If there were no other factors at work, fine, but people are watching. Weasels in the press can sense that we've been up to something, even if they don't know what it is.*

*Have you gone soft, my love? I thought you had more gumption than that. What happened to the man who would be king of Grouse Mountain?*

*I'm in the real estate business, I'm willing to take risks, but this is beyond the pale.*

*Has your ambition gone to sleep? Has the fire gone out? If it has, are your feelings for me just as feeble?*

*No Daisy, don't even think that. But it isn't as simple as you say. Forrest isn't alone. He has men working for him.*

*Olson and Flood? They're not working for him, take it from me.*

*But what if—*

*What if we fail? Stick with me, dear, and we won't fail...*

There was a long, long silence with only shuffling sounds. I had no idea what they were doing. Then another curious exchange occurred:

*Oh darling, you are—*

(Slap!) *Don't call me that.*

*I'm sorry.*

*Did I give you permission to call me that?*

*No, Miss Tyler, you did not.*

*Now lean over the table.*

*Yes, Miss Tyler.*

What I heard next was a sound I recognized from when I was a child and Father was cross with one of us. It was the sound of a stick striking someone's bottom!

For a while I shut my eyes and covered my ears in embarrassment, then I resumed listening. As I remember it, here is what I heard:

*There you go. Now do you want to please me?*

*Surely you know that I always want to please you.*

*That's what I like to hear.*

*Oh darling...*

*I warned you not to call me that.*

*My mistress.*

*That's better.*

When finally they opened the office door and closed it behind them, I confess that I simply wanted to get out of the building as quickly as possible. I hadn't the courage to go open the drawer and view the files. Out of cowardice, I missed my second chance.

What I did see looked like a ledger of income and expenses having to do with Mr Taggart—on the income side, some names were familiar—Reifel, Celona—while the expenses side included a firm of detectives and various officers with the Provincial Police. Without context, I realize that all this is probably meaningless.

Millie darling, I hope you will forgive me, for I am new at this. I hope you will trust that next time I shall be less of a disappointment, and that I shall remain—

Your loving friend,
Gracie

MILDRED FOLDS GRACIE'S letter and places it on her bedside table, wondering what can possibly be going on. Obviously Mr Crombie and Miss Tyler, like Jack and Mrs Spratt, have discovered areas of compatibility both sexually and financially, and Miss Tyler is, so to speak, holding the reins. And yet, it is not uncommon for two people to enter a relation with quite different plans; from tracing her career, it seems obvious that Daisy is a woman who never did anything except for money.

Which leads to her connection with the local Klan. While washing her face, Mildred thinks back on her research in preparation for Mrs Crombie's book club party—including her husband's fortuitous investments in real estate. Surely a man like Crombie wouldn't use his own money if he could help it.

Having turned her steamer trunk into a makeshift dressing table, she sits cross-legged on the floor and, in unforgiving daylight, takes stock of a face she finds all too ordinary and by no means pretty. By dusting with powder, darkening and shaping the eyebrows and applying a risqué shade of lipstick, she manages to achieve a certain drama—an art that Daisy Douglas Tyler seems to have mastered.

Dressed now, Millie stands before the dresser mirror (her room is too small for a full-length view, but no matter, for there is not much shape to assess) while following the money back to its most probable source.

The Klan. If one adds up initiation fees, as well as the price of merchandise such as robes, swords, bibles and the like, by now there must be a considerable amount of money in Klan coffers—and Vancouver's underworld contains plenty of men who know how to break into a safe.

A woman like Daisy isn't about to settle for bank interest. So what has been done with Major Forrest's "locally invested funds"?

A subject of interest to Mr McCurdy, she expects. And to her as well, in a different respect.

# CHAPTER 24

SINCE LONG BEFORE the "pansy craze" took over New York's caba-
rets and nightclubs, the New Fountain Hotel on Cordova Street
has been known for its philosophy of benign tolerance and, when
called for, willful ignorance. Staff are hired for their capacity to
perform their duties like blind men in a gathering of nudists.

Unlike blazingly bright, barn-like drinking factories like the
Kingsway, where working-class men sit and drink their beer
in austere misery, the New Fountain's interior has remained
unchanged since the turn of the century when the saloon and
the gin palace predominated.

Under a patterned tin ceiling and beneath the patchy amber
light of a central brass chandelier, a series of plaster arches divide
the area into sections, creating an ideal layout for various groups
of like-minded individuals to engage in discreet gatherings—
especially in the Ladies and Escorts area, where men and women
are accommodated who are not necessarily dressed as such.

Upholstered stools at the bar invite drinkers to strike up new
acquaintances, while banquette seating in the corners allows for
more intimate conversations to take place.

McCurdy makes his way past tables occupied by robust
women and clean-shaven young men until he locates Miss Wickstram at a corner table, looking sporty in a knife-pleat skirt, pale
green shirtwaist and no lipstick, with two glasses in front of her,
one empty, and a cluttered ashtray.

McCurdy is served a whiskey sour by a chubby young fellow
with a possibly false moustache and a fixed smile of general
equanimity.

Mildred waits for the waiter to move on, then leans forward.
"This is going to have to be quick, Eddie. A friend has invited me
to her birthday."

"Pull the other one, Millie, you and your friend are kicking it up with the fairies at Ma's speakeasy. The birthday cake is ten years old and it's made of plaster of Paris."

"Oh dear, that's right Eddie, you're a newspaperman. It's easy to forget that." She lights one of her disgusting Middle Eastern cigarettes, a process necessitating three safety matches, swearing under her breath as she blows a plume of smoke in his direction.

"Millie, whatever happened to your posh lighter?"

"I dropped it. At a place I don't wish to return to."

Her expression darkens, then snaps back to business. "Do you remember when I mentioned a story that might pry you out of your room? When you were in the Golden Empire, or whatever they call a dope-induced coma?"

He looks about the room. "I'm surprised you found the time to do research. You seem otherwise occupied these days."

She puts her head at an angle and smiles with one side of her mouth. "Surely you're not jealous, Eddie."

"*Confused* is the word, I think. Both you and General Newson seem to have switched allegiances. Joined the other side, so to speak."

"I hate sports metaphors."

"Very well. I mean to say that you are shagging another woman."

"*Shagging* isn't the right word. *Exploration* is more like it. It's a question of how far one chooses to travel."

"In any case, at least you're keeping up with the times—it's very à la mode in Germany, I understand. If you can sing, you might put on a tuxedo and join a cabaret."

"For that show of support, I shall up my charge by five dollars. But you will get a series out of it, so stop sulking and listen."

"You don't look exactly chuffed yourself, frankly."

"Actually, I am feeling a bit shirty." A long, smoky pause while she searches for *le mot juste*. "Eddie, do you remember when you were shot at?"

"Do you have to ask?"

"Well I fancy what I have to tell you is rather like that."

"Somebody shot at you too?"

She searches for a clever way to say this, and finds none.

"The Grand Goblin tried to rape me."

"Good heavens, Millie, surely you're joking!"

"Do I look as though I'm joking?"

No, she doesn't. You can't fake that look. "Forgive me. It's just that the Goblin part is a bit surreal. Spit it out, sister. Tell me your story."

"I finagled an invitation to a meeting at Glen Brae—the pile they've rented for a hundred and fifty a month. I was taking a look around, and he, and I..."

A long pause follows. McCurdy examines his whiskey sour, which has become more so.

"I... resisted. Successfully." She nods as though to remind herself.

Clearly it could be worse, but not by much.

He cleans his glasses while she blows her nose, puts away her handkerchief, takes a long, deep drag of her cigarette, then another, then sits back as poised as ever.

"Millie, I'm waiting for you to tell me that you called the police. Obviously the swine should rot in gaol."

"That wouldn't have been wise, Eddie. At the meeting I recognized several coppers."

"Oh, I see. I'm afraid I get the picture."

"And there were no witnesses. It was what people call a one-on-one transaction..."

McCurdy sees the film come over her eyes again, so he quickly moves on. "Well, in any case, if *revenge* is too strong a word for you, I recommend what the general would call a *punitive action*."

The term seems to cheer her up. "Eddie, that is precisely what I have in mind."

"And I assume that the series of articles you propose bear upon your recent... experience."

"Correct. But just because I have a personal interest in the subject, do not think for a moment that I'm doing this for nothing."

"Millie, you're turning into a battle axe."

She uses two more safety matches to fire up another cigarette. "Where do you wish to start?"

"Not with the details of your assault, please. It'll only upset my stomach."

"Very well, let's start with the Klan. As you probably know, today's Klan has nothing in common with their ancestor but the regalia.

"It's a sort of *Birth of a Nation* fan club as I understand it."

"Also like a football club."

"Sporting yobbos, sort of thing—who support the club by shelling out for dues and merchandise?"

"Correct. Its members are its customers. But unlike your football club, its existence depends on its ability to constantly acquire *new* members."

"Seeking new blood, like a leech. Well, I suppose it's a living."

"Or you could say it's a case of expand or die, like a single-celled germ. When they run out of new members in one town, the sales force moves on to another. It's a big country, with hatreds yet to be mined. Which brings us to my personal villain, one Luther Forrest, now Grand Goblin of the Vancouver branch, after founding chapters in California, Idaho, Oregon, Washington and Alaska. And that is where our series—"

"A series about the business plan of the KKK? Where do we publish this—*Success* magazine?"

"Don't be snide. You don't know about Indiana."

"I never hope to. Indianans are bible-thumping, cow-tipping rustics who like to play basketball."

"The home of basketball, that's true. But also once the home of three hundred thousand dues-paying Klan members. In Indiana, for the past several years, it has been impossible to get elected without them. Now math was never my forte, but at seventy-five dollars a membership it adds up to a lot of dues, not to mention the price of robes, hoods, Klan water—"

"So I take it we're about to make a big splash in the *Indianapolis News*."

"Very funny. I must say, if this is what you call creative thinking, it's no wonder you can't write a decent poem."

"That was uncalled for, Millie."

"You're pouting again. I'm sorry, but at times I find you unbearable."

"Is that the upshot of our discussion? If so, I should like to pay my bill, take my leave and jump in front of a passing tram."

"Surely not before I tell you about Daisy Tyler."

"Daisy *Douglas* Tyler?"

"The same. One item unmentioned in her publicity material is that she founded a parallel women's chapter in Indianapolis, called the Queens of the Golden Mask. It was billed as a temperance and eugenics movement, but really a woman's auxiliary for the Klan, with its own dues, robes and all the rest."

"You have to hand it to the American entrepreneur. The can-do spirit in action."

"Except that earlier this year, her frontman, Grand Dragon Stephenson, was convicted of kidnapping, rape and murder. He was a piece of work—biting was involved. There was an inquiry and some government members went to gaol. Along the way, membership in the Klan collapsed—and with it, the Queens of the Golden Mask."

"Another rapist—is it a contact sport with them?"

"No, it's something men do in their spare time, usually while drunk. In any case—"

She stops in mid-sentence as her eyes swivel up. McCurdy turns in his chair and looks above him at the clean-shaven young American from the Kingsway Hotel, with the excellent teeth and small pistol.

"Mr Johnston. We meet again."

"Yes indeed, suh. I trust you have recovered from the tanning you got at the Kingsway."

"No permanent damage, thanks to you. Let me introduce you to my friend, Mildred Wickstram."

"We've met."

McCurdy takes a closer look from one face to the other, and it all fits.

# CHAPTER 25

THE TWO POLICEMEN stop to admire the enormous circular towers on either corner of the building—the unusual vaulted windows and intricately carved trim capped by rounded roofs with nipple-shaped points.

"Sir, why do people call it the Mae West House?"

"I wouldn't know, Mr Quam. I suppose people find it preferable to the *Imperial Palace*."

"The place is a filthy mess," Quam says, noting the unmown lawn, the unswept floor of the verandah and the railings dappled with pigeon shit.

"Surprising, isn't it, Constable? Their sheets always seem clean enough."

Hook lifts the heavy brass ring (tarnished green-grey) and slams it against the door plate, twice. Inside, the crack of metal on metal echoes throughout the house. No response. He slams down the knocker again, several times, until they can hear footsteps on the hardwood floor.

With the slide and click of a deadbolt, the door opens just wide enough to reveal a scraggy fellow in a suit a size too small, from whose cuffs protrude a pair of veined wrists, raw hands and calloused knuckles. Drooping beneath the long nose, a walrus moustache fails to soften the dry, feral face peering at them from under Vaseline hair.

"Yeah? What is it?" A set of ice-grey eyes take in the uniforms: "Oh. Good day, officers. And what kin we do for yuz today?"

"Sir, I am Detective Sergeant Hook of the VPD, and this is Constable Quam. We are making general inquiries about an incident last week. I wonder if we might come inside for a moment."

"Are y'all expected?"

"We haven't scheduled an appointment, if that's what you mean."

"Well, that's mighty unfortunate. The Impurial Palace is not open to visitors at this time."

"I gather that. We thought the absence of visitors might make this a good time for a casual chat."

"This is private property. Do y'all have a warrant?"

"We're not undergoing a search, sir. Just a friendly chat."

"We thought we'd drop in while we were in the neighbour-hood," Quam adds, unnecessarily.

The door doesn't widen, and its occupant doesn't move. "Either way, you can't come in, suh. I got orders of Major Forrest."

"Actually, it's Mr Forrest we'd like to speak to, sir," Quam says.

"Mr Forrest has always been very supportive of the police," adds Hook.

A pair of frown lines appear above the bridge of a hawk nose. He draws back slightly, scratching his chin with two ragged fingernails. "Maybe so, but—"

A second face appears in the doorway, equally feral but clean shaven and with a scar beneath the left eye. His suit is a better fit, marred only by the heavy object in the side pocket of his coat.

"What's this about, Gainer?"

"Jessup, these two policemen here want to speak to Major Forrest."

"The Grand Goblin would be pleased to speak to you gentle-men, but that ain't possible at this time. Major Forrest has an injury. He is confined to bed."

"What sort of injury, sir? Nothing serious, I hope."

"An accident on the stairs. Took a fall, hit his head and cut himself. The doc says bedrest should see him out."

"Good to hear it, sir."

"Awful sorry to waste your time, officers. Maybe call next week. Mind you call first. Good day."

The two policemen descend to the front walk and head for the street. "I wonder if you noticed, Mr Quam, that the subject of a warrant seemed to come up rather quickly."

"Americans are very serious about their private property, sir. But even so, I found them most unwelcoming."

"Reminded me of Joe Celona's bouncers at the Belmont Caba-ret." Hook ignites an Ogden's. "If Mr Forrest requires protection, I wonder who from."

# CHAPTER 26

*Hello, operator speaking, MUtual exchange. Are you there?*

*Here is SEymour 330, Hotel Vancouver. MUtual 491, please.*

*I will connect you now.*

SWITCH

*Hello, are you there? Here is Bird, Rabinowitz, Farris and Sweet, operator speaking. How may I assist you?*

Mildred speaks with her plummy voice, though she is careful not to overdo it. (Operators can detect a fake posh accent every time.)

*Operator, I should like to speak with Mr Sweet.*

*And your name please?*

*Miss Mildred Wickstram.*

*Certainly. I shall connect you with his secretary, whose name is Miss Brice.*

SWITCH

*Here is Mr Sweet's office, Miss Brice speaking. How may I be of assistance?*

Now Mildred switches to another voice—the one she employed in Whitehall when placing calls for the general, to ensure quick service and a good connection; the voice that says, *I am speaking on behalf of a very important man about very important matters.*

*Miss Brice, I seek Mr Sweet's council on urgent business. It is a confidential matter—*

*I understand, Miss Wickstram. Please hold.*

In the distance she can hear a male and a female voice in discussion; when she is reconnected it is the male voice speaking. It seems the plummy accent did its work.

*Here is Tristan Sweet. Are you there?*

The voice belongs to a man in his twenties, a Canadian who has spent enough time in England to smooth out the consonants and round the vowels.

Thanks to her Badminton theatre classes, Mildred knows that the first order of business is to seize the audience's attention.

*Mr Sweet, thanks awfully for taking my call. My name is Mildred Wickstram, and I was assaulted by a member of the Ku Klux Klan.*

As expected, a long pause at the other end.

*Ah. Ah. Yes. I believe I understand you. And, well that is... yes. Very well. I see. He assaulted you. Did he strike you? Are you injured?*

*No, it was more of a... personal sort of injury.*

Another pause. A clearing of the throat.

*Ah. Yes, of course. Point taken. Have you spoken to the police?*

*I do not feel comfortable with the police, and with good reason.*

*Oh. I see... Well actually, I don't see.*

*No, I didn't expect that you would. As you can imagine, this is a difficult thing for me to discuss over the telephone. I called your firm hoping that...*

She pauses, breathing in a way that suggests emotional upheaval, a damsel in distress. *Excuse me, just give me a moment...*

*Please don't distress yourself any further, Miss... er, Wickstram. Can you come to my office at eleven o'clock tomorrow morning?*

*I can, and will. Thank you ever so much, Mr Sweet.*

As captain of the Badminton field hockey team (Southwest School Championship, 1913–14), Mildred found it of utmost importance to conduct sufficient research before choosing one's offensive line.

The firm of Bird, Rabinowitz, Farris and Sweet are known for taking liberal positions on matters of race and politics. Mr Bird, a member of the Canadian Socialist Party, gained notoriety for having represented (albeit unsuccessfully) a boatload of would-be immigrants from India; and Mr Rabinowitz (*son of a Rabbi*) is, obviously, a Jew.

The senior partners are wealthy, middle-aged men with houses in Point Grey, and have for months been arguing a number of drawn-out cases involving a longshoremen's strike and a Tsimshian man accused of murder; feeling the pinch after so much pro bono work, these men are no doubt busy chatting up their roster of wealthy clients, in order to fluff up the corporate pillow.

Further research indicated that the firm tends to win its battles on technical issues—not by making stirring speeches that win headlines but lose cases, leaving the client morally victorious but in gaol nonetheless.

This is the sort of lawyer she wants.

Though her case is scarcely likely to interest one of the partners, their record must surely affect their choice of *junior* partners.

Her conclusion: Tristan Sweet is her man. A junior member of the firm who has not yet argued a sensational trial.

Granted, Mr Sweet has won several cases, but none has appeared on the front page of a newspaper—suggesting that he could well be susceptible to taking a knight-in-shining-armour role, defending the damsel in distress.

Having played the role over the phone, she must now decide how she is to approach her audience in person. Assuming that she is a few years his senior, she decides to play the well-bred, experienced woman—amused, knowing and ever-so-slightly flirtatious.

Mildred is not especially fond of such tactics as a means to achieving what she wants from a man; but in a negotiation, the party with the weaker position must work with what she has.

THE OFFICES OF Bird, Rabinowitz, Farris and Sweet are located on the sixth floor of the Metropolitan Building, a brick shoebox on Hastings Street situated near the Supreme Court and steps from the Vancouver Club, where lawyers continue the arguments over consecutive whiskies and soda.

For the role, Mildred has chosen her volley afternoon dress, whose V-neck scoops a shade lower than strictly necessary so that a slight cleavage merges with the bodice, forming an arrow pointing downward. She has covered her head with a cloche hat, her hands with cuffed gloves and her feet with matching pumps.

In the mirror this morning she practised lifting her chin ever so slightly, as a woman bearing up in a difficult time.

Inside a pair of etched glass doors, a matronly receptionist in a tweed jacket invites her to be seated, with a smile that says she is expected.

With a murmur of thanks, she sits in a leather club chair and gazes about, taking mental notes. On one wall, dominating the room, a series of exquisitely fashioned, truly frightening masks: a long-haired creature with a single black eyebrow and lips pursed, two sharp-toothed bears, and birds with enormous curved beaks. From her reading-up, Mildred knows that they were obtained as payment for securing the acquittal of a pair of Kwakiutl Indians on murder charges.

Fine as payment in full, but for a reception room hardly the thing to cheer up a distressed client.

Her prospective lawyer strides into the room, looking about the age she expected but taller, with dark hair swept over one eye, eyebrows like French accents and the studied focus she associates with the Oxford debating team.

"Miss Wickstram, how do you do? I'm Tristan Sweet. Welcome." He shakes her hand as though afraid he might break it. "Please come into my office."

Viewed from behind, his suit looks bought off the rack but altered to fit the waist and shoulders; holding the door open for her, he displays a club necktie, tied four-in-hand with deliberate carelessness.

"I see you've been to England, Mr Sweet."

The corner of his mouth twitches; he isn't comfortable being observed this early in an encounter, not to mention the feeling that someone is taking notes.

"My undergraduate degree is from Oxford—on a Rhodes Scholarship," he quickly adds.

"Very classy I should think, given that your senior partner is a Socialist."

That twitch again. "Actually, my father is a pastry chef."

"*Sweet*: Isn't it curious how people can resemble their names, like characters out of Dickens. And your father a pastry chef! Well if that isn't sweetness..."

The twitch becomes more pronounced and the cheekbones redden. "Yes, I suppose that might be so. Please Miss Wickstram, take a seat."

Having thoroughly rattled her host, Mildred casts an innocent gaze about the office.

Overlooking the neighbouring roof, sparsely furnished with a leather-topped desk and two library chairs—the office's inhabitant is decidedly a junior partner. One wall is occupied by framed certificates, while on the opposite wall is a large photograph of a group of uniformed men, perched on and around a strange-looking truck in what appears to be a snowfield. Looking more closely, she recognizes Mr Sweet among them.

"Where was that picture taken, Mr Sweet?"

"Vladivostok," he replies. "The Siberian Intervention. I was seventeen and they didn't know what else to do with me. So I was seconded to protect the Yakutsk railway station from the Bolsheviks."

"And it seems you were unsuccessful, if we are to believe Comrade Stalin."

"Not entirely. They didn't attack us, which was the main point. Perhaps we frightened them off. But we're not here about my heroic tour of duty, Miss Wickstram."

"Quite right, Mr Sweet. I wish to engage you in a lawsuit, on a contingent fee."

An extended pause follows. She remains silent while he wonders how to begin.

"Miss Wickstram, from speaking to you on the telephone, my, er, understanding was that we are dealing with a case of attempted rape. This is a serious criminal charge, with a possible penalty of life in prison."

Mildred replies a bit more snappishly than intended. "Oh no, Mr Sweet. You are mistaking me for a silly bloody fool."

He appears taken aback, perhaps because her expression momentarily revealed the extent of her anger. She executes a dismissive shrug, smiles demurely, then sets out on the path she prepared beforehand, lying awake at night, trying to expel the memory that keeps returning like a stuck record: *Just lie back and enjoy it, sugar...*

"Miss Wickstram, would you like a glass of water?"

"No. No, thank you. Mr Sweet, I hope you're not mistaking me for a helpless girl looking for pro bono representation. Please understand that this is not a criminal case. My purpose is to earn us both a good deal of money."

His nostrils flare momentarily, making her think of a spaniel with a whiff of roast beef. "Please explain, Miss Wickstram. I'm all ears."

"As you well know, to press criminal charges would be a sticky wicket. With no witnesses present to prove beyond a reasonable doubt, the court requires 'visible' injuries—for which the defence will produce a bystander who saw one fall downstairs, possibly drunk—and evidence of 'fierce resistance,' which is to say visible injuries on the accused as well. This line of questioning will inevitably touch on questionable morals: Has she ever partaken of alcohol? Has she ever, tipsy or not, exhibited a provocative way with men? If unmarried, was she a virgin before the alleged assault? If still a virgin, would she be willing to submit to examination? If not, then why not—"

"Miss Wickstram, you've ably described the argument—are you sure you wouldn't like a glass of water?"

"No, thank you. My wish is to undertake a civil suit, where the yardstick is not proof but the balance of probabilities."

"You've been reading up, I see. Well you're quite right, that is another game entirely."

"What I propose is what you lawyers somewhat derisively call a 'seduction suit,' under what legal scholars call, even more derisively, the 'heart balm statutes.' You are, of course, familiar with these terms?"

"Of course. But don't you think a seduction suit is a bit inadequate in a case of attempted rape?"

"Punitive damages, Mr Sweet. Compensation for pain and suffering, for diminished marriage prospects. Put a man in gaol and he'll cast himself as the victim of a bitter woman. Take away a man's money, and he must carry the shame that a woman got the better of him."

"I shouldn't put it quite that cynically, but I take your point."

"In this case, our precedent is *Gibson v. Shackleton*, 1915. The plaintiff claimed that Shackleton promised marriage, on condition that she yield to his advances. Which she did, and he jilted her, and she sued. The court ruled that willing intercourse was irrelevant to the breach of promise, and awarded considerable damages."

"And did Mr Forrest promise to marry you?"

"He certainly did—what do you take me for? I'm a ruined woman. My reputation is in tatters. I shall have to marry a foreigner." She refrains from shedding a tear, not to egg the pudding.

Mr Sweet appears skeptical. "This is a serious charge. Can we prove it?"

"We don't have to. Shall I explain?"

"Please do."

"Do you have an ashtray? I hope you don't mind if I smoke."

"Oh thank heaven, I was hoping you would ask that."

They bring out their respective brands, a kind of meeting of the minds. He lights her cigarette with his silver lighter so that she doesn't have to fumble with her safety matches. They take a moment to savour the relief and relaxation a delayed smoke has to offer.

Mildred continues. "As you know, even a civil case requires evidence. My evidence is a blood-soaked dress—it's *his* blood, not mine."

"*His* blood? The court will require an explanation."

"It happened when he jumped on me, pulled my dress up and was fumbling with his... Mr Sweet, must you blush like that? It's unnerving."

"I'm sorry, but it's all so..."

"Anatomical? Gynecological? Sexually exciting?"

The blush deepens. "Let us say that it invites unwelcome... imagery."

"My point is, just as he was completing the act, he had a sudden nosebleed."

"And where was he at the time?"

"On top of me, as I told you. Where else would he be? You should see my dress."

"Ah."

"Dear Mr Sweet, I am sorry to introduce such vulgar matters to a young, sensitive lawyer."

The eyebrows converge: "Miss Wickstram, I think you'll find that we don't appreciate sarcasm in this office."

"Few people do. But they don't like it when one says something straight on, either. Very well, fine, let's speak plainly. He wasn't trying to pick my pocket, he was about to insert his penis—"

"Stop it, Miss Wickstram, clearly we are dealing with a case of forceable rape."

"Only if a criminal charge is laid. Otherwise it's a brief dalliance."

"Technically, I suppose."

"Then suddenly he developed a nosebleed and bled all over my dress. Nosebleeds happen at the most inconvenient times. That is my version of the story. Mr Forrest's may differ."

Mr Sweet's ears seem to prick up, giving Mildred a glimpse of the fox within. "Continue, please," he says, producing a foolscap pad and unscrewing his fountain pen.

"In addition, I wish to sue the Klan, which Mr Forrest represents as Grand Goblin. The evidence is in previous speeches about the sanctity of womanhood. I can provide them to you. The press feeds on hypocrisy and will snap like trout."

He watches her carefully, while two ribbons of smoke silently drift slowly upward. "So I take it you're after bigger game than Luther Forrest."

"Correct. I wish to collect damages not only from Mr Forrest and the Klan organization; I also seek damages from the gentlemen present in the Imperial Palace that evening—among whose number were a prominent cleric, two aldermen, three policemen and an MLA. The papers make a meal of familiar names."

"Damages for what, Miss Wickstram?" He leans back in his chair making a wigwam of his fingers.

"For failing in their duty to protect a lady's honour. But do you think they will be eager to appear in court with their hoods off, defending their presence at a KKK meeting where a woman claims to have been seduced? That alone would be enough to destroy several careers."

By and large, she can see that she has won over Mr Sweet, though there is no telling whether it was her argument or her bodice.

"From this, Miss Wickstram, I assume you are looking for an out-of-court settlement, without actually going to trial. Were we to proceed, what would you consider reasonable compensation?"

"I'd like it to be as unreasonable as possible."

"So the defendant is to suffer financially—and publicly, as the amount of the settlement itself becomes news."

"Mr Sweet, who was it who said something about *repaying a wicked man in his own coin*?"

"I'm sure I don't know, but it rather sums up lawsuits at their best."

"In military terms, I propose what an acquaintance calls a *punitive action.* For Lord Kitchener, this involved slaughter and plunder. I wish to plunder Mr Forrest, and slaughter his reputation.

"I want him to remember this for the rest of his life. As, I'm sure, will I."

### KLAN SEDUCTION LAWSUIT FILED
### Grand Goblin Charged
### Max Trotter
### Staff Writer
### *The Vancouver World*

A local woman, whose name is under publication ban for safety and modesty, has sued the Ku Klux Klan organization on a charge of seduction, with battery as an aggravating factor.

The writ, filed under the Seduction Laws, names Luther Forrest, the Grand Goblin, along with others present in the so-called Imperial Palace (formerly Glen Brae) at a meeting last September 11, at which Jane Doe claims she was persuaded to participate in a sexual liaison with a promise of marriage. Subsequently, she claims, Mr Forrest recanted his proposal.

Also charged are the Grand Klaliff, Dr Ambrose Walker; two Cyclops, Jessup Olson and Gainer Flood; four unnamed Nighthawks and an unstated number of Ghouls. Klan supporters who were also present at the meeting are said to include three policemen, two aldermen and an MLA.

The plaintiff claims damages, material and punitive, in excess of a hundred thousand dollars. She is represented by Tristan Sweet, a partner with Byrd, Rabinowitz, Farris and Sweet, a firm known for its defence of Orientals, Indians and Socialists.

Mr Forrest, who is presently recuperating from an injury, was unavailable for comment at press time. Through a spokesman, he vigorously denies that marriage was ever discussed.

Since the Vancouver branch opened, the Ku Klux Klan has proved surprisingly popular with temperance groups and the Asiatic Exclusion League. Already it claims to have enrolled over eight thousand members in under a year. (Informed observers say that the figure may be an exaggeration.)

With regard to the Klan itself, yesterday in the Legislature, mixed emotions were expressed by MLA Major Burde, speaking to a motion censuring the organization for its disparagement of Roman Catholics: "I object strongly to putting Negros and Catholics on the same plane. At the same time, they will have done a service if they run Japanese, Hindoos and Chinamen out of BC."

# CHAPTER 27

THE FIRST CONSTABLE on the scene gained entry by breaking the door, then galloped across the room to open a window and air the room out—never mind that a howling squall was carrying on outside. Gusts of wind are causing the corpse to swing gently, like the pendulum of a grandfather clock.

The constable is now standing guard by the door, while a second is stationed outside the front door, awaiting the ambulance.

DS Hook has been assigned to lead the initial investigation—a post that, in a case involving violent death, normally goes to a more senior member. Maybe Hook is being oversuspicious, but he wonders if someone on the force wants to put him in a difficult position, for the Klan is popular among several officers. Some admire their anti-Asian position; others view the KKK as a Protestant bulwark against Papist domination. And there are always a few temperance cranks on the force.

Thanks to Chief Barfoot's eagerness to please the rank and file, a recently promoted outsider can always depend on being first up for any assignment likely to be controversial, gruesome or, as in this case, both at the same time.

Constable Quam holds a handkerchief over his nose. "What an awful smell."

"Yes, Constable, they always stink. Keep in mind that Forrest didn't *intentionally* shit himself." Hook is well aware of the pong, having dealt with several suicides at Rugeley Camp—recruits who feared what was to come in the field of battle, or who had grown tired of the rain and the mud and the boredom, or who could no longer stand the homesickness.

Most soldiers shot themselves (for convenience if nothing else), but there were others who, by training or instinct, couldn't quite manage to aim a pistol at themselves and pull the trigger.

(In fairness, it's harder than it looks.) With the availability of rope, hanging was the second choice.

As the squall eases, and the swinging carcass of Grand Goblin Luther Forrest gradually reaches equilibrium, Hook takes mental notes for the inevitable report, to be filed in triplicate: *Deceased wearing the white robes of the Ku Klux Klan. Hood cast aside, lying on floor. Cord of the robe cause of death by hanging...*

The two policemen contemplate this marionette with the plum-coloured face, kept upright by a single string.

"It all seems quite open-and-shut, sir. Do you think he left a note?"

"Not unless he committed suicide."

"What do you mean?"

"Something doesn't sit right—don't you agree?"

Clearly, for Quam, the answer is no. The constable's face takes on a certain weariness: "You're saying that it's more complicated, aren't you, sir?"

DS Hook steps closer to the corpse and points above the head. "Quam, do you see where the cord is tied to the fixture? What kind of a knot is that?"

Quam holds his nose and looks more closely. "I have no idea, sir."

"I take it you weren't a Boy Scout, then."

"I was 4-H. The club is very strong in Manitoba."

"Ah. Well, that knot is called a clove hitch—used for quickly tying, say, a boat to a mooring or a horse to a post. Now look closely at the noose itself. What do you see?"

"I see a hangman's noose, sir."

"Well done, Constable, you just put your finger on it."

"Put my finger on what? Are you being sarcastic again, sir?"

"Not a bit. Do you see the regulation thirteen coils? Such careful work, when a simple running knot would have been sufficient. Why would he take the time to fashion a traditional hangman's knot, then use a simple clove hitch at the other end and not tie it properly?"

"Because it was faster, I suppose."

"And yet there was no reason for our man to hurry. The door was shut and locked. Eternity was at hand."

With a sigh, Quam stops to think. His eyes grow moist with effort. "I'm afraid you've lost me, sir."

"Did you see *Birth of a Nation* a few years ago?"

"No, I was too young. Anyway, I prefer comedies."

"It could be that someone hastily tied the clove hitch, while someone else held the body up—with difficulty, because the victim was resisting at the time."

"Or he could have done it himself in a hurry, just to get the thing over with."

"Point taken, but now let's look at the physics of it. What did our man stand on to secure the cord?"

"Obviously it was that stool in the corner—it's on its side, don't you see."

"And a good ten feet away. Now imagine yourself with a noose around your neck, hauling off and kicking the stool that's holding you up with such force that it lands that far away. Quite an achievement, wouldn't you say, constable?"

"Was he a football player?"

"I would think it far more likely that someone *else* kicked the stool."

"Sir, I take it you're seriously suggesting that some other party hanged Mr Forrest."

"Not hanged, Mr Quam. Given the thirteen coils and the occupants of the house, I think the correct term is *lynched*."

Quam takes a moment to process this detail, then brightens. "Still, it must have been him who locked the door—don't you see, the key is on the inside of the door?

"A house this size usually has more than one set of keys."

The constable's eyes dart about like those of a cornered animal, then take on a look of resignation. "And there is something to complicate things further. Isn't there, sir?"

Hook reaches into the side pocket of his tunic and comes up with a copper bullet casing. "Do you know what this is, Mr Quam?"

"It's a bullet."

"Not exactly. It's the *casing* for a bullet. A bullet that has been fired."

"Where did it come from, sir?"

"An associate left it at the station, to prove something. But since you don't know what a bullet is, I don't suppose you know what kind of weapon fired it?"

181

"I'm not a ballistics expert, sir." Quam is beginning to look ill, not just from the stench but from the mental effort.

"Surely, Quam, you agree that something is off."

"Pardon me, sir, but you tend to make everything seem a bit off."

"In any case, while we're in the building, perhaps we might just as well take a look around."

"Surely we need a warrant, sir?"

"Foul play is suspected, Mr Quam. I thought we agreed on that."

IT TAKES ONLY a few moments to establish that the entire second floor has been recently abandoned. Two rooms show signs of long-time occupation and a hasty exit—unmade beds, dresser drawers gaping open like tongues, stray socks on the floor.

"Someone was here but now they're gone," observes the constable.

"Very good, Mr Quam. People dodging a summons tend to make themselves scarce. Especially with a hanged man just down the hall."

Closer to the staircase, they come upon a former library that appears to function as a warehouse for Klan products, complete with price tags. The two policemen rifle through the racks of robes ($9.50), headgear ($3.50) and the shelves packed with Klorans, boxes of Klansman cigars, bottles of Klan Water, Klan flags and helmets, piano rolls with Klan songs, a crate of Kluxers Knifty Knives, and a bookcase containing *The Clansman, The Rising Tide of Color against White World-Supremacy, The Menace of Modern Immigration* and *The Ku Klux Klan in Prophecy,* as well as issues of *The Watcher on the Tower, The Fiery Cross* and *The Pillar of Fire.*

Curiously, the bookcase also contains what are apparently non-Klan publications: *The Protocols of the Elders of Zion* and The International Jew.

"It's almost like a business, isn't it, sir?"

"Constable, I think you've hit the nail on the head."

Quam narrows his eyes, suspecting sarcasm, but he remains silent.

Assuming the room was once a library, there had to be a storage room of some sort for books. Hook ducks behind the racks, sidles his way around the perimeter—and there it is.

Pushing a white curtain of satin gowns aside, he opens the door to what has become a cabinet for weaponry. On the far wall, a set of shelves contains .45 caliber Smith & Wesson revolvers and a Thompson submachine gun. On another wall hang baseball bats and truncheons, while on the third wall is a rack of six .30-03 Springfield rifles and a tripod for sniping.

From a box of ammunition he extracts a bullet. If the elevator operator was correct, and the person who shot at McCurdy used a Springfield rifle, it might narrow things down, somewhat.

Dear, Dear Millie,

This can only be a short note, for I must feed and exercise Miss Carr's sheepdogs. I am happy to do so because my poor landlady is run ragged by bad tenants.

There is a man downstairs who complains about every little thing and, we suspect, beats his wife—his third wife, I am told. He has fingers like bananas. Why she hasn't left him is beyond me.

Then we have the tenant who refuses to pay her rent and refuses to leave without official notice.

What with shovelling coal and fielding complaints and going to and from city hall, Miss Carr is being ground down to a husk, and I fear for her health if she doesn't spend more time painting.

Meanwhile, everyone in the Legislature is a-twitter about goings-on at the Liquor Control Board. According to Gwendolyn, my former employer Mr Taggart arrived for an appointment with the Attorney General, and when he emerged from Mr Stalker's office, his face was bright crimson, his hands were bunched into fists and his eyes were redder than whatever they were before. On his way out, he picked up Angela Fleet's typewriter and flung it to the floor, then overturned her desk!

Mr Taggart hasn't been seen or heard from since. I don't know what to make of it—and there are too many rumours for one letter.

Oh please, we must have a visit if ever we can—if only for an hour. Knowing you are so close and yet so far, sometimes I feel as if I shall die!

Your loving friend, Gracie

# CHAPTER 28

AFTER A GOOD dinner of bubble and squeak, while the sun is still up, they go for a ride on the motorcycle.

As always, Jeanie rides precariously sidesaddle on the pillion seat, with her arms wrapped around his waist. He planned to acquire a sidecar but hasn't on the pretext of affordability, when the truth is that he wants to preserve the memory of their first ride together.

Today, however, it provides an opportunity to temporarily put aside the worry that has been dogging him all week. A motorcycle demands mental discipline; let your thoughts wander and you will find yourself lying on the ground, and with Jeanie behind him, holding on, trusting him... it clears the mind.

But, of course, the minute they get home he begins to fret about it all over again.

Usually Jeanie's time of the month is heralded by a headache or a sore back or a bout of staccato chippiness; but none of those symptoms have occurred, and now he is searching his mind for a way to broach this delicate subject.

Of course he's used to hearing male terms for the event (*on the rag, the curse*) but has never discussed it with a female, least of all his mother. In his understanding, it was a mysterious business that only women knew about, and it involved blood.

Due to the product's association with triage bandages, Kotex ads have been a staple of newspaper advertisements since the war (*If it's good enough for our soldiers, it's good enough for us!*); but as with women's undergarments in the Eaton's catalogue, it isn't a subject suitable for mixed company.

As a result, Hook can only wait for news, like a war bride.

Meanwhile, the days seem peppered with omens. Everywhere he looks he sees advertisements for Clapp's Baby Foods or Johnson's Powder. It's as if every second woman on the street is pushing a pram.

At the kitchen table over tea, Jeanie is talking about her day.

"I met Annie Tompkins at Woodward's Meats, and we walked down Hastings for bits and bobs, and then we stopped off at the White Lunch for tea—blimey, it's only September but it was bloody Baltic this morning! And poor Annie! They're skint with the mill at half shift, and Gannon is down to sellin' a bit of rum on the side—you won't grass on them, will you, ducky?"

"I'm off-duty, pet. Your husband hears everything, the Detective Sergeant hears nothing."

"I knew that, don't know why I asked. Anyway, I've been thinking about the two telephones you mentioned a while back, and told Annie about it, and what do you s'pose she said?"

"I can't imagine. What did she say?"

"Oh come, use your noodle, ducky. Who do ye s'pose would want to throw listeners-in off the track? Badly enough to pay for two telephones?"

"Oh. Well I suppose if you put it that way—"

"Bootleggers, luv. Not some bloke like Gannon without a pot to piss in, but a major punter with an ice wagon or a dairy wagon, with the emblems and everything... you aren't listening are you, luv?"

"Pet, I am listening to every word. I shall look into that idea. You are a very observant woman—sometimes I think you'd do a better job at this than I do."

"Now you're just being silly. But there's something else on your mind isn't there? Is it about the time of the month, ducky?"

He can feel his face turn red, so there's no denying it. "Well actually, to be perfectly honest..."

"I know, the train *is* late. So are ye feelin' strung up about it?"

"Certainly not, pet. If you were to be, er, in the family way, we would carry on, and I would love you just as deeply." Of course, to deny that he worries is a bald-faced lie. But it is the only safe thing to say, or she'll wonder *why* he is worried, what he is worried *about* and worry herself sick about his worrying.

Jeanie never lies, though surely she must be capable of it—after all, laughing and lying is what makes humans different from the animals. But she has never lied to him, and that is what counts.

She looks him in the eye with a furrow between her eyebrows. "I know it would mean a big change for us."

He reaches across the table and puts his hand over hers. "Let's take a wait-and-see attitude, pet. Let's just take things as they come."

She grins into her teacup. "Either way, ducky, tonight should be pretty safe, I expect."

They stand and hug one another tight for a while. Her shoulder smells like fresh-baked bread.

DISAPPEARANCE AROUSES SUSPICIONS
Former LCB Chairman Nowhere to be Found
Max Trotter
Staff Writer
*The Vancouver World*

Government employees and MLAs are baffled and alarmed by the sudden disappearance of Clyde Taggart, following his ouster as chairman of the Liquor Control Board.

Contacted by telephone, his wife admitted to feeling "calm but concerned." Pressed further, she added, "When I spoke to him on the telephone, he mentioned something about a *rocket attack*—he served in the trenches, you know."

Observers disagree on what exactly Mr Taggart meant by the words "rocket attack."

Mr Taggart is a skilled political operative, and he is surely unhappy about being sacked. Indeed, witnesses report that, following a meeting with the Attorney General, Taggart, livid with rage, destroyed government property and caused office girls to fear for their safety.

Whether or not Taggart seeks revenge, it would not be the first time the stench of scandal has stained the reputation of the LCB. Corruption has been a by-product of the industry ever since W.C. Findlay, the Prohibition commissioner, was convicted of importing trainloads of illegal rye.

Anonymous government sources suggest that no one should be surprised if Mr Taggart has taken a page from

Mr Findlay's playbook and hightailed it to Seattle with his ill-gotten fortune, never to be seen again.

Comments Deputy Minister Bertram Bliss: "Something fishy is going on with Mr Taggart, and the Attorney General's department will jolly well get to the bottom of it."

# CHAPTER 29

BEHIND THE GLASS, Chief Barfoot is hosting a meeting with the mayor, two aldermen and a woman Hook thinks he has seen before but can't remember where or when: in her thirties, with her dark hair pulled back into a severe bun and sharp features devoid of makeup, wearing the long skirt and high-necked blouse of a schoolteacher.

With his round tortoiseshell glasses reflecting light from the window and an unlit cigar clamped beneath his paintbrush moustache, Mayor Taylor is talking animatedly, directing his speech primarily to the female member of the group, who seems to need convincing. She appears to be taking notes, despite the fact that there is a stenographer in the room—an indication that, by keeping a record of her own, she wishes to ensure that there will be no "misunderstanding" as to who said what.

Pausing for breath, Mayor Taylor lights his cigar; the two aldermen, Garbutt and Cottrell, follow suit. Smoke billows above the table as though from a locomotive, and soon the meeting will be all but invisible to anyone on this side of the glass.

But the fact is, DS Hook could not give a shit about these people or their argument, having spent a miserable hour pounding with two forefingers at the keys of a Royal typewriter, by the "hunt-and-peck" method. He nearly suffered a hernia carrying the thing to his desk, and now his hands are raw from untangling jammed type bars, and black from handling carbon paper that smudges everything.

And to think he used to complain about ink stains.

From the martini glass on the table beside the victim, through the meeting with hotel staff, the search of Cunning's suite, the meeting with Mr Patterson, the visit to the Crombie residence, the Imperial Palace—that and more must be itemized and

189

described and filed in triplicate. Corpses must be described, witness responses noted...

According to the manual, this is not police work, so there is no question of paid overtime. Just another unpaid chore to go along with Constable Quam—more unpleasantness, unmentioned when he joined the VPD.

Which means he'll be late for dinner. Jeanie's roast will be dry and the turnips will be cold, and she will be disappointed.

Perhaps it's time to invest in a telephone, even though it would spell the end of their privacy—a telephone is a loudspeaker sitting in the parlour, demanding everyone's attention, buttonholing people for whatever purpose the caller wishes, taking precedence over whatever is happening in the life of the recipient. Still, like the home radio, one can see its value for keeping in touch.

On the far side of the glass, the volume and pace seem to have quickened. The stenographer is finding it hard to keep up, even in shorthand.

He focuses on the face of the woman at the table and tries to place it—then curses aloud as another pair of type bars jams together. Trying to pry apart the two greasy crossed fingers, he becomes aware of a shadow behind and above his shoulder, and from the smell, which today puts him in mind of a mouldy spice tin, he knows who it is.

"Mr Quam. What is it, please?"

"Yes, sir, it is I. You should know that the lab report on the sample from under the bed in Gordon Cunning's hotel room has come in. Nothing to report."

"Nothing at all?"

"Nothing, sir. It's the same with the sample from Mrs Crombie's house."

"How disappointing. And what about the gin sample in the locker?"

"Better news, sir, depending on how you look at it. The bottle in the locker is almost *all* wood alcohol." ·

"And?"

"A bit of juniper is all, for taste. It would take no time at all to kill you."

"So it appears that the two died from different causes."

"Exactly, sir. The bottles in Mrs Crombie's bathroom and Mr Cunning's suite amounted to pure coincidence, as I pointed out from the beginning." Quam's face brightens at the prospect of having been right, for once.

"Not necessarily, Constable. Not without an autopsy on Mrs Crombie. And our chief has ruled that out."

"These are frugal times, sir. We must all tighten our belts."

"True for you, Mr Quam—but that is not the entire reason."

"You're going to suggest something more complicated, aren't you, sir?"

"Should the two victims turn out to have died of tainted alcohol, it could cause a panic. The liquor business would suffer. Taxation income would fall through the floor. Meanwhile, the PPA would dearly love to fan the flames. And all this trouble, just because someone may or may not have been murdered?"

"Sir, if I may say so, you paint a cynical picture."

"War makes cynics of us all."

"So where does that leave us, sir?"

"Back to where we started, Constable—with nothing except for the gin bottle in the locker to suggest that Cunning didn't die of natural causes."

"Well at least we have that to hold onto."

"Not necessarily. This might be what someone *wants* us to think. Someone could have planted the bottle in the locker for another reason."

"So Mr Cunning may have been killed by something else entirely?" Quam's eyes tear up, then turn inward.

DS Hook sets fire to an Ogden's and returns his attention to the typewriter, on the assumption that the constable will leave now.

Quam clears his throat. "One more moment, sir, if I may. If this is a good time to speak." The constable takes a deep breath.

"Do you have something to get off your chest, Mr Quam?"

"Something to discuss, if you don't mind."

"Not at all, please carry on." In fact, the last thing he wants right now is to entertain Quam's tiresome wig-bubbles.

The constable looks about for an empty chair; finding none, he returns to the desk and continues. "Sir, it seems to me that, in general, to be perfectly frank, it seems that, as a partnership, we have failed to, in a word, gel."

"Gel in what sense, Mr Quam? Do you mean, as in *gelatin*?"

"In the course of the investigation, I've noted a certain... a certain lack of rapport."

Hook must admit that this is true. He has often felt an unbecoming urge to lay hands upon his teammate and beat him to death. At the same time, he must also admit to himself that what underlies his distaste for the man is the fact that *he didn't serve*—despite having no obvious, McCurdy-like handicap. (He has never known a man to be declared too stupid to serve.)

Sometimes Hook wonders if in surviving the war he has taken it upon himself to represent the dead. Every so often the urge comes over him to to speak for every soldier who entered the meat grinder and didn't come out; or those who returned, who currently line the streets and pack the nuthouses.

Upon arrival, the first responsibility for any returning soldier was to conceal what the folks at home didn't want to know. Those who failed to do so were checked into Essondale Hospital for the Mind and the newly built Acute Psychopathic Unit, there to receive electric shocks, lie in a cold bath for days on end, lose a chunk of their brain or die *from exhaustion due to...*

"Are you listening to me, sir?"

"Yes, Mr Quam. Point taken. And I apologize for my snide remarks. Most unprofessional. My wife has warned me against sarcasm."

"Thank you, sir. I appreciate that. But in any case, I've been thinking about things, and I've come to a decision about my... my future."

"And how do you see your future, Mr Quam?"

"With the Dry Squad, sir. I have applied for a transfer."

"Ah yes, the Dry Squad. Would that would be Sergeant Rocco's bunch?"

"He's the officer in charge, yes."

As a Redhat, Hook became more than familiar with officers like Rocco, whose value lies in the fact that after an encounter with the officer, charges or not, an offender will recoil from ever meeting him again, on duty or—worse—in plain clothes, waiting outside the mess hall, late at night. At Rugeley, men feared and hated the military police, and some officers thoroughly deserved the sentiment.

"The Dry Squad offers a solid opportunity for advancement, sir. The department is expanding by leaps and bounds."

"I applaud your ambition, Mr Quam—but *expanding*? Are you certain? It's been my understanding that cutbacks have occurred in all departments."

"Not so with the Dry Squad, sir. Word has it the budget has doubled. And it's a chance to do some old-fashioned police work—where you know your man straightaway and can arrest him without filling a form in triplicate. To be honest, sir, your sort of case is too complicated. I'm losing sleep with all the thinking that has to be done. It's given me headaches, sir."

"Yes, headaches are an occupational hazard."

"The Dry Squad is the force of the future, sir—meeting criminals head-on, dealing with them decisively, enforcing the law with a steady hand..." As his enthusiasm takes hold, one hand unintentionally forms a fist.

"Put that way, Constable, the Dry Squad might be just your cup of tea."

"That's what Sergeant Bigsby said when I handed him my application and curriculum vitae. He said, 'With your level of experience and your physical size, you're just the sort of man we're looking for!'"

DS Hook rises to his feet and the two men shake hands. "Well, Constable Quam, I wish you the best of luck."

"Thank you, sir. And the same to you."

Just as Quam turns to leave, an involuntary question blurts from Hook's mouth: "Mr Quam, if I may ask, why didn't you serve?"

"What?"

"In the war. Why didn't you serve?"

"Oh. That. Well you see, when I reached minimum age I was at bible school."

"Pardon me, Mr Quam? *Bible school*?"

"Yes, sir. Calvin Bible College in Calgary. It was suggested that I defer until my ordination in '18. They were running out of chaplains on the front line, and I might be more useful comforting the men than firing a rifle. The brass didn't expect that, by November, the war would be over."

"Nobody did, Mr Quam. We thought it would go on forever."

LAWSUIT TO EXPOSE KLAN SECRETS
Questions over Death of Grand Goblin
Ed McCurdy
Staff Writer
*The Evening Star*

Lo, the Goblin is slain
Never to gobble again
Evils accrued
A maiden has sued
His Gremlins have much to explain.

Mr Luther Forrest's apparent suicide, said to be due to a seduction writ claiming enormous damages, has focused unwelcome attention on Klaliff Walker, two American "Cyclops" and others currently living in Glen Brae mansion, notably Miss Daisy Tyler, the newly appointed Chairman of the People's Prohibition Association, whose former associate was one D.C. Stephenson, Imperial Wizard of the KKK in Indiana.

A prohibitionist and "defender of Protestant womanhood," Mr Stephenson was convicted of raping and murdering one Madge Oberholtzer. Put delicately, bite wounds were an aggravating factor.

Sentenced to life imprisonment and refused clemency by Governor Jackson, Stephenson retaliated with a list of officials on the Klan payroll that included the governor himself. A flurry of resignations and criminal charges followed, and membership lists plummeted in a state that was once a Klan stronghold.

As it turns out, the remaining leadership at the Imperial Palace have proven remarkably coy about explaining themselves. Two Cyclops, Jessup Olson and Gainer Flood, have yet to respond and seem to have gone to ground. Likewise the Imperial Klaliff, who goes by the name Dr Ambrose Walker but has been identified by a researcher as one Albion Early, who is not a doctor but a part-time veterinarian from Ohio suspected of supplying illegal drugs to two-legged animals.

According to a reliable source with police connections, all three officials have since disappeared without a trace, leaving an empty safe behind.

Knowledgeable observers suspect that these men arrived in our city as virtual outlaws, fleeing the implosion of the KKK in Indiana amid a flurry of lawsuits and criminal charges; that they resettled in Canada one step ahead of American policemen and summons servers; and that they chose Vancouver, which offered a bumper crop of allies through the Woman's Christian Temperance Union, the People's Prohibition Association, the Asiatic Exclusion League and service clubs.

It seems that in Vancouver today there is a sucker born not every minute but every thirty seconds.

A number of local dignitaries at the Klan meeting in question are understandably reluctant to acquire a public association with what may well be a group of American swindlers on the lam.

No one is suggesting, nor should we, that any of the men subject to Jane Doe's lawsuit are guilty of a crime—it was not their concern whether a woman was about to be raped upstairs.

Yet observers have to wonder at the number of parties with an interest in seeing Luther Forrest dance at the end of a rope.

# CHAPTER 30

CONSTABLE QUAM'S FIRST night in his new position has proved a revelation, though not necessarily a pleasant one.

Complicated as his time with DS Hook seemed, with the Dry Squad life has become even more so, albeit in a different way.

Quam was brought up to view complication as the business of "experts"—parsing this and that, examining things in little pieces. It was not a part of his upbringing. As his father would say: "Son, you need to know the time, not how to fix a watch."

Father would be proud of his acceptance into an elite unit. During his morning of instruction and grounding he was told that he had been selected for his "even disposition," together with a willingness to disregard "the unpleasantness attached to the work." He also learned that the unit has a high turnover rate; that many officers transfer out within weeks, men who find the "unpleasantness" too much and night work a strain.

Quam feels he is up to the challenge. Frontline police work is not for men who get squeamish at the sight of blood. Nor is it the end of the world for police to set aside regulations that, followed to the letter, would allow criminals to sneer at the law and murderers to run scot-free.

Thanks to recent legislation, the Dry Squad has freed its officers to deal with suspects as they see fit.

The team he has been assigned to is one of the most seasoned on all fronts. Sergeant Rocco has on more than one occasion shot a fleeing suspect in both thighs at fifty feet. Constable Simpson, an ex-carpenter, can spot a trap door or a false wall easily and swings an axe like a faller. Constable McNamara's sawed-off shotgun (also called a *riot gun*, depending on the circumstances) speaks for itself: last year it blew off the hand of a Maltese seaman who gestured with a stiletto in a threatening way. The wharves have had less trouble with foreign sailors since then.

Quam recognizes his colleagues as tougher, more experienced officers from whom he has much to learn.

For one thing, he would like to know how his fellow plainclothes officers manage to dress so well on a clothing allowance that provided him with one serge suit from Woodward's whose jacket pulls at his armpits, plus a shirt that makes him sweat, and two collars. Yet here stands Sergeant Rocco in three-piece hunting tweeds and a paisley tie. Combined with his shaved head, two signet rings on the left hand and two sets of visibly callused knuckles, the outfit befits a hunter of more urban creatures.

Similarly, Quam admires Constable Simpson for his expensive hobnail boots, custom-fitted with iron toe pieces that can smash a door—or a tibia.

Quam's first raid was a classic of its kind, carried out with military precision and the brutality of invading Goths.

The target was a small chicken farm at the end of Prior Street, with a barn and a modest but cozy dwelling with latticework on the verandah and a freshly whitewashed front walk. The squad had received a tip from an anonymous source (a rival probably) to the effect that a local farm was operating a covert delivery business by telephone using the code "Two dozen eggs and a redbreast chicken." From here, gathering evidence was a simple process of tracing the telephone and making the call.

Having gathered on the verandah, at a signal from Rocco, McNamara shot out the living room window (known as a *wake-up call*) while Simpson demolished the front door with an axe. Quam stood by with a sledgehammer, ready to follow the other three into the house and smash the furniture to bits.

In the front hall, after McNamara fired another blast into the ceiling, the homeowner appeared at the top of the staircase, a look of weary fatalism on his face as he watched Simpson's axe splinter the walls in a search for disguised doors. Quam, meanwhile, undertook a search for concealed compartments that made shards of the fireplace and kindling of the mantle.

Upstairs, above the crash of smashing wood, Quam could faintly hear the terrified wails of children.

Having experienced a close-up view of McNamara's shotgun, the farmer (whose name was Culbert) reluctantly showed them to a hidden door at the back of a closet; it led to a cavernous, windowless addition behind the kitchen containing all the equipment necessary for the manufacture of whisky, including a fifty-gallon mash barrel, a copper wash boiler, a copper dome, a copper gooseneck and coiled tubing.

Simpson set to work with his axe, punching holes in the fifty-gallon barrel so that the cellar would be flooded, while Quam made use of his sledgehammer to reduce the distilling equipment to lumps of copper.

Always with a nose for a stash, Rocco suspected that there was more to be found, and after a period of persuasion, Mr Culbert led them to the chicken barn behind the house, to a room that could only be reached by ladder (the body heat from below made it a good location for aging liquor). The barrels stacked against the wall were quickly dealt with by Simpson, producing torrents of amber liquid and eliciting an outraged chorus of squawks and shrieks from below.

Destroying property is strenuous work. By the time Culbert was safely locked in a cell (somewhat the worse for wear), it was good thinking on McNamara's part to have put by several bottles of Red Chicken as a pick-me-up.

Constable Quam quickly became used to routine procedure: break down the door, smash the windows, terrorize everyone in the house, destroy everything breakable and throw the man of the house in gaol.

One target was a blind pig whose owner had failed to maintain good relations with competitors and the VPD, and whom Quam rather admired for his ingenuity—a spot in an alleyway where one could throw an amount of money into a cellar well and in moments a hand would appear with a bottle. It was one of the cleanest arrests Quam had ever seen—when the hand appeared, Simpson clapped a cuff on it.

It was common knowledge in the force that the owner had got himself in the bad graces of Joe Celona, whose administration oversees trade in illegal liquor. From the first day, Rocco made it clear that Celona himself was not a target the Dry Squad should pursue, the stated reason being his value as an informer on smaller bootleggers. The arrest statistics made the compromise worthwhile—why nail one lawbreaker when you can raid dozens?

As well, it does not escape Quam's notice that, in enforcing the liquor laws, his team rarely ventures beyond Union Street, Hogan's Alley, Hawks Street and the Fairview shacks, with one foray into Little Italy to destroy the homemade wine operation of a family from Naples, after a call to Rocco from a helpful neighbour.

What does trouble Quam from time to time is the growing suspicion that, in some instances, raids are taking place for purposes other than upholding the liquor laws. This came to mind with regard to the comely war widow with two children who conducted an "open house" on Dunlevy, and seemed to feel, to judge by her language, that she had been singled out by Simpson because of a previous personal relation that proved unsatisfactory.

When Constable Quam entered the Dry Squad and was told about "unpleasantness attached to the work," the picture that came to mind was of body fluids, broken bones and bloody noses, not moral confusion.

From time to time he feels the urge to talk to a knowledgeable outsider, to ask, Is this the normal thing? He knows instinctively that it would be unwise to voice such thoughts to Rocco, Simpson and McNamara, who go about their work as cheerfully as your neighbourhood butcher.

And, of course, police duties have a positive side. For one thing, members of the Dry Squad enjoy an ample supply of free product and are spared the overpriced, diluted hooch available from the LCB stores.

On the other hand, something about the work keeps him awake at night. And he needs his sleep.

He once brought up this complicated matter for discussion with DS Hook, who seems to enjoy thinking so much. Hook's only response was that he found the constable's observations "interesting."

THE FINE POINTS OF LIQUOR ENFORCEMENT
Selectivity Is Key
Ed McCurdy
Staff Writer
*The Evening Star*

While the Liquor Licensing Act is
Enforced with clubs and axes
Drys are appeased
The brewers are pleased
And the Liberals hoover the taxes.

"No one expects you to live on a policeman's salary."

This may sound like a joke of the same ilk as, "If you want to know the time, ask a policeman." But both aphorisms carry the weight of hard-earned experience, whether applied to a drunk waking up in gaol without his watch or a constable supporting a family on $2,250 per year.

According to a member of the force who must remain nameless, to have a viable career in policing one must take, shall we say, a nuanced view of law enforcement procedure and to whom it should apply, and be willing to follow custom in accepting small rewards from the public for a job well done.

Our mayor himself has set the tone, having been elected while a fugitive from charges of embezzlement in Chicago. Meanwhile, on what is supposedly the other side of town, Joe Celona, the mayor's friend and fellow horse-racing enthusiast, presides over two of the most popular hotels in the city, the Maple and the Balmoral, where entire floors of rooms remain fully booked for months on end, even during the off-season.

To establish a close relationship with the business community, aldermen with stellar reputations eagerly join the mayor in accepting invitations to the Belmont Cabaret or on a yacht cruise, with Mr Celona furnishing "live entertainment."

Nor, as an example to youth, should one gainsay the entrepreneurial spirit of "Blondie" Wallace, a Celona associate who has managed, on a boxing teacher's salary, to acquire a fleet of moving and storage trucks for, one has to presume, purposes other than moving and storage.

For their part, committed as they are to the maintenance of public order, members of the Dry Squad eschew Point Grey and the West End, whose residents content themselves with an orderly glass of sherry in the privacy of their living rooms.

For effective enforcement (and acceptable arrest statistics), better to concentrate on the kitchen bars and Greek grocery stores in the East End, where crimes result more from need than greed.

It is an unspoken edict that the frontline soldier in the provincial "war against bootlegging" must combine selectivity with deterrence. Selectivity—because in the case of the well-heeled, the cause of justice is so easily thwarted by their devilishly clever lawyers. Deterrence—because prosecution is more efficient when the suspect can't afford a lawyer to press a lawsuit.

For example, in one case, after ransacking a house on Union Street and turning the furniture into toothpicks, officers found a single bottle of whisky in a room large enough to hold several cases. Officers were not pleased by the smug look of innocence on the offender's face.

The offender became less smug when he woke up lying in a ditch outside Haney with two black eyes and a fractured arm (shortly after that, he moved to Calgary without filing a complaint).

In the same vein, a remarkable number of small-time bootleggers seem to have had the audacity to "violently resist arrest" and arrive at the station with bruises and broken ribs, unexplained incontinence and difficulty swallowing.

Asked about this element of violence in enforcement, a spokesman for the Attorney General's office replied: "A critical disease calls for strong medicine. British Columbians jolly well understand that."

For the men on the front lines of the war against bootlegging, it appears that law enforcement officers have found that there is more than one way to skin a cat.

# CHAPTER 31

MCCURDY AWAKENS TO the sound of a key in the door—obviously it's not Miss Wickstram picking the lock again.

He settles under the covers, thinking that it is someone trying to enter the wrong room, soon to realize their error.

But no. It isn't.

He sits upright in bed just as a short man in an expensive tweed suit marches in, grabs the reporter's pajama shirt (tearing it nearly in two), flings him onto the carpet, inserts one knee in the small of his back precisely at kidney level and presses the barrel of a pistol against the back of his head.

"Sir, you are under arrest. You are suspected of the importation and sale of illegal liquor."

"Are you out of your mind? In a *hotel room*?"

"Shut up."

The knee digs hard into his right kidney. Another boot with a hobnailed sole is positioned on top of his head, jamming his face into the carpet and producing a continuous whistling in his ear.

He understands now. He has made an enemy of the Dry Squad. As with the piece on the royal visit, his latest column has upset certain people, and this time there is no armed American to intervene.

"Officer, just out of curiosity, where is your evidence?" He asks this through the side of his mouth, knowing the question to be a silly one; indeed, it draws a jolly laugh from the other three men in the room, and another rap in the head with the pistol.

"Never mind, officers, I know where the evidence is. It's waiting for me at the station."

"Shut up." The knee probes further into the kidney, just short of causing damage.

Through the whistling in his ear, McCurdy hears boots clomping about, along with the sound of ripping fabric, of drawers being heaved open and their contents dumped onto the floor. They seem in no particular hurry; in fact, as they work they discuss sports scores.

"Gentlemen, can we talk? I'll confess to anything you like—"

The man above him snickers and the knee bears down. "It's not that easy, mac." Then he turns to his fellows: "Mr McCurdy wants to confess."

Again the other visitors join in the merriment. Everyone is laughing except for the man on the floor.

AN HOUR LATER he is seated on a stool, still in his ragged pajamas, with his head between his legs, trying to catch his breath, staring down at the former contents of his stomach.

He lifts his head—gingerly, because the whistling hasn't gone away, and one never knows about brain bleeding when one has been knocked out cold.

Stealthily gazing back and forth, he takes in a stone block wall, a barred window, a metal cot and a bucket, everything painted the colour of pus. At the end of the room he can make out a set of floor-to-ceiling bars with an oblong opening, waist high and big enough to admit a shallow bowl.

He straightens up a bit. As suspected, he is in a holding cell, in the basement of the station on Powell Street—a floor known for its soundproofing.

The officer in tweeds, the one with hard knuckles and sharp knees, looms over him. Nearby, a younger officer, a big fellow in a cheap suit, sits on the metal bunk with a sheet of paper and a pen in his lap, watching with small watery eyes.

The better-dressed officer smokes a leisurely cigarette and regards McCurdy with the dispassionate eye of a craftsman surveying work to be done.

"There. Did you see that, Constable Quam? A closed fist just between the ribs and just below the rib cage. With minimum effort, you get maximum effect.

"Remember," he continues, sounding like a technical instructor, "it's all about bruising. You don't want bruising. You want the suspect to walk into court without a mark on him."

He slaps his own stomach gently. "The softer areas don't bruise easily, even if the innards are turned to porridge. But the face and head, they bruise more easily because there's more blood vessels. For that, there's a trick you can use—hand me that telephone book, would you?"

Constable Quam produces a Vancouver directory and hands it over.

The officer delicately removes the reporter's glasses and hands them to Quam, who places them in his lap with the pen and paper. Then, placing the closed telephone book against the side of the reporter's face, he continues the tutorial:

"You see, Constable, the key is to distribute the force of impact over a wider area, the way a boxing glove does." And with his cigarette still dangling from his lips, he forms a fist and swings.

McCurdy flies off the stool, which overturns on top of him, and remains on the floor, semiconscious. The whistling in his ears has become a siren. The cold cement against his cheek eases the throbbing like an ice pack, but it is short-term relief, because he knows this will continue until he signs the confession form, which means signing up for a year's hard labour.

McCurdy doesn't like pain. If Mr Tweed Suit keeps this up, he knows he will fold like an omelet.

Dearest Gracie,

I do so look forward to your letters!

It is terribly sad that I have not been able to go to Victoria, but having one day off per week, if then one factors in five hours each way on the ferry, plus road travel, it would take the entire holiday just to get there and back, with scarcely time to visit at all!

You have been so helpful to my American friend, who is investigating the Ku Klux Klan for an organization in Indiana. Honestly, they are the most dreadful people!

(I had an altercation I will tell you all about when I see you, but which is far too embarrassing to write about, other than in French.)

As you probably know, the KKK have made quite a splash here since their arrival and are viewed as quite respectable, having secured alliances with the Asiatic Exclusion League, the Citizens' League and the People's Prohibition Association. They are on friendly terms with the Masons and Odd Fellows as well. It is said that they are even planning to sponsor a baseball team!

Even so, they make a peculiar sight marching down Granville, with their burning cross and their pointed hats and their *Keep Canada White* banner. It is hard to imagine that an upright citizen would wear such a costume—other than as a disguise, for their ranks are said to include an aldermen and even an MLA.

My friend says that they are up to no good and wishes to commend you for your service to America as well as to the province. I have no idea what it is all about really, but it sounds terribly important and, if nothing else, you and I will have something to reminisce about when we do see each other—which I hope will be soon!

Don't worry about the files, darling. The fact that that one page involved Taggart was of great interest to a regular client; and your experience with Mr Crombie and his new, shall we say, associate, is infinitely more enlightening than whatever else is in that drawer.

Both my friend and my client are dying to know more about this relationship. If you or Gwendolyn hear any more tidings about this mystery woman, do tell!

Your loving friend,
Millie

BOOTLEGGING "CRUSADE" ANNOUNCED
"Crime Wave Must End," Stalker Declares
Max Trotter
Staff Writer
*The Vancouver World*

In his first legislative address since his appointment, Attorney General Boris Stalker declared a "Crusade Against Bootlegging."

In his speech, the Attorney General deplored organized criminals such as Italian immigrant Joe Celona and the Jewish Reifel family but asserted that an even more deadly consequence of this wave of alcohol crime is the corrupting influence of bootlegging on the body politic—not only in attracting foreign criminals to our province, but also in making criminals of ordinary citizens.

"No community in the province, no matter how small, is without a bootlegger who was once a law-abiding taxpayer but who has crossed the line into criminality—and in so doing, is making criminals of his neighbours."

Mr Stalker was not available for questions, owing to legislative duties. In his place, Mr Bertram Bliss, spokesman for the Attorney General's office, met with reporters on the steps of the Legislature for a spirited exchange.

Asked if the Crusade Against Bootlegging is not in fact a campaign to stuff government coffers with liquor profits and taxes, he replied: "I say, old chap, better to stuff the people's coffers than to line the pockets of criminals." Bliss added that the measure has the firm endorsement of the People's Prohibition Association. "If they support the crusade, I should jolly well think it behooves others to follow suit."

On whether the use of the term *crusade* might be seen as an appropriation of a Christian reference to describe what is really a taxation issue, Mr Bliss replied: "Perhaps you had better ask the Woman's Christian Temperance Union, who are behind the Attorney General one hundred per cent."

# CHAPTER 32

ON THE SCREEN below, three men in sombre suits and doffed hats pose in front of a stone wall, inspecting a *fallbeil*—a compact yet massive steel contraption made of iron, with a bench at one end, a spout and bucket at the other end, a blade about ten feet above and sawdust on the floor below.

The title card reads: "In Germany, a trader in contraband meat known as 'the Butcher of Hanover' was beheaded for murdering and dismembering twenty-six young men..."

"Would you look at that," Hook says. "You have to appreciate German engineering."

"Built to last," McCurdy agrees. "It'll be chopping off heads for years to come."

In preparation for the meeting, this time it is McCurdy who has brought a mickey of Wiser's Deluxe, for he is in an unusually generous frame of mind.

"Be assured that I didn't buy it from the LCB store."

The reporter uncorks the bottle and hands it to DS Hook, who takes an appreciative sip. "A fine beverage," he replies. "Its origin is not my business."

"My point is that I am most grateful to you, Calvin. I tell you, Sergeant Rocco nearly crippled me."

"Well at least you *look* quite healthy."

This is true. As McCurdy has learned, with a Dry Squad interrogation all damage is internal. The ringing in his ears has finally begun to subside, but the bruises to his kidneys and bones will take longer.

"They're a highly motivated team," Hook adds, "though with their training, I'm not sure arming them was a good idea."

This is also true, as McCurdy knows first-hand. Having a pistol pointed at one's head isn't as bad as being shot at, but it's no fun.

"In any case don't thank me, Ed, thank Constable Quam. He alerted me to the situation, which even he found a bit much. I managed to persuade Rocco that your criticism of the force is part of your cover—that you're an undercover agent and must be protected at all costs. Rocco sends his apologies, though he cautions against publishing more unfair articles."

"Here's to Constable Quam," McCurdy says. "I shall thank him in person."

"Actually, the strategy was my wife's idea. Jeanie put it to me this way: 'Convince them he's important, that if they don't let him go they've bit off their own goolies.'"

"Your wife has a shrewd mind. I'm not sure I envy you in that respect."

Hook shrugs and sighs as if to say, *What can you do? The die is cast.*

McCurdy raises the near-empty bottle: "A toast to all the lovely ladies."

"I've been meaning to ask you about the less-than-lovely lady I saw in the chief's office, hobnobbing with the mayor..."

On the screen, a "tri-state tornado" has devastated the American Midwest; a new invention called Radiovision has enabled the first synchronized transmission of pictures and sound; and a counterfeit artist by the name of Artur Reis has destroyed the Portuguese economy with a pyramid scheme. Following that, a series of short clips appear in which unsmiling dictators, with chestfuls of medals and golden hairbrushes on their shoulders, parade before adoring crowds—Horthy in Hungary, Zog in Albania, de Rivera in Spain, Hirohito in Japan, General Pangalos of Greece...

GULLIVER ILLNESS SPARKS EXECUTIVE COUNCIL SHUFFLE
Deputy Ministers Hold Levers of Power
Cecil Harmsworth
Staff Writer
*The Beacon*

As per previous reports, Attorney General Boris Stalker has moved temporarily into the premier's office, in a major shuffle arising from Premier Gulliver's sudden illness.

Observers in the know have begun to wonder, Is Gulliver fit for duty? Or, as another government official put it, "Does the premier have the physical strength to lead the crusade?"

According to the premier's physician, Dr Seth Kettle, Mr Gulliver incurred a stomach ailment on the train from Ottawa after engaging in tense negotiations over the freight rate. Dr Kettle reached a diagnosis of viral gastroenteritis, likely caught from another passenger. "Trains are mobile incubators, really," he added.

Contacted by this reporter, a spokesman for the CPR had this to say: "Food storage on our passenger trains is always fresh and of the highest standard."

Dr Kettle has prescribed tonics and a period of bed rest. "We will take all precautions," he said. "He is, after all, our premier."

Some observers wonder if Dr Kettle has made the correct diagnosis. Dr Morris Blackwell points out that "symptoms of food poisoning can mask a more serious underlying condition." An anonymous government member noted darkly: "Gordon Cunning complained of stomach pains as well."

With the recent departure of Gen Victor Newson from the Liberal side, the Legislature is teetering on the brink of collapse; with an election all but upon us, many caucus members worry that Mr Gulliver has become a political liability.

As Attorney General and now acting premier, Boris Stalker was unavailable for comment, citing urgent business.

Questioned by this reporter, Gen Victor Newson, the newly independent MLA, assures British Columbians that he has no plans to bring down the government at this time: "It would be unconscionable to afflict taxpayers with the disruption and expense of another election, especially when current anti-bootlegging measures are having some effect. But the battle will not be won by defeating the bootleggers. It will be won when we get rid of the booze."

For the present, Harlan Crombie, a long-time ally of the Attorney General, remains solidly in command of government forces in what some call "the war on bootlegging."

"I would trust Mr Crombie with my own mother," Mr Stalker was heard to say on Thursday. "Believe me, the crusade is in good hands."

Until the premier is well enough to walk into the Legislature to face his critics, Acting Premier Stalker will oversee procedural duties, while Deputy Minister Bertram Bliss will partially assume the duties of the Attorney General. "Mr Bliss will oversee day-to-day details under my supervision," the Attorney General said, over CFYC Radio. "The overall direction of the department will not change."

Mr Bliss, speaking on the same broadcast, agreed: "I shall be speaking with Mr Stalker on an hourly basis. He is still our Attorney General. I am humbled by the responsibility and jolly well determined to do my duty."

Such reassurances are welcome indeed. Nonetheless, observers are troubled that, for the time being at least, an unelected public servant is in charge of the justice system.

"A decidedly untoward tactic," commented Opposition leader Henry Pooley. "Boris Stalker and his henchmen have virtually taken over the running of the province. This whole affair makes a mockery of British democracy."

# CHAPTER 33

THE PURCHASE OF the sofa took weeks to accomplish—not because they disagreed, but because they couldn't make up their minds, either together or apart.

For hours they walked the floors at William Worrall and must have sat on a hundred sofas before choosing a model that looks much like the overstuffed sofas at home, but with practical upholstery that will wear well and resist stains. Once they have a rocking chair and an area rug to cover the fir floor, they will have a proper living room fit for company.

Hook sits down gently, fires an Ogden's and leans forward on their new couch so as not to spill ashes on the fabric. When Jeanie has settled back comfortably, he asks, choosing his words carefully, "Pet, I need to ask you something."

Her eyes remain closed. "If it is what I think it is, no developments as yet."

"That isn't what I want to bring up. Not this time." He knows that he has been acting like an immature worrywart and that worry is contagious. Sometimes it's best just to keep one's mouth shut.

"No, it has to do with other, *intimate* matters." Even to his wife, he can barely say the word out loud.

She gives him the straight-on look that sees right through him. "*Sexual* matters is it you're saying?"

"That would be the word, yes."

"Ducky, you're blushin'!" She reaches over and puts her hand on his upper thigh. "If there is something you want or don't want, you must tell me, do."

"No. No, it's not that, not at all, far from it. This is a case that involves others. It has to do with... hitting."

She takes her hand back with a frown: "Aye, many marriages are like that. Men can be brutes, especially the drinkers."

"That's not what I meant, pet. I meant... the other way around."

"And what would be the other way around?"

"Such as when the woman does the hitting."

"Do you mean whipping and that sort of goings-on?"

He nods. "Something like that, yes."

"It's the public schools—Eton is famous for it." She smiles with one corner of her mouth. "Would you like that, ducky?"

"No! No, pet, I mean... my question is part of an, an investigation."

"Of a disorderly house, you mean?"

"No, it concerns an individual who occupies a certain... position of authority."

She starts to giggle. "You mean while another bloke bends over with his skivvies down?"

He waits for his wife to recover her composure, for this is a serious police matter. "No, pet, not that. I'm talking about the, er, person of interest's *social* position. Actually, it's a *government* position."

"Goodness. Is it the toff who speaks for the premier? I'll bet *he* likes a good caning. I've heard toffs are flogged so often in public schools that some of them come to like it when they grow up. In London there are clubs where rugby men get their arses whipped by large, buxom women. They say the chancellor of the exchequer is a member of one."

"You must be joking!"

"That's what I hear tell. And I shouldn't be surprised if that sort of thing goes on in Victoria, it's so Jolly Olde England and all that."

"In any case, the female in question is neither large nor buxom."

"I doubt that is a necessary requirement. Mind, I've not seen such goings-on myself."

"How do you suppose such a relation is arrived at? How does a fellow persuade a lady to come to... an agreement as to the, er, details of the punishment? Or is it the lady who takes the initiative?"

Jeanie thinks about this a moment.

"I should think she draws him in. Some of the women at the greengrocer talk about things of that sort—tricks to keep their husband's interest. Mrs Walsh says garters are the ticket. Garters are the only present her husband ever gives her that's not a kitchen appliance. And there are others what say they must get themselves all dolled up with lipstick and perfume."

"So it's a matter of costume and makeup?"

"Of course, ducky. Why else spend good money on such things?"

Hook remembers McCurdy's description of the mousy woman in the chief's office, seemingly with the ability to transform herself from worm to butterfly at will. To judge by Max Factor advertisements, beauty is big business now. Thanks to modern science, it is possible, given sufficient skill with brushes and pads, for a woman to look like anyone she wants. It's a sobering thought...

Jeanie is watching him closely, her head tilted to one side and a half-smile on her lips. He kisses her cheek: "I assure you, pet, that you don't feel you have to get all dolled up for me."

"Not you, ducky." She looks down at his trousers. "Not yet, anyway."

# CHAPTER 34

SLOUCHED OVER THE bar in the Lumberman's Club, McCurdy drinks in silence, cocooned in gloom with a grim sense of foreboding, of having made a hash of his life. Where did he go wrong? Which decision put him where he is now? It's the stuff of sleepless nights and multiple whiskys.

Unlike his forebears, he has no supreme being to appeal to or to blame, having determined that there are many gods, who take turns farting about with the world for their own amusement. *So God created man in His own image...*

As a child, he loved limericks. He liked to memorize and recite them. He even won a contest in the *Toronto Telegram* at the age of thirteen—he doesn't remember what he wrote, but it involved a convenient rhyme for a public figure. By that time he had become an aesthete of the genre. Having tired of Edward Lear's repetition of the first and last line, he immersed himself in the work of Algernon Swinburne:

> There was a young man from Dundee
> Who buggered an ape in a tree.
> The results were quite horrid:
> All arse and no forehead,
> Three balls and a purple goatee.

At no time did McCurdy envisage himself approaching forty with these childish rhymes a mainstay of his career and that the lowest of literary forms—limericks and muckraking—would be his bread and butter, much less that they would make him a target of snipers and goons.

Imagine, to die over a limerick!

McCurdy sips his drink, idly watching as a rat glides along the baseboard of the wall opposite as though it were on tiny casters, then stops and looks at him sideways. He has heard that when you get a good look at a rat it means that there are a dozen more nearby, and if it doesn't run for it, you're infested.

Truman, an experienced bartender, has seen patrons in this mood before and serves the usual without speaking. When a man sinks into a brown study, best keep one's distance.

By the time McCurdy emerges from the Lumberman's Club it is supper hour, when citizens have gone home before heading out again for drinks and the movies. As he steps somewhat unsteadily downstairs, Hastings Street is nearly empty of traffic, except for the black McLaughlin ambulance with whitewall tyres now idling by the curb.

As he stops to admire the highly polished machine, the passenger door opens briskly and a cuddlesome nurse in a white uniform climbs out. In her twenties, she has round pink cheeks like a plaster cherub.

Since the war, men have regarded nurses as angels come to earth and McCurdy is no exception. As she moves toward him he feels the urge to put his arms around her, but instead he tips his hat. "How do you do, madam?"

She doesn't smile or reply. Instead, she reaches toward his face with something in her hand as though about to wipe his nose—and before he has time to properly assess the situation, she pushes what might well be a Kotex pad precisely over his mouth and nose. He smells something sweet and immediately falls backward, to be caught in the arms of two strapping orderlies in white, who bundle him into the rear of the vehicle, hop in behind him and shut the door.

The ambulance pulls away, turns right on Main Street and disappears. The scattering of pedestrians who have stopped to watch, now with nothing more to see, continue on their way.

# PART III

*Her heart was broken perhaps, but it was a small inexpensive organ, and in a way she felt things had been simplified.*

—Evelyn Waugh

# CHAPTER 35

TAKING THE FIGHT TO THE ENEMY
Increased Police Powers Bring Results
Cecil Harmsworth
Staff Writer
*The Beacon*

The Bootlegging Crusade marches forward.

With hands untied by government red tape, officers are finally able do their job effectively and criminals need not be treated with kid gloves. Enforcement may now be unexpected, and while the interrogations may be tough, the sheer volume of guilty pleas speaks to their success.

"The holding cells are bursting," observed Deputy Warden Chas Older, "and there will be hundreds more to come. If this continues, there will surely be a need for more facilities."

Less enthusiastic is Joe Naylor of the so-called One Big Union: "It puts working men in gaol and is making British Columbia a province of snitches."

However, whether for or against, this reporter could find no one who would deny the program's effectiveness.

Thanks to tougher measures against profiteers of illegal alcohol, officers on the front lines have clipped the wings of bootleggers, who poison their customers and deprive the province of tax dollars that could ease the plight of veterans, victims of crime and the poor.

In outlying areas, travelling informants, acting as salesmen, loggers and teachers, have broken the code of silence that is all too common in small communities.

As arrests reveal the extent of the problem, there is evidence that public opinion has begun to turn against liquor criminals. In Yale, known bootleggers were visited by fellow citizens in masks and white robes who set fire to outbuildings containing vats and other illegal equipment. In Fernie, men in similar costume arrived at the home of a local bootlegger in the dead of night with torches and threatened him with hanging for the harm he had vested on their community.

A statement from Mrs Albert McDuff of the People's Prohibition Association reads, "Thanks to the acting premier, British Columbians have made remarkable progress in the fight against alcohol abuse. If only Boris Stalker had been in power in 1917, our province would now be booze-free."

Independent MLA Victor Newson agrees: "We find ourselves in this situation thanks to timid, hypocritical concessions to booze profiteers on the part of the previous Attorney General. Protesters against Stalker's program, rather than interfering with traffic, might better lay their complaints at Gordon Cunning's grave."

HE AWAKENS IN a bed not his own. He smells something sweetish—chloroform?

*So that's what it was. And she was so pretty.*

Lazily he opens his eyes. The ceiling and walls have been painted institutional white. (With the help of a few hundred cigarettes, they will gain the same pus-like patina as the holding cells at the station on Cordova Street.)

*What new hell is this?*

He turns his head gently this way and that. Oddly the room is not square nor oblong but triangular. To his upper left, a square window is situated too high to reach and is covered with heavy metal mesh. *Better safe than sorry...*

He reopens his eyes and gently raises his head from the pillow, which produces a wobbly feeling and a sensation of bubbles popping in the brain.

*Chloroform, for certain.*

He remembers the handsome McLaughlin ambulance and the face of the apple-cheeked nurse. *So pretty...*

He lifts his arm and sees that he has been dressed in institutional pajamas, striped cotton, not unlike mattress ticking. He rises to his elbows and looks down at his feet: surprisingly, he is still wearing his shoes and socks. Only in a hospital do men wear street shoes and pajamas.

Has he had an accident? Is he in a recovery room at St Paul's Hospital? If not, then he has been... shanghaied? Certainly not kidnapped; kidnappers are freelance, they don't run hospitals.

Someone wants him to disappear but hasn't the stomach for killing (there was enough of that in the war) or, worse, they want information and the killing will come later.

A former acquaintance, a communist by the name of Sparrow, told him that the interrogator's first order of business is to convince the prisoner that the situation is his own doing. Do not believe them, but do not show it.

Other pointers from Sparrow come to mind: Do not volunteer information. Always appear co-operative. Feign some sort of brain damage...

"What in holy hell are you doing here?"

Was that a voice in his head? *No.* There is someone else present.

He rolls over and is startled to see what looks to be his reflection across the room. Is the wall a mirror? He can't tell without his glasses—*where are my glasses?*

In a panic he lurches left, away from the wall—and to his immense relief there they are, neatly folded, on a white metal bed table that seems to be bolted to the floor.

*What sort of hospital bolts things to the floor?*

Winding the temples around his ears, across the room he sees an identical bed containing a gentleman in identical pajamas, lying on his right side propped up on one elbow, looking back. The man has a cauliflower ear, so it can't be a mirror.

"I repeat, what the feck are you doing here?"

"Somebody chloroformed me on Hastings Street and put me in an ambulance. Other than that, I haven't the faintest idea. Do *you* know what I'm doing here?"

"You're that bloody reporter, are you not? The one who writes defamatory columns with idiotic rhymes."

"I am that man, it is true."

Looking closely at his roommate, McCurdy recognizes the slightly battered features of Clyde Taggart. He vaguely remembers unkind remarks characterizing Taggart as a human vacuum cleaner sucking up money for Cunning, or something of that sort.

"You're the snake who wrote that libel about Liberal bagmen. Impertinent bastard. You deserve to be horsewhipped."

McCurdy vaguely remembers the column, something about suspect donations funnelled through Taggart's "family business"—always in quotation marks, because with his political activities it would come as a surprise if Taggart entered his office at the Firestone company more than once a year, let alone operated the city's main supplier of tyres. He remembers that the accompanying doggerel contained the rhymes *tyre* and *liar*, *whither* and *slither*.

"Ah. I do beg your pardon. Please be assured that there was no animus behind it. I had a column to fill. The truth of the matter is that I had two hours before deadline and it was the only idea that came to me at the time. Surely, Mr Taggart, you've encountered such a situation in your line of work."

Taggart scratches the stubble on his chin, eyes narrowed, evaluating the disparager sitting across from him. McCurdy looks back with complete indifference. Taggart's face, handsome in a workmanlike way, has taken a punch now and then. His hands, unnecessarily large, are farmer's hands, the hands of a man who has risen above his class, but not by much.

After what seems like a half-hour, Taggart nods briskly: "Under present circumstances, I accept your explanation. I suggest we set the matter aside."

"And what *are* the circumstances, Mr Taggart? If I may fire back your first question, what are *you* doing here?"

Taggart heaves a sigh. "It's a bit embarrassing, but I lost my temper with the Attorney General. I threatened to divulge sensitive information, and my outburst was not appreciated. But it stuck in my craw to be thrown away like a bald tyre."

"And you are in the tyre business, after all."

"What are you implying?"

"Oh, nothing. What sort of sensitive information do you have to divulge?" As he asks the question, McCurdy feels for a nonexistent notebook. "What sort are we talking about?"

Taggart laughs ruefully. "Listen McCurdy, a liquor-licencing system is mother's milk to machine politics—plumbing, really. Think of it as an irrigation system for making the garden grow."

"And the product could be anything from cognac to anti-freeze."

"That has been an issue, I agree. As chairman of the LCB, my task was to minimize the public embarrassment. But all that's behind us now."

"Behind us, perhaps—but do you have any idea where we *are*?"

"Oh, yes. We're in Woodlands, formerly the Provincial Lunatic Asylum. With so many crazies after the war, the place is under constant renovation. We're in the isolation annex for men. If you could look through that window up there, you would see the exercise yard at BC Pen. Our building is called Maple Cottage. I know the facility well—served on the building committee for four years."

"At a staggering per diem, if memory serves."

"You newspaper people are always carping."

"Only when there's something to carp about."

"Last year, you practically crucified Gordon Cunning over a dead nanny and a Chinese houseboy. It almost cost him the election."

"In which he resorted to some remarkably dirty tricks. His opponent's life is in ruins, I understand."

"In a close election, sometimes a personal attack is the only tactic left. I knew Gordon for years. We played sports together. We were drinking mates."

"He was fond of martinis, I understand."

"He was. I could never understand it—a puddle of gin as far as I can tell. But he was a good egg, and my best mate. Stalker is in another league entirely. He has no friends, only henchmen, willing to dirty their fingers on his behalf."

"You mean he wants to be premier."

"Oh, that's the least of it."

"Then what's the rest?"

"Let's call it perpetual incumbency. That's how they think, McCurdy. No politician wants to envisage leaving office—Stalker least of all."

"Are you suggesting he's a midget Mussolini?"

"McCurdy, take it from me, politicians are imitators to the core. No man runs for office who has an original thought in his brain. In politics, the question isn't What do I believe? but Who shall I imitate? Who do you think Stalker is imitating when he calls an emergency, pushes the need for leadership and makes his adversaries disappear? If it walks like a duck and quacks like a duck..."

"Mr Taggart, you paint a gloomy picture."

Taggart takes a seated position on the edge of his cot, rubbing his head with one hand as though to calm himself down. "And it gets gloomier. Here we are in the booby hatch—and with worse to come."

"I might have known there's worse. Fine, spit it out."

"Woodlands is known for its advanced treatments: fever therapy, insulin shock, radium. Dr Freeman's speciality is lobotomies. One or two a week, I'm told, plus a few for violent offenders in the BC Pen next door."

"To stay in practice, I suppose."

"Apparently it calms them right down. Real bruisers become meek as mice. By the way, you might as well call me—"

Taggart abruptly puts one palm behind his good ear and puts a forefinger to his lips. McCurdy can hear footsteps outside. They come to a stop outside the door, followed by the jingle of keys.

Moving quickly, Taggart lies back under the sheets. "I'm going to pretend to be asleep now. Don't talk to me." And closes his eyes.

Seeing no reason not to keep his own eyes open, McCurdy watches as the door opens and in steps a prematurely bald man of about thirty with a ragged moustache he trims with his teeth, in a none-too-clean white shirt with sleeve garters, a greasy tie and an enormous white apron of the type used by lab workers and butchers. He is pushing a metal cart containing a line of syringes on a miniature rack, as well as bottles of pills, a carafe of water and a metal cup. The wheels squeak like an approaching mouse.

McCurdy forcibly reminds himself to appear co-operative and grateful and stupid.

The attendant consults a clipboard. "Let me see—Mr McCurdy, isn't it? Good to see you're awake, Ed."

McCurdy looks up at him, deliberately goggle-eyed. "Are you the doctor? Am I awake?"

The attendant laughs with practised good humour. "You are indeed awake, sir. Can you remember what happened to you?"

"I've been asleep. I think I must have passed out."

A nod of encouragement: "Well done. Sorry to say, but you hit your head when you fell. This is why you were sent to us, for observation, don't you see. By the way, do you know where you are?"

McCurdy resists saying something snide about what *caused* him to pass out. (*Appear co-operative.*) Instead, he scratches his head like Stan Laurel in *Mud and Sand*: "Let me think... Yes. Gee, I think I hit my head. So that means I must be in the hospital!"

The attendant smiles as though genuinely pleased. "Right again, Ed. I see that it's all coming back now. What an encouraging sign. Probably all you need now is a good long rest. We all need a good rest now and then..."

The attendant plucks a filled syringe from the wagon and bends down to whisper in McCurdy's ear in an entirely different tone of voice, giving the patient a full blast of his appalling breath: "You and I know the reason you're here, Ed. So let me give you a piece of advice: don't *ever* think you can sneak out of Woodlands. I'll be just downstairs—or my assistant will. And you do not want to meet my assistant."

McCurdy has nothing clever to say in reply. Having abandoned the pretence of care, however momentarily, the attendant has made the situation seem all too real.

"But no need to bother our heads with such matters," the attendant says. "Believe me, Ed, we will to do everything possible to help you get better."

"Thank you, sir. I appreciate your help."

"That's the spirit!" He pats the patient on the chest, then gently rolls up McCurdy's pajama sleeve, checks the needle for air bubbles and prepares to inject. "You might feel a bit of a pinch."

"What are you giving me, Doctor?"

The attendant swabs his arm with alcohol. "Just a relaxant to help you rest. Nighty-night, Ed."

Before dropping off, McCurdy notes that the attendant seems to be sweating chicken fat. Our man is definitely *on* something, which might be of use...

HE AWAKENS FEELING jittery, sweating copiously. He just had a terrible dream, like a Boris Karloff photoplay.

He opens his eyes, looks about and is no longer sure that it was a dream.

He turns his head to the left: excellent, there are his glasses, folded and placed on the table like an old friend waiting patiently, arms crossed. He winds the temples around his ears, and through the lenses contemplates the now-familiar figure of Clyde Taggart seated across the room, on the edge of his cot, watching him.

"About time you woke up, McCurdy. Thought you might be dead."

"*Dead?* Why would I be dead?"

"They're not too particular about dosages here. Sometimes they overdo it."

"If you don't mind me asking, how do you know that?"

"I was on the board, remember? I hear all the scuttlebutt. I have colleagues still serving, holding their noses for the per diem."

"You must have a high tolerance for smell."

"Oh wonderful, an idealist. In any case, the place gave me the creeps then and it still does."

Thinking of his own profession, McCurdy decides not to press the integrity issue.

"In any case, good morning, Mr Taggart."

"Actually, it's past midnight, to go by the light outside."

McCurdy looks up at the window—definitely too far up to reach without a ladder—and yes, the world beyond the grate is pitch dark.

"He gave me a shot of something. What time was that?"

"I'd say late afternoon."

"Did he give you a needle as well?"

"No. I pretended to be unconscious, remember? When you're already out cold, that's when they worry about overdose—*obvious* overdose. So they lift your head and place a pill on your tongue. I move it to one cheek and spit it out later."

"I'm not sure I wouldn't rather be asleep."

"That's what they'd prefer too. They like to keep patients isolated from time and place so nothing riles them up. No tomorrow, no yesterday: a permanent neverland. It means fewer staff are required."

"You use the word *patients* but really we're prisoners, aren't we?"

"That's more or less the size of it. Under the circumstances you might as well call me Clyde."

"I notice that Dr Freeman's grooming is less than antiseptic."

"Because that wasn't Dr Freeman, Ed. That's Rollins, a semi-trained attendant, one half-step above a thug."

"And stoned, I notice. I'd say he's hopped up to the scalp."

Taggart's eyes narrow. "How do you know that?"

"His pupils are so dilated you can barely see his forehead."

"He's a dope fiend? Needles sort of thing?"

"Probably not. I'd bet on laudanum—he was happy as a clam and sweating like a Turk. Plus the breath, of course."

"Laudanum is all over the place here. Cheaper than morphine, keeps patients manageable—which, again, saves on staffing costs."

"I suppose they've taken away our clothes."

"And everything else as well, except our shoes, obviously. So that we can walk over to the main hospital—to the treatment rooms, the electric chair, the padded confinement cells, the operating theatre. Oh yes, they're fully equipped."

"Before Rollins came into the picture I seem to remember you mentioning *lobotomy*. That's an alarming word."

"It is indeed. Around these halls they're as common as haircuts."

McCurdy looks at the unreachable window, then at the reinforced door at the end of the room. "I'll say it again: you paint a gloomy picture, Clyde."

"Oh you think so? Wait until you meet Dr Freeman!"

# CHAPTER 36

*McCurdy has been kidnapped. Please meet
me under the Birks clock.—M. Wickstram*

DS HOOK KNOWS nothing about Mildred Wickstram other than
that she is an associate of McCurdy's, a casual acquaintance
who supplies him with particulars and has seen him through a
number of crises he's brought upon himself. He pictures her as a
typical scion of some upperclass school for girls, with buttoned
gloves and a fondness for croquet.

To his surprise, the person waiting underneath the Birks
clock at Georgia and Granville turns out to be a compact figure
in a plaid shirt, denim work pants and a flat tweed cap pulled
down over one eye. As he approaches this person he can descry a
moustache, neatly penciled above the lips. He wonders what the
world is coming to when women go about dressed as golfers and
sailors, and men masquerade as rowing enthusiasts and grouse
hunters. Don't people want to look like what they *do* anymore?

(Like most things, he expects that it has something to do with
the war.)

"How do you do, Officer Hook." She steps forward and shakes
his hand with a surprisingly firm grip. (He resists the urge to
give her a bone-crusher in return, out of spite.) "Please come
with me."

Hook accompanies Miss Wickstram through pedestrian
traffic, turning right on Hastings, without exchanging a sentence.
By the time they cross Carrall, their destination has become clear
and the reason for her workman's getup.

Of course. The Lumberman's Club. These women will be piss-
ing in the men's loo before long.

It's late morning, so only a few tables are occupied by the all-night poker players, who glance blearily at the intruders then go back to their cards, having recognized the uniformed copper as one who is known to ignore the legal status of the place, on duty or off. For DS Hook, this has become the only place in Vancouver where he feels comfortable, other than at home.

"Morning, Officer Hook. An early visit, I see."

Truman is tending bar, looking terrible. His right eye is the same purple as his nose, and he seems to have lost a front tooth so that he has a slight lisp.

"Good to see you, Truman. You look like you've had a rumpus with my colleagues in the Dry Squad."

"Not this time, Calvin. Stopped a fight between two regulars—veterans, good fellas I thought, but they resented the intrusion."

"I've warned you about this before. You didn't bring out the billy club. Just because they were veterans, you made an assumption."

"I admit that's true," replies the bartender, looking abashed; then he turns to Hook's companion, standing behind him facing the door.

"And who might you be, sir?"

She speaks in a guttural alto that is good enough for Truman: "Malcolm Wickstram is my name. My friend Ed McCurdy sends his best wishes."

"Yes sir, of course. Sign the membership, please."

The bartender hands a pencil to the new logger, who provides an unreadable scrawl of a signature.

"Done. What'll it be, gentlemen?"

"Whisky please," Mr Wickstram says, "with a splash of water to release the aroma."

"What aroma are you talking about?"

"I was only joking."

"Nothing for me I'm afraid," Hook says. "I'm on duty."

"Suit yourself." The bartender shrugs. Just as he turns to fill their orders, the door opens to admit another ambiguous figure—tall and lean, walking with the spring of an athlete.

Hook is beginning to feel lightheaded. The evidence before him almost suggests the existence of a third gender.

They engage in a handshake, surprisingly ordinary: "Howdy, Officer, my name is Johnston. Hollis Johnston. I reckon we have something to discuss."

Mildred sits back in her chair, lights a cigarette and watches as Hook and Johnston exchange accreditations. Never having witnessed Holly in her official capacity, it comes as a mild shock to discover a different version. One never knows the whole person, even a lover. Perhaps not even a fraction.

Hook suppresses his unease at the creatures before him. It's not that he didn't know about the existence of such people—confirmed bachelors, spinsters, roommates of long standing; he has no argument with their right to be on this earth, and never has. The difference is that such people were somewhere else, over there and not on public display—thus, by unstated agreement, avoiding the letter of British law.

Since the war, so many things about the nature of human beings have been pried open and exposed, things that were formerly considered best hidden. It provokes one to reconsider the difference between men and women: Is this the thin edge of some sort of wedge? And if so, what is the wedge?

As an officer of the law, Hook makes every effort to put all this out of mind and to listen to Mr Johnston as a fellow officer on a case.

"Sergeant Hook, first you should know that for the Pinkerton Detective Agency, BC is our biggest client in Canada. Fact is, your law enforcement, fine though it may be, lacks manpower and resources. That's where we Pinkerton's folks come in.

"But it's a ticklish situation. As a private contractor we can't be suspected of breaking Canadian law. We have to be pretty darned careful."

Hook gazes wistfully at Miss Wickstram's glass. How he wishes the conversation were happening in an officers' mess, where men can temporarily shed their mental uniforms and be straightforward. But this isn't a mess, and they're not in the army.

"And you are here on what orders?" He asks this in a toned-down version of his Redhat voice.

Abruptly, the Pinkerton's person switches to another role—or rather, another version if him- or herself.

"I am seconded to undertake the transition of Daisy Douglas Tyler back to the USA, where she is wanted for embezzlement and grand larceny in the state of Indiana."

Hook fires up an Ogden's. "Welcome to British Columbia."

"Thank you, suh. We at Pinkerton's have a long history with this great province."

"Forgive my ignorance, sir, but what is going on in Indiana that has anything to do with BC?"

Johnston leans forward—the eager officer, explaining everything. Mildred lights a cigarette, leans back and watches.

"As I mentioned to Miss Wickstram here, Miss Tyler was the force behind Mr D.S. Stephenson's domination of the Ku Klux Klan in Indiana. She seems to have envisaged the Hoosier Klan as a form of shadow government, guiding the legislature of the state of Indiana under the banner of temperance, race, immigration and the flag."

"A powerful combination anywhere, I should think."

"Correct. But there is another factor. Detective Sergeant Hook, in your experience, surely you are aware that certain women have the ability to control gutless men. Daisy had such a hold on Stephenson. But in the end, he was proven to be a degenerate skunk and now he's in gaol. Daisy was about to be deposed, so she emigrated to Canada."

"And has done well for herself."

"Correct. In fact, all indications suggest that Miss Tyler aims to turn BC into Indiana north, and that Harlan Crombie is her Stephenson."

IT OCCURS TO Mildred that this scenario reinforces one of McCurdy's pieces—perhaps the one that inspired someone to try and shoot him. When a hack lays open a sensitive topic at a critical time, one that implicates important people, it is like a dentist approaching a nerve—there will be a response. All of which suggests the possibility that McCurdy is in a ditch somewhere, or at the bottom of Burrard Inlet, wrapped in logging chains.

But that is not the only reason she finds the conversation disturbing.

She doesn't care for Holly's tone of voice—and not because she is impersonating a man. This isn't the voice of the woman with whom she has been sharing her bed. It is the voice of a soldier, an ambitious soldier, a well-lubricated cog in a machine. A soldier who takes orders and hunts people down. Who carries a pistol and is ready to use it without hesitation.

It all reminds her too much of the war. Putting aside the accent and pitch, she sounds like a lieutenant reporting to a captain, every sentence expressing her solidarity with the team and its objective.

At Whitehall, Mildred was under orders to listen in on conversations for verification, in case of a difference of opinion later—for example, over what was said before orders went out that killed a thousand men. All for the purpose of covering the superior officer's behind, of course. One consequence was that the hello girl learned things she would rather not know.

"I wonder, Mr Johnston," she interjects, "if we might return our attention to the original subject of the meeting: Mr McCurdy's disappearance?"

"Miss Wickstram, I wouldn't have brought this up if it wasn't relevant," Holly says—a bit snappishly, Millie thinks.

A long pause follows. Hook lights an Ogden's; Mildred lights something Turkish; Holly checks her pocket watch.

"I agree with Mr Johnston," Hook says, at last. "A reporter has disappeared without explanation. A reporter who has gone out of his way to antagonize well-defended institutions, including the Klan. Based on evidence I'm not at liberty to divulge, the Vancouver branch is capable of such violence."

"I reckon McCurdy is dead more likely than not."

Mildred's cigarette quivers. "Do you really mean that, Mr Johnston?"

"Millie, that's your third cigarette in a half-hour."

"You're changing the subject."

"Well if you want me to tell you the honest truth, with the Klan you never know for sure. They either hang people in public to send a message, or they make them disappear, never to be seen again. This specially applies to *aliens*—that's what they call non-members who speak out against them. They snatch 'em up, shoot 'em, then take the body someplace remote and bury it. You folks up here have a lot of territory to bury folks in. Sorry to say, but that's my opinion of it."

DS Hook lights another Ogden's. He was not prepared for this. Vancouver has had its fair share of kidnappings—there is no end of hand-wringing over "white slavery"—but a kidnapping and murder would be unprecedented.

"Truman, I think I'll have a small whisky after all."

They sit back in silence while the bartender brings over a whisky, a gin and a glass of tap water for Hollis Johnston— probably the most dangerous drink of the three.

"I don't cotton to bringing you folks down any further, but there's an additional matter to consider. Millie, you had better bone Detective Sergeant Hook up on the other situation."

*Bone up*: Mildred is suddenly back at Badminton school and Hollis is Matron Webster, poking her with a horny forefinger and telling her to get cracking.

"Yes, Mr Johnston. I suppose so." She takes a deep breath and prepares to tell her sorry tale.

"First of all Sergeant Hook, you should know that I am the person behind the Klan lawsuit. My suspicion is that Mr Forrest killed himself—or was murdered, if that rumour is true—on my account." Mildred remembers lying awake at night, wishing Mr Forrest dead. She didn't think it would actually happen.

DS Hook takes a moment to mentally parse her words and find an appropriate response. Observing Miss Wickstram's breathing pattern and the cigarette trembling between her manicured fingers, he decides to, for want of a better word, lie.

"Miss Wickstram, there is evidence that can't be divulged at this time, that suggests your assessment of the cause is wrong."

"That is very gentlemanly of you. In any case, Luther Forrest's death is unfortunate, but irrelevant. I still want his money."


LCB FIRE IGNITES FIERY SPEECH
Stalker Brings Legislature to Its Feet
Max Trotter
Staff Writer
*The Vancouver World*


The LCB outlet on Dunsmuir Street was a blur of flame by the time firefighters arrived, and a tangle of charred posts and beams in less than an hour. Some witnesses claimed to have heard an explosive blast, while other reports involved a whooshing sound. One observer claimed to have heard a high-pitched whine that may have been a rocket.

The general opinion is that the fire was not accidental, but a case of arson—and if so, who is to blame? We must keep in mind that the notion that a wooden building filled with flammable liquid meeting such an end by accident is not entirely out of the question.

Harlan Crombie of the LCB was quick to ascribe the destruction to bootlegging interests. For his part, in a statement Attorney General Boris Stalker saw the incident as part of a wider conflict.

In an impassioned speech before the Legislature, Stalker, as acting premier, called on British Columbians to "face the fact that we are under attack by an insidious enemy, an enemy without a country, without uniforms, without purpose and without rules.

"For the past five years, British Columbians have lived in a fool's paradise—unaware that, with the lifting of the War Measures Act, a cap was released and a boiler blew open, spewing out anarchists, Bolsheviks. Anyone with an agenda or a grudge is now free to seek ways to destabilize society."

Mr Stalker concluded with these words: "There is every reason to call a state of emergency."

Liberals rose to their feet, many crying: "Hear! Hear!"

# CHAPTER 37

MCCURDY IS ALMOST glad to hear the key in the door. Other than chewing on overcooked slop, he spent his day listening to a review of Clyde Taggart's complaints—chiefly over the hypocrisy of everyone other than himself. Reminding himself of his friend Sparrow's tips on successful incarceration (*Make friends with people you don't like*), he refrained from mentioning a few items concerning a certain Liberal bagman named Taggart, a hardened ward heeler who knew just who to pay and who to punish.

The door opens and Rollins enters, followed by two not unexpected visitors. The gentleman wears a white lab coat, with the inevitable stethoscope hanging from his neck. His oblong head is topped by a balding pate, surrounded by thick black hair, like an egg in a nest. He keeps an unlit billiard pipe clenched between his teeth, which he takes out of his mouth only to speak, and by the droop in his lower lip it is clearly as much a part of him as his tongue. He exudes the engaged calm of a scientist dissecting an interesting toad.

His female companion is none other than the cherubic nurse McCurdy encountered before passing out on Hastings Street. Today she is wearing a criss-cross apron and white nurse's cap. Like her superior, she affects a professional mien, with her clipboard and pencil at the ready.

In a pathetic attempt at flirting, McCurdy puts on a funny sad dog face and tries to catch her eye. She glances down, meets his gaze and immediately returns to her clipboard, finding it far more interesting.

Taggart is the first to receive medical attention, providing McCurdy with the opportunity to watch the grisly duet in action.

"Ah, Mr Taggart. And how are we today?"

Taggart smiles, dog-like, pathetically grateful. "Much better Dr Freeman, I'm glad to say."

"Good, good, good. And about those hot flashes—how are we coming along there?"

"Also much improved, thanks to you."

"No more spasms?"

"Steady as a rock." Taggart makes a fist and smiles like an idiot.

Dr Freeman raises a fist as well, to demonstrate solidarity. "Good show. I don't mind telling you that when you first came to us we were very worried. We're glad to have brought you back from the brink—isn't that so, Nurse Butterfield?"

She tilts her head sympathetically. "Very much so, doctor. We are all very much relieved."

"Good, excellent, well done." Now Dr Freeman's face takes on a concerned expression McCurdy doesn't believe for a second. "Unfortunately, there remains the risk of a coronary or cerebral apoplexy. But thanks to modern science, we now have medications to lower your level of stress—and the other option, of course, is surgery."

He takes a silver penlight from his pocket. "Now let's have a look at those pupils."

On cue, Taggart rolls his eyes upward as Dr Freeman leans forward to examine each one and Nurse Butterfield makes notations with a pencil. "Minor myosis. Full coordination. Retraction normal. Fundus normal. Inflammation minor." He straightens and puts his penlight away. "For the present, everything looks absolutely first-rate."

Having completed one assessment, Dr Freeman and Nurse Butterfield turn toward the new arrival, assessing McCurdy with eyes as bleak as a winter sky.

"And who might we have here?"

Nurse Butterfield consults her clipboard, as though she didn't know. "Doctor, his name is Edward McCurdy. Preliminary examination indicates substance abuse disorder, and he is anecdotally prone to obsessive fixations, eruptive, violent outbursts, and violations of civility and respectability. When we arrived on the scene, he was less than co-operative. Because it was a public place, we administered a sedative before he had the ability to lash out."

"Well done, Sheila. In dealing with a dangerous fit of lunacy, public safety comes first."

"That was my thought as well." Sheila casts a sad, sympathetic smile at the patient on the bed, who contains his outrage because a fitting reply would only confirm the diagnosis.

Nurse Butterfield hands her clipboard over to Dr Freeman. For a few moments he peruses the report with knitted brow, then nods as though to say, *Everything is as I suspected*, and turns to the patient.

"Mr McCurdy, do you know why you're here?"

*Do not volunteer information.*

*Appear co-operative.*

*Feign stupidity.*

"Doctor, I have no memory of it whatsoever."

A slow nod, as though the patient has said something significant. "Are you familiar with the term *dementia praecox*?"

"No Doctor, I have no idea. Does it have to do with my teeth?"

A sound erupts from Dr Freeman's throat that is somewhat like a chuckle. "Good to see that you're eager for me to explain your behaviour. Put in layman's terms, *dementia praecox* is characterized by hypomania, with attendant psychotic episodes evidenced by delusions and disorganized behaviour, followed by the depressive attack that confined you to your bed. Does that sound familiar?"

"It certainly does. I put it to the ups and downs of everyday life. Was I wrong?"

"Not necessarily. But there comes a point where what you call 'the ups and downs of life' become a clinical issue—whether it is what we call a 'manic' phase or a 'depressive' phase, you reach the apex or the nadir of the cycle and become a danger to yourself and others.

"Left untreated, these fits will become worse. At this moment, you may *seem* stable, you *feel* stable, but believe me, you are far from stable. The cycle will intensify until full-blown psychosis takes over, and another violent episode occurs, along with destruction of property and danger to your friends and colleagues."

As described, it sounds as though he is in gaol—the difference being that there will be no hearing, trial or sentence.

"But not to worry, Mr McCurdy. You have come to the right place."

The doctor smiles benignly as he turns to Nurse Butterfield: "Nurse, we will leave these gentlemen to their thoughts."

It occurs to McCurdy that not once has he seen Freeman blink. *Are all these people on drugs?*

The two angels of mercy head for the door, stopping to confer with the attendant, who has been waiting patiently in a clean apron, a freshly brushed blue suit and a crisp shirt and tie, with his tea caddy filled with emulsions, pills and other medical miracles. And hypodermic needles, of course.

Dr Freeman strikes a wooden match and lights his pipe. "We are finished here, Mr Rollins. Carry on. Keep up the good work."

The door closes behind them, leaving behind a woody, smoky, nostalgic smell.

Rollins approaches the two patients with his cartful of dope, beaming like a man who has just shaken hands with the pope. To go by the light from the window, it is almost dark; it's time to be put to sleep.

He produces a vial, sticks a needle through the cork, pulls the plunger, and fills the barrel with amber liquid. "Isn't he wonderful? I tell you, the province is lucky to have him. Patients from all over the world seek him out."

McCurdy nods like a credulous dolt. "He is very impressive. It must be an honour to work alongside such a man."

"It certainly is," Rollins replies, as though McCurdy has gotten right to the heart of it. "I tell you, the staff worships the ground he walks on—and if you knew the time and effort he puts into a case..."

The attendant's encomium to his superior is interrupted by Clyde Taggart—as the latter emits a sudden leonine roar, springs from his bed like an overweight panther and wraps his right arm around Rollins's neck, while the left hand snatches the needle from between his fingers and immediately jabs it straight into his bottom.

A sharp intake of breath as Rollins's eyes widen in surprise, then roll upward and he flops to the floor.

Looking satisfied, Taggart lays the now empty syringe neatly on Rollins's cart, then sits beside McCurdy on the edge of his cot.

"He was getting on my nerves," Taggart explains.

Silence follows. Neither man knows quite what to say or do next.

Contemplating the inert body at his feet, and choking back the panic welling up in his throat, McCurdy takes a long, deep breath. He may be in a madhouse, but he has no wish to be driven insane.

"Tell me, Clyde," he says with enforced calm. "Why did you do what you did just now?"

Taggart shrugs his shoulders. "Fed up with Freeman and his lies. When two goons are hauling you into a lorry, kicking and punching is hardly a *spasm*. Sons of bitches!" Taggart begins to turn red again.

"Easy there, Clyde. According to the press, you were acting like a madman."

"I knew Crombie was Stalker's man. I knew what was coming. I knew the protocol. I'd be shuffled away to a minor department—Education was what I expected. But that wasn't the offer. I was threatened with an investigation, with criminal charges assured unless I fucked off and kept my mouth shut. The bastard had a file on me. Doctored, of course. I told him I have files of my own, and they're not doctored, and that I intended to use them. I shouldn't have said that. I should have kept my powder dry."

"For a bureaucratic duel, in other words—files at dawn."

"Very funny. The material I have on Stalker and his ilk would bury any man."

"And what about the file he has on you? My source tells me it's a fat one."

"Oh really? How do you know that?"

"I'm a muckraker, remember? My question is this: Are you certain Stalker's file was compiled by Stalker?"

Taggart frowns. "What do you mean, Ed?"

"If the file is as thick as that, when was it compiled?"

The frown becomes a scowl. "I don't follow you."

"I'm suggesting that a file that size isn't put together all at once. Criminal accusations take time to cook up."

A long pause while the implication dawns on Taggart, who is torn between delivering a rebuttal or a punch in the mouth.

"I think I know what you're about to say, and it's impossible."

"Do you mean for Gordon Cunning to throw you off the train?"

"Gordon Cunning and I played hooker and tighthead prop with the Gaiters—do you know what that means?"

"I was never a rugby fan."

"We were mates in sports and in life. We watched each other's back. Brother Masons. Brothers in arms. Do you know what *that* means?"

"I'm afraid I haven't experienced such a touching friendship. I'm envious. At the same time, as someone experienced in politics, I should think—"

"Shut up, Ed. You're starting to sound like my wife."

Taggart's right hand has become a fist. McCurdy chooses to change the topic.

"Believe what you will, Clyde, we have more pressing matters at hand: there's an unconscious man on the floor. You put him there. He's bound to wake up. What do you see as our options at this point?"

"Our only option is to escape. That should be obvious, even to you."

"So you can trot out your damn files on Stalker? Fine, away you go. It's your funeral."

"Think again, Ed. I know about this place. We're scheduled to go under the knife."

This gives McCurdy pause. "Again, you paint a terrible picture."

"*Desperate* would be my word for it." Taggart indicates the prone body on the floor with the toe of his shoe. "Look at Rollins down there. Use your head. Think of this as your one opportunity to get out of here while you still have what passes for a brain."

"I take your point." McCurdy has nothing more to say; in fact, as far as he is concerned Taggart just clinched the argument. "But what do you have in mind? Even if we were to make it out of the building, we're in pajamas issued by an insane asylum."

"We'll have to strip him."

Despite the unsavoury prospect of wearing the attendant's clothing, they set to work. McCurdy is surprised to find Rollins's jacket and shirt less sticky than expected. "He seems to be dressed in his Sunday best."

"Maybe it's to impress Dr Freeman. Or maybe he has his eye on Nurse Butterfield."

They divide Rollins's clothing according to fairness and fit. Taggart wears the shirt and trousers, whose cuffs are above his ankles. As for McCurdy, the jacket drapes like a bathrobe, and he is still in pajama bottoms. All in all, the two look like a vaudeville comedy team.

McCurdy reaches into the inside jacket pocket and finds a billfold containing four dollars, which they divide equally in case they become separated. In an outside pocket he finds a ring containing several keys.

"What about wearing his apron?" Taggart suggests. "It would at least cover your bottom half."

"Too clean. It would practically glow in the dark."

As fully dressed as possible, they hoist the nearly naked attendant onto McCurdy's bed, put the covers over him and head for the door.

Taggart finds the correct key on the fourth try (cursing after each one) and gingerly opens the door. They enter a central area shaped like a British 50p coin, with a stairway on one side. "As I remember the floor plan, the attendant's quarters are a flight down. One of these keys is bound to fit."

"What are we after? Money?"

"Trousers." Taggart indicates the fabric covering McCurdy's legs. "Your pajamas are a dead giveaway."

They ease their way down a set of concrete steps to a landing with a bronze fire extinguisher on one wall and a door in another.

"We could also do with a torch," McCurdy suggests.

"And a billy club for that matter."

McCurdy takes the keys from Taggart and gives the lock a try, then tries another key; his hands tremble as he inserts each key one by one, until he realizes that he has been inserting them upside down. By now he is all but convinced that none of this is really happening and that he is asleep in his bed at the Castle Hotel.

"Useless turd," mutters Taggart.

Suddenly the key turns almost by itself and the knob turns just as easily. McCurdy gives the door a shove and it jolts open. They look inside—and stand frozen on the spot.

The creature standing just inside the doorway is a good three inches taller than either of them. He wears a stained white shirt and trousers of some heavy white material. He could be taken for a house painter, except that he is smiling, or rather grimacing, displaying a set of teeth that have been filed into points, like the teeth of a shark.

It becomes immediately apparent that the reason Rollins got himself dolled up was not to impress Miss Butterfield but because he was about to go out for a night on the town, leaving his "assistant" in charge.

Out of the creature's open mouth comes something between a laugh, a roar and a shriek.

In unison, the two escapees whirl away from the apparition in the room, run straight across the landing, stumble downstairs and lunge through the outside door, thanks to a panic bar installed in case of fire.

They stop to catch their breath. They are in a boot-shaped, gravelled, open space between three buildings, opening at the toe.

"Over there is the new annex for bath cures. I was on the approval committee."

"Bully for you. But what are we going to do now?"

McCurdy approaches the gap. In the light issuing from the main building he can make out an acre of gardens to the right (vegetables, to go by the pong of manure); next to that, a gravelled driveway leads away from the principal entrance through an expanse of lawn dotted with ornamental trees and shrubs, down to an open gate with pillars on either side, next to the cement wall with wrought-iron filigree that encloses the property.

"Best that we split up, Ed. The fecker can't run in two directions."

To McCurdy it sounds like flipping a coin over life and death. "I take your point, but where the hell *are* we?"

"Beyond that wall is Columbia Street and the end of the Kingsway. On the other side of the road is the railway and the river. I recommend we try—"

The door to Maple Cottage crashes open. Without saying goodbye, they plunge forward in opposite directions, veins spurting adrenaline—Taggart to the garden, McCurdy across the lawn, like waterbucks chased by a crocodile.

Now McCurdy hears footfalls on gravel, an unhurried, confident jog bearing down upon him. *The luck of the draw.* An extra jolt of fear rattles his sternum as the creature makes that terrible sound again, forcing him to speed up despite his aching, wheezing lungs.

Further in the distance, near the doors to the main building, somebody is shouting in the voice of a normal adult and not the shriek of their pursuer, which suggests that they have awakened the evening watch.

Now McCurdy hears the snuffle and whine of dogs—who, like his pursuer, must also have sharp teeth.

Surely this has to be a nightmare! Surely he will wake up with a start and a gasp, wondering what he drank or took last night! Unwilling to take that chance, he hurtles across the lawn, a frantic, doomed, condemned sinner trying to outrun the hounds of hell.

Seconds later, he hits something like a tripwire and plummets face-forward into the clipped grass, bruising his jaw and skinning the palms of both hands. He rolls onto his back, pushes his glasses back up his nose, reaches for his foot—and extracts a croquet wicket. He flings away the U-shaped piece of wire, struggles to his feet and can now see in the dim light that he has blundered into a pitch—seven wickets and a centre peg, now an obstacle course for his benefit.

He hears those confident steps, closer now, and some distance behind them the jingle of chain collars and the expectant panting of dogs who have caught the scent. McCurdy scrambles to his feet, runs for it—and two strides later he is flat on his face again, with more bruising and a split lip. In the near distance he hears quicker steps, and the sharp breathing of a man at full run. Back on his feet, flinging himself toward a hawthorn tree, he receives a shove between his shoulder blades that causes him to pitch forward into another tree—this one a crabapple, to go by the thorns tearing at his flesh.

Defeated, done for, finished, McCurdy flips over to a seated position with his back against the tree trunk and looks up at the creature's face, with his terrible teeth on display—when all at once two shadows leap, not on him, but on the back of the creature, who is thrown off-balance and tumbles onto the lawn.

Seizing on this unexpected opportunity, McCurdy scrambles to his feet and sprints flat out toward the gate, so intent on reaching his target that he scarcely hears the growls behind him, or the screams.

# CHAPTER 38

*Hello, operator speaking, SEymour exchange. Are you there?*

*Here is SEymour 120, Vancouver Police Department. Operator speaking, how may I assist you?*

*I have a call for a Sergeant Hook.*

*I will connect you now.*

SWITCH

*Hello, are you there? This is Detective Sergeant Hook speaking.*

*I have Sanford Pickles of BC Collateral on the line. Will you take the call?*

*Certainly. Thank you, Irene.*

Hook knows BC Collateral well, with its spinning LOANS/ SELLS neon and plate-glass windows filled with its forlorn merchandise. When he served with the Point Grey constabulary, to survive on a constable's salary he made full use of the service, hawking his father's watch on multiple occasions to tide him over at a relatively modest two per cent a month. He knows Sanford Pickles as a principled businessman who will not sell collateral prematurely at any price, and will not accept as collateral a man's spectacles or false teeth.

*I will connect you now.*

SWITCH

*Calvin, are you there? It's Sanford Pickles.*

*Good to hear from you, Sanford. How's business?*

*Fair to middling, Calvin. And yourself?*

*About the same. So what's the story?*

*One of my clerks had a hinky customer in the box with two watches and a ring. Could be one of the goons I seen in the paper.*

*What'd he look like, this fellow?*

*A shifty bird, talked like a cowboy.*

*And the ring, Sanford? Are you sure it isn't an earring?*

*No, it's a man's ring. A fake ruby with something that looks like a Military Cross.*

*Does the cross have a drop of blood in the centre?*

*Ah, so that's what it is. It's where the royal cypher ought to be. Damn disrespectful if you ask me. But the paper said these birds were packing, so we weren't gonna take him on. Gerry let him have three fins for the lot.*

*Very wise. Sanford, can you keep him occupied? We'll be there in ten minutes.*

*Not fast enough, I'm afraid. He took his money and went that-away. Oh, goddammit to hell.*

*Keep your shirt on, Calvin. I had a boy ankle after him down the street. Saw him go into the Maple Hotel.*

It occurs to DS Hook that the top two floors of the Maple Hotel comprise one of Joe Celona's whorehouses. It's possible that the stolen earrings were used to purchase a service, therefore not pawned with the rest.

*We're on it, Sanford. On behalf of the force, thank you for your co-operation.*

*Only doing my civic duty, Officer. But I want the stuff back when you're finished. And if it's stolen property, I want my fifteen dollars.*

WAVE OF CRIME STRIKES THE CITY
Robberies Signal Moral Deterioration
Cecil Harmsworth
Staff Writer
*The Beacon*

As though the suspected arson attack on a Liquor Control Board outlet were not sufficient cause for public alarm, a recent series of holdups involving guns has called attention to a wave of crime unleashed by the legalization of alcohol.

Two office girls, a service station attendant, a Chinese grocer and a streetcar conductor were robbed at gunpoint of sums ranging from four dollars to twenty dollars. Two pocket watches were stolen (a Tod & Manning and an Elgin family heirloom) and a pair of rhinestone button earrings the victim scrimped for months to buy.

In each case, the perpetrators covered the lower part of their faces with handkerchiefs in American outlaw style and were armed with pistols. Victims described the men as speaking with southern American accents and addressing them as "yous" and "y'all."

Alderman Henry Garbutt remarked: "This is yet another sign of the moral deterioration of the city under our current mayor."

Responded Mayor Taylor, facetiously: "Alderman Garrett would find moral deterioration in an overripe vegetable."

Observers agree that our mayor would do well to follow Attorney General Stalker's lead and begin to take crime seriously.

# CHAPTER 39

HOOK HAS COME to a decision he knows will haunt him in the future: the decision to be a clever fellow.

*When cleverness arises, lies flourish.* He forgets who said that, if indeed he ever knew, but the speaker wasn't just banging his gums.

He is about to betray his partner. *Ex*-partner, truth be told, and thick as old barn wood, but a fellow officer nonetheless, who trusts his word.

After asking around the station, he manages to locate Constable Quam in Leonard's Cafe, seated halfway down the counter and tucking into a slab of blueberry pie with a large scoop of vanilla ice cream.

Hook's misgivings increase; nevertheless he continues. "Mr Quam. Just the man I'm looking for." Hook has never felt like such a phony. When he was caught lying as a boy, his father would beat him with his belt to within an inch of his life. Which only happened once, but the fear of it has stayed with him.

Quam looks up like the little boy who stuck in his thumb and pulled out a plum, but as soon as he sees who it is his face becomes wary and apprehensive. "Hello, Sergeant Hook."

"Constable, you have some pie on your upper lip."

"Sorry, sir." He uses his napkin to wipe off the purple moustache. "I was just having a spot of lunch."

DS Hook takes the stool next to him. Quam exudes the old sour apple smell and an air of incomprehension. Hook lights an Ogden's and reaches for the ashtray. "There's something you might want to know about Mr McCurdy."

Quam reluctantly sets his fork down. "You mean the informer? The one who writes for the paper?"

"That's the bird."

"I assure you, sir, Sergeant Rocco had no idea he was one of ours."

"Of course he didn't. No reason why he should have. In fact, that's what I'd like to talk about. I was a bit short with you folks there, when in fact you should have been commended. I want to apologize for it."

The eyes grow misty. "Sir, you're not being sarcastic, are you?"

"Not a bit, Mr Quam. I really should have known better. The Dry Squad's conviction record speaks for itself."

Quam reflexively brushes a few crumbs from the sleeve of his cheap jacket, which has already gone shiny at the elbow.

"And as for the McCurdy fellow, it turns out that your first instincts were as sound as a pound."

The constable frowns: "Sound in what way, sir?"

"Oh, didn't you know? He's disappeared."

"Disappeared?"

"Into thin air. Oh, he was up to something, we're now certain of that. There are discrepancies in his receipts and suspicious gaps in his reporting." DS Hook says this with not a clue as to what he is talking about.

Quam's toddler forehead forms something like a frown. "Do you know, sir, I'm not at all surprised. Sergeant Rocco said he was damned queer."

"A bit light on his feet, you say? That could be as well. In any case, give Sergeant Rocco my congratulations—kudos from DS Hook."

"Sir, are you quite sure you're not being sarcastic?"

"Far from it, Constable." Hook gets up as though about to leave. "And by the way, tell Rocco good luck with the Maple Hotel bunch."

Relieved at having switched to another subject, Quam goes back to his pie before the ice cream melts. "The Maple Hotel is Joe Celona's place, sir," he says with his mouth full. "Sergeant Rocco says it's off limits. Orders from the mayor's office."

"I believe him. And that's what makes it such a rum situation."

"A rum situation? How so, sir?" Quam looks sadly at his empty plate; if he were alone, he would lick it clean.

"It seems there are a couple of grifters from the States selling whisky out of one of the rooms. Canadian Club, premium product. For some reason they think being in the Maple makes them immune to raids from the Morals Squad, the Dry Squad—from anyone. I can't imagine why."

Quam stops wiping his mouth. "You can't?"

"Are *you* being sarcastic now, Constable?"

"Certainly not, sir. But it seems obvious to me that they are hiding behind Mr Celona."

"By heaven, I think you're right. Well the cheeky buggers!"

"Very nervy of them I must say."

"You're not whistling Dixie, Mr Quam. Hiding under Celona's coattails, taking the brothel king for a sap? They must have bigger balls than a Jersey bull."

"They really are asking for it, sir. Mr Celona will not be pleased when he finds out—which he will."

"Indeed. I should expect a police raid would be a blessing in comparison."

"You know, sir, you make a good point." Quam's face takes on a brighter cast at the prospect of occupying the moral high ground, for once.

"Well, I must be off. Remember to give my regards to Sergeant Rocco."

"Bet your life I will, sir."


BY NOW QUAM knows the routine well.

The raid is scheduled to occur in the small hours of the morning, when the occupants are most likely to be inside and asleep, or drunk. This time there are no crying children involved, which is a good thing. Of late he has had troubled dreams along those lines.

The desk clerk was fully alerted about Room 327 and knows what is about to take place there. Other guests on that floor have been directed by the management to remain in their rooms or leave the building.

Now comes the approach.

With torches in hand, they creep up the three flights of stairs in the usual order: McNamara in the lead with a loaded shotgun, followed by Simpson with his axe, then Rocco with pistol drawn, safety off. Quam, the least experienced of the quartet, takes up the rear, with a pistol in one hand (safety on) and a torch in the other, being responsible for backing up, banging up and retrieval in case of injuries. (Another blessing, for his fire-arms training was over in an hour.)

After positioning themselves on either side of Room 327, and on a count of three from Rocco, McNamara's shotgun blasts a hole where the lock once was, whereupon Simpson puts his hobnail boot to the door; all four officers lunge through the wreckage and into the room. Rocco's torch reveals a double bed, where two men simultaneously sit bolt upright, on high alert. Quam recognizes Olson and Flood from the visit to the Mae West house—the two Klansmen supposedly protecting the unfortunate Mr Forrest.

"Police! Stay where you are!"

While Gainer Flood gropes frantically under his pillow for his weapon, Jessup Olson, the faster of the two, leaps to his feet with a .45 revolver extended in front of him. It takes him a second to choose which copper to shoot, and he pays for his indecision when a blast from Simpson's second barrel sends him reeling backward, roaring and cursing, with a scattering of bloody dots on the front of his union suit. Seeing that the odds are stacked against them in this confined space, Gainer Flood rolls off the bed, crawls underneath it like an alligator, comes out the other side and makes for the window, pausing to squeeze off a shot that misses Rocco but takes off a piece of Simpson's ear. (The injury will earn Simpson the nickname "Gremlin" for the rest of his career.)

Still at the door, Constable Quam is standing by.

Aiming in a hurry, Rocco fires his .38 Special twice but manages only to hit Gainer's left thigh, enabling the suspect to push off with his right, roll through the window onto the fire escape and half-tumble down the metal steps, turning at intervals to fire erratically at the window above.

Rocco hugs the wall to one side of the window as McNamara reloads his shotgun and takes the other side, while Quam crawls to the wounded Simpson, now lying at the foot of the bed, swearing. Shoving his side arm under his belt, Quam pulls a sheet from the bed, tears off a strip and attempts to staunch Simpson's bleeding ear.

AT THIS MOMENT, outside the Maple Hotel entrance, DS Hook is in the act of parking the BSA when he hears muffled gunfire inside the building, followed by louder shots that echo off the walls in the alleyway to his left. He draws his side arm and runs into the dimly lit alley, just as Gainer Flood alights from the fire escape.

Now staggering toward Hook, dragging one foot behind him, Flood lifts his revolver for an easy shot and pulls the trigger, but the mechanism fails to fire. While Flood swears at his weapon, DS Hook holsters his pistol, steps smartly up to the suspect, grabs him by the front of his union suit and smashes his forehead into the offender's face, flattening his nose and producing a gusher of blood. Flood's injured leg buckles, he topples backward onto the cobbles, and there he remains—writhing, clutching his thigh and moaning imprecations in the name of Jesus.

From a window three floors up, Rocco's bald head appears, catching a ray of morning sun. "Hook, you fucking bastard! Goddamn you, there's no booze here, not a drop!"

"I'm surprised to hear that, sergeant! That's certainly not what I was told! I guess it must have been another rumour!"

"Pull the other one, Hook! You've got us in a real mess up here!"

"Nobody dead, surely to God?"

"No—but no thanks to you!" With an inaudible curse, Rocco disappears inside.

(This understandable resentment on the part of the Dry Squad will dissipate when the team receives a commendation for bravery from Chief Barfoot, as well as mentions in all the newspapers for having apprehended two armed and dangerous American criminals on the lam.)

Flood continues to roll back and forth on the ground, clutching his thigh, wiping blood from his face with his sleeve, swearing continuously. DS Hook drops onto one knee to check the man's vital signs, which seem to be in reasonable order. Satisfied that the suspect will remain alive for the time being, he retrieves the useless .45 from the cobbles and stands up.

As sunlight trickles through low-hanging clouds and spills onto one brick wall, Hook lights up an Ogden's and heaves a sigh of relief.

Still, he has a bad conscience. His treatment of Quam has left him feeling vaguely ashamed. Jeanie would not be pleased.

# CHAPTER 40

SEATED IN A ditch a half-mile down Kingsway, McCurdy relaxes somewhat.

With the dogs otherwise engaged, he sees no benefit in trying to put more distance between himself and Woodlands, especially given the two alternatives: either to thrash through thickets and crawl over fallen trees or to stroll along Kingsway, a bleeding man in institutional pajamas waiting to be plucked off the road by police or an ambulance, then strapped into a straitjacket and bundled off to captivity.

He could do with a drink or a snort or a puff, or anything really, lacking which he crawls away from the road until he finds an inconspicuous spot beneath a monkey puzzle tree. There, he wraps himself in Rollins's jacket, assumes the foetal position and waits for morning...

Well past dawn he is jarred awake by the abrasive complaint of a pair of crows on the ground a few feet away, eyeing him sideways like proctors at an exam. When he begins to stir they scold in earnest, batting their wings up and down for emphasis.

He curses the vile creatures, then realizes that the crows are doing him a good turn when he hears the rhythmic grinding of steel tyres on cement, along with the heavy, hollow clop of horseshoes.

He mutters an apology to the the crows, who flutter to a nearby log to discuss.

Back in the ditch by the edge of the road, he fogs his spectacles and wipes them with the tail of his pajama top, wondering, Is there any point in planning *anything*?

Moments later, a farm wagon turns off Columbia Street onto Kingsway. Painted Irish green and with *McCormack* printed on the side, it is pulled along by a draught horse with some variety of skin disease; but though rudimentary, it at least holds the promise of a leisurely ride to Burnaby.

He waits until the wagon passes in front of him, then climbs out of the ditch and scurries after it. Reaching to within arm's length of the tailgate, he grips the top edge and jogs along until he establishes a rhythm; then, skipping on one foot, he places the other foot on the deck overhang and vaults over the tailgate and into the wagon, feeling rather athletic for once—

And finds himself thigh-deep in sheep shit.

The wagon is carrying a load of fertilizer for distribution to gardens all over the city. Manure has become a saleable commodity given the dwindling number of horses in the streets.

At this close distance, the stench is nearly enough to knock a man out. He turns to the front of the wagon, where the driver hunches over the reins, oblivious to the smell and, more important, to the acquisition of a passenger.

By the time the wagon reaches Burnaby, the reporter is draped over the tailgate like a discarded rag doll. The unfamiliar sensation of a right turn clears his mind sufficiently that he senses it might be time to do something.

In a what-the-hell frame of mind, he heaves one leg out of the muck, rolls over the tailgate and tumbles onto the road. From a seated position he breathes in deep gulps of delicious air as he watches the farm wagon recede into the distance.

Behind him is a picket fence enclosing a kitchen garden, next to Chuck's Grocery. To his right is a billboard, advertising, oddly, the Devonshire Hotel. Pleased that at least he is no longer in the wilderness, he struggles to his feet and makes his way up Rumble Street to the Interurban Railway.

AS A GENERAL rule, a member of the male gender is permitted to stink of sweat, tobacco, rotten teeth, liquor or all four combined.

But not sheep shit.

In any North American city in 1925, the most offensive stink one can emit is the smell of the farm. The farm is what half the population came to the city to escape. The farm is an affront to everything the city stands for.

However, as it is with a skunk, an offensive rural stink can be a social weapon if you brazen it out—if only because the smell of the farm is the smell of their parents. As such, it brings on feelings of guilt over having abandoned the homestead. You are shunned, but respectfully. They make way for you to pass by as they would a crippled veteran. McCurdy contemplates a future piece on what prominent men smell like, and shelves it for later use.

On the tram, he hands the driver a dollar and stares him down while the fellow provides change, ostentatiously holding his nose. When he turns to seat himself he finds that the aisle has been cleared, to make room for this special passenger.

Twenty minutes later, stepping off the streetcar at Main Street, he walks purposefully north, looking like something out of an Uncle Remus story, bleeding from scratches and scrapes, wearing an ill-fitting coat and soiled institutional pajamas. Yet nobody stares at him or comments. On passing, pedestrians look straight ahead and unemployed loiterers examine their fingernails.

As he limps down the sidewalk, he forms a plan—a pathetically short-term one, but a plan nonetheless.

He will make careful use of the rest of his share of Rollins's money by securing a room for a maximum of thirty-five cents under an assumed name. Then he will use a nickel to telephone DS Hook and to find out whether the police are looking for him.

For all he knows, they are hunting him down as a dangerous lunatic. And in the case of the toothy creature he heard screaming, is a charge of criminal negligence waiting for him as well? On the whole, it paints a gloomy picture of his prospects. In the face of everything else, potential snipers from neighbouring rooftops are of minor concern.

*The first step is to gather information.* He wonders where he learned that, then remembers that he is a reporter by trade.

He steps into a cigar store, buys a *World* for five cents (a dollar fifty-five left), seats himself on a bench in front of the plate-glass window and reads.

On page two, below the fold, he finds a Trotter item that simplifies his situation, if only slightly.

INMATE MAULED BY DOGS
Institutional Success Story Recovering in Hospital
Max Trotter
Staff Writer
*The Vancouver World*

An inmate at Woodlands hospital named Charles Setter is recovering from multiple puncture wounds after being attacked by the institution's watchdogs. The animals had been patrolling the grounds to discourage pranksters, who frequently breach the fenced perimeter in order to taunt the inmates, defecate on the lawn and harass the staff.

It is probable that Mr Setter exited the building by means of a fire door. Still, police are baffled as to why an inmate was permitted to venture outside on his own. An ambulance attendant reported that, while being taken to hospital, Setter was raving about chasing someone.

Dr Walter Freeman, who supervised Mr Setter's treatment, noted that Mr Setter had only recently been taken from the segregation facility and transferred to the main building, as he was deemed no longer a danger to himself or others.

Dr Bigney, the eminent surgeon who treated Mr Setter, regrets the incident. "It is a crying shame," he said. "The patient has made such progress. With Charles, we had every hope of a remission or a cure."

While many will sympathize and express hope for Mr Setter's recovery, it must be noted that Mr Setter's story is a strange one.

Two years ago, a neighbour accused Setter, a roofing contractor, of having stolen his dog. Not receiving a satisfactory response, he called the police, and two constables came to Setter's home, where they encountered a number of animal skeletons stacked on the south side as though to bleach in the sun.

In the back porch was what appeared to be a butcher's table, together with a bone saw, a meat saw and a cleaver. Acting on a hunch, an officer inspected the kitchen icebox, where he found a stack of wrapped packages, carefully labelled.

In the front parlour, another officer discovered a central table displaying a collection of dog collars. The collars were later identified by distraught owners whose dogs had disappeared, some of them years earlier.

"That collar belonged to my Skye terrier," testified Mrs Wade Brown. "It is heartbreaking to think that dreadful man ate Rosie."

Upon his arrest, Mr Setter confessed straightaway. It was during this early interview that officers observed how the suspect had filed his teeth into points. Mr Setter explained that he had served a year for burglary in Pentonville Prison, London, and had filed his teeth as a means of protecting himself from violent convicts.

Neighbours were able to cast little light on Mr Setter's habits or personality.

"He was a quiet fellow," commented one neighbour. "He tended to keep himself to himself."

"We spoke once in a while," added another, "but I couldn't look at his teeth."

Sentenced to three months for the theft and slaughter of domestic animals, Mr Setter was sent to Woodlands upon examination by the prison nurse and was confined to Maple Cottage, a segregation unit for potentially violent patients.

The two dogs responsible for the Woodlands attack, Buster and Cliff, will not be destroyed, due to Mr Setter's past history with dogs. Mr John Spriggs, their trainer, spoke on the animals' behalf, noting that Alsatians can sense hostile intentions in humans and may react in defence of their species as a whole.

As Mr Spriggs observed: "The dogs can tell if you like to eat dog."

# CHAPTER 41

THE PHOTOPLAY AT the Pantages this week is *Pretty Ladies,* in which ZaSu Pitts plays a comedienne whose husband leaves her for a chorus girl.

As always, he and McCurdy will leave during the newsreels, but Hook decides to bring Jeanie to *Pretty Ladies* on Saturday, for she likes cheerful endings, and given the sort of movie it is, the heroine will inevitably recover and find true love.

"Jesus, Ed, you look like shit on a shingle. And what in the deuce are you wearing for trousers?"

"These? They're called pajamas, Calvin. You should be pleased the manure has dried, otherwise I'd clear the theatre."

On the screen below, the German *Schutzstaffel* perform a peculiar stiff-legged march down Unter den Linden street; then in Italy, Mussolini sticks his chin out before parliament, and a title card notes that he has banned the Italian Socialist Party. Then RAF bombs pacify rebellious tribesmen in Waziristan. Then General Pangalos disbands the Greek parliament. Then what appears to be a fashion item: that women have taken to wearing radium lipstick that glows in the dark.

DS Hook opens a mickey that claims to be Bacardi rum but could just as well be transmission fluid.

"*Kidnapped*, Ed? By a *nurse*? Along with Clyde Taggart? Isn't it more likely that you fell down while drunk or muggled or on the powder and were hospitalized for your own protection?"

"Goddammit, Calvin, that's exactly why I didn't report this at the station. With you I was hoping at least for a fair hearing. Do you think I hallucinated Clyde Taggart, like a pink elephant?" He opens his pajama top. "And how about these lacerations and contusions—did I put them there myself?"

"Well I doubt that, but still—"

McCurdy produces a newspaper, folded in eight, from the side pocket of his oversized coat. "Now read this."

"I can't. It's too dark in here."

"A man was mutilated by dogs. He said he was chasing someone on the Woodlands hospital grounds. With this in mind, ask yourself where *these* came from." He pulls out the front of his pajama shirt. "Do they remind you of hospital pajamas? Or do you think I stole them from the hospital and ripped them to shreds on a lark? Jesus, man, what do you take me for?"

"Would you please calm down, Ed? The Orientals over there are beginning to take notice." The policeman hands over the mickey of rum. "Have some of this for heaven's sake."

McCurdy takes a swig, after proposing a toast to mental health.

After a pause, DS Hook relents. "Oh, fine. All right, then. Barring evidence to the contrary, I choose to believe you, though nobody else will."

"So if I were to say that Boris Stalker is at the bottom of it—"

"To implicate the Attorney General, you'd need a whole passel of evidence. Do you have *any* evidence?"

It strikes McCurdy that, without Clyde Taggart, he has absolutely nothing. "I expect a corroborating account soon."

"I look forward to it. Meanwhile, what are you going to do now?"

"Haven't the slightest idea. I'm staying at the Scat Inn for thirty cents a night. Bedbugs are complimentary."

"Well, looking on the positive side—"

"Oh Jesus, here comes Samuel Smiles."

"Would you listen to me? As of now, nobody is looking for either you or Mr Taggart—let alone two nutters on the loose. For one thing, the public is in a panic over terrorists and criminals, and we are undermanned because the funding is going into Stalker's bloody bootlegger crusade. Just go back to your hotel, take a bath and put on some decent clothes."

"Calvin, if you'll recall, not long ago the Dry Squad raided my room, with the desk clerk's blessing."

"The Dry Squad aren't a threat to you anymore. And we'll see about the desk clerk."

On the screen below, Babe Ruth has collapsed after binging on hot dogs and soda before a game. Rushed to hospital, he is to undergo ulcer surgery while a nation gathers around their receivers waiting for news with bated breath...

Millie dearest,

Oh darling, the other night I was feeling too lonesome. Gwendolyn was out for the evening as she usually is, though I'm glad to say she is no longer with a different gentleman each evening, having settled on a young man named Wilber who fixes bicycles and autos, and I think sells them too. He seems quite nice, though I am a bit put off by his blackened fingernails.

In any case, I decided to go to a photoplay, and for company I invited Miss Carr.

The Dominion was showing *The Sheik*, which stars Rudolph Valentino, who has become quite a hit with the ladies. (I have heard men refer to him as "Vaselino" and regard him as more than a little fey, but I think they are just jealous!)

To be frank, I doubt that I could fall in love with a kidnapper and potential rapist just because he saved me from another one, especially when both men have a tendency to knock a girl about.

As for Miss Carr, I'm not sure she had ever seen a photoplay before. Early on, she began to make comments directly to the actors, aloud, in a voice well above a whisper. (And well above the piano player as well.) She seemed to think the actors could hear her criticisms. People were shushing all around, and I am afraid that she quite spoilt the entertainment for everyone.

Speaking of entertainment, the Legislature is all a-twitter about a letter, rumoured to be written by the missing Mr Taggart, that promises documents showing the Liberals to be guilty of all manner of corruption—at the LCB where I work, and especially over the business dealings of Mr Beaven, Mr Munn and even Mr Crombie!

Independent MLA Victor Newson says that he intends to bring down the government over it, and plans to make it the issue that defines the next election.

I have never seen Mr Crombie so upset—considerably more so, may I say, than he was by the death of Mrs Crombie!

Oh Millie, it has all taken a strange turn. To begin, it turns out that the person Mr Crombie has taken on as an adviser to the LCB is none other than Daisy Douglas Tyler, the American woman who runs the PPA. Well I never! Mind you, they behave with great propriety in public. But knowing the nature of their private association, it seems positively weird!

Gwendolyn says that the whole building is a tangle of rumours, private alliances and intrigue; Millie, there is something positively <u>French</u> about it!

Please darling, write back soon and tell me about the scandals swirling around the Ku Klux Klan. Here we get only the sketchiest of details, and Victoria must surely be tame by comparison.

I must say that British Columbia has become unexpectedly racy!

Your forever friend, Gracie

# CHAPTER 42

AT THE CHECK-IN counter of the Castle Hotel, DS Hook pounds the brass bell repeatedly until the desk clerk ambles out of the office, looking sleepy and irritated—until the VPD uniform has its effect and he transforms into the Concerned Host.

"A very good day to you, Officer. And how are we this afternoon?"

"We are fine this afternoon, thank you, sir."

"And how may I be of some assistance?"

"I need to speak with Mr Edward McCurdy—is he in his room?"

The desk clerk's voice tightens, as does his face. "Ah yes, Mr McCurdy. I'm sorry to say, Officer, that we haven't seen Mr McCurdy for several days now." His tone implies, *And I hope we never do again.*

"Sir, I caution you that your sarcasm is overdone. In any case, when he does check in, please give him the following message: that Detective Sergeant Hook dropped by to commend him on a job well done, and to say that he will be in contact tomorrow and will keep him abreast."

The desk clerk's gaze grows cold. "Beg your pardon, sir? *A job well done?*"

"Very much so. We couldn't have solved the case without him."

"Solved? Mr McCurdy *solved* something?"

DS Hook leans over the counter as though speaking in confidence. "McCurdy is one of the best undercover detectives in the country. I'm not at liberty to say more. Please keep it under your hat."

He flicks a conspiratorial wink, turns briskly and exits the hotel, passing two fellow guests in cheap suits and hobnail boots who have been listening from behind their newspapers.

Moments later, almost as though on cue, Mr McCurdy himself enters the lobby. The two newspaper readers glance at the new arrival, glance at each other, fold their newspapers and leave the building.

The desk clerk's nostrils flare as McCurdy approaches, though his face remains a mask of professional politeness. "Welcome back, Mr McCurdy! Very good to have you back, sir."

"Thank you, Rodney. I'm touched. Have there been any messages for me?"

"Actually, a Detective Sergeant Hook was here just moments ago. He wished to commend you for, as he put it, 'a job well done' and to say that he will contact you tomorrow."

"Excellent. Now I'll have my key—and no visitors or calls, please. I wish to take a long, hot bath."


### WHAT THE ATTORNEY GENERAL KNOWS
Cecil Harmsworth
Staff Writer
*The Beacon*

It has taken a crime wave to do it, but finally the Government of BC has emerged from its moderationist cocoon and has opted to take action.

To assess the current sorry situation, one must first understand the forces lurking behind it.

It has long been known that foreign elements have been steadily working to undermine the moral fibre of white Christian British Columbians and to assert values particular to their race.

One tactic among many is to ply the white working man with alcohol and drugs.

Behind the epidemic of drinking, bootlegging and alcohol deaths is a syndicate of foreign conspirators who feel free to spread their poison, encouraged by permissive laws and lax enforcement.

Meanwhile, defenders of the public good can only look on, helpless, stymied by laws that, although intended to preserve and protect us, have been twisted to accomplish precisely the opposite.

The current Crusade Against Bootlegging is well named. For white Christians it is a war of survival.

But the tide is turning.

Thanks to the combined efforts of civil, provincial and federal police on the front lines, and thanks to laws that put the onus on the wrongdoer to explain himself, our prisons are bursting with miscreants reaping their reward at the treadmill and the crank.

As Deputy Minister Bertram Bliss remarked, "We'd have a thousand more if we had the prison space." Indeed, this reporter has learned that a committee has been struck to examine possible locations, estimate costs and make recommendations.

Upon his ascension, Attorney General Stalker has sent the message loud and clear: "Bootlegging and its attendant vices will no longer be given free rein in our province. It is high time for British Columbians to take a stand."

Stalker's message is a clarion call to arms, inspired by Paul in Ephesians 6:11: "Put on the full armour of God, so that you can take your stand against the devil's schemes."

Our Attorney General is doing the Lord's work. Let us wish him godspeed.

# CHAPTER 43

LIVING IN WALDO, DS Hook never got into the church-going habit. Father and Mother attended for social reasons only, as did everybody—what else was there to do on a Sunday?

The only church in town was Waldo Church—basically a wooden house rounded at one end to suggest an apse—and it was firmly non-denominational, since nobody in Waldo could agree on the time of day, much less how to get to heaven. As a result, Pastor Uphill spoke about whatever happened to be on his mind that week—usually something uplifting about someone in the village who did something nice for someone else or an appeal to help out a neighbour who lost a body part in the sawmill.

Jeanie's family are died-in-the-wool Methodists. For Methodists, church-going is a sacred duty, and she gets chippy if he doesn't join her at Grandview Methodist on a Sunday morning.

All in all, he doesn't mind. It's a chance to wear his good suit, and Jeanie dolls up nice. The music is tuneful and well sung by the choir, and he finds he has taken to some of the hymns: "Holy, Holy, Holy" has a soft sweetness to it, though he finds "Before Jehovah's Awful Throne" a bit ominous, and "Onward, Christian Soldiers" calls up memories of doomed, over-the-top assaults ordered by the likes of Victor Newson.

Still, at Grandview Methodist, the primary challenge for Hook is the effort it takes to stay awake during the sermon. More than once, Reverend Sutherland's ministerial drone has occasioned a sharp elbow from Jeanie, when a too-conspicuous snore escaped from his nostrils.

This week, Sutherland's sermon is based on the theme "Love Thy Neighbour":

...In the current civic atmosphere of suspicion—when neighbours spy on neighbours, when undercover policemen prowl the streets, the gaols are filled with the accused, and when every week it seems a new public enemy is uncovered—it behooves us to pay attention to the words of Leviticus 19:16–18:

*Thou shalt not go up and down as a slanderer among thy people; neither shalt thou stand idly by when thy neighbour's life is at stake. Thou shalt not hate thy brother in thine heart, but reprove him openly. Thou shalt not bear any grudge against the children of thy people, but thou shalt love thy neighbour as thyself...*

To DS Hook, the upshot of it is that every last person in Vancouver is going to hell, except for Jeanie.

Which is fine with him.

After the obligatory handshake with the minister, Hook and Jeanie hop on the BSA, which is parked around the corner, and roar away together, her arms around him as they speed straight down Fourth Avenue (deserted, stores and bank closed), then along Marine Drive to Spanish Banks.

As with many memories, one of their first encounters has become a marital tradition. Italian fishermen tending their nets recognize the pair and wave.

Walking down to the beach, he hoists her onto a waist-high log and they look across the water at the city, muffled in a greyish-brown cloud, with the Birks clock and the cornice of the Sun Tower and the sawtooth mountains looming above them. In the streets of the city, ant-like shapes whiz about to the hum of tyres, the croak of auto horns and the harsh, kazoo-like moan of a St Paul's ambulance.

"Ducky, I have something to tell you."

Hook inhales deeply, bracing for what, to judge by her serious expression, is not good news.

Jeanie continues, staring at her hands folded at her waist. "I don't know how to say it, love, so I'll say it right out. I'm not up the duff."

Hook takes a minute to absorb this. He is surprised by the pang of sadness he feels beneath his rib cage.

"If there is more to tell, pet, please tell me."

"Aye, there is more. I've been searching my mind for the right words. Men are awful squeamish. Most don't want the bloody details."

"Don't forget the war, pet. There's not much left that will make me squeamish."

She pauses and looks down at her hands again.

"There was something in the toilet, ducky. Never mind what it was. And there was blood. Gina Corelli's sister Chiara is a midwife, and she told me what it was. Called it a 'blighted womb.' It sounds like a disease. Ducky, it isn't like we lost someone—there was nobody there in the first place." Tears form in her eyes, more wistful than sad. "I'm not blarting, ducky, don't worry."

"Is there more, pet? Does this mean you can't... in the future...?"

"Oh blimey, no! Chiara said it happened to one of her women and she went on to have a dozen."

"Well, I wouldn't want to go that far."

"They're Catholics, ducky. Being Protestant, you can make use of your barber."

She half-smiles: "Something for the weekend, sir?"

EVERY WEEK AFTER church, maybe as a gesture of rebellion against her dour parents, Jeanie likes to have a good time on "the holiday."

And for Sunday entertainment, there is nothing to compare with Happyland.

Situated in a park at the eastern edge of the city, Happyland enjoyed only modest attendance when first constructed; now, thanks to the new electric tramline, the park is bursting with visitors—especially on a Sunday afternoon, when stores and theatres are dark and radio is nothing but sermons and hymns.

For his part, Hook likes nothing better than to bring Jeanie to Happyland, where the dimples appear when she smiles, and he hears her laugh out loud.

Hook could do with a bit of happiness right now. He has barely made a dent in the Cunning case, has run poor Mrs Crombie into the ground and has double-crossed his ex-partner. In return he has a bottle of wood alcohol in a staff locker, whose obvious purpose was to throw them off the track. (It would take a remarkably lax murderer to leave the poison behind.)

But to throw them off *what* track?

The question itches him like one of Quam's impenetrable thoughts. Was it some sort of hoax? What was he intended to think?

That, and the martini glass.

Otherwise, there's little to refute the suggestion that both victims died of natural causes. Certainly nothing that will persuade Barfoot to dig them up for analysis...

While Hook broods, Jeanie squeals with delight.

They are on the Ferris Wheel, at whose apex the city lies before them, bounded by endless sea, endless forest and a wall of mountains with spikes on top; then, before the thrill has had time to set in, you are brought back to earth, to repeat the cycle until the motor winds down and you descend in jerks, back to where you started.

Hook can't enjoy the ride properly. It reminds him too much of work.

He also endures Shoot the Chutes, on which, having stood in line for a half-hour, they ride down an artificial waterfall, which is rather pleasant except for the wet clothes.

Then they visit the Educated Horse, a snake charmer and the Ganges River crocodile. They don't venture into the bingo tent, because neither of them holds with gambling—Jeanie by Methodist tradition, Hook because he never wins.

By prior agreement, they save the best for last: the new Giant Dipper roller coaster, which features a sixty-foot drop at a speed of over forty miles an hour—fast enough to make Jeanie squeal with delight, with no trace of sadness at all.

# CHAPTER 44

BATHED, FRAGRANT, FRESHLY dressed and having had neither a drink nor a pharmaceutical boost in a few days, McCurdy is feeling positively top drawer.

It occurs to him that, despite the low food quality, men seem to come out of gaol in better shape than when they went in. Is imprisonment good for one's health?

He makes a note on this for a future piece about prison life or about the poor eating habits of British Columbians or about both combined. Or about a famous felon who just got out and has lost weight. Diet stories are always a reliable wheeze.

However, first things first—which is to contact his former cellmate, Clyde Taggart.

*DUnbar exchange. Are you there?*

*Operator speaking, SEymour exchange. Castle Hotel calling.*

SWITCH

*Taggart residence. Are you there?*

*DUnbar exchange. Castle Hotel calling.*

*Please make the connection.*

SWITCH

*Here is Mr Ed McCurdy.*

*I wonder if I may speak with Mr Taggart, please?*

*I'm sorry, but Mr Taggart isn't here at present.* (The voice on the line is the voice of an icicle.)

*Do you know when he'll be back?*

*Mr McCurdy, I know who you are. You are the reporter, and you know the situation perfectly well.*

*Ah. Then I assume I am speaking to Mrs Taggart.*

A long pause follows.

*This is she. What is it you want, Mr McCurdy?*

*Actually, I wonder if I might come around. So that we might have a chat.*

*And what would be the purpose of that be?*

*Mrs Taggart, I've been in touch with your husband.*

*I see. Have you really?*

Perhaps it is the crackle and hiss of the telephone line but, from the voice on the other end, he detects no hint of either curiosity or relief; no "Where is he?" or "Is he alive?"

*Mrs Taggart, I thought you might wish to know what happened to your husband—unless of course you've seen him already...*

From the silence that follows, he begins to suspect he has been disconnected—or perhaps she is consulting someone with one hand over the receiver.

*Hello? Mrs Taggart? Are you there?*

*Yes, Mr McCurdy, you may stop by. Tomorrow around noon, assuming you're awake and sober.*

Located in Dunbar Heights near an Indian reserve, the Taggart residence is a handsome Craftsman summer house beside a salmon creek, a sylvan retreat built by a man who made a great deal of money in timber or fish.

Behind the house is a small stable and a fenced area where two riding horses munch on grass.

Finding himself thirty minutes from downtown, McCurdy might as well be in Rupert's Land. He is grateful for the newly constructed streetcar, which is able to trundle him to Dunbar and back to civilization.

As far as Taggart's wife is concerned, from her voice he expected either a bitter, browbeaten creature or a battle axe. Neither one turns out to be the case.

The woman standing before McCurdy is a few inches taller than him; *statuesque* comes to mind, as does *amazonian* and, less charitably, *horsey*. She wears sporting togs, though for what sport is open to question—a pair of knickers, a brown jacket with a velvet collar and ankle boots. She could be dressed for a day of golf, shooting, riding or cycling. She is certainly not dressed for keeping house.

He clears his throat and executes his most unthreatening smile. "Good afternoon, Mrs Taggart. Forgive me for barging in on you."

"Good afternoon, Mr McCurdy. I read your columns regularly."

By her expression he can't tell if this is a good thing or not. "As I mentioned on the telephone, I was in touch with Mr Taggart—"

"During your stretch in Bedlam," she interrupts. "I know about that." She has a slight Irish accent. The expression on her face says, *I'm waiting to find out why you're bothering me.*

Temporarily thrown, he has run out of conversation.

She emits a conspicuously patient sigh. "Well you'd better come in. You mustn't be fainting on the verandah."

As he follows Mrs Taggart into the front hall, he works on an alternate assessment of her character: no doormat but a cool customer, with the alert equanimity of someone who has done a great deal of planning.

"So you have spoken to Mr Taggart, then."

"I have indeed."

*Then why did you agree to meet?* he wonders as she leads him into the living room.

The exterior of the home may be rustic, but cottage life has no part in the decor. There are no trophies, no decapitated animals or stuffed fish; in fact, if not for the Donegal rug, he could have stepped into an Art Deco salon, or perhaps a walk-in refrigerator.

McCurdy sinks into a leather club chair that delivers an infantile sensation of being enveloped in a cold bosom. Mrs Taggart looms over him like the Statue of Liberty with a cigarette. For a brief moment he suspects that he may be out of his league.

"I shan't offer you tea because I can't stand the stuff myself. In any case, from your reputation I expect yourself will want a real drink."

"Yes, I know about my reputation. Perhaps you have some heroin or cocaine."

A mirrored bar has been installed in one corner, with the makings of every drink on the menu of a luxury hotel. She produces a brand of whisky that can't be had in BC, pours several fingers into two cut-glass tumblers, then spoons in cubes of ice from a silver bucket.

"Mrs Taggart, are you aware that the Attorney General threatened your husband with criminal charges over his work with the LCB?" He listens for the sound of ice cubes rattling. Nothing. She turns to face him: the two crystal glasses are steady. Her eyebrows suggest amused assessment. Her brow looks as though it has never had a wrinkle in its life.

She sits in the chair opposite and crosses her legs; usually that is a prelude to flirting, but not in riding pants. "Clyde told me all about it. He made some threats of his own, which is how he ended up in the bug house. He does that sort of thing. It's part of his personality."

McCurdy probes further. "If Clyde were to go to prison—God forbid—who would run the Firestone tyre business?"

"I would, of course. I own it." She shrugs, modestly. "Firestone Tire and Vulcanizing is my business, my property, established by me. Mr McCurdy, can I refill your glass?"

"You own a *tyre shop*?"

"I don't install them myself, if that's what you mean." She gets up, turns her back and heads for the bar. "I saw there were more and more autos on the roads. It came to me that tyres would wear out more often than autos. I obtained the licence for Firestone Tires, and it has gone well. Next we plan to open a Woolworth's. We don't think the economy will continue to soar, and people will want cheap products."

She sets his glass on the table, sits and crosses her legs. "Franchising is the future of retailing, Mr McCurdy."

"Thanks for the tip." He gets out a handkerchief, fogs up his lenses and wipes them carefully. "It's strange, but in the business directory, Firestone Tire and Vulcanizing is listed as belonging to Clyde Andrew Taggart. I take it that's for banking purposes."

"Clyde's signature is essential. I couldn't rent a telephone without it."

"Except, with everything under his name, having your husband in prison would put you in quite a pickle."

She takes a sip of her drink—rather more than a sip, actually—then sets it on the table and lights a cigarette. (By her manner, McCurdy is not tempted to light it for her.)

"I said that Clyde was furious with Stalker; actually, we were both furious."

McCurdy winds his glasses around his ears, leans forward and looks her in the eye, knowing his eyes to be magnified to twice the normal size: "Except that the timing doesn't make sense, Mrs Taggart. As I mentioned to your husband, when he was canned from the LCB, Stalker had barely moved into his office. Rather than coming up with these charges, isn't it more likely that Stalker *came across* them?"

"And your point is?"

"My point is that it seems more likely these charges originated with Mr Cunning."

Mrs Taggart takes a sip of her whisky with a shudder that, to McCurdy, carries a hint of theatre. "That would devastate Clyde. He and Gordon go back—"

"I know. Real mates they were. But drastic situations demand drastic measures. For the Liberals, the LCB is a cash cow and a millstone around the neck, both at the same time. It may have required human sacrifice. That's politics—but you'll think I'm just a cynic."

She heaves a sigh; if he were trying to score a point, he has succeeded. "In any case, Mr McCurdy, Clyde won't hear a bad word about Gordon Cunning. They played sports together, joined up together. Mates for life and all that."

"Many veterans feel that way. Did he serve?"

"Yes. But he doesn't talk about that." She puts out her cigarette and lights another.

Seeing an opportunity, McCurdy rises to his feet, so that now he is looking down at his hostess, for the first time—a manoeuvre Victor Newson always uses to put one at a disadvantage. "Well, I shan't take up any more of your time. I must be going."

Mrs Taggart stands, and again he feels short and squat. "Of course, Mr McCurdy, I'll see you to the door."

They are both standing up now, but neither moves. He looks into her eyes, the colour of root beer.

"Oh by the way, Mrs Taggart, I've been admiring your decor since I arrived. Especially your custom-built bar."

She glances behind her as though to make sure it is still there. "Oh. Yes. Well thank you, Mr McCurdy. We did have it custom built."

"And I couldn't help noticing your martini glasses. So contemporary."

She turns to face him. Her eyes flash, though her brow is as smooth as ever. "Mr McCurdy you're getting at something. I do wish you would come out with it."

"I see that you keep a stable, Mrs Taggart. I hope you keep a supply of strychnine. For killing rats, I mean. I hear there's an infestation."

A long pause, which McCurdy has no intention of breaking. In every negotiation, financial or otherwise, there comes a silence, and the one who speaks first is exposed.

"Excuse me a moment, please." And without further explanation she abruptly retreats through the front hall into another part of the house.

*Was it something I said?*

Either she has abandoned the room or has gone for reinforcements.

He returns to the bar, helps himself to another whisky, then scans the array of crystal glasses lining the shelves around bottles of Taggart's unobtainable booze. Yes, indeed—only five martini glasses, when they usually come in sets of six. A stroke of luck, given that the entire meeting was a bluff. He wonders how he managed that.

CLYDE TAGGART APPEARS with a broad smile in the archway leading from the front hall and reaches out with both arms as though for a manly hug.

Standing by his side, Mrs Taggart gives him a gentle nudge, so he settles for a thumbs-up. Wearing a starched shirt with gold cuff links, he could pass for a professional sports champion—a middleweight boxer with the cauliflower ear.

Seen together, they look like a famous couple—or at any rate, a couple who *should* be famous. Mrs Taggart seems not the least unnerved, a tough nut to crack. Based on their conversation so far, McCurdy considers himself fortunate that she returned with her husband and not with a shotgun.

He stands up, aware that the two of them still tower over him. "Clyde, what the devil were you hiding from *me* for?"

"Have you forgotten your profession, Ed? You're a reporter, and a rather nasty one at that."

"He practically accused me of murder," Mrs Taggart says. "He has rather a lot of nerve."

"Now, Wanda, Ed may say outrageous things but he is an experienced reporter. He knows better than to spread libelous accusations without evidence. Isn't that right, Ed?"

"I wouldn't dream of it." They seem remarkably relaxed and unthreatened. McCurdy is on his guard.

Taggart crosses to the bar. "Care for a drink, Ed? Scotch?"

"Perhaps just a splash." A shift has occurred in the balance of power now that he faces the two of them, a pair greater than the sum of its parts.

Having replaced Mrs Taggart in the leather seat across the coffee table, her husband raises his glass: "To the man with pointed teeth!"

They clink glasses. In his peripheral vision, McCurdy can see Mrs Taggart easing her way along the opposite wall to watch more closely.

Taggart sips his drink. "Ah, that's the stuff. So tell me, Ed, how did you make your way back to Vancouver?"

"I rode to Burnaby in a wagon full of sheep manure."

"Oh dear. That sounds smelly."

"And you, Clyde?"

"I took a taxi from downtown New Westminster."

"I beg your pardon? You took a *taxi*?"

"Wouldn't you know, the driver was a dyed-in-the-wool Liberal. We met at a party gathering. I remembered his name. It's an excellent habit to get into."

"Quite. I must remember that."

Mrs Taggart, arms crossed, leans against the wall beside a replica of *The Kiss*, a gaudy piece of gimcrack by an Austrian named Klimt. She lifts her glass: "Didn't I mention it? Clyde is a Houdini when it comes to getting out of trouble."

"Not necessarily, Mrs Taggart," McCurdy replies, and gives her the benefit of his thick lenses. "Sometimes he requires assistance."

She lifts one eyebrow and ignites a cigarette.

Taggart intervenes: "You're right, Ed, it's true. We do work as a team. We compromise. We agree to disagree. Anything my wife may or may not do on my behalf is... in my best interest."

"Mr Cunning underestimated the strength of our marriage," Mrs Taggart adds. "Gordon was a bachelor after all. But that's all in the past, now."

Taggart produces a cigar and takes his time lighting it. "Ed, you'll remember that Stalker has his documents and I have mine. I believe you referred to a 'bureaucratic duel.'"

"Ah, yes. Files at dawn."

"Correct. Well, dawn has broken and we're giving you the first shot."

"Think of yourself as our champion," Mrs Taggart says, with barely a hint of irony.

Taggart smiles. "You of course know the saying: 'The best defence is a good offence.'"

"I was never much at sports."

"Nor at fighting a war, if I remember correctly."

Mrs Taggart is mixing herself a cocktail at the bar. "Don't be mean, darling. He has bad eyesight, obviously."

*Two minds are better than one.* McCurdy has begun to experience the distinct feeling of having been snookered. "So I take it that I'm to do your dirty work for you."

"After all, that is your profession," Taggart says.

"I think it will play much better as a series," Mrs Taggart says. "Don't you, darling?"

"Much better," Taggart agrees. "For momentum."

"Say, one item per week?"

"We've already mailed a covering letter to General Newson and followed up with a telephone call. Your employer is most enthusiastic. He expressed hope that this will finally expose the rot at the heart of the government.

Taggart checks his pocket watch: "Oh dear. Ed, I'm afraid we're going to have to make this a brief visit."

"Ah yes, of course. You must be a busy man."

He places a hand on his wife's shoulder. "Actually, before you arrived we were packing my things. I'm booked on the Continental Express to Toronto. It leaves the station at three-twenty."

"Clyde is to spearhead the campaign to repeal the Temperance Act in Ontario. At a remarkable per diem, I might add."

Her husband nods, happily: "To be frank, Premier Ferguson's government is desperate for the tax income."

"It only took a telephone call," Mrs Taggart adds. She lifts an eyebrow in Taggart's direction. "Clyde would run the country if he could keep from shouting at people."

# CHAPTER 45

DS HOOK HAS just been summoned to the chief's office. It's his second invitation since he was brought onto the force. Based on previous experience, his mind turns to the worst—that he is to be fired or demoted, and with payments owed to William Worrall for the sofa.

His fellow officers on the other side of the glass pass back and forth, flicking glances in his direction out of morbid curiosity.

Based on the chief's message, *Join us, please*, he knows that there is a third person present. What's the complaint this time? He ransacks his mind for possibilities—Patterson? The manager of the Hotel Vancouver? It's been over a week since he questioned them. Or is Crombie still holding a grudge? So many potential enemies in such a short time.

Chief Barfoot looks like a man with a serious hangover, and his eyes have rings of flesh around them.

"Good morning, Detective Sergeant Hook."

"Good morning to you Chief Barfoot, sir."

"How is the family?"

"Very well thank you, sir."

Hook joins them at the long walnut table. He looks up to acknowledge the visitor, and it takes an effort to conceal his surprise.

"Detective Sergeant Hook, allow me to introduce you to Hollis Johnston of the Pinkerton Agency. Mr Johnston, this is Detective Sergeant Hook, who has been on the case."

"Very good to meet you, suh."

"Likewise, Mr Johnston. Welcome to Vancouver."

Hook meets Miss Johnston's steady eye. As they shake hands they hold each other's gaze, a silent pact that their previous encounter will not be mentioned.

277

"Mr Johnston has brought us fine weather, it seems."

"I understand you folks get a passel of rain," Johnston says.

"Yes, indeed we do," Hook agrees. He wonders if it is possible for a conversation in Vancouver to occur without mentioning the topic.

"Got a taste of it during that storm a piece back."

Hook remembers Luther Forrest's body swinging gently from the ceiling, his blackened face and wet crotch—another war story to go with the others. "Yes, that was indeed quite a storm."

Barfoot interjects: "Well, gentlemen, I say we get right down to business. To begin, thanks to first-class work by members of the Dry Squad, and of course Mr Hook here, our two fugitives are now in custody."

The chief produces a bulldog pipe and lights it with a kitchen match—a signal that Hook may fire up an Ogden's, which he does, gladly.

The chief continues, between thoughtful puffs. "These two individuals, Jessup Olson and Gainer Flood, underwent an extensive interrogation led by Constable Simpson. I should mention that, though suffering a gunshot injury, Simpson volunteered for the duty. In the end, both agreed to co-operate—once Simpson threatened to set them loose on the streets to take their chances with Joe Celona. They invaded his territory, and Celona regards it as a capital crime."

It puts Hook in mind of the war, where a man could be shot for a variety of offences.

"So far, the situation is well in hand," the chief continues. "And this is where the Pinkerton's men come into the picture. Mr Johnston, you have the floor."

Johnston turns in Hook's direction, eyes stripped of emotion— a professional law enforcement officer delivering a report to a complete stranger. DS Hook could just as well be the opposite wall. "Mr Hook, I have been seconded to undertake the repatriation of Daisy Douglas Tyler back to the State of Indiana, where she is wanted for embezzlement and grand larceny—"

The chief cuts in: "And this is where we bring Mr Hook up to speed. As the officer in charge, you are to arrest Miss Tyler on a charge of conspiracy to murder. Once in custody, it is decided that Pinkerton's will offer her the option to accept extradition instead."

"Which is everyone's preference, far as I understand," Johnston adds.

The chief nods. "In British law, *mens rea* is a difficult charge to prove. It's damned tricky to establish a state of mind."

As far as Hook is concerned, establishing his own state of mind often comes as a challenge, let alone someone else's.

The chief rises to his feet, indicating that the meeting has drawn to a close.

"Of course, it goes without saying that none of what we have discussed here will leave this room."

Hook agrees wholeheartedly, knowing that fellow officers on the other other side of the glass have taken up lip-reading.


GULLIVER AGREES TO LEADERSHIP REVIEW
Province in Need of "New Energy"
Max Trotter
Staff Writer
*The Vancouver World*


With their government about to fall on a vote of no confidence at the next sitting, the Liberals under John Gulliver have called for a party convention on October 26, at which there will be a "leadership review."

Inside observers note that the surprise announcement is a reflection of waning support for the premier within the party. As well, the fact that Mr Gulliver agreed to such a review suggests that he wishes to put off an election he is all but certain to lose.

Gen Victor Newson, the Liberals' self-appointed nemesis, condemned the announcement as "a cynical attempt to subvert the will of the people." Conservative leader John Bowser concurs: "It is a constitutional outrage, and a dark day for British democracy."

Others suggest that the convention signals a desire among party members for a change of direction, and a sense of forward momentum after months of drift. "It is a cracking good opportunity for Liberals to unite under a single vision, and for voters to have a clear choice as we move forward with new energy," said a spokesman for the Attorney General.

During an interview on CFYC Radio, Liberal MLA Duff Patullo, member for Prince Rupert, said: "While we pray for the premier's recovery, the Attorney General has been juggling two portfolios for weeks."

Added MLA Horace Wrinch, member for Skeena: "When surely serving as acting premier is a full-time job."

The two MLAs declined to reveal their allegiance but, when asked specifically about Attorney General Stalker, Mr Wrinch replied: "Nobody doubts that he has done an exceptional job under exceptionally challenging circum-stances."

The Attorney General categorically denies aspiring to the top job: "My loyalty to the premier is firm. Such talk is just more mischief-making by the press."

# CHAPTER 46

WORD HAS FILTERED through the precinct that Quam was cash-iered from the Dry Squad and is plenty blue about it. Hook feels responsible, though Quam is unsuitable for the work, lacking the necessary inner rage when circumstances demand.

Once again, he feels the urge to look up the constable and have a chat. This time, however, it is for a respectable reason.

Sure enough, he finds Quam in Leonard's Cafe, seated on what looks to be his usual stool at the counter, tucking into a slab of peach pie with a scoop of vanilla ice cream on the side. Hook decides not to beat around the bush: "Well, Mr Quam, I understand you've suffered a disappointment."

Startled, Quam looks up with fork in mid-air, causing the overloaded scoop of pie and ice cream to drop back onto the plate.

"Oh. It's you, sir. Pardon my French, but I hope you're not here to gloat about my misfortune."

"Constable, gloating is the last thing on my mind."

"And no sarcasm, sir, please. I got a whiff of it there."

"Not a word of sarcasm, I promise you. Every word I say will come straight from the heart."

Quam looks down at his pie, sadly. "Well, the truth of it, sir, is that I was not up to the job."

"Ah. I've been in the same position myself."

"You have, sir?"

"Oh yes. In fact, hardly a day goes by when I don't feel decid-edly inept. But what was it did you in? I hope it wasn't the Maple Hotel fiasco."

Quam temporarily forgets about his pie. "Well, as you know, sir, when transferring to another unit, one is on six months' pro-bation. It took less than a month for me to be deemed unsuitable.

I have an 'unsuitable attitude' is what the report says. And they were right. My attitude *was* unsuitable. I hoped for straightforward police work, only to discover that, with the Dry Squad, work is rarely straightforward. At times it felt more like politics than law enforcement. At other times it felt like we were committing a crime."

Hook sets fire to an Ogden's. He finds it unsettling to hear this from the constable, as though a pet dog has begun to speak in complete sentences.

"Mr Quam, sometimes it occurs to me that, whether we know it or not, *everyone* is in politics."

Quam thinks about this for some time, stirring ice cream into his forkful of pie. "Did you know, sir, that Leonard's changes its pie fillings to go with the seasons?"

"No, Mr Quam, I must admit that I didn't know that."

"Well it's true, sir. Leonard said so himself. He said he meant it as a sort of celebration."

"Beg your pardon? A celebration of what?"

"Well I asked him that same question, sir. He said it was about the seasons."

"Mr Quam, I'm impressed. You observe unusual things. Please consider rejoining the team."

BOOTLEGGING BY ANOTHER NAME
A Crusade of Weasels
Ed McCurdy
Staff Writer
*The Evening Star*

Those whom connections allow
Have lucrative fields to plough
While tipplers pay
Liberals make hay
Milking the hundred-proof cow.

Documents provided to this newspaper by a former member of government indicate beyond doubt that the so-called Crusade Against Bootlegging is in fact a publicly funded version of the Chicago gang wars, where rivals vie for an ever-greater share of the loot.

If true, then the Liquor Control Board can only be described as a family tree, a crime syndicate and a slush fund combined.

Especially fortunate have been board members Alan Beaven and Chester Munn, whose oversight of the supply chain over the past two years has proved a blessing to their nearest and dearest, and whose qualifications for their appointments have yet to be established.

With its inferior products, stratospheric prices and a near-sadistic list of regulations as to where, how and when a workman can buy a glass of beer, the board is already heartily disliked to the point of hatred.

With Attorney General Cunning in charge, Clyde Taggart was tasked with keeping the department from becoming an election issue—an uphill battle, to say the least.

It can hardly be a coincidence that Mr Taggart has disappeared without a trace. (Rumour has it that he was one step ahead of the summons server.)

Now, the LCB's newly installed chairman is Harlan Crombie, a long-time ally of Attorney General Stalker. Seemingly, Crombie has been tasked with keeping the pigs inside the pen and ensuring that the stink doesn't annoy the neighbours—so that the LCB may continue to serve pork to Liberal supporters and achieve an electoral victory.

Recently uncovered evidence suggests that Mr Crombie's efforts at animal husbandry are doomed to fail; in fact, already the public has begun to smell a rat.

# CHAPTER 47

SEATED AT HER corner desk with pencil and foolscap, Grace prepares to take minutes. So far there is nothing to write.

While waiting for someone to open his beak, she draws a noose and gibbet.

Seated at the head of the table, Mr Crombie stares into space with eyes that are like the wet black pebbles you see on the beach at low tide. His pipe is clenched so hard between his teeth that Grace wouldn't be surprised if he bit the stem in two, and by the way he drinks from his water glass, she shouldn't be surprised if it contained something other than water.

As for Mr Beaven and Mr Munn, their faces have become wrinkled and diminished, like partially deflated gourds. Beneath Munn's eyes are what look to be purple hammocks. Beaven's teeth have turned yellow from chain smoking.

The silence goes on and on, not a word spoken, all three staring at the table as though it might contain a hidden message.

The suspense in the air is almost as thick as the smoke by the time Bertram Bliss slips through the door, holding a rolled-up copy of *The Evening Star* in his fist. And his expression has soured—no hail-fellow-well-met smile pasted beneath his waxed moustache.

He slaps the newspaper down on the table the way a teacher will use the strap for emphasis: "Gentlemen, we are in crisis."

The three board members look back at him like patients about to receive the bad news. Grace's hand has begun to tremble with excitement; she only hopes she will be able to read her shorthand later.

Hands clasped behind his back, Mr Bliss leans forward so that he hovers over the table like a man looking down a well. "Gentlemen, the Attorney General's office, in fact the government as a whole, is faced with a spot of hellish bloody bother that, I regret to say, originates with the Liquor Control Board."

As he speaks, the three men seated at the table seem to shrink into themselves, like cuttlefish.

"You, gentlemen, are not suspects at present, but I think all of you bloody well know that the individual came from this very table, and that his name is Clyde Taggart."

Three sets of shoulders ease, somewhat.

"To say that the Attorney General is deeply disappointed would be an understatement. This individual has chosen to put sensitive, privileged information into the hands of none other than Victor Newson, who has already sworn to bring down the government. Just think of it—an embittered former appointee revealed party secrets to an enemy *of his own party*. There are countries in Europe where such an act would justify a charge of high treason."

"Indeed, the guilty cur should hang for it," Mr Crombie says, relieved at having been been exculpated.

"I say amen to that," Mr Munn agrees.

"Hear! hear!" Mr Beaven says, before breaking into a fit of coughing.

"For the present, the damage is done. Before the next sitting of the Legislature, we can be jolly well certain of a steady barrage of damaging dirt in Newson's bloody scandal sheet, meted out in droplets like Oriental water torture.

"Gentlemen, the Attorney General initiated a crusade. Now we must prepare for battle."

Even writing in shorthand, Grace is put to the test trying to keep up.

"Of course it goes without saying that the accusations made by Newson's paper are false from beginning to end. Expert opinion has it that the documents cited are forgeries.

"Gentlemen, that is our strategy on the first scrum. Our second line is that documents exist from trusted sources implicating Conservative Party operatives, who may or may not be holding Clyde Taggart hostage, and may have extracted these falsehoods through beatings—or worse.

"It would be an irony—bloody reporters love irony—if we were to rescue Mr Taggart unharmed and secure his co-operation in time to set the record straight before the election."

INSIDE THE DOOR they share a hug and a kiss—a gesture not of passion but of mutual understanding. Mildred reminds herself that it shouldn't come as a disappointment. It isn't as though one might marry (apart from the obvious issue, she has no intention of marrying anyone); yet all the same, one must expect to undergo a period of heartsickness at the end of an affair.

Without speaking, they sit side by side on the floor beneath the window, because the bed doesn't seem right for the conversation they are about to undertake.

More silence, while each wonders how and where to begin.

On Mildred's bureau are some items Holly gave her: the sharpened metal comb for wounding, the one-inch iron ball wrapped in hemp cord for cracking skulls, the lock-picking apparatus, the old-fashioned hat pin that could skewer a man like a brochette. Not the sort of gifts a girl expects from a swain, but appreciated nonetheless.

And the experience has rescued her from boredom for a while, which may be the best one can hope for. She will hang herself rather than become a schoolmarm or nurse. Which leaves the other profession, if only she weren't so fussy about men's body odour and bad breath.

For Holly, the situation is surely simple and clear. She is not about to leave her profession or her country for anyone—unlike Mildred, who has already done both and would rather not do so again.

With this in mind, she decides to begin with a legal quip: "So my love, are we an open-and-shut case?"

Holly takes a deep breath, then nods. "Oh honey, I declare you're close to the nub of it."

"In the sense of 'close, but no cigar'?"

Not a laugh, but at least a smile: "You know I don't hold with your cigarettes."

"Would you prefer that I smoked a pipe?"

Holly grins with her American teeth: "When you're older, maybe. My mam in Boonville smoked a pipe."

Mildred reaches over to take Holly's strong hand, places it in her lap and holds on. "How long, do you think?"

Holly's brow furrows. "D'you mean, how long have we got? Or d'you mean, how much longer 'fore we close the case?"

"Both, I suppose. It's the same timetable, isn't it?"

She nods. "I reckon the operation is coming to a head. I expect that, by rights, we should have the suspect on her way back home within a week."

"So we *might* have a week left."

"That appears so, honey. 'less you hanker to become an American."

"Not to second-guess a Pinkerton's man, but why can't you just arrest her now and get it over with?"

"Well dang, there's the bugger of it. Daisy has flown the coop. She hasn't taken to the woods, and her Packard hasn't been seen crossing the border. But your Sergeant Hook is more fit than others I met. I reckon we'll track her down pretty quick."

"How can you be so certain? She's a cunning one—we must respect that."

"That's so, but never in her born days did Daisy lift a finger 'cept for money. Follow the money, and there you'll find her."

"I must mention this to Eddie."

"You do that."

Silence—not a pause, but the end of anything to say.

When something is over, Mildred prefers it to be over. She can bear the humiliation of being left, but will not have her nose rubbed in it.

"Darling, did I mention? I have made plans for a short journey. I want to call on a friend in Victoria. I shall tell my supervisor that I have a touch of the flu—nobody will check. They're afraid it's *that* flu. These days, people worry they'll catch it over the telephone."

"And your pal in Victoria—is it male or female?"

"We were cabin-mates during the voyage. Gracie is like my adoring younger sister."

"That sounds plenty good. Makes me feel better too."

"So, you won't have to move. You can stay here if you like. I shall speak to the matron, and you'll find the keys under the mat."

"No need. I can let myself in."

# CHAPTER 48

AS SOON AS McCurdy steps into the manager's outer office, his vision is immediately captured by the crucifix adorning the bosom of the pretty young woman behind the Underwood. His eyes lift to where they belong—too late, to go by her look in return.

*Brazen it out.* He removes his glasses and cleans them with his handkerchief.

"Excuse me, miss, but I couldn't help notice your typewriter. I use an Underwood myself. I'm Ed McCurdy of *The Evening Star*. I believe I have an appointment with Mr Tremblay."

With a skeptical lift of an eyebrow, she checks her appointment ledger, then speaks, with the voice of an oboe. "Surely, Mr McCurdy. Let me just check with him, shall I?"

"Thank you, miss."

She rises, crosses the room and leans through an inner door, affording McCurdy a fine view of her derrière.

Turning back, she gives him an accusatory scowl, along with "Mr Tremblay will see you now." And returns to her desk with her chin in the air.

The office decor is the equivalent of a three-piece tweed suit. Seated behind his desk, the manager makes a point of finishing some paperwork before greeting him—yes, that old trick.

When the manager finally deigns to look up, McCurdy is examining the oil painting on the wall to his right: "Would this be a Milne?" he asks.

The manager smiles under his moustache, pleased and proud. "Monsieur McCurdy, you have a keen interest in art, I think."

"Never cared for Milne though. Way too fussy. Give me Harris any day."

The manager's smile fades: "Very good then, Mr McCurdy. I believe you wish for an interview, yes?"

"Yes indeed, Mr Tremblay. At *The Evening Star*, we believe our readers wish to keep abreast of the most luxurious hotel in the empire." McCurdy says this with a face as straight as a statue.

The manager's smile (which could be mistaken for a smirk) returns: "You are most welcome, *monsieur*. It is good, I think, to keep warm relations with the public."

"Quite. In particular, we would like to focus on your superior services, as seen from your own point of view."

"Ah. Of course. In service we are second to none in the world. We spare no effort to satisfy our guests, I say this."

"The personal touch is what counts."

"It can make all of the difference, *monsieur*."

"Is that why you have two telephones on your desk?"

"I am not sure I understand the point of your question," Mr Tremblay says, looking at his two telephones as though for the first time. "Why would I *not* have two telephones?"

"Of course. A man in your position needs a second telephone for, shall we say, sensitive requests. Requests that may or may not stretch the limits of the law. A confidential service requiring a separate number, corresponding to a storage room, wired to one of the instruments on your desk. Personal service, Mr Tremblay. It's what separates a good hotel from a great hotel."

The manager glares at the the two telephones as if they were responsible. They stare back at him, like one-winged ducks with rounded bills.

"Mr McCurdy, I do not think I wish to continue this interview."

MCCURDY EXITS THE office in time to see the receptionist hurriedly take her seat at the typewriter. He tips his hat, "Good day to you, miss."

"He was a pig," she replies.

"Beg your pardon, miss?"

She inserts foolscap into the roller and begins to type loudly, as though to confuse a potential eavesdropper. "Cunning was a filthy beast who thought he could put his hands wherever he wanted."

"Rather forward, was he?"

"I'll say. He ordered women like room service. Entertained them at all hours of the night."

"Shocking behaviour, I should say, in a public official."

"Not that he was the only one." She applies correction fluid to a page. "In fact, I've submitted my resignation."

"I don't blame you. One expects a higher standard here."

"Yes, sir. I'm paid to work for a swanky hotel, not a brothel."

### STALKER TO CHALLENGE GULLIVER
#### "Challenging Times Need Strong Leadership"
Max Trotter
Staff Writer
*The Vancouver World*

Inside observers who must remain anonymous have confirmed that, on Monday next, Attorney General Boris Stalker will announce his intention to challenge John Gulliver's position as party leader and premier.

Asked for confirmation or denial, Deputy Minister Bertram Bliss dismissed the suggestion: "The press is, as usual, making a mountain out of a molehill. Any rumour to sell newspapers."

Observers note that Mr Bliss's response came short of an outright denial. Mr Stalker has, of late, emphasized the need for unity in waging the "crusade against bootlegging," which he terms "the moral equivalent of a state of war."

Despite these denials, such rumours offer hope that the Liberal convention on October 26 may turn out to be, not an "unparliamentary stage show," as feared by the Opposition, but a genuine contest.

# CHAPTER 49

MILDRED IS PLEASANTLY surprised by the *Princess Kathleen*, its size and luxury and appointments: a miniature ocean liner first class with wood-panelled lounges and staterooms, an enormous dining room with crystal chandeliers and white-jacketed waiters, and ship's officers strutting back and forth with rows of brass buttons in front and gold stripes on their sleeves, and elastic bonnets over their posh white caps as protection from the rain.

Outside, the sea is liquid slate with white ruffles.

Seated before an immaculate white linen tablecloth, she admires the weight of the cutlery, then picks up the menu and decides on the potted game sandwich and a glass of lemonade.

At the bottom of the menu is an additional note: *Invalids or passengers on a diet please consult the chief steward for specially prepared dishes.* On the back is an advertisement for a "Honeymoon Special" on the midnight boat.

A bit much really, for a journey of less than sixty miles—all a part of the province's perpetual campaign to assure the public that it is a "world-class" destination.

Passengers, in the effort to seem world-class themselves, behave as though this is only what they deserve, imagining themselves to be Kathleen herself; at a neighbouring table Mildred overheard a diner comment that the asparagus wasn't sufficiently crisp, and the waiter seemed so shocked and hurt that she took back her complaint and gave him a generous tip.

All in all, a memorable contrast to Millie and Grace's second-class voyage to Canada, during which passengers were by no means subject to scurvy but it was wise to bring a supply of fruit to supplement the diet of oxtail soup, brisket and farina pudding.

Mildred steps out onto the passenger deck just as the vessel passes a series of small islands so close by that she feels a childish urge to reach out and stroke their mossy pelts and the smooth orange trunks of the arbutus trees. She can imagine elves living there, fairies as well.

She reflects on the amount of space one can cover in a mere fifty-eight miles. Surely there can be no better way to put distance between oneself and the end of an affair than this first-class passage across the sea, in miniature.

As the *Princess Kathleen* approaches Victoria Harbour, Millie leans over the railing, soaked with mist, and can make out what she knows to be the Empress Hotel, an enormous French chateau with Tudor arches and Gothic teeth. Turning to the starboard side, she sees what looks to be a Greek temple built by a hedonist; as they draw nearer she can make out Poseidon, god of the sea, on one corner of the building, so this is obviously the ferry terminal.

Now she can see Grace standing in front of a Doric pillar, looking a bit older and a bit tweedier, and a bit uneasy, with the pinched look of a person who has carried high expectations and now experiences a sudden feeling of unease—either that Mildred has changed her mind and remained on the mainland, or that the coming thrill will turn out to be not very thrilling after all.

Mildred raises her hand over her shoulder as though holding up a bright spotlight. Grace looks her way and starts to wave back frantically, jumping up and down, and it appears that, yes, she is the same girl she was; and when she runs across the dock and they wrap their arms around each other, temporarily at a loss for words, she even smells the same.

At length, she manages a whisper: "Millie, I'm so glad you're here."

"And already I'm glad I came."

ON FIRST LOOK, Victoria puts Mildred in mind of Mr Wells's time machine, except that the machine would have to transcend geography as well.

As they walk along Government Street they could be in the streets of a Victorian town, albeit on a Lilliputian scale, for the Douglas-firs in nearby Beacon Hill Park easily dwarf the downtown architecture, casting the city as a miniature Ipswich crammed between the forest and the sea. Along the way she listens to Grace, who can't stop talking and is gushing over with happiness, talking what Mildred would ordinarily call sentimental rot but which, on this occasion, serves as a reminder that one can like another person not for their ability to interest one, but for one's ability to interest them. She remembers her mortification upon realizing near the end that Holly sometimes found her rather boring. In comparison, Grace's spate of nervous prattle is like spring rain on her face.

Up the hill toward the Douglas-firs, on Simcoe Street overlooking the bay, Grace and Gwendolyn's boarding house is an enormous rectangular shed facing sideways onto the street, with brown and white walls, a front gable looming over the entrance and many windows of varying sizes. Upstairs, a pair of peach scanties are hanging from a windowsill to dry.

In the front hall, Grace introduces her to a stocky woman Mildred can only describe as formidable. She wears a hair net and a velvet band above hooded cobalt eyes, above a set of broad cheekbones, big arms and hands, and has what looks to be caked paint on the skirt hem below her apron.

Seated on the floor to Miss Carr's left is a monkey.

A green monkey, with a black face, it has outraged eyes and pointed yellow teeth. From its mouth comes something between a growl and a hiss.

Mildred returns her gaze to Miss Carr's face, whose eyes seldom seem to blink. *Do I need to apologize for angering her monkey?*

"Oh dear, Miss Carr. I'm afraid that your monkey doesn't like me."

"Don't jump to conclusions, Miss Wickstram. Woo is in fact smiling. When she doesn't like someone, she tries to bite them. And usually succeeds."

"Well, I am glad she didn't do that!"

"Woo's problem is that she is over-aware of people's intentions. I'm glad to say that she thinks yours are honourable." When Miss Carr smiles, her face becomes all dimples and cheeks.

From the front door to the stairway is a gloomy, windowless journey, owing to the fact that both front rooms have been turned into accommodation, their doors shut and locked. Upstairs, the same is true—in fact, it seems as though every useable square foot of the house has a tenant living in it; she wouldn't be surprised if the linen closet was fitted with a cot.

"You described her perfectly," Mildred whispers.

"Did I? When?"

"In one of your letters."

"Oh yes, now I remember." Grace blushes slightly. "Thank you, Millie. I don't think I write very well."

"Well you do. But in any case, I appreciate the forewarning. If I hadn't been mentally prepared for Woo, I expect I might have screamed."

Grace laughs. "It really is an unusual household. How odd the way things seem perfectly normal when you've been around them for a while."

"She is a formidable woman, but I expect she has a soft side."

"Don't count on it. Last winter a tenant found his room too cold. She caught him trying to sneak an extra scuttle of coal into the furnace and pushed him into the bin."

Once upstairs, to get to the guest room, one must cross through Miss Carr's studio, which is as Grace described, with an easel holding a painting covered with a dust sheet, and several other paintings, facing inward against the wall, observed by a silver cat.

Two doors have been set into the far wall; on one is a painted bear's head, as one would find on a totem pole. The landlady opens the other door and is about to hand Mildred the key when a voice downstairs shrills, "Miss Carr, you must come down here at once!"

Miss Carr winces: "That would be Mrs Webb. She speaks to me like I'm a servant, though I have told her not to."

"Miss Carr! Are you listening?"

"She traipses around the house in a negligee. She refuses to use the trash bin because it is too much trouble."

"I know you can hear me, Miss Carr, and I am losing patience!"

"She leaves laundry everywhere."

"Miss Carr! I want you now!" The screech has transitioned to a scream.

The landlady trudges wearily out the door and heads downstairs. Below they can hear her say, "Mrs Webb, I have called the plumber. There is no need to howl like a banshee..."

Mildred uses the key to open the door without the totem pole design and enters what Miss Carr referred to as the doll's house—a room meant for a midget, whose steep gable roof begins four feet from the floor. A tiny window at the far end looks down onto a dog kennel, a small vegetable garden, and cages of chickens and rabbits.

"Millie, I do hope you don't bump your head."

She sets her overnight bag on the bed. "I think it is perfect. No room for anyone but me."

"Good. Come down to our flat when you're ready. We'll have tea and Gwendolyn will join us when she returns."

GRACE AND GWENDOLYN's flat consists of two tiny bedrooms, a tiny living room and a kitchen that could be the galley on a modest yacht.

Grace puts down a pot of tea, a plate of scones, butter, steel utensils and a small jar of gooseberry jam. "Gwendolyn is at a tea dance. She has dropped Wilber and gone fishing again. She says it was his fingernails, but I suspect it was his prospects."

"An old-fashioned girl, I take it."

"And here in Victoria she fits right in. In Victoria, time stopped in 1901."

"And you, Gracie? How is your love life?"

"On hold for the moment. As Miss Carr puts it, 'At present I prefer animals with four legs to animals with two.'"

"I have sometimes had that feeling myself. Do you mind if I smoke?"

"Oh, heavens no, I'll fetch you an ashtray."

It is an odd feeling to be with someone so eager to confide in one, when the feeling is not mutual. Mildred expects that she won't tell Grace about the Grand Goblin incident. She would rather not hear her experience reflected back with exclamation points. Nor will she dwell on her sojourn with Holly, for it might make Grace nervous.

Grace returns with a glass ashtray stolen from a coffee shop, and Mildred lights a cigarette with a match after three tries. She will retrieve her lighter even if she has to break into the place herself. The Grand Goblin may have taken away her dignity, but he's not taking away her lighter.

Grace sits down again. "Gwendolyn took up smoking the moment we arrived. I think it looks trashy to be seen smoking in public, but she says it's the fashion—Oh! And here she is!"

Grace rises to greet Gwendolyn at the door, and Mildred watches them share in a ritual hug, absorbing the contrast between the two young women; it is not difficult to see why one girl is invited to tea dances and the other is not.

Grace is more or less as remembered, but with round eye-glasses on her nose and a nascent fleshiness beneath her chin; Mildred can easily imagine her at fifty, working in an office as the loyal assistant to a deputy minister or the vice-president of a financial institution.

By contrast, she would not have recognized Gwendolyn if she met her in other circumstances, for she has been not so much restyled as reparcelled, having lost perhaps twenty pounds, with bee-stung lips that positively glow (radium, possibly), eyebrows plucked and pencilled into precise arches, and hair bobbed as short as a government office would allow.

"Millie!"

But when she faces in Mildred's direction, Gwendolyn is the same girl she remembers, with the puckish expression that made her laugh on the train as she recounted the antics of the men in the lounge, their inability to tear their eyes away from her chest. Likewise, her lips and makeup are just a cover for the same mouth, the same slightly goofy smile and the unexpectedly hearty hug Mildred remembers from the day the three of them parted company at the ferry.

"Gwendolyn, how you've changed!"

"Yes, Millie, I have. I like to think it is my new self."

"And I sincerely approve."

"I'm so glad. I was afraid you wouldn't." They sit down and join hands across the table. "How long can you stay? Please say it will be a long time."

"I'm on sick leave. I can get away with it for a few days. Dr McCurdy will telephone a daily report to the office."

"It is nice to have a co-operative doctor."

"Yes, it is."

"Well you must certainly stay until Monday afternoon. Mr Stalker is going to announce his challenge to the premier. He is a spellbinding orator."

"Gwendolyn, you're joking!"

"No I'm not, Gracie. Miss Langdon is burning up the lines telephoning the press. Every paper in the province will be sending someone down, even the *Prince Rupert Optimist.*"

Mildred knows Prince Rupert is to the north, possibly somewhere near the North Pole. She has been lax in forming an understanding of regional geography. In a place so enormous, what is the point?

### STALKER ANNOUNCEMENT ON MONDAY
## Opposition Urges Caution
## Asa Moore
### *The British Colonist*

Attorney General Boris Stalker has scheduled a major announcement for Monday afternoon, less than a week before the Liberal Party Convention.

According to his spokesman, Bertram Bliss, "Mr Stalker has been thinking long and hard about the future of the province, and about his own future as well. Any more than that I am not at liberty to say."

Newspaper reporters from as far away as Fort Nelson will be in attendance. This reporter has learned that CFYC Radio has already begun making the necessary preparations to broadcast the event.

Not everyone, however, is looking forward to the announcement with such enthusiasm.

Conservative leader John Bowser has suggested that Mr Stalker is engaging in an abuse of power: "He is using his bully pulpit to herd the press like cattle. Manipulating the news for political ends is hardly the work of a gentleman."

MILDRED WAKES UP to the sound of screeching on the stairway outside. She pads across Miss Carr's studio and peers out the door in time to see the landlady disappear around the corner, leaving a trail of tin pots and pans on the stairs and, at the bottom, a woman with a zinc pail over her head that previously held brown liquid.

Returning to her room, she stops upon hearing another kind of screeching, this time from a violin being scraped back and forth, repeated without variance and with steely concentration, producing a sound that causes her skin to grow goosebumps all over.

Over a breakfast of kippers, beans and tea, Gracie provides context to what she saw and heard. "Mrs Relish is in arrears with her rent, and Miss Carr was trying to confiscate her pots and pans. The violinist is the Dankworths' eleven-year-old daughter whose determination would be admirable if one didn't want to strangle her."

So when Gracie announces that Mildred must come out and meet the dogs, it is a welcome invitation, although she has had few experiences with dogs and most of them have been unpleasant.

Over the next half-hour, she learns a good deal more about English sheepdogs than she really wanted to know, for they are huge drooling, farting creatures with shaggy coats embedded with debris, muddy paws and wet beards, who think it fun to jump up and push one onto the ground, then to thrust their snouts into one's private area.

For Grace, the dogs make life in Victoria worthwhile; for Mildred, it will take more than that.

By the time the two women return inside for elevenses, Mildred is muddy from head to toe. With only one change of blouse and skivvies in her overnight bag, everything must be hand-washed and hung up to dry, leaving Millie in her spare shirtwaist and a dowdy checked skirt from Gracie that has to be tied around the waist with twine not to fall around her ankles.

Meanwhile, downstairs, the dreadful concerto goes on and on like a cat crying out in pain.

# CHAPTER 50

THE FOUR WOMEN leave the boarding house early on Monday in order to arrive in time for the announcement, which they look forward to with varying degrees of interest.

For Mildred, her observations will amount to crisp copy for Eddie, while for Gracie and Gwendolyn, Stalker's announcement might have a direct bearing on their future. Miss Carr expects nothing but another pack of lies from a liar-in-chief.

As they walk down the hill toward the Legislature, they make sporadic conversation about nothing much, until Grace mentions the untimely death of Gordon Cunning.

"It was a dreadful thing to happen," Grace says. "Poor Mr Cunning."

Miss Carr throws her a skeptical look: "He was a terrible man by all accounts. When a terrible man dies, I don't see why one should waste one's time feeling sorry."

"Boris Stalker is worse," Grace says.

"He certainly is," Gwendolyn agrees. "He gives me the willies. Walks around the Leg like he owns the place."

They stop while Grace extracts a stone from her shoe. "Maybe he plans to," she says.

"When he doesn't like someone," adds Mildred, "he makes them disappear."

"He sounds positively Russian," Grace says, and they continue on their way.

"I should never date a Russian," Gwendolyn says. "They seldom smile, and they're too fond of dill..."

The city appears below them, uniformly grey except for Captain George Vancouver, glittering in the mist. To their right is the grandiloquent Empress Hotel.

In front of the Legislature they can discern perhaps a

hundred people milling about, giving out a steady murmur like a gentle washing machine. Most are members of the press—reporters in shabby suits and misshapen fedoras, photographers with their Speed Graphic cameras and pouches full of spare bulbs. When the four women reach the perimeter of the lawn, they see that they are the only females present, other than the bronze Queen Victoria who has turned her back on everyone.

On the Legislature steps, a platform has been rigged to provide a flat surface wide enough to accommodate dignitaries; front and centre are a lectern and a microphone whose wires snake down to the bottom of the steps. There a table has been set up to hold a varnished wooden box with knobs, switches, coloured buttons and a semicircular dial. Perched on a stool by the table is a man wearing rounded metal headphones, smoking a cigarette.

On either side of the platform, flagpoles fly the Red Ensign and the Union Jack. On the front of the pedestal is a placard containing another image of the Union Jack, together with the legend *Keeping the Faith*.

On the lawn near the steps are six men in band uniforms, chatting, smoking cigarettes and blowing spit out of their horns—trumpet, alto horn, tenor horn, euphonium and tuba.

The event occurs right on schedule: as the twelve o'clock gun sounds at Work Point Barracks, the musicians break into an abbreviated version of "The Standard of St. George." With the concluding quarter note, Attorney General Stalker strides out of the building onto the platform in a light grey kilt (presumably the Stalker tartan) with a matching tie and a dark tweed jacket.

"Dear Lord, he thinks he's Robert the Bruce," Miss Carr comments.

Through the door a retinue emerges, consisting of a dozen or so dark-suited backbenchers along with the two members of the Liquor Control Board, Alan Beaven and Chester Munn.

Over to one side Bertram Bliss supervises the scene, like a stage manager before the curtain rises on Act I.

The Attorney General turns his head from side to side, nodding to some and pointing with his forefinger to indicate that he recognizes someone (whether he does or not is another matter) while he waits for the applause to die down, which doesn't take long.

After tapping the microphone gently, and upon receiving confirmation from the radio technician at the bottom of the steps, he produces a sheaf of paper from an inside pocket, places it on the lectern, smooths out the folds, clears his throat and begins his prepared statement.

> *Greetings to you, citizens of British Columbia. And greetings to you, gentlemen of the press. I extend special greetings to the radio audience, sitting by your receivers.*
>
> *I shall move straight to the point. The reason I have called you here is to announce my candidacy for premier of this great province.*
>
> *After long and hard consideration, after consultations with some of the best minds in the Commonwealth, I have determined that we British Columbians stand at a critical moment in our history.*
>
> *My friends, the province is in a crisis—a crisis of leadership.*
>
> *We live in exceptional times. The foundations of our traditional way of life are cracking under pressure. Fundamental Christian values are eroding. Waves of foreigners pound our shores. Rule of law is under siege by radicals and agitators.*
>
> *In short, the centre is not holding. Without decisive leadership, things fall apart. Anarchy will be unleashed on our world...*

Miss Carr turns to Mildred: "Who said that, Miss Wickstram? It sounds familiar."

"Yeats, actually. We memorized it at Badminton. In fact, every phrase he utters sounds like something I've heard before."

"You know," Gwendolyn says, "I think Mr Stalker is wearing shoe lifts."

> *My friends, as a great man once said: "Exceptional times require exceptional actions, and exceptional actions require exceptional men..."*

"Heaven help us, now he's stealing from Samuel Smiles," Mildred says. "Can Wellington be far behind?"

> *Sadly I say to you that, here in British Columbia, at present, we are not led by exceptional men. We are being led by ordinary men. Men who should be tilling the land and plying their trades.*
>
> *Fine men. Honest men. Hardworking men. But not exceptional men.*
>
> *My challenge to the leadership of the Liberal Party has one purpose and one purpose only: to create a team of exceptional men who will lead this province to an exceptional future.*
>
> *Here at the edge of the world, we will create a bastion to defend the British way of life...*

At this moment, Mr Stalker pauses, then looks up from his text with a puzzled expression. A dark red blotch appears beside his tartan tie, followed by the shriek of a rifle, and he crumples to the floor.

# CHAPTER 51

*Hello, operator speaking, CAstle exchange. Are you there?*

Here is SEymour 120, Vancouver Police Department. Operator speaking, how may I assist you?

*I have a call for Detective Sergeant Hook. I will connect you now.*
SWITCH
*Hello, are you there?*
Detective Sergeant Hook speaking.

*I have a Miss Chan Jingheung on the line, sir. An Oriental woman. Will you take the call?*

*I will, Irene. Thank you.*

*I will connect you now.*

*Detective Sergeant Hook speaking. Are you there, Miss Chan?*

*Officer Hook, excuse my intrusion, please.*

*Nei hou, Miss Chan. Could you speak up, please?* (Clearly the caller is not comfortable using the telephone.)

*Yes. I'm sorry. Is this enough?*

*It is. What is it you wish to speak to me about?*

*Mr Hook, my call is about Mr Crombie. He has come home, in a...*

*Yes?*

*He was... very excited. He told me to go disappear now. I thought he meant that I should go away from his sight, but I think I am dismissed. I started down the hall to the kitchen, and he shouted and blocked my way. His face was very pale. I ran to the study and I closed the door.*

*I understand, Miss Chan. What happened that caused you to telephone the police?*

*I heard him run upstairs, and then I heard the sound of glass breaking in the bathroom.*

*Do you mean like a mirror or a window?*

*No, no, Officer Hook. It was bottles. He was smashing bottles, one after the other. Big bottles, small bottles, every bottle, I think.*

(Suddenly, Hook realizes his error. *Blast! You stupid, stupid, stupid git!*)

*Please tell me this, Miss Chan. Did you ever do Mrs Crombie's shopping for her?*

*Shopping?*

*Yes. Groceries and the like.*

*Sometimes, yes. When we ran out of something.*

*And was your errand sometimes to the pharmacy?*

*The pharmacy. Oh yes, of course. Mrs Crombie was very fond of the martinis. She said it helped her nerves.*

*Miss Chan, the police will be at your front door in fifteen minutes. Please watch for us. Goodbye.*

Without waiting for her reply, Hook hangs up, jumps to his feet and turns to the adjacent desk, where Quam's short, stout fingers are plugging away at a report.

"Mr Quam!"

At the sound of Hook's voice, biscuit crumbs spray from Quam's mouth and onto the report. "Yes? Yes, sir?"

"You must come with me at once. Now!"

The constable scrambles after him, as Hook worms his way between the desks, jostling shoulders and leaving a trail of mild curses in his wake.

"I take it that this is an urgent matter, sir."

Hook stops and turns, feeling feverish: "We only tested the martini bottle from the Crombie home, Quam! What about the other bottles? The stomach bitters, the iron tonic?"

"What about them, sir?"

"She had already gone through the first bottle of Patterson's, and the maid fetched a replacement. Did we think of that? No! We tested the replacement!"

"I didn't think of that."

"Nor did I, Quam, nor did I."

"That is all most unfortunate. But if the original bottle is gone, what is the hurry now?"

"Because Crombie didn't know that either. He only knew the rumours. He assumed his wife, as a secret alcoholic, would drink anything that contained alcohol—but it was the *eucaine* she was after! Knowing Patterson, I'll bet that every single tonic in the room is laced with it."

"Sir, that is not what the law intended—"

"Shut up, Mr Quam! The point is that, not knowing Mrs Crombie's drug of choice, her would-be poisoner would have poured wood alcohol into every last bottle in the bathroom—the bottles Crombie is smashing right now while we stand here with our fingers up our arses!"

"Sergeant Hook, we must go there at once."

"I fully agree. And by motorcycle."

*WHAT WERE YOU using for brains?*

While Quam hoists his bulk onto the seat behind him (again he smells like sour apples), Hook retracts the kickstand with his heel, cursing his own stupidity.

Hook failed to keep up with the times, this age of secret vices. When an intoxicating drug becomes illegal, does a man simply go without? (*You can rob a lady of her virtue, but you can't rob a man of his...*) As with booze, what one gets is alternate suppliers to fill the demand, with substances gleaned from the herbalist and the veterinarian.

The BSA was never so sluggish as it is with Quam seated behind him, and Hook can hardly breathe with the constable's death grip around his rib cage. Obviously, this is Quam's first time astride a motorcycle: he is worried about staying upright and tends to overcompensate. During the first few turns, he leans his bulk with the tilt of the machine, causing the motorcycle to nearly capsize.

After the machine comes close to sprawling on its side and spinning out on the cobbled road, taking half their legs with it, Hook yells over his shoulder, "Sit upright, for God's sake, and hold still!"

Obediently, Quam sits very still; now Hook is forced to manoeuvre with a refrigerator behind him.

Riding onto the lawn of the Crombie house, Hook sees the curtains in a front window move; as the two policemen struggle off the motorcycle, Chan Jingheung has already opened the front door.

"Officer Hook. Officer Quam. Come in now, please."

They follow the tiny woman through the vestibule and past the front parlour, whose dour Scottishness is relieved only by the presence of a modern coffee table Jeanie would detest.

The three of them stop at the bottom of the hall stairs to listen. Above them, the sound of breaking glass seems to have subsided; in its place they can hear the crunch of shoes stepping on the shards.

"Has anything happened since we spoke, Miss Chan?"

"Very sorry but I have been in the study, sir. His face was like..."

"Don't mistake me, you are not at fault. You did the prudent thing. Well done."

She leans forward slightly, palms together. "Thank you."

As her employer's legs appear at the head of the stairs, Chan Jingheung silently retreats into the study and softly closes the door.

From behind, Quam whispers into Hook's ear. "Sir, what is the next step? What's our strategy?"

Hook holds up his hand for silence, not because he is listening for something but because he hasn't the foggiest idea himself.

The soles of Crombie's shoes make a faint cracking sound as he descends the stairs—every bit the lord of the manor except for his right forefinger, which is bleeding from a small cut. He sucks on it as he takes in the two officers below, with something like a smirk on his fat lips.

"Brazen it out," Hook whispers.

"What does that mean, sir?"

"It means shut up."

"Yes, sir."

"I'm surprised to see you, Officer Hook. I don't remember calling the police." Crombie exudes, or is attempting to exude, an air of authority. He stops his descent partway down in order to maintain the advantage of height. "Your chief gave you fair warning, it seems to me."

DS Hook executes a smart salute. "Terribly sorry to disturb you, Mr Crombie, but we received a distress call."

"From some sort of crank, I suppose," Crombie says, giving his bloody finger another suck.

"The call was a call from a concerned passerby—isn't that so, Constable Quam?"

"What is that, sir?"

Hook is grinding his teeth again—the man is useless in a bluff. "Isn't it so that the call came in from a concerned citizen, passing by on the sidewalk?"

"Oh. Yes, that is true, sir. Very true. Someone said he heard the sound of breaking glass inside the house and thought it should be investigated."

Crombie frowns, on alert. "Sergeant, what broken glass is your man talking about?"

"Maybe the same glass that is now stuck in the soles of your shoes, sir. To hear the caller, someone must have been up to their ankles in broken bottles."

"Ah." Crombie produces a pipe and goes through the ritual of filling and lighting, buying time to think. "Well I suppose you probably know already."

"Know what, sir?"

"About my wife's... problem."

"Oh. Yes, sir. No disrespect to Mrs Crombie, but we encountered rumours of alcoholism—is that not true, Constable?"

"Quite true, sir," Quam agrees, without really knowing one way or the other.

"I can see that such an illness in the family might be an awkward business for a man in your position."

"You've put your finger on it, Mr Hook. As Liquor Board chairman, it behooves me to ensure that there is no alcohol in my house whatsoever. But as you well know, the pharmacy acts as a second liquor store for people who don't want to pay the proper tax—"

"Or who wish to avoid undue attention."

"That is possible as well. In any case, I investigated the contents of her medicines, and my wife's deception became obvious. I found it most upsetting."

"I can sympathize, Mr Crombie. After such a long marriage, such a discovery must have come as a shock—almost like discovering one's wife is a dope fiend."

"Yes, indeed. And I am still in a state of shock. Now if you have no more questions, I would ask for privacy at this time."

Silence. Crombie towers over them, leaning against the railing, nursing his bloody finger and smoking his pipe. The two policemen are expected to apologize, put their hats back on and disappear. But they do not move.

DS Hook clears his throat. "Actually Mr Crombie, I hate to bring this up at such a difficult time, but we have reason to believe you murdered your wife."

Behind him, Quam emits a barely audible gasp.

Another long pause follows. Crombie takes his pipe from his mouth and studies it. He seems almost amused by the suggestion. "And where did you people come up with such a preposterous notion?"

"Well it has to do with Mr Cunning, sir. The last Attorney General, Mr Gordon Cunning—you'll remember him."

"No need for sarcasm, Officer. I hope you know that your chief is about to receive a harassment complaint."

"Sorry, sir, that just slipped out, my mistake. In any case, what we did was to follow a trail of assumptions we believe you made—false assumptions, as it turns out.

"When Mr Cunning's death was reported, like many others, including the press, you suspected the cause to be adulterated alcohol, which had raised fears that an American epidemic was spreading north. Your next assumption was that, if your wife was poisoned in the same way as Mr Cunning was poisoned, the two deaths would be seen in that light. So you laced all Mrs Crombie's apparent sources of alcohol with wood alcohol.

"But we policemen proved to be more dense than you expected. There was no autopsy done on either corpse, despite your demands. To goose the investigation, and since Cunning was drinking martinis at the time, you planted a bottle of adulterated gin in a locker in the basement of the Hotel Vancouver, thinking you might nudge the police in that direction. Unfortunately, Chief Barfoot's arse remained tight as a clam."

Hook takes a pause to observe Crombie—outwardly calm, even amused, but with his pipe squeezed tight in his fist and his finger bleeding freely.

"Now it seems you've been breaking every Patterson's bottle in your house, to eliminate the source of what killed your wife. That is my thinking at the moment, sir. What is your own opinion?"

"My opinion, Officer, is that you have devised a clever story that has nothing whatever to do with the facts."

"I agree, sir. With no evidence in the bathroom to test, even if we exhumed your wife and found she was poisoned with wood alcohol, it would prove nothing."

Hook lights an Ogden's while Crombie treats him to the same scornful smile he received in the chief's office. "I think I've heard quite enough. Gentlemen, now that you have barged in, accused me of a dreadful crime and admitted to a complete lack of proof, I'd like you to leave at once."

"Yes, you are perfectly right, sir. We can't prove you murdered anyone. Except, sir, that's not the reason we're here. It's not to arrest you at all. It's to arrest Miss Daisy Douglas Tyler. And I believe Miss Tyler is in your house as we speak."

Crombie's smile disintegrates. Hook smokes his cigarette; Quam begins to say something but receives a sharp elbow to the ribs (McCurdy having once told Hook about the inadvisability of breaking an impasse).

"Harlan, who are these men?"

As though having been introduced on stage, Daisy Douglas Tyler is standing in the kitchen doorway in a loose fitting cocoon coat with exaggerated buttons and a cloche hat over one eye.

To Hook's albeit inexperienced eye, Miss Tyler is not so much dressed as *in costume*. This version is not the mousy creature he saw in the chief's office, let alone the evangelical figurehead McCurdy described; this time she seems to be impersonating Pola Negri, the dusky seductress in *Bella Donna*.

"It's the police," Crombie says. "They have been making wild accusations against me, and now they want to start in on you."

Hook produces his warrant card. "Detective Sergeant Hook, Miss Tyler. And this is Constable Quam. We are here with orders to arrest you on a charge of counselling to commit murder."

Miss Tyler's eyes widen with innocence, the southern belle after an improper suggestion. "Good Lord, officer, *murder*? How absurd. Do you mind at least telling me the name of my victim?"

"Luther Forrest. He was hanged—rather expertly, I might add—by Mr Gainer Flood and Mr Jessup Olson, on your instructions. They have given a full confession."

She seems not in the least rattled by this. "And you believe those two? Y'all have seen their criminal records? Well I declare right now, that dog won't hunt."

"It's not for me to believe or not believe, Miss Tyler. My orders are to bring you in to the station, where you're free to explain why the dog won't hunt. Once we—"

Crombie interrupts: "Don't say another word, Daisy. I think it is time to call my lawyer."

"I see no need for that." Miss Tyler produces a Browning pistol from the folds of her voluminous coat and holds it by her side casually, her eyes focused on Hook's upper torso. "Harlan, I want to go home."

Crombie seems taken aback by the direction things have taken. "Really, Daisy, I don't think this is—"

"Don't contradict me. We go back—*now!*" Her "now" is not unlike the yowl of a cat.

"Yes, Daisy," Crombie says, and joins her by the kitchen door.

"I advise you gentlemen not to follow. Back home, I could shoot a possum in the eye."

"So it says in your resumé. But you failed to hit a man standing in front of the Lumberman's Club."

"The quarry made a sudden movement. It happens."

As Crombie and Miss Tyler disappear into the kitchen and out the back door, Hook scolds himself for having left his side arm in his locker, knowing that he was about to arrest an American.

Outside, the door of an auto slams shut behind the house, followed by the rumble and roar of a Packard Twin Six and the sound of wheels spinning on gravel.

"What are we going to do now, sir?"

"Constable, why do you think we brought the motorcycle?"

"We are going to *chase* them? Unarmed?"

"No, Mr Quam. *We* are doing nothing of the kind. Telephone the station and alert the border police at once. Then I advise you to hop on the tram."

THE BSA REQUIRES four tries at the starter pedal before the engine turns over—probably in a snit about overheating—but then it fires up, loyal and true, and Hook takes off down Arbutus Street, plowing through a slot between a streetcar and a laundry truck, glad to know that Jeanie can't see this.

The motorcycle threads its way down Arbutus with its cobbles, its slippery tram rails and oil spills from raddled, leaky engines, trying to avoid the cavernous potholes and the unexpected antics of new drivers.

Hook calculates his chances.

On the plus side, he knows where they are going and the shortest way to get there: the Pacific Highway, opened two years ago and paved all the way to the border. He also knows that a motorcycle is more manoeuvrable than a luxury car. As long as they are in the the city he is able to keep the Packard in view.

Working against him is the fact that a BSA, at full throttle, can manage no more than fifty-five miles per hour, whereas a twelve-cylinder Packard will easily hit eighty on smooth pavement and in a straight line. Though he has never seen it himself, he knows the road to Washington to be as straight and smooth as the part in Valentino's hair. Once they get past Brownsville, he will never catch up.

INSIDE THE PACKARD, the smell of leather, oiled wood and gasoline has been outmatched by the pong of Harlan Crombie's fearsweat. Dark patches stain the fabric beneath his armpits; he has a dead man's grip on the handle above the passenger door.

Unlike her passenger, Daisy Douglas Tyler is thriving in her element—the element of risk. She focuses like a race car driver, foot to the floor, pushing the Packard up to sixty along Kingsway, barely slowing down when traffic funnels into New Westminster, then swerving around a flatbed full of lumber and clipping the side mirror of a Royal Mail lorry. Handling the shift lever like an expert, she veers into the oncoming lane to pass a moving van, forcing the Packard up to seventy as they cross the Fraser River on a two-decker bridge with a train clattering overhead. Returning to their lane, she then has to quickly swerve right, again into the oncoming lane, in order to pass a Green Stages passenger bus.

As for their pursuer, threading between vehicles speeding in opposite directions, Hook manages not to entirely lose sight of the Packard, although its superior speed leaves him increasingly behind.

A half-mile ahead, Crombie covers his eyes. "Darling, don't you think—"

"Never call me darling!"

"Oh. Yes, dear. Yes, mistress... It's just that—"

"Shut your mouth, Harlan, do you hear me? Just shut up!"

Slamming the pedal to the floor, she squeezes out another five miles per hour as they take the turn at Brownsville onto the Pacific Highway—only to gape at what is just ahead.

Livestock.

Crossing the highway, a herd of cows has created a bovine wall. They are being driven to the opposite side by a man wearing overalls and a straw hat and carrying a switch from a crab-apple tree.

Stamping frantically on the brake, Daisy swings the steering wheel hard left—too hard for the Packard, which leans over on two wheels with the momentum tugging outwards. The auto is drawn across the road until a few inches from the bank, when the left front wheel collapses, causing the machine to roll forward, cornerwise, over the verge, then into the ditch—throwing Harlan Crombie through the windscreen, while Daisy Douglas Tyler caroms off the ceiling like a lottery ball in a cage.

After sliding for what seems to be several minutes, the Packard comes to rest on its side in a stream of muddy water.

The man herding the cows rushes over to the accident scene, leaving his cows to mill about in the middle of the road or to sample the grass on the verge.

Beyond the cows, the horns of northbound traffic are croaking their displeasure.

Having tested his machine to the limit, Hook comes upon the scene moments later, brings the motorcycle to a fast stop, then gingerly eases forward. All he can see through the cloud of dust are the shapes of cows lumbering about, until he catches sight of two wheels spinning in the ditch, and a man in a straw hat, peering down at the prone, half-submerged body beside the grille.

BORIS STALKER SHOT DEAD
Shocked Audience Witnesses Assassination
Max Trotter
Staff Writer
*The Vancouver World*

On Monday, while announcing his challenge to Premier Gulliver for the leadership of the Liberal Party, Attorney

General Boris Stalker fell to an assassin's bullet, witnessed by hundreds of onlookers and heard by hundreds more on radio.

Herb Kergin, member for Atlin, termed it, "The most shocking thing I have seen in all my years in politics. It's the sort of thing that happens in Russia."

Says Horace Wrinch, member for Skeena, who was standing behind Mr Stalker when the shot was fired: "I have no doubt that the shot came from the Empress Hotel, from one of the upper floors."

Bertram Bliss, spokesman for the Attorney General, assures the public that unprecedented police resources, both municipal and provincial, will be brought to bear in tracking down the perpetrator, and that the RCMP has been consulted. "The public can jolly well be sure that we will leave no stone unturned."

Already, after preliminary inquiries at the Empress, police have brought certain details to light.

Investigators now know that the fatal shot was fired from a top-floor garret room on the southwest corner.

According to Inspector Forbes Cruickshank of the Provincial Police, officers have determined that the assassin was familiar with the layout of the hotel, so that he was able to identify a corner turret room as providing the best view of the Legislature steps.

The murderer seems also to have been familiar with hotel procedure: the room was not broken into, which implies that he used a key—which he could have obtained from the room rack in the desk manager's office during the lunch-hour changeover.

According to Officer Cruickshank, that is the most likely time for lapses in security to occur: people going to lunch tend to leave on time, whereas, when coming back from lunch, tardiness is more likely.

Says an employee who requested anonymity: "If you stop to assist someone, it will make you late getting back from lunch. It's the human thing, don't you see."

Others, however, dispute this complaint over lunch times, which hotel manager August Wimble described as "a smug and superficial assessment on the part of organized labour."

As Wimble explained, "Extending one's lunch robs the employer of precious time for which he pays dearly. It is one more tactic of union agitators to milk the system."

On the other hand, there remains the possibility that the suspect simply picked the lock.

Asked how it was possible for a man to pass through the hotel carrying a sniper rifle, Manager Wimble referred to the annual Victoria and Seattle inter-club tournament that is currently taking place. "This weekend, every second gentleman in the lobby was carrying a golf bag."

Considering the death of Mr Stalker's predecessor as Attorney General, alarming rumours have it that the position has come under a curse. Asked for comment, Anna Feglerska, the noted psychic, said: "It is possible that our justice system no longer produces justice, and so karma has taken over the task."


PROMINENT PAIR IN SERIOUS AUTO ACCIDENT
Max Trotter
Staff Writer
*The Vancouver World*


A respected government official and a leader of the temperance movement have sustained serious injuries after a high-speed accident at the entrance to the Pacific Highway.

Harlan Crombie, chairman of the Liquor Control Board, and Daisy Douglas Tyler of the People's Prohibition Association are in hospital after their auto went off the road near Brownsville while attempting to avoid colliding with a herd of cows crossing the road.

According to records, the construction of the Pacific Highway entailed expropriations by the Department of Public Works, some of which called for the splitting of large tracts of land, chiefly potato fields and pasture. In this case, the pasture belonged to Willard Stewart, a dairy farmer near Brownsville with seventy-five cows. The particular cows in question formed a herd of twelve cattle, driven by farmhand Lyle Tizzack.

Mr Tizzack, sole witness to the accident, described the scene: "Might have been the new pavement, because I never seen an auto travel that fast. She rounds the bend at the old Yale Road going seventy-five at least. There was nothing I could do but try and calm my cows."

The incident may reignite local unrest in Surrey over what is perceived by many as government bullying, Victoria having rammed the legislation through without consultation. As John Catherwood, Conservative member for Dewdney, remarked, "Any farmer in the riding could have told Gulliver that overpasses were needed. How many people must die before the premier admits to having made a mistake?"

Added Mr Stewart, the property owner: "That damn road cuts straight through my property. Without an overpass, these speed demons will devastate my herd."

Now receiving treatment in Royal Columbian Hospital, the two victims are in what is described as serious but stable condition.

Dr Ronald Barrows, the attending physician, reports that, at present, the prognosis is mixed: "Miss Tyler has suffered broken ribs and a broken collarbone, as well as facial injuries caused by impact with the steering wheel. Mr Crombie's condition is less heartening, for he crashed through the windscreen. He has suffered a fractured skull and remains in a coma. How long he will remain in that condition is an open question at present, but we are reasonably hopeful for at least a partial recovery."

Further inquiries have established that, when Miss Tyler has sufficiently recovered as to be moved, she wishes to be transferred to Indiana, USA, to be closer to her home.

"This is a body blow for the city," commented Mrs Albert McDuff, General Secretary of the People's Prohibition Association. "Daisy Douglas Tyler was the heart and soul of the temperance movement in British Columbia. She will be sorely missed."

# CHAPTER 52

IN VANCOUVER, THE transition from September to October entails a precipitous drop in temperature. As though at a signal, stratus clouds converge into nimbus clouds, the rains begin, a dank chill descends and it becomes clear to citizens that, for the next three-and-a-half months, they will be living at the bottom of the sea.

McCurdy turns in his copy to the receptionist rather than appear in the main office—where he is bound to be noticed, then summoned by the general for another vicious wig-bubble that has emerged from his elderly mind.

Newson's store of resentment and blame operates like the magma at the centre of the earth—tap into it and you have an eruption, and are apt to be burnt to a crisp.

At the same time, the general's convictions are balanced by a robust amount of self-interest. With Cunning unmasked, Stalker dead and the government in chaos, Newson's priorities, like the province itself, will return to normal. McCurdy has no doubt that he will be persuaded by advertisers to take a less disruptive position, both at *The Star* and in the Legislature; he will be encouraged to take a more nuanced, balanced position on the issues of the day, and the events of yesterday. He will put up no resistance when a street is named Cunning Avenue and a school becomes Boris Stalker Academy, to commemorate two public figures who stood for the British Way of Life, along with the current roster of immortalized railway executives, coal barons, imperial warriors and, of course, Prince George, the cocaine enthusiast, said to be in preparation for a tour of South America after scandals involving the heiress Poppy Baring, as well as the Duchess of Argyle...

Turning down Granville Street, McCurdy heads for the CPR dock where he is to meet Miss Wickstram, freshly back from Victoria with more details about the assassination—one of several nasty crimes worthy of this reporter's attention at the moment, unless the others become lost in the glare. Her onsite observations will provide colour to a prosaic account of Liberal malefactors.

He looks forward to her arrival, although with reservations.

It strikes him that he and Mildred have, more than once, seen one another at low tide, so to speak, occasions when unfavourable aspects of one's character come out of hiding and scuttle about for all to see.

Perhaps that amounts to some sort of love—to see the worst and not recoil. Not a high standard perhaps, but it will do for now.

OFFICIALS MUM ON MURDER
Questions Go Unanswered
Ed McCurdy
Staff Writer
*The Evening Star*

The reader, while wracking his brain
Surely has cause to complain
When officials are mum
The police deaf and dumb
And reporters are driven insane.

As the public reels from the recent series of unprecedented events, newspapers attempting to report are hampered by a shroud of secrecy.

Police and government spokesmen remain coy, some say inappropriately so, about the specifics of three deaths—a former Attorney General, a leader of the Ku Klux Klan and the wife of a deputy minister—or whether any connection exists between them; instead, they take shelter beneath the umbrella of an "ongoing investigation."

The two men involved in Luther Forrest's death have pleaded guilty only to abetting a suicide; and there remains the possibility that Mrs Crombie and Mr Cunning died by inadvertently consuming tainted alcohol.

Asked about exhuming the two bodies, Chief Barfoot replied: "We will require hard evidence before we undertake a wild goose chase at taxpayer expense."

In sum, perhaps Boris Stalker put it best when he said, just before meeting his tragic end: "Things are falling apart."

As for the assassination, officials have likewise declined to answer questions concerning either the sniper's identity or the weapon used, though a knowledgeable veteran of the trenches, when pressed, was heard to comment: "I tell you one thing only—that shot did not come from a Ross rifle."

DS Hook stops reading, puts down *The Evening Star* and turns to his wife: "What do you think, pet? Are things falling apart?"

"Ducky, you know how reporters exaggerate. It can't be as bad as all that. I fancy Mr McCurdy is egging the pudding."

"I'm sure you're right, pet," he says, and kisses Jeanie on the cheek.

— END —